MW01265692

Fuzzy ERGO SUM

By Wolfgang Diehr

Pequod Press

FUZZY ERGO SUM

A Pequod Press Science Fiction Novel

Manufactured in the United States of America
Second Edition 2011

V 10 9 8 7 6 5 4 3 2

ISBN: 978-0-937912-17-1

On the cover: Alan Gutierrez, Fuzzy Ergo Sum, 2011
(*www.alangutierrez.com*)

Pequod Press
P.O. Box 80
Boalsburg, PA 16827

www.PequodPress.com

For

H. Beam Piper

who inspired me

&

John F. Carr

who encouraged me.

PROLOGUE

John Morgan looked up to see out of a portal hoping for a view of the planet, but all he could see was the surface of Darius, Zarathustra's inner moon and the Terra-Baldur-Marduk transfer station for passengers from ship to shuttle. As with most hyperspace ships, the portals were on the ceilings due to the spherical design of the craft, so, for the convenience of the passengers, video displays were also provided throughout the ship. Artificial gravity originated at the core of the ship and radiated outward, forcing the designers to construct the floor-plan in concentric circles outward from the center, much like a Terran onion.

It was an efficient design that was comfortable for the passengers if not for the crew. Near the core of the ship, where crew quarters were situated, the floors curved noticeably while in the outermost levels the curvature was so slight as to be easily dismissed.

This was John Morgan's first trip to Zarathustra, though far from his first planet-fall. He had seen several other planets such as Mars, Terra, Yggdrasil, Nifflheim, Gimli, Baldur, Thor, Fenris and especially Freya. Morgan was looking for someone and hoped to find him on Zarathustra.

It had taken a lot of planning and money to get here. He had invested tens of millions of sols to get a working control of the local company. As a major shareholder in the Charterless Zarathustra Company, he would have access to files and computer databases that would help him in his search. He had used this same method on every planet he had visited. In the past he even hired private investigators, bribed planetary officials and, when necessary, used blackmail.

A soft feminine voice from a loudspeaker informed passengers making planet-fall to go to shuttle dock 7-A in ten Terran minutes. As many passengers were accustomed to other world's time units, the interviewer's always reminded them that ship time was based on Terran standard. Morgan hustled back to his room, inspected it thoroughly to be sure nothing was left behind, collected his luggage and sealed the room behind him.

In the corridor he opened his wallet to make doubly sure that his portfolio card was safe. In a universe where communications depended on hyper-ship couriers it was necessary to keep financial records in a portable form. Bank account balances, stock shares and other information was recorded and encoded on the card, along with the bearer's thumbprint, retinal scan and a DNA sample. Only the person possessing all three could authorize access to the card. As a final security measure, there were matching microchips implanted in the card and in some random location inside the bearer's body. If the portfolio card and its owner were more than ten feet apart, the card would not function.

Every time the card was accessed any changes were automatically recorded and transmitted through secure frequency to all outgoing hyper-space ships. The information would be retransmitted to every port where the ship made planet-fall. Financial transactions, planetary news, police reports and other information were also updated world-to-world in this manner. If stolen it was impossible to use. If lost, there was hell to pay to get it replaced. Once satisfied that everything was in order, Morgan hurried off to the shuttle dock.

On the journey from Darius to Zarathustra the flight attendant gave a brief seminar about the planet below. "Zarathustra is roughly 2% larger than Terra but has only .95134 of Terran gravity. The lower gravity is due to the lesser density as opposed to Terra, which is the densest planet in the Sol System. The Zarathustran day consists of twenty-four hours, twenty-three minutes and fifty-nine point nine-one seconds in Terran units, closely mirroring a Martian day. Local time is based on a twenty-four hour clock with the hours lengthened to accommodate planetary rotation. Seconds and minutes are Terran standard, but the Zarathustran hour is 61 minutes long. If you do not have a multi-zone watch, Zarathustran time pieces are available in the gift shop in the Mallorysport spaceport.

"The Zarathustran year is approximately 396.1 days. There is a Leap Day every ten years. On Leap Day the clock is reset to account for 0.09 seconds gained in the Zarathustran day. This makes Zarathustra unique from many other Federation worlds where T-time is the standard.

"The axial tilt of the planet is roughly 11.2 degrees as opposed to Terra's more extreme 23.4 degrees. This means seasonal change is far less variable than on Terra and many other planets. Seasonal change is only significant near the polar regions of the planet, though cold snaps are not uncommon at the extreme north and south. While the equator is typically warmer than the rest of the planet, it does not reach the extremes common to the equator on Terra. This is due to the greater distance of the planet from its primary, which is a K0 star. Were it not for the less extreme axial tilt, most of Zarathustra would be unbearably cold.

"Darius, the inner moon, is one fifth the size of Zarathustra, unlike Luna which is one fourth the size of Terra. Like Luna, Darius controls the Zarathustran tides. Unlike Luna, Darius rotates on its axis once every six and a half days. It completes an orbit around the planet every 32.97 Zarathustran days. Xerxes, the second moon, is roughly one-half the size of Darius and twice as far from the planet's stratosphere, so tidal effect is negligible."

The brochures tended to compare the planet with Terra in its pre-atomic era, but to Morgan it looked more like Freya; blue water, green landmasses, wispy cloud cover…and maybe the man he was looking for. Morgan stopped paying attention to the attendant in favor of the portal. Zarathustra grew large as the shuttle approached. Unlike the great spherical hyperspace ships the shuttle was designed around an egg shape. As such the portals were on walls instead of ceilings.

Absently, he extracted an old photo from the inner pocket of his jacket. The picture was laminated to preserve the image. It was a picture of a man somewhere in his late twenties to early forties. He possessed one of those faces that defied exact age classification. He would be much older, thought Morgan, maybe scarred or bearded. For all he knew, the man in the photo could have changed his name and had reconstructive surgery on his face.

Morgan let out a long breath. He had the same thoughts before every planet-fall, like his subconscious was telling him how impossible his search was. He had spent fifteen years searching for a man with a twenty year head-start. He might not even be alive, anymore. The universe was a dangerous and unpredictable place. That was the possibility that disturbed Morgan the most; he wouldn't be able to kill a dead man.

I

"Mot shuka! Fak hat-zu'ka!"

It was early morning and everybody was hungry. As such it was *Bal-f'ke*, Red Fur's, responsibility to find food for his tribe. He was the best hunter and thinker so he was made the *kim-chu*, the leader of the tribe. Red Fur didn't like being the leader but he didn't want his tribe to make dead, either. A tribe worked best when a wise one led them.

As the leader, Red Fur led the hunting party to find *hat-zu'ka*, a main source of meat for the Fuzzies. When the *hat-zu'ka* stood on their hind legs, they were nearly as tall as the people. They also had strong jaws with sharp, buck teeth. The *hat-zu'ka* was a burrowing animal that liked to chew the bark of trees. They moved about on all four legs as did every furry animal that the Fuzzies were familiar with, but would stand on their hind legs to fight if they had to.

Red Fur didn't see hunting as a chore, regardless of the potential danger. Hunting was fun if one wasn't too hungry, and *hat-zu'ka* were tricky and dangerous if one wasn't careful. The challenge of hunting difficult prey could also be fun, provided nobody was seriously hurt.

Red Fur signaled Healer, Silver Fur and Makes-Things to move to the right and for Little One and Stonebreaker to move left. Even though he knew the *hat-zu'ka* could not hear him speak, he preferred to use hand gestures when hunting with the tribe. Little One tended to talk too much and distract the others from what they were doing, so nobody was allowed to speak until after the attack began.

Red Fur waited until everybody was in position then signaled to attack. Healer, Silver Fur and Makes-Things moved in throwing their pointed sticks while Little One and Stonebreaker cut off the escape of any *hat-zu'ka* that tried to run.

He watched as two of the *hat-zu'ka* fell dead or wounded while the other two launched themselves at Little One and Stonebreaker. Using his axe, Stonebreaker chopped one of the *hat-zu'ka* in the head and it immediately fell and stopped moving. The other *hat-zu'ka* attacked Little One who barely managed to avoid its sharp teeth by forcing the shaft of his chopper-digger into the beast's open maw.

Red Fur moved in quickly and used his own chopper-digger to kill the *hat-zu'ka* before it could hurt Little One.

With four *hat-zu'ka*, there was enough meat for the whole tribe to fill their stomachs. The members of the tribe who stayed behind would be unhappy that they could not hunt while caring for the young but glad for the meat. It used to be much harder to find enough meat for everyone but lately there were fewer *gouru* in the skies. It had been many-many days since he had seen the last one. This was a good thing; less *gouru*, more *hat-zu'ka*, and fewer people being carried away.

As expected the camp Fuzzies were happy to see the *hat-zu'ka*. There were Tells-things, the eldest and Little One's mother, Runs Fast who was Red Fur's mate, Climber who was Stonebreaker's mate and Sun Fur who was still too young to take a mate. The infants, three males and two females, did not yet have names.

As *kim-chu*, Red Fur doled out the meat making sure that the females and infants were fed first, then the males. If any hunters were still hungry they could go out and find more food, but the females with infants had to stay with their young. There were some things the males simply could not provide.

After the meal, Red Fur congratulated Makes-Things for the pointed throwing sticks and asked how he had come up with them.

"Watch *shimo-kato* use horn on *shikku*," Makes-Things explained. "Think if I have horn like *shimo-kato*, can make *hat-zu'ka* dead fast. Not work on head but in hand. *Hat-zu'ka* fast. Not catch with pointed stick, get mad, throw stick like rock. Hit *hat-zu'ka*. *Hat-zu'ka* make dead. Make more pointed sticks for throwing,"

"You very wise," Red Fur said, "maybe find way to make throw-stick go very far, kill *shikku*?"

"Not know how," Makes-Things admitted. "Not make arm longer."

A strange noise from above interrupted the ultra-sonic conversation. Red Fur looked up and saw two hands of melon seed shaped birds with no wings; one of them was larger than all of the rest combined. The birds flew overhead and continued on for a moment before stopping.

Makes-Things observed that no birds could fly without wings or stay still in the air and said so.

"Not birds," Red Fur said. "Made-things, like pointed sticks for throwing."

"Made-things?" Makes-Things considered for a moment. "Who make such things?"

"People," Red Fur said. "People not like us. Wise people."

The melon seed shaped things lowered down to the ground. Makes-Things asked, "What they do?"

"Leave sky. Go to ground." Red Fur thought for a moment, then said, "Get Stonebreaker, Healer, and Silver Fur. Tell Little One stay. We go look at fly-like-bird made-things."

*   *   *   *   *   *   *   *   *

"Is this the right place? the taller man asked. The shorter man checked his map then nodded. "All right, we have a lot of digging to do and every inch of dirt has to be analyzed, labeled and stored. When we are done, there must be no sign that we were ever here."

"Break out the excavation robots," the shorter man ordered. "Make sure they are all programmed to strip off the surface in two inch layers. All equipment must be cleaned before moving on to the next level. There must be no contamination between the layers. I want every square foot photographed and scanned before surface removal. Any and all fossils will be photographed then carefully removed, bagged, tagged and stored for reburial."

Six men armed with digital cameras and other equipment moved over the area with almost mechanical precision and coordination. Next, robots painted in the fashion favored by military ground units rolled out of each of the smaller vehicles and lined up as if awaiting inspection. Several men, all dressed in camouflaged fatigues, quickly opened the chest panels of each robot and tapped away on the internal keypads. Once they were satisfied with the programming, the panels were sealed and the robots would begin carefully removing the small plants and rocks before stripping-off the topsoil. Everything would be bagged, tagged or potted for replanting and stored in the warehouse ship, the largest of the contragravity vehicles.

"All contragravity vehicles and equipment must be camouflaged in the next thirty minutes," the taller man demanded. "Remember, from 0945 to 1015 all equipment must be out of site and powered down to avoid satellite detection."

Another man ran over to the first two. "Updated weather report, sir. We can expect about three inches of rain tomorrow evening."

The taller man swore blasphemously. "Can we get the canopy up in time to prevent contamination?"

"Yes, with the robots' help."

"Do it." The taller man looked about quickly then made another announcement. "Remember, no smoking or dropping trash or even spitting on the ground. We were never here and the landscape must reflect that. All surplus material will be thrown into the mass/energy converter. Anything strange comes up, Geology and Paleontology will be consulted. Any dangerous wildlife comes around use the sono-stunners; absolutely no gunfire! Bronson, if you use that bow of yours, you good and damn well better police-up the arrows afterwards. And if I catch anybody pocketing sunstones, well, I guarantee they will not like what happens next. All right, let's make it happen, people."

"What are we going to do about the sunstone flint?" the shorter man asked. "We'll have to break it up pretty badly to get at the sunstones."

"According to Geology, this was a pretty seismically active area some millennia back. Broken flint could be explained away by that. And with a little heat and pressure we should be able to reform enough of it that it won't raise any eyebrows when or if it's ever discovered. By that time I expect to be on Freya with a pretty little gal to keep me company."

"Do you really think the haul will be as large as projected?"

"According to Geology, this will be the largest single deposit of sunstones on the planet."

"That's what I don't get," the shorter man said. "Why didn't the Chartered Zarathustra Company find this before we did? They've had, what, twenty-five years to study this planet?"

The taller man shrugged. "Sunstones were discovered by accident by a non-company man. That was, I don't know, ten or twelve years ago. The company was happy to let prospectors do all the work. Why not? The CZC owned the planet out-right, so they were the only people who could legally buy the stones. Nobody knew that there were concentrated deposits until Native Affairs Commissioner Jack Holloway discovered Yellowsand. But by then most of Beta continent was one big Fuzzy Reservation."

"Okay, then how did the Boss get into the picture?"

"Ah, he was on Zarathustra back then. When he left, he took along every geological survey map he could lay his hands on. When he got to Terra he looked up some brain-boys who studied the maps and other information." The taller man shrugged. "Then they did their thing and determined that this was the most likely location for a major deposit. Beats hell out of me how they did it, and I don't really care. We just do our job and get the Nifflheim out before we get caught."

*　*　*　*　*　*　*　*　*

"What make do?" Red Fur asked. Makes-Things, Healer and Gold Fur were hiding in the brush with their leader observing the strange, almost completely furless giant people. Even stranger were the things that looked like people without legs that moved back and forth putting other things together. "How move with no legs?"

"Not people," Makes-Things said.

"Have arms. Have head," Healer argued. "Makes put together thing like Makes-Things."

"Is made-thing," Makes-Things said firmly, "like melon-seed birds. See Big One's walk out of flying things? See Big Ones open no-legs thing? Open live-thing it make dead. No-legs thing not make dead."

Red Fur and the others were forced to agree with Makes-Things. They couldn't understand how such made-things were possible but they could see that the Big Ones could do many wondrous things. At one point, a big *shimo-kato* charged into the Big Ones' camp and destroyed one of the no-legs made-things. The Big Ones used another made-thing that created a loud humming sound and the *shimo-kato* staggered and fell. A hand of no-legs made-things picked up the *shimo-kato* and carried it into the big melon-seed flying thing. When they came out again there was no *shimo-kato*.

"Look," Makes-Things said. He was pointing at the no-legs made-thing made dead by the *shimo-kato*. Its shell was ruptured open and the interior spilled out onto the ground. There were things that looked like thin vines of every color, a brown fluid that was too thick to be blood and other things without comparison. "Inside all made-things!"

"Big Ones make fly-things," Silver Fur stated. "Make work-things. Big Ones' very wise."

"Make friends with Big Ones," Healer suggested. "Big Ones help us. Teach us how to make fly-things."

Red Fur was hesitant. The *shimo-kato* made dead by the noise-things scared him. The noise things also hurt his ears. There was a small trickle of blood coming out of Makes-Things ears. "We watch. See what Big Ones do. Big Ones more powerful than *shimo-kato*. Make *shimo-kato* dead. Maybe make us dead."

II

The pseudocrustacean blissfully gnawed away at the bark of the featherleaf tree completely unmindful of any potential dangers that could be lurking in the nearby forest. This was typical behavior for a representative of its species as it had virtually no natural enemies.

The land-prawn, was a nasty little thing, which is how nature and evolution designed it to be. It ruined everything it came near in its constant search for food. Most creatures avoided the land-prawn. It didn't even associate with its own kind. Were it not for the fact that it was a parthenogenetic female that reproduced asexually, its species would have been long extinct.

So it was a bit of a shock when it found itself suddenly bereft of a head. Standing over the now decapitated creature was a small hairy biped holding a metal weapon with a leaf-shaped blade at one end and a counterbalancing metal ball at the other. The newcomer, a male, was little more than a foot and a half tall itself with a round head, big ears and a tiny snub nose. The hands that wielded the weapon enjoyed the advantage of opposing thumbs.

The tiny humanoid looked down at its kill with disproportionately large eyes then a smile came to him as he flipped the dead pseudocrustacean onto its back. Two solid strikes on the underside with the ball end of the weapon cracked open the shell allowing the furry biped to scoop out the gooey insides and stuff it into his mouth, which he did with gusto. When the meat became harder to dig out, the little being used his weapon to chop off one of the land-prawn's mandibles to use as a pick allowing him to get at the more difficult to access morsels. When done eating he turned around and raised his weapon above his head with both hands and proudly stated, "Yeek!"

Jack Holloway, semi-retired sunstone prospector and active Commissioner of Native Affairs, quickly pulled a small device out of a pocket and shoved it into his ear with one hand while holding a movie camera in the other. The camera was catching the Fuzzy rite of passage into adulthood while the ear device, an ultrasonic hearing aid, allowed him to understand what the Fuzzy was saying, or would have had he inserted it sooner.

Baby Fuzzy is too excited to pitch his voice in the human audible range, Jack thought with a smile, and he should be excited. *Baby made his first kill. He's a man, now.*

Jack took as much pride in the Fuzzy's accomplishment as any parent watching his son hit a homerun or hit a bull's eye the first time he picked up a rifle. And why shouldn't he? Hadn't he discovered and adopted the first representatives of *Fuzzy sapiens zarathustra*? The Fuzzies had come a long way since that fateful day when Jack Holloway discovered a small golden furred creature in his shower stall.

"I should have put more thought into Baby's name," Commissioner Gerd van Riebeek said. "He's a bit too big to be called 'Baby' anymore but he can't grasp the idea of changing it to something else. I should have called him 'Harry' or something."

Little Fuzzy, Mike, Mitzi, Mama Fuzzy, Ko-Ko and Cinderella ran over to congratulate Baby Fuzzy on his success. Little Fuzzy was slapping Baby Fuzzy on the back in a surprisingly Terran display of congratulation and affection, and then produced a pipe. The elder Fuzzy lit it and took a few puffs then offered it to Baby. The younger Fuzzy took a puff and coughed once then shook his head.

Just as well, Jack thought, *Baby* Fuzzy *still has a lot of growing to do and tobacco might stunt his growth.* The sapient being from Terra turned off his movie camera and joined the sapient natives of Zarathustra in offering his congratulations to the new hunter with Gerd.

"I would have thought Baby was still too young to hunt land-prawns," the xenonaturalist commented. "Near as I can figure he's about the equivalent of a human child around eight to ten years old. He can't be more than four Z-years old."

"Children of primitive cultures grow up quickly, Gerd," Jack said, "or they might not get to grow up at all. If a damnthing or flock of harpies killed all of Little Fuzzy's tribe then Baby would have to fend for himself. He's big enough to wield a chopper-digger so he's ready to learn how to hunt and survive."

"Hardly seems necessary with Pappy Jack around to protect them," Gerd observed.

"Well, Fuzzies and humans have only been together for a little over two years, you know. Their culture will take a while to adapt. Besides, we don't want them dependant on us for everything. Better they maintain their way of life as much as possible even with us looking out for them. That's why I made the North-East quadrant of the reservation a Terran *verboten* zone. Keep the Terran-humans away from the Fuzzies there and maybe they'll develop naturally without our screwing them up."

"Then why didn't you have him make his own chopper-digger instead of making him that metal one?" Gerd argued. "Terran speaks with forked-tongue, I think."

"Actually, Little Fuzzy had Baby make one out of a zarabuck antler," he countered. "He did a real fine job, too. Then Little Fuzzy told him to bring it to me and ask if I wanted to trade for a metal one."

Gerd raised an eyebrow then said, "That's great! They keep their skills and they use barter to trade up. We'll have to tell Ruth and Dr. Mallin about that. Hey, I'll bet we could even get a market for Fuzzy artifacts going off-world. We should talk to Victor Grego about the marketing possibilities."

"That sounds like a good idea. Those damn Baby Fuzzy hats are still popular on Terra, Gimli and Baldur, last I heard." Jack considered a moment then said, "We should open a Native Museum like the ones on Uller and Yggdrasil. Fill it up with Fuzzy tools, wax figures and whatnot. We can move Goldilocks' statue into it…or better, in front of it…no, wait, we just build it on the edge of the park near her statue. We could set up a viewing room for all the movies we took way back when we first discovered the Fuzzies. It would be educational and something for the tourists to gawk at. I'll bet the Fuzzies would get a kick out of it, too."

"Looks like Baby's gearing up for another go," Gerd said, as he watched Baby Fuzzy raise his weapon and move off into the forest. "You know, I expected him to attack the legs like Mama Fuzzy, but he runs by it and spins around like Little Fuzzy."

"Little Fuzzy worked with him before sending Baby out. Come on. It'll be interesting to see what he does with a second kill." Jack turned on his movie camera and followed the Fuzzies with Gerd close behind. "Too bad Ben is missing all of this."

"Where is our Colonial Governor anyway?"

"He's back at Government House doing his job…and hating every minute of it."

*   *   *   *   *   *   *   *   *

"How the Nifflheim did I let myself get put in this position?" Colonial Governor Bennett Rainsford yelled. "I want a recount, damn-it!"

"Usually it is the loser that demands a recount, Ben," Victor Grego, CEO of the Charterless Zarathustra Company, offered, "It was a fairly close election but you took it with a 10,000 vote lead."

"Wrong. I lost. I wanted out of this job. Nifflheim, I never wanted it in the first place but Commodore Napier boxed me in."

Grego shrugged and tried to keep from smiling. "Granted, it's a dirty job but somebody has to do it." *And you like the job more than you want to admit.*

Three Fuzzies playing together outside had heard the outburst and came to investigate. "Pappy Ben," the female asked, "You angry at Pappy Vic?"

"No, Flora," Ben said. "We are just talking loud like Big Ones do sometimes."

"Not angry?" Grego's Fuzzy Diamond asked. "Not fight like on vid?"

"Vid?" asked Ben.

"Diamond watches a lot of old Western movies," Grego explained. "He's just making certain we don't go out back and have a shootout."

"No, Diamond," Rainsford said. "Pappy Ben and Pappy Vic are still friends and everybody is happy."

"Go play with Flora and Fauna, Diamond, while Big Ones make big people talk about government," Grego added.

"Hokay, Pappy Vic," the Fuzzy agreed.

The Fuzzies scampered out and left the big people to their discussion.

"My mistake was in not running like hell when my appointment was up," Ben muttered, careful to keep his voice low lest it further upset the Fuzzies. "Two years was all I was supposed to be stuck for. By then we were supposed to have an operating legislative body and proper elections."

"Then why did you run in this last election?"

"Gus talked me into it," Ben admitted. "He said we needed to have at least two candidates for a proper election and nobody wanted to run against Juan Takagashi. I figured he would take this election hands down. I mean, Nifflheim, I didn't even campaign!"

"People vote their wallets," Grego said. "That's why I voted for you, too."

"Betrayed!" the Governor howled, then added dramatically, "*Et tu, Veek-tor?*"

"I fail to see what the problem is. You're governing a relatively small population, the treasury is in the black, thanks to the sunstone mining agreement, and you have very little that actually needs your attention."

"On the contrary I'm facing a few sizable problems. One of which is the influx of immigrants who landed here expecting to get rich," Ben argued, "only to find all the best land is already taken. These people need food, shelter and employment."

Grego rubbed his jaw then said, "Employment won't be too much of a problem. The Company is still scrambling to fill positions vacated when the Pendarvis Decision smashed our charter. People took off in droves looking to get in on the free land grab. More got arrested for aircar theft and others ended up working for you to fill slots in the police forces. I lost some good security men that way. Immigrants I can happily find jobs for…within reason."

"That helps but won't do it all." Ben shook his head as if to clear it. "In fact, you should be a little worried yourself about the population increase."

Grego raised an eyebrow. "Why me?"

"Because our agreement has you on the hook for planetary services. In the last year the population of Zarathustra has increased by over ten percent. That means greater demands for power, sewage treatment, communications and medical care for starters."

"Well, for the most part we are already situated for that. Home

Office always planned for Zarathustra to expand and grow, meaning more people to work for it and a larger population base to draw that work-force from." Grego stubbed out his cigarette before continuing. "We have sufficient resources to provide power for ten times the current population, as well as sewage treatment. Actually, most of the sewage is separated from reclaimable water and put into a mass/energy converter. More sewage equals more power. Same goes for non-recyclable trash. Thank Ghu we don't just dump garbage into land-fills like they did on Terra back in the first century AE, let alone spew sewage directly into the oceans! Medical is more of a problem, I'll admit. Hopefully, we can get some qualified doctors and nurses from the influx of immigrants."

"There will also be an increase in the need for schools and housing. The schools are on your plate, but the housing is on mine, plus increased law enforcement. Pretty soon the treasury will go from black to red." Ben opened a drawer in his desk and extracted two headache pills. "I'm going to be chewing on these things like candy before too long."

Grego thought for a moment then said, "Why don't you look into what other new governments did to generate revenue? Taxes are out, but there are tariffs on imports you could impose, for example."

"Hmm…I'll put Millie on research. You might be onto something there."

*   *   *   *   *   *   *   *

"Gerd, Jack, good to see you back." Ruth waved as the men and Fuzzies approached. "That little problem is getting bigger."

"You'll have to be a little more specific," Jack propted. Problems abounded for the Commissioner of Native Affairs.

"Fuzzy sanitation measures. The Fuzzies have been ranging further and further from the Reservation to 'bury the bad smells.' Well, a couple of Fuzzies were nearly trampled by a zarabuck because they ranged so far out. We need a better way of dealing with this."

Jack looked around at the numerous plots of overturned earth. It looked like a major gopher convention was in town. "We need a Fuzzy-sized latrine and a king-sized septic system to go with it. And a training vid. I think I have an idea."

Jack turned on his heel and marched into his office where he sat down in front of the viewscreen and punched in the code for Victor Grego's office. Within seconds the homely face of Myra Fallada, Grego's secretary, filled the screen.

"Mr. Grego's office. May I help…oh, Mr. Holloway! Is Mr. Grego expecting your call?"

"I'd be worried if he was," Jack said with a smile. "I just had an idea and I need his help with it."

"I'll see if he is free." The screen went dark with a bright CZC logo shining in the middle. The logo changed color in spectrum order; red-orange-yellow-green…before it shifted to blue the screen changed to Victor Grego.

"Jack, good to hear from you." Grego shook his hands together in traditional screen-greeting style. "Your timing is pretty good. I just got back from visiting Ben. Myra says you need some help with something?"

"I do, and it might make you some profit." Jack explained the problems with the Fuzzies and the need for an isolated waste disposal system.

"Yeah, I've been having the gardener swap out the soiled earth in my private garden since Diamond moved in," the CZC Head admitted. "A scaled down series of commodes on a heavy-duty septic system should do the job. A self-cleaning model might be best, at least until the Fuzzies understand how it works. Maybe adapter seats, like those used for potty-training young children, would do the job in most households. Yeah, I think we could pull in quite a bit of profit from that. Okay, assuming this takes-off, where do we send your royalty checks?"

"Royalties?" Jack thought for a moment. On some planets the ideas of government employees became the property of the government. "Send half to the Treasury and take the cost of installing the latrine here out of the other half."

"I think that would come out of the Fuzzies' sunstone revenues, Jack," Grego replied. "I'll talk it over with Ben and see what he says about it."

"Fair enough." Jack glanced out a window at the plods of earth. "Any chance we can get an advance on that and get started right away?"

Grego laughed. "I'll have an excavation and installation team out there tomorrow evening. We'll cut costs by pulling it from the marketing budget. I'll have to get a film crew out there for advertising and the training film after the latrine is up, though."

"Sounds good," Jack said. "I'll get my family ready to be film stars."

III

"For the love of Ghu would somebody get me a damned drink?"

Allan Quatermain and Natty Bumppo looked up from their jigsaw puzzle at the large unusually hairy sapient sitting up at the table with them in a wheelchair. Actually, all three of the table's occupants were extremely hairy but in the case of the Fuzzies it was a standard racial characteristic. Fuzzies, usually upset by sudden outbursts from Big Ones, took this sudden flare-up in stride. In the last few days they had heard it many times before.

"Dok'ta say no *coktail-drinko*, Pappy Gus," Allan said.

"*Likka* make livah go bad if not wait," Natty added.

They grow up so fast, thought Gus Brannhard. "I know, I know. But, Great Satan! A man could die of thirst in this place."

"If Pappy Gus thihsty, got wateh to drink," Allan offered.

"That stuff is murder," Gus muttered under his breath. "I wouldn't have cut back on my drinking if I'd known this was going to happen. I'd have tried to store it like a camel."

Allan and Natty had been unswervingly solicitous of the big man's health since he was admitted to the hospital, only leaving his side for necessary trips outside to bury bad smells and then just one at a time. Moreover, they adhered strictly to what Doctor MacTaggert ordered by preventing Gus from sneaking in a bottle of bourbon by bribing an orderly the day before. The orderly barely escaped with his hide intact when the Fuzzies caught him with the bottle hidden under his jacket. The hapless man had walked into the hospital room when the two Fuzzies raised their heads, sniffed the air and launched themselves at the orderly with chopper-diggers swinging wildly.

The orderly, sensing discretion would be the better part of valor, ran back out of the room where he collided with another orderly carrying a tray of food. Both orderlies went down, the tray went up and the contents rained down over both of them. Gus was laughing so hard at the display he forgot to be angry over not getting his hooch.

"Dok'ta say wait month so a'fishul liveh not go bad," Natty Bumppo reminded Gus for the *nth* time.

"Need time to a-jus' to body," Allan Quatermain added.

Gus wanted to argue but knew it was pointless. On almost anything else the Fuzzies would take his word as gospel, but a doctor saying Gus would hurt himself if he drank alcohol made them adamant to protect their Pappy even against himself. All Fuzzies were taught to trust doctors at Hoksu-Mitto, the Wonderful Place, when they first came in from the wild. They had to or else the medical teams would never be able to do work-ups and blood draws. So when a doctor said 'do this' or 'don't do that' the Fuzzies accepted it without question. Even if their Pappy disagreed.

Gus was considering other methods of sneaking in some libations when a visitor entered the room. The Fuzzies yeeked excitedly, then lowered their voices to the audible level yelling, "Pappy Jack, Pappy Jack!"

"Jack! Save me from this hirsute Temperance League," the Colonial Chief Prosecutor exclaimed.

"They're too tough for me, Gus." Jack Holloway smiled, as he ruffled the Fuzzies' fur. "Besides, it would take Science House another three months to grow you a new liver if you pickle that one too soon."

Gus swore blasphemously under his breath. "A cigar, then?"

"No smokko, eit'er, Pappy Gus," Allan reminded. "Dok'ta say so."

"They got you there, Gus. These two would make great babysitters."

"I should have named them Tomás de Torquemada and Konrad von Marburg," Gus growled.

Jack took a seat across from the cantankerous attorney. Gus put on a real show but Jack could tell he was enjoying the game with the Fuzzies, and maybe he was teaching them responsibility. "In a few weeks you'll be back to your evil old ways. Just be patient."

"A patient patient should be considered an oxymoron," he grumbled. "What brings you to this unholy den of morality?"

"Just visiting you, actually." Jack pulled a piece of red licorice out of a pocket and gave half to each Fuzzy. The Fuzzies thanked him and started in on the treats with gusto. He turned back to Gus. "I thought you might like to know that Baby Fuzzy is now an adult by Fuzzy cultural standards."

"Really? Good for him." Gus stroked his thick facial hair. "It seems like only yesterday he was hiding in my beard playing peek-a-boo."

"Well, we really don't know what the growth-rate and life expectancy of a Fuzzy is, yet," Jack explained, "so Baby could be anywhere from three to ten years of age, and the equivalent of a twelve to thirteen year old Terran child. Khooghras become breeding adults at eight."

"Khooghras only live about thirty Terran years," countered Gus, "assuming they aren't killed by something other than old age."

Jack raised an eyebrow at the litigator. "I didn't know you had been to Yggdrasil."

"I haven't been, but I read some legal precedents concerning Terran commerce with the Khooghras back during the Fuzzy Trial. Never know what might come in handy against a shark like Coombes. I have been to Mars, Baldur, Thor, Loki, Shesha and Freya, but that's about it."

"Freya?" Jack ruffled Natty's hair. "Any little Gus's running around there? The women are almost impossible to resist and are inter-fertile with Terrans, you know."

Gus made a sour face. "Freya was the second planet I hit after leaving Terra. My mind was on other things at the time. I'd forgotten that you'd been there." Gus absently stroked his beard. "That was, what, thirty years ago? I might have missed you by a few months or so."

"Give or take a few years. There are times that I wish I had stayed there, but I like my life here just fine, even if I am trapped behind a desk most days." Jack glanced over at Allan and Natty and thought of his own Fuzzies. "I wouldn't trade my life here for all the sunstones in the world."

"Speaking of sunstones how have the diggings been?"

"Well, as you know, I only go out on weekends and then only if the weather is good," said Jack. "But I hit one of the richest loads I ever saw just before I found Little Fuzzy. Or he found me, I should say. It's no Yellowsand, mind you, but with the improved microray scanner Henry Stenson made it takes less time to find the good deposits. If I was selling them I'd make as much in those two days a week as I did back when I was working the digs full time." Jack reached under his shirt collar and extracted a leather pouch. He spilled the glowing contents into his hand and showed them to Gus. It was several polished sunstones. "This is just my 'walking around' stash."

Gus was no expert but he estimated that there were a good 25,000 sols worth just in Jack's hand and the pouch still looked to be more than half full. He let out a low whistle. "You're not selling them?"

"One or two here and there, but for the most part I'm storing them up against either my retirement or my death. Don't get me wrong, I still have a lot of good years left, but there are far more behind than ahead of me and a sensible man makes provisions for the future."

"Guess I should do the same," Gus said thoughtfully. "Now that I'm a family man again, I should make provisions for Allan and Natty if something should happen to me."

"Family man again?" prompted Jack. Gus usually played very close to the vest when it came to his past.

"Did I say 'again'?" Gus shook his head as if trying to clear it. "Lack of suitable refreshment must be affecting my mind."

*   *   *   *   *   *   *   *   *

Ruth van Riebeek was exhausted. In addition to her duties at the Reservation, she still worked two days a week in Mallorysport with the Fuzzy Adoption Agency and the Fuzzy Protective Services Agency. That meant flying out to Alpha Continent twice a week. The mornings were not a problem since the three hour time difference worked in her favor. Ruth could get up at her normal time and set the aircar on automatic while she ate a leisurely breakfast during the trip out. With the time difference Ruth would arrive at the same time she left. The problem was in the stresses of the day followed by a three hour trip home. If she left at 1700, between the time difference and the travel time it would be 2300 when she arrived home.

Last Monday was a truly horrific day. There was the Fuzzy Family that was fed only table scraps and garbage by the adoptive family. Some people couldn't make the mental leap to accept that Fuzzies were people, not pets. A male, his mate and an infant Fuzzy had to be returned to the Reservation. The adoptive family was being charged with neglect and abuse.

Ruth simply couldn't understand how anybody could mistreat a Fuzzy, or a human child, for that matter. As a student of the psycho-sciences she could understand the traumas and mental defects that could create the propensities in a person, but to actually be faced with such a monster was a different matter.

Ruth flipped through her paperwork and one report caught her eye. "Lynn, what is this about an adoptive parent refusing to feed Extee-Three to his Fuzzy?"

"Actually, they both, the *pappy* and *mummy*, claim that their Fuzzy doesn't like Extee-Three," Lynn replied. "They lay it out and the Fuzzy just ignores it."

A Fuzzy hating Extee-Three! she exclaimed to herself. "Has anybody else tried feeding the Fuzzy?"

"Jeff tried. He said the Fuzzy nibbled at it as if to be polite, but no more than that."

"Let's get that Fuzzy in here and see what he does if he has a choice between Extee-Three, live land-prawn or something else…um…goofer meat, maybe. I want to see what he goes for first."

"I'll call the Garzas and arrange for them to bring Zorro in."

Zorro? The names people hang on Fuzzies!

"Good. I'll call Dr. Mallin and Juan Jimenez. I think they'll be very interested."

*   *   *   *   *   *   *   *   *

Since the Big Ones set up camp near Red Fur's tribe the game became progressively scarcer each day. Whatever the Big Ones were doing was scaring away all the animals. Except the *zuzoru*; nothing scared *zuzoru*. If anything, they were attracted to the Big Ones' camp. Red Fur's hunting party had no trouble collecting enough for everybody, but Red Fur and a few others disliked *zuzoru* although they would eat it when nothing else was available. Little One would only eat it if he was very hungry, while Runs Fast would eat *zuzoru* at every opportunity.

There was also the problem with Makes-Things' ears. They always hurt and he couldn't hear right. To him there was always a sound like a strong wind blowing even though the air was still. Red Fur believed it was caused by the noisy made-things that the *Koo-wen* used to make the *shimo-kato* dead. Healer sent Climber up into a rogo tree to harvest some *li-kou*, the healing plant that sometimes grew on tall trees. Runner caught a *hikwu* for the stinger venom. Healer used two flat rocks to pound the *li-kou* into a powder, and then added the venom and some water until it formed a thick paste. This was gently dabbed into Makes-Things' ears, and then covered with a wrapping of grass that went around his head. The surplus paste was wrapped into large leaves to be used later. The *li-kou* paste would be good for up to four hands of days if a little water was added when it dried.

To find fresh game, the hunting party traveled South until they spotted a *shikku*. Red Fur wanted to try to kill the *shikku* for the meat but Climber and Stonebreaker objected.

"*Shikku* big-big," Climber complained.

"*Shikku* run fast," Stonebreaker added. "We not run fast like *shikku*."

"Have pointed sticks for throwing," Red Fur argued. "We get close, throw pointed sticks, *shikku* make dead."

"*Shikku* big-big," Climber insisted. "Too big to carry back."

Red Fur had to agree that Climber had a point. He looked to Makes-Things.

After he had paced around the camp a few times, Makes-Things had an idea. "Use outside part to pull good to eat inside part," he explained. They would make the *shikku* dead and then cut off the hide and drag the usable parts in it. Climber was skeptical but Red Fur was the leader so she would go along.

Since Little One was not with them this time, and they were far from the Big Ones' camp, Red Fur spoke in his normal ultrasonic voice and laid out his plan of attack. Stonebreaker and Climber stealthily crawled behind the *shikku* while Red Fur and Makes-Things worked their way to the front.

The Fuzzies had just gotten into position when something startled the *shikku*. The beast leaped forward straight at Makes-Things. Red Fur jumped up and threw his pointed stick catching the *shikku* in the neck.

The animal reared up in pain, but not before crashing into Makes-Things, knocking him several feet back. Stonebreaker and Climber ran up quickly from behind to assist Red Fur. Climber leaped twice his height into the air and came down on the *shikku's* back, driving his sharp stick deep into the animal's hide.

Stonebreaker, disdaining the sharp stick, swung his coup-de-poing axe into the *shikku's* haunch. The three-way attack quickly brought their prey down. A final swing of the axe into the animal's skull finished it.

Red Fur ran to Makes-Things. The battered Fuzzy was still breathing, but unconscious. "Climber, make run fast!" he ordered. "Bring Healer!"

Climber turned and ran towards camp.

"Stonebreaker, cut *shikku* skin. Make drag-thing for Makes-Things and another for good to eat parts."

"We bring *shikku*? Makes-Things hurt bad!"

"Everybody still get hungry. Need good to eat things."

Stonebreaker was still skinning the *shikku* and Makes-Things was just waking up when Climber returned with Healer. A quick examination revealed that Makes-Things had a broken arm and leg.

"This bad," Healer said. "Not hunt. Might heal not right."

Makes-Things looked around then had another idea. "Get sticks and *shikku* skin. Wrap around broken parts. Make straight." Healer did as directed and fashioned a workable splint for the injured limbs. Makes-Things still needed to be dragged back on the hide, but he would live.

Back at the camp Red Fur called the tribe together. "Hunting not good here with *Koo-wen* scaring away *hat-zu'ka*. Soon, eat only *zuzoru*. We must move to place without Big Ones."

"Makes-Things not walk," Healer countered. "It many days before he can walk."

"We wait for Makes-Things to heal. Then we go," Climber said.

"Maybe have nothing to eat if stay," Little One added. The young tended to think with their stomachs.

Red Fur spoke up. "*Shikku* big. Have meat for many days. Have *zuzoru*. Not go hungry."

The rest of the Fuzzies agreed that hunger was not the problem and nobody wanted to leave Makes-Things behind. There was a discussion about what to do if Makes-Things was never able to hunt again.

Red Fur thought hard. Everybody contributed to the welfare of the tribe. Then Red Fur got an idea.

"If Makes-Things not hunt, then he will make things for everybody. New pointed sticks for throwing, maybe new things we never see before. Makes-Things very wise."

"What about the Big Ones?" Tells-Things demanded.

"We watch Big Ones," Red Fur declared. "See what they make-do."

"Maybe make friends with Big Ones?" Tells-Things asked. She was interested in the made-things that could make a *shimo-kato* dead as were all the tribe.

"Hope so," Red Fur replied. "Not want Big Ones for…" Red Fur hesitated. There was no word in the *Jin-f'ke* language to explain what he feared. So he created a new word, one than meant bad not-friends; *fuk'voko*. "Not want Big Ones for *enemies*."

IV

The group of men silently collected their luggage and then left the terminal. Once outside, the apparent leader of the group hailed a taxi.

"We would like a hotel near the edge of town," the leader said.

"Close to or away from Junktown?" the cabbie asked, with an edge of humor in his voice.

"Junktown?" the short man asked.

"I was just pullin' your leg, Pal. If you hafta ask ya don't wanna go there," the cabbie explained. "It's a slum."

"Actually, that would be fine," the taller man said.

The cabbie shrugged. The taxi flew over a series of abandoned warehouses, dilapidated homes and empty factories. The group remained silent until they were in a room at the Alibi Inn.

"Why did we have to take rooms in a dump like this?" the short stocky man with thinning red hair asked. "I'll bet they don't even have a robotic cleaning crew."

The room, while passably clean, was shabby compared to the better hostels on most Federation worlds. The owner of the Alibi Inn was a greasy shifty-eyed man with a ridiculous comb-over who fancied himself a sportsman. The floors and walls of all the rooms had animal skins on them, but nothing larger than a zarabuck hide. The mattresses were the only things that seemed halfway new, and were still well used. The group suspected most of the business done in the hotel was hourly instead of nightly.

"Two reasons, Dr. Rankin," the leader explained. "We do not want to attract undo attention, and here, in a location where morals are low and unemployment high, we will find the muscle we need to do the manual labor. I already have an inside track on who to see and who can be trusted."

Unlike the rest, the leader was schooled in the legal sciences. He was six feet tall and clean-shaven with thick gray hair. The skin on his face looked a bit tight, suggesting some form of plastic surgery, possibly even bone restructuring. There were faint scars on his throat that indicated vocal reconstruction to the trained eye, which could explain the rich baritone voice. Then there was the way he walked, as if he were having trouble maintaining his balance. But the most striking thing about him was his eyes. They conveyed a sense of sincerity that made a person want to trust anything he had to say. When he spoke everyone listened.

"Dane is quite correct," agreed the balding man with an ebony complexion. "However, I think we should get some bodyguards first. I would hate to be at the mercy of some of these morally and financially bankrupt locals. We should have had the advance party arrange that for us before we got here."

Dane turned to the dark-haired man sitting on a bed. "Lundgren, can you hack into the local constabulary databases to find us some likely prospects? Ex-cops who were on the take would be ideal."

"It will take a little time if they changed all the passwords after the Charterless Zarathustra Company lost its charter, but it's doable."

"Good. Let's get to work."

* * * * * * * *

John Morgan collected his sidearm from the security desk. Colony worlds allowed for the carrying of weapons, but they still had to be registered upon planet-fall. The entire process took over half an hour, mostly due to the background check. Once finished, he strolled out of the terminal and hailed a taxi.

"Where to, Bubba?"

Morgan looked at the driver with a quizzical expression. "What is a 'Bubba'?"

"Old Terran expression, like 'Mac" or 'pal'," the cabbie explained. "No offence intended. That's how I address all my fares."

He thought it over for a moment. On Terra cabbies addressed fares as 'sir', but colony worlds tended to be less formal. Mars Colony, for example, used 'partner' to address unknown persons, a practice derived from the early days of colonization. Well, when amongst barbarians, do as they do.

"Very well, ah, Bubba. Transport me to the CZC Company House."

"Yes, sir."

Morgan hadn't decided whether or not to stay at a hotel or to take advantage of his position as a major stockholder and stay at Company House. In either case, he needed to meet with the Charterless Zarathrustra Company CEO. He intended to do a lot of work there and it would be best to start off on the right foot. Home Office held Victor Grego in high regard, especially after his negotiating a deal with the local government that kept the CZC well in the black. A background check revealed that Grego had run successful operations on three uninhabited planets before coming to Zarathustra. He was a stern taskmaster, yet his employees liked and respected him. Grego could be a powerful ally.

Or a very powerful enemy.

*   *   *   *   *   *   *   *   *

"Nifflheim, what a dump. I've seen some ghettos on backwater planets before, but this place is worse than even a Yggdrasil hovel. What did you want to meet me here, for?"

Several people in the diner glanced at the booth where the two men, obviously from off-planet, were drinking coffee.

The taller of the two men noticed the turned heads and cautioned his associate. "Keep your voice down, Duncan."

Duncan "Ripper" Rippolone, a short, stocky man with almost white-blonde hair, pale blue eyes, and a deep tan snorted at his companion. "What'd I say, huh? Think anybody in this dump of a town gives a hoot in Nifflheim what I'm talkin' about? Gimme a break, Tony."

Anthony Nicholovich Anderson, a tall, wiry, light skinned man with a thick shock of red hair, rolled his green eyes in exasperation and spoke in a low voice so as not to be overheard. "We do not need to draw attention to ourselves, Ripper, especially in this Junktown, as the locals call it. Besides, we are here on business. In our business, getting noticed by anybody, cop, local, innocent bystander, whatever, is bad."

Ripper had heard the 'business' speech many times before, usually right before engaging in whatever enterprise he and Tony were about to undertake. "Enough, already," the shorter man said, as he unconsciously lowered his voice. "Well, if you're so hot to go unnoticed, maybe we should roll around in the mud a bit to blend in better with locals. I know the drill, Tony. Hell, I've heard it enough times."

"And yet it always fails to sink in," Anderson said. "Like that time on Baldur…"

"Hey, you promised to stop harpin' about Baldur. I could remind you about that time on Thor…"

"You have made your point, Ripper," the larger man sighed. "Just humor me and keep your voice down. I have been here for six months and can tell you that these are not people to antagonize. Once we have attended to our business, you can whoop it up all you like…on the ship home. We'll get you an adjoining room to mine at the Alibi Hotel here in Junktown. There we can lay low and avoid attention."

The two men left the booth after Anderson dropped a few sols on the table. He was only too aware of the eyes of the other patrons on his back as he and Ripper walked out of the diner. Outside, he spotted a newsstand and bought a newspaper, one made of real paper. Only colony worlds still bothered with newsprint.

"You got a plan to take him with us, yet?" Ripper asked.

Anderson took a deep breath and let it out slowly. "That…is a work in progress. I will have a better idea what to do after we meet with our contact. It is just about time for our appointment, so hail a cab."

Ripper pressed the call button on the side of a building. "Hey, yeah. You said you'd tell me who that was after I hit planet-side. It's been about half an hour since we met up, already."

"I didn't want to discuss it until we were well away from too many ears. His name," Anderson said, "is Raul Laporte."

* * * * * * * *

To say that Company House was a large building was a bit like saying Mount Everest was a fair-sized hill. It was enormous. Company House had eighteen levels, not counting the penthouse or sub-surface areas, with each level consisting of four to six floors, each floor being typically two stories high. Each floor contained over 250,000 square feet. Many of the levels were left vacant with an eye towards filling them later as the company grew. This was a building constructed to last for centuries, if not millennia. The framework and foundation were lined with iron collapsium. It was prohibitively expensive but guaranteed to outlast everything save the planet itself. Nickel collapsium lined the outer walls of the building rendering it immune to anything man or nature had to offer short of a direct nuclear blast or large meteor strike. Bomb shelters, though considered by many to be superfluous, made up thirty percent of the sub-levels.

The plumbing and ductwork and power distribution wiring were also designed to last forever. It wasn't feasible to install pipes and wires that could corrode and breakdown within walls and flooring that were nearly impossible to remove. As such the wiring was made of copper and silver alloys housed in super-insulating plastic, the air shafts lined with collapsed tin and the plumbing with collapsed aluminum.

Because of the shear size of the building, normal transportation was out of the question. There were over twenty elevator stations strategically located for vertical travel, but each floor needed additional travel aids. Conveyor belts were built into the center of every main hallway allowing for speedy movement from section to section.

If there was a drawback to the building, it was the energy utilization. Though powered by a Matter/Energy converter, the building was always hungry for more power. Elevators, conveyor belts, computers, lights, machinery, vehicle recharging stations plus the energy needs of Mallorysport; all took a toll on the power supplies. On paper an M/E converter looked like it could power an entire city from the potential energy of an apple. The reality was considerably less. Much of the energy released in an M/E converter was used to sustain the matter to energy conversion matrix. More energy was used to control that matrix…heat dispersal, energy dampening, energy distribution…at the end of the day less than thirty percent of the potential energy was diverted to run the machines and lights of Company House, a building capable of holding the total sapient population of Zarathustra, Terrans and Fuzzies alike.

As such, all non-recyclable waste was diverted to the M/E converter. As this proved insufficient, plumbing was designed to separate human waste from reclaimable water and feed it into the voracious converter. Every kilowatt was carefully tracked and logged by the company computer. Even a mild irregularity of a few thousand kilowatts had to be researched and accounted for.

The shareholders screamed bloody murder when they saw the bill for the construction project, but settled down when the CZC made the money back in the second year after construction. By the third year all agreed that it was money well spent. This was the building that held the Charterless Zarathustra Company and its CEO, Victor Grego.

Victor Grego was just finishing a conference call about a mysterious, though minor power drain with the various department heads when Myra walked into the office. She patiently waited while Grego made his good-byes then announced that he had a visitor. "It's a Mr. John Morgan, sir." Myra was slow to warm up to people, be they Terran or Fuzzy, and was especially frosty to those she felt shouldn't bother her boss.

"John Morgan?" Myra nodded. "What is his business?"

"He says he's a stockholder, Mr. Grego. I ran his name and verified his portfolio card. He holds 300,000 shares, sir."

Grego let out a low whistle. That many shares made him a serious heavy-weight in the Home Office. Only Grego himself held more shares… at least on Zarathustra. "Best we not keep Mr. Morgan waiting, Myra."

Myra nodded and left the office while Grego reached for a cigarette. He changed his mind when he considered the possibility that John Morgan might be a non-smoker. *Best not to start off on the wrong foot with the man.*

The first thing that struck the CZC CEO when Morgan entered was that he was wearing his gun belt. "Did you find something unsatisfactory, Mr. Morgan?"

Morgan looked confused as he answered. "I don't understand."

Grego indicated the sidearm.

"Oh. On the flight in I learned that people on Zarathustra typically went around armed everywhere. I was just trying not to look like a tourist. And, please, just call me 'John,' Bubba."

Bubba? "No problem, John. And, please, call me Victor." The two men shook hands then Morgan took a seat in front of the desk.

"Ordinarily, you would be correct. However, we check our arms before entering court houses, police stations and secure facilities…like Company House, except in special circumstances." Which made Grego wonder who fell down on the job at the front entrance. Chief Steefer would have a few things to say about that. "Anybody entering the building is required to check their guns at the security desk, unless they are accompanied by me. Law enforcement is exempt from this rule, of course."

"I appreciate the crash-course. That also explains why the security man at the entrance insisted on taking my ammunition, too. On Freya men carry guns, knives or swords pretty much everywhere. We only check our firearms when taking audience with the nobility," Morgan explained. "When meeting with one's peers it is actually an insult to go unarmed."

"Really?" Grego found himself interested and leaned forward. "Why is that?"

"It suggests that they consider you to be completely harmless," Morgan explained. "Like a woman or a child."

Grego showed his toothy smile and leaned back. "Well, in that case I accept the compliment of your carrying that cannon while meeting with me, and hope you will not be insulted that I neglected to be similarly armed."

"No offence taken, Victor. I have been to enough Terran Federation worlds to know that Freya is the 'odd-duck' with that particular tradition. I'll be happy to take it off." Morgan stood and removed his gun belt and hung it from a peg on the wall that Grego indicated. He noticed that Grego's gun belt on an adjoining peg held a Martian Special 9mm. Good for accuracy if lacking the stopping power of his own .457.

"I never went armed on Terra, and only for my first week on Mars. I had a little misunderstanding with the police before I put them away for the duration of my stay." Morgan turned away from the gun rack and noticed the floating replica of Zarathustra and its two moons, Darius and

Xerxes, illuminated by an orange light that simulated the local sun. "That's some time piece you have there, Victor."

"I had it made shortly after I set up my office here, oh, about fifteen years ago. I'll have to introduce you to the craftsman who made it."

Grego changed the subject by inquiring what John Morgan needed from his office.

"I do have a few questions. I am conducting an investigation for my own purposes. I am considering increasing my holdings in the company and want to make sure my investment would be sound."

Most investors paid people for this sort of thing. Morgan took a more hands-on approach. Grego respected that. "Okay, shoot."

"Well, I was reading the company reports and I saw where you justified using Company resources to make Terran Federation Space Forces Emergency Ration, Extraterrestrial Type Three…"

"Make that Terran Federation *Armed* Forces Emergency Ration, Extraterrestrial Type Three," interrupted Grego. "A slight name change to avoid copyright infringement."

"Ah, yes…but the ingredients are the same? Isn't there a patent on that, as well?"

"I had legal look into that. The patent expired long ago. I guess nobody thought to spend money to protect a product that was universally despised."

"I can well believe that! Anyway, then there was the research and development of Hoenveldzine… I see it has two names here."

"I'm sorry to interrupt again, John, but the brand name is different because Dr. Hoenveld discovered the long-chain molecule in the Extee-Three, but the name got hijacked before he could name it. I mollified him by putting his name on the scientific nomenclature, and slapping the publicity accepted name on as the brand. He gets his name in the history books and we keep the brand name for the public."

"And the brand name comes from… ?"

"From the Fuzzy language meaning 'Wonderful Food'."

Morgan grimaced. Apparently he had tried Extee-Three at some point. "In the reports you claimed that these actions were to generate good will from the colonial government and put a good face on the CZC, something you desperately needed after word got out that you had planned on putting a bounty on Fuzzy fur hoping to trap them out before their sapience could be proven."

Grego visibly winced at being reminded of some of his actions prior to the Fuzzy Trial. "I barely escaped being brought up on charges for some of my…activities at that time."

"I can imagine. But I would like to know what you were really thinking when you used the company's resources to, ah, help the enemy, so to speak."

Grego considered the question for a moment then decided to give a straight answer. When in doubt, tell the truth and be prepared for early retirement. "Truth be told, I didn't think about much of anything other than helping the Fuzzies. It was easy to plan atrocities against them when they were in the abstract, but when I found Diamond in my quarters and got to know him I realized just what I had done and was going to do—and felt more than a little sick about it. The Fuzzies needed food and medicine and the Company was the only thing on the planet that could provide it."

"You also said that you simply heated up some farina in a titanium skillet and the Fuzzies accepted it as Extee-Three. Why go to the trouble of reproducing the entire formula when it would be much cheaper to simply produce titanium heated wheat?"

"Ah, well, I considered it, but Fuzzies have almost identical nutritional requirements that we do. Simple wheat cakes wouldn't meet those needs and might cause digestion and evacuation problems over time. Fuzzies are carnivorous omnivores, just like humans, but tend to go heavier on the meat than we do. Feeding Fuzzies bulk wheat, even if they like it, would be much like a bread and water diet for us. The complete Extee-Three recipe would keep them healthy."

"I see," Morgan nodded. "You did a good job of justifying it in your report." Morgan flipped through his notes. "You also commissioned the 'Fuzzy Phone' with a Mr. Stenson, but then cancelled it after one run."

"I don't know how well you studied our recent history, but Fuzzies used to speak exclusively in the ultrasonic range," Grego explained, "The Fuzzy Phone translated their voices into the human audible range. Then Diamond, a Fuzzy I adopted, learned how to pitch his voice so that the phone was no longer needed. I did still pull a small profit by selling them to Jack Holloway as training aids at on the Rez." Grego explained the name and function of the Fuzzy welcome training center.

"You also managed to get the concession on Extee-Three here on Zarathustra, which is the only planet in the Federation where you can turn a profit on that stuff. I fed some to my pet kholph on Freya, once. He didn't like it worth a damn."

Grego laughed out loud. "That's what my chief chemist at Synthetic Foods, Malcolm Dunbar, said when he fed it to the kholph over in Science Division."

Now it was Morgan's turn to lean forward in his seat. "You have a Freyan kholph, here?"

"I'll check with the lab and see if we still have any. I guess I should mention that we are starting a new product line aimed at Fuzzies."

"Oh? Different varieties of Extee-Three?"

Grego sat a bit straighter. "That's not a bad idea, actually." Grego scribbled a note on his office pad. "Maybe land-prawn flavor…but no, it's the Fuzzy Flush." Grego explained about the sanitation needs of the Fuzzies and the problems involved. "When Fuzzies still lived a nomadic life-style, it wasn't a problem, but with all the Fuzzies adopted into Terran families and the population density on the Rez, the Piedmont and the various Fuzzy villages, more effective sanitation measures need to be taken. And we can expect a good return on the investment, too. Seat adapters will be simple formed plastic. That will have the highest return, I think."

Morgan scribbled a note on his pad. "Fuzzies and humans have been interacting for two years and this is the first time this issue came up?"

"Well, Fuzzies typically see to themselves, unlike Terran infants and pets. If a Fuzzy needs a little…personal time, he simply goes outside with his chopper-digger and attends to it on his own. I have heard that some people install something like a cat-box…"

"You seem to be doing well with products aimed at Fuzzies."

Grego smiled his overly toothy grin. "You better believe it. Profits are actually up a good ten percent over our pre-Fuzzy days. Saddles for the dog mounts, lint brushes for collecting loose Fuzzy hair, the Extee-Three…hell, at a tin of Extee-Three per Fuzzy a day, with 5,500 Fuzzies currently living on the Rez, the Piedmont and Alpha Continent villages, we sell almost a ton and a half worth a day, not counting the military and emergency supplies sales or the purchases made by people who adopted Fuzzies.

"And, that number is climbing almost daily as more Fuzzies come in from the wild. Shoulder-bag and chopper-digger production alone keeps us hopping. We're also testing alternative weapons and accessories for the Fuzzies; halberds, swords, crossbows…Diamond is very fond of his epee, for example. Instructional games and toy sales are also way up."

The two men went over a few more reports until Morgan ran out of questions.

Grego leaned back and affected an air of calm. "So, did I pass?"

Morgan closed his notepad and stuffed it into a pocket. "I really shouldn't discuss it until my research is done, Victor. I have a lot more snooping to do, if it wouldn't be too inconvenient."

"Fair enough," Grego agreed. "Have you found a place to stay, yet?"

"Not yet. I came in straight from the spaceport."

"The apartment below my penthouse suite is kept available for visiting dignitaries. It is easily as good as any five star hotel accommodations. You must stay there and I will not take no for an answer. I can also set you up with a company aircar and driver. Meanwhile, how about a guided tour of the company? Chief Steefer can take you around and even get you into the lab to see the kholph, if you like."

Victor Grego is a very forceful individual, Morgan thought. "Very well, I accept both offers, provided the Chief isn't too busy…"

"He's always too busy, but he'll jump at the chance to take you around. I imagine he'll take the opportunity to inspect the security arrangements while conducting the tour." *Plus he'll give you a subtle grilling and let me know what he finds out*, he added to himself.

Grego screened the Chief, who was indeed busy but could break away for a couple of hours. After John Morgan left with Chief Steefer, Grego called up the employee list. After scrolling down a bit he spotted a familiar name; Akira O'Barre. Grego thought for a moment trying to remember how he knew that name. Failing that, he opened her personnel file. There it was. Akira was one of the secretaries working for Myra when Grego brought Diamond in looking for a Fuzzy-sitter way back when he first discovered Diamond asleep on his bed. Akira had since been transferred to Records Division on Myra's recommendation. She was a top-flight file clerk with superior computer skills. She had also proved to be a capable assistant manager, too.

Grego made another call, this time down to Record Keeping. "Akira, could you come up to my office, please? Don't tell anybody where you are going and take my private elevator up. I'll send it down for you."

"Yes, Mr. Grego."

Grego screened-off and sat back in his chair. He wished he still had Ruth Ortheris—correction—Ruth van Riebeek on the payroll. She was used to all the cloak and dagger stuff from her time in the Terran Federation

Navy as an undercover operative. She did a good enough job on the CZC, after all. But she was gone and Grego had to make do. Akira O'Barre was a bright young woman, according to her personnel file. Hopefully, she would learn a little about what John Morgan was up to.

After a moment's thought, Grego called down to Science Division. Juan Jimenez' face appeared on the screen.

"Juan, Chief Steefer is bringing down a VIP. Give him the five centisol tour. And wear your guns when you greet him."

Juan couldn't keep the surprise off his face. "Wear my guns? Here? If you say so, Victor."

"The VIP is from Freya. It's a sign of respect…."

*   *   *   *   *   *   *   *   *

"This building must be ten times the size of the Charterless Freya Company's headquarters," Morgan observed.

Juan Jimenez, complete with gun belt, John Morgan and Chief Steefer stepped off the conveyor belt near an elevator in Science Division. "I've never been to Freya myself, so I couldn't say," said Jimenez. "Company House is about 650 feet by 500 feet at the base and around 2200 feet high not counting the transmission towers. However, we left Company House after that last set of double doors. Science Division is an annex connected by this long corridor. Still, the main building is the largest structure on Zarathustra." He turned to Steefer. "Chief, I understand you were on Freya during your time in the military. What do you think?"

"I didn't spend much time at the Charterless Freya Company's HQ, but I recall it didn't look as big from the outside," replied the chief. "Of course, it was built for an inhabited planet some three or four hundred odd years ago, and I recall it was being expanded on when I left."

Jimenez nodded. "Company House was designed and built when the CZC owned the planet outright," he explained. "Almost everything is here under one roof. Production Division, warehousing, the power plant, you name it. Science Division and Prison House are the only real exceptions. We had expected to fill the building in about one hundred years as the company grew along with the profitable exploitation of the planet."

Morgan nodded. "And now?"

"Well, the Fuzzies, through no fault of their own, did cause a hiccup in our long-term plans but Victor managed to get us through it and we are back on track, more or less."

"Indeed. I would have expected Science Division to be turned over to the colonial government after the charter was invalidated."

"Ah, Victor managed to hang on to it in the same deal he brokered to maintain planetary services and mine sunstones at Yellowsand."

Morgan nodded then turned back to Steefer. "Oh, Chief, let me get that." He reached over and plucked a few hairs from Harry Steefer's parade perfect uniform. "I can see that you are a man who takes pride in his appearance."

"The legacy of my time in the Service," said Chief Steefer with a nod. Then he pointed at his thinning scalp. "These days I have to hit myself with a lint brush several times a day to keep up with the fall-out."

"Why not use follicle replacement ointment?"

"I prefer to look my age and not delude myself with cosmetics." The chief ran a hand through his thinning hair. "I might just shave it all off when it starts to look really bad, though."

"So, you were on Freya, Chief?"

The Chief was taken off-guard by the sudden shift in topic. "Ah, yes, sir. It was about thirty-six years ago as a raw lieutenant straight from the academy."

"Really? What princedom were you stationed in?"

*   *   *   *   *   *   *   *   *

"Thanks for coming up on such short notice, Juan."

As soon as Akira left his office, Victor Grego summoned Juan Jimenez. Ordinarily, when something was bothering him he would have called Leslie Coombes. Unfortunately, Coombes was on loan to the Colonial Government as Acting Colonial Chief Prosecutor, while Gus Brannhard was laid up, as a favor to Ben Rainsford. Leslie Coombes was the only lawyer on the planet whom Gus would admit to being his equal. Fortunately, Grego had found that Juan Jimenez made an excellent sounding board once he was confident that he could speak freely without fear of repercussion.

However, Juan still tended to jump like a raw recruit being barked at by a drill sergeant when Grego called. He had come straight up to Grego's office without removing his gun belt.

"Mr. Morgan was just leaving the lab when you called, Victor," replied Jimenez. He never stumbled over using Grego's first name anymore. Back when he first replaced Leonard Kellogg as head of Science Division it took a concentrated effort on his part to use the CEO's first name, as was the prerogative of all division heads. Somewhere along the way the two men became more than company officers. They had become friends.

"That is what I wanted to talk with you about." Unlike when he was speaking with John Morgan and Akira O'Barre, Grego met with Juan Jimenez on the balcony. Meeting with a division head from behind a desk would have implied that he was being called on the carpet. "What do you think of our Mr. Morgan?"

Jimenez considered a moment before answering, then shrugged and said, "He seems like a good guy. Of course, if he's head hunting he might just be putting up a likeable front to catch us off-guard. I was a little surprised when he walked in with that planet-buster on his hip. Thanks for the heads-up about putting on the belt." He patted the gun belt then looked surprised to find he was still wearing it. Sheepishly, he hung it on the peg next to Grego's.

Grego gave a short laugh and took a drink from his highball. "It seems he got the impression that colonists traveled everywhere armed. He isn't completely wrong, of course."

"I noticed Morgan was particularly enamored with the kholph. I think he might be a little homesick. I offered to let him have a young one since the mated pair produced three offspring, but he politely declined. He said the young need to be kept together until they reach mating age, then they need to be separated quickly." Juan took a drink from his iced tea. He never drank on company time. "Do you think he's a head hunter?"

"That I can't be sure of. I had a chat with Akira from Records. Morgan will be going through the sales records, product placement reports and who knows what else? Akira will be keeping us informed on everything he does. Meanwhile, Chief Steefer will do a background check on him."

Jimenez leaned forward. "Good idea...wait...Akira O'Barre? She'll likely try to put a ring in his nose and lead him around by it. I've heard some stories...."

"Don't tell me about them! I want plausible deniability." Grego finished his drink. "We'll keep our ear to the ground and see if there are any rumblings."

V

To look at him, one would never think that Raul Laporte was a respectable businessman…nor should they. He was tall, lean and swarthy with slicked-back hair and a black handlebar mustache that instantly summoned to mind the image of a cartoon villain. A long reddish scar marred the left side of his face an inch from the ear completing the almost stereotypical image of a thug. But Laporte was more than just a mere thug…he was a criminal artisté. Since his arrival on Zarathustra he managed to get into a sunstone fencing operation, extortion, stolen goods, racketeering and even an information brokerage that traded in CZC and Terran Federation Naval secrets, not to mention his connections to numerous robberies and the occasional murder.

As the owner of The Bitter End, a nightclub in Junktown, Laporte had access to every lowlife on Zarathustra. This allowed him to act as middleman for most of the criminal activities in Mallorysport and especially in Junktown. However, hard times had befallen Laporte. Sunstones, once the sole domain of the Chartered Zarathustra Company for legal purchase from prospectors, were now on the open market for anybody to buy, undercutting his illicit gem fencing operations. The information brokerage died out when the Pendarvis Decision smashed the Chartered Zarathustra Company's charter, resulting in the CZC no longer buying secrets, or even having any worth keeping. That left him with plain vanilla robbery and extortion.

Not for the first time Laporte considered taking over Leo Thaxter's various ventures of shylocking, protection and money laundering, but as long as Thaxter was alive—even in prison—he presented a danger. All it would take is a big enough case against one of Thaxter's cronies or henchmen and they could slap old Leo into a polyencephalographic veridicator and make him talk about how this, that or the other person was connected and quicker than you could say 'lawyer', everybody gets busted. In fact, most of Thaxter's enterprises were already in shambles, the result of his being connected to the Fuzzy faginy ring and its CZC sunstone vault caper.

Laporte sat behind his desk and absently sharpened his knife. This was something he did whenever he had to do some thinking. One of the benefits of living on a colony world was that everybody carried weapons, so he didn't stand out by lugging around such a large bowie knife. Ironically, the major drawback of living on a colony world was that *everybody* carried weapons and they were not at all reluctant to use them. Laporte had to be very careful when and whom he tried to strong-arm.

For instance, no amount of money would ever entice him to take on, say, Jack Holloway. Everybody who ever tried was now dead and buried. For that reason alone Laporte would avoid antagonizing Holloway directly or indirectly. So, when the two men in front of his desk suggested he do just that, Laporte picked up his whetstone and methodically worked his blade.

"Whattaya think, Mr. Laporte?" Duncan Rippolone inquired.

"I think what you ask for is suicide," the gangster stated. "That is what I think."

"Oh, come on," the shorter man argued, "this is a two-bit backwater planet—"

"With a population just over one point one million and growing, and with a spaceport controlled by the same company that manages the prison," Laporte finished. He stabbed his knife into the top of his desk for emphasis. Laporte liked to do that for the intimidation factor it provided.

The numerous scars in the desktop attested to how often he used this tactic. "Let's say you manage, against all odds, to grab up Gus Brannhard. How do you plan to get him off-planet? They'll veridicate every person who even looks like they'll buy an off-world ticket. And Brannhard tends to stand out in a crowd."

"We could disguise him—" Anderson started.

"That's meaningless to a cop with a DNA scanner," Laporte interrupted. "When Brannhard was appointed Colonial Chief Prosecutor they took his DNA, did a retina scan, mapped every scar and blemish and even X-rayed his teeth and skeletal structure. There was an attempt to kidnap a public official on Loki a few years back. They drugged him up, pasted a fake beard on him and tried to get him off-planet. They would have made it if the beard had stayed on. After that they took the precautions I already mentioned. Rainsford was quick to follow the Loki example to protect his cabinet. Fingerprints can be altered, retinas can be covered with implants, scars can be removed and teeth and bones can be worked on, but DNA comes with a lifetime guarantee."

"DNA can be masked," Anderson said. "How do the scanners work, here?"

"A swab of saliva is dropped into a receptacle and the scanner breaks it down almost instantly," Laporte replied, as he pulled his knife out of his desktop and started working it again. "Hard to beat that."

Rippolone snickered and Anderson glared at him until he settled down. "On Terra, a person's hand is placed in a box-like contraption that reads DNA instantly. They were brought into use over a year ago because the out-dated scanners that are still in use on the colony worlds are now beatable."

Laporte put down his knife and whetstone and looked squarely at the taller man across from him. "Beatable how?"

Anderson produced a small capsule from a pillbox and handed it over to Raul Laporte. The capsule was no different from what one might purchase at a drugstore to counter the symptoms of a common cold.

"How does it work?"

"You keep it in your mouth until you see a cop with a scanner come your way. Then just bite into the pill and swish it around. For the next fifteen minutes, you have somebody else's DNA in your mouth. It only works on the saliva, so it is useless on the newer scanners."

"Where does the DNA come from?" Laporte turned the capsule over in his hand.

"Homeless types, bums who were paid off for a blood sample," Anderson explained. "People with no criminal records."

"How many of those pills you got?"

"Forty pills," supplied Anderson. "Five for each DNA signature with eight different signatures. Color coded so you can tell them apart."

"In case they retest anybody more than fifteen minutes apart," Rippolone added. "If they get wise to one sample we just switch to another."

"I see." Laporte returned the capsule to Anderson. "Now all we have to do is get the bag on Brannhard, fit him with contacts, shave his whole body and arrange for a new identity and get him to cooperate when you shove that pill in his mouth. Sure, nothing to it."

"I realize this presents a significant challenge."

"A challenge is hunting a damnthing on foot in a loincloth armed with a knife," Laporte interrupted. "This is just plain impossible."

"Whazza damnthing?" Rippolone asked.

"Local carnivore," explained Anderson. Unlike his associate, he had read-up on the local flora and fauna during his time on Zarathustra. "Three horns and seven kinds of mean."

"The point is that we have no way of grabbing him up without getting the whole planet in an uproar. Brannhard used to get people out of a jam with the law. The fact that he now works the other side of the fence hasn't hurt his popularity one bit with his former clients, partly because he recuses himself when an old client is prosecuted. And almost everybody he has personally prosecuted is still in jail. You won't find many people willing to help with this caper. Grabbing him will be relatively simple, but getting him off-planet will be a major bitch and a half."

"This will take considerable study and planning," Anderson agreed.

"Gentlemen, I fail to see how taking part in this caper in any way benefits me while the numerous downsides are readily apparent," Laporte said, as he resumed sharpening his knife. "While I personally would like to see Brannhard gone, he would simply be replaced by somebody else, like Coombes, who is currently keeping his seat warm. I have made some very dangerous, not to mention powerful enemies on this planet. I barely escaped indictment after the CZC robbery, even though I had nothing to do with that."

Laporte leaned forward and pointed his knife at the two men and said with special emphasis, "I don't need to make any more enemies in the government than I already have. Especially, Holloway. He tends to shoot back first. Brannhard and Holloway are as thick as thieves…if you will pardon the irony of that expression."

"Who is this Holloway you refer to?" Anderson asked. "Is he a player?"

"Jack Holloway is most definitely a 'player,'" Laporte explained, as if to a small child. "He is a close personal friend to Grego, Rainsford and Brannhard, as well as being the Native Affairs Commissioner and one hell of a gunfighter. He's killed more men than I ever expect to. So many in fact that when somebody draws on him they call it suicide."

"Aw, you colonists always exaggerate about these things," Rippolone said. "I'll bet I could take him if I had to."

"Feel free," Laporte smirked. "I'll send flowers to your next of kin. By the way, what is your interest in Brannhard, anyway? You seem prepared to go to a great deal of trouble to get him off-planet alive."

"Our organization has had prior dealings with your Colonial Chief Prosecutor," Anderson supplied. "There is an open contract on his head and we intend to collect."

*   *   *   *   *   *   *   *   *

Juan Jimenez returned to his office in Science Division to find Dr. Mallin patiently waiting on the couch. Juan couldn't help thinking that Dr. Mallin always took a seat on a couch if one was available. He wondered if it was an occupational habit or a subconscious cry for therapy.

Jimenez welcomed the psycho-scientist then took a seat in the chair across from the couch. "So, Ernst, what can I do for you?"

"Have you heard from Ruth van Riebeek, today?"

"I just got back to the office. Let me check." Jimenez went over to his desk and checked his viewscreen messages. There were a few of the usual fare; various sub-division heads wanting his approval for one thing or another, the weekly complaint from Anton Bayley about this or that. Finally, there was the message from Ruth.

He checked his watch and concluded Ruth would be at lunch. He scribbled a note to call her after 1300 hours and then returned to his chair opposite Dr. Mallin. "I missed her call while I was out. Does she need something from Science Division?"

"Actually, no." Dr. Mallin leaned forward. "She wants my expertise in the psycho-sciences and yours as a naturalist."

This got Jimenez's attention. There wasn't much call for him to work in his field since he was promoted to head of Science Division. "What would she need both of us for? Our fields are pretty far apart, and Gerd is a xenonaturalist. He would be better qualified than me, especially since I now spend more time running this division than practicing my vocation."

"Ruth doesn't want to drag Gerd over to Mallorysport without good reason."

Better to bother me, he thought wryly. "Over what?"

Mallin showed his secretive smile. "It seems that she found a Fuzzy that doesn't like Extee-Three."

Jimenez had to admit that it was unusual, but variances in dietary habits were to be expected in sapient beings.

"This Fuzzy also passes on land-prawns."

That caught his attention. "A Fuzzy that doesn't like land-prawn? What about the other hokfusinated foods, like the juices and candy we produce?"

"According to Ruth, the Fuzzy, whose name is Zorro, can take it or leave it."

Jimenez digested the information. "So she's wondering if it could be something psychological, like maybe Zorro doesn't want children, physical, maybe the Fuzzy is sick, or maybe even some new mutation in the Fuzzy's genome?"

"Yes, that sums it up. I will admit to looking forward to talking to this Fuzzy, excuse me, to Zorro."

"I'll have to bring Dr. Hoenveld in on this." Jimenez went back to his desk and took a seat. "We'll have to do some blood draws and look for pathogens, do a full body scan and check for parasites…"

"Be sure to get me a good scan of the brain," Mallin added. "There could be a physical cause for aberrant behavior. I want to rule that out before I delve into his psyche."

"Good thinking, Ernst. I'd better bring Victor in on this, too. Hmm… Jack Holloway will need to know…but I imagine Ruth will take care of that."

Dr. Mallin asked, "Do you think we might be overreacting to an isolated case?"

"No. First of all, we don't know if this is an isolated case or the beginning of some sort of epidemic. A pathogen that inhibits normal behavior could be very damaging to any species. We need to get ahead of this if we can."

"Assuming that it is a pathogen, of course," Dr. Mallin said.

"What else could it be?" he asked, his hands outspread.

*   *   *   *   *   *   *   *

"Sir, you need to see this."

"What do you have, Hendrix?"

Hendrix indicated a screen to his left. Several red silhouettes were grouped together. They were somewhat anthropomorphic though very small compared to Terrans.

"Fuzzies?"

"That's my guess, sir."

"Do they know we're here?"

"We don't have audio, yet, and we still need to get the translator up."

"What's the holdup?"

It had taken all night to get the canopy up in time to block the surveillance satellites. The canopy was constructed of a lightweight fibroid weave designed to refract infrared light and muffle ultra-sonic noise, and it was very heavy and hard to setup.

"Ah, Nifflheim," the leader grumbled. "Well, priorities are priorities."

"What do we do with them?" Hendrix glanced back at the screen. "Stuff them in the mass converter like the damnthing?"

"Only as a last resort. Killing Fuzzies is bad for your health—if you get caught. This area doesn't have any outposts or human inhabitants. Those Fuzzies won't even know what a Terran is. We just stick to our own area and hope they do the same."

"And if they come snooping around?"

"Give them enough Extee-Three to hold them until we're done. Hey, tell everybody to stop shaving until we bug-out. Maybe they'll think we are big Fuzzies. At the very least it would confuse them if they try to I. D. us later."

The leader signaled for the screen to be turned off then called some men over to him. "You all heard that?"

They had.

"We have weeks of work to do here and if we are discovered it will all be for nothing. So let's be careful and above all, don't mess with the Fuzzies. I'd rather be busted for illegal prospecting than murder any day."

One man spoke up. "Maybe we should pack it in and try again after the Fuzzies have moved on."

"This is a one-shot operation, people. Too much money and time went into this for us to just pack it in. We will never get another chance like this."

VI

John Morgan had wasted no time in getting to work. Grego arranged for a suite of rooms below the penthouse for him. It was easily as large and well-appointed as anything in an affluent hotel on Terra, just as Grego had promised. The décor was tastefully done in post-modern colonial Zarathustran. No animal heads adorned the walls. Instead, there was a collection of native artifacts from several worlds. The newest additions were of Fuzzy origin. On the floor there was a large damnthing-skin rug in front of a fireplace that could burn real wood.

Climate control in the building eliminated dust from the air and maintained the humidity at optimal levels, eliminating the need for regular maid service for an empty room. There were signs that someone had been through the room, and recently. Morgan extracted a small device from his suitcase and waved it around the room. Nothing happened.

I guess Grego has the maid staff go through each suite before anybody takes occupancy, Morgan thought, *not a sign of a surveillance device anywhere in here, though.*

Victor Grego also assigned him an office near the file rooms and even sent over a secretary to assist him. Morgan suspected the secretary, Akira Hsu O'Barre, was reporting his movements back to Grego. That was fine with him since anything else would have denoted a lack of healthy suspicion on the part of the Company CEO. It also made up for leaving his room un-bugged.

Morgan got busy first thing the next morning. He inserted a microdisc into his computer terminal and ran a security program that would block anybody from tracking his virtual activities, then plugged a back-up drive that would store all his research. Everything he did on the terminal from that point on would be completely untraceable.

"Here are the files you requested, Mr. Morgan." Akira stood in the doorway with an office box in her hands. Despite the best efforts of Terran civilization to eliminate hard-copies, paper still accumulated in every office in the Federation. "These are the environmental reports, geology reports and the meteorological trends of the last twenty-five years. I also have that study on Zarathustran background radiation you requested."

"Thank-you, Akira. Just put it all down on the desk. And call me 'John.'" Morgan quickly cleared a section of the desk and Akira set the box down. "No point in being so formal."

"I think this would go a lot faster if you used the computer," the young woman pointed out.

"I have an affinity for print, I guess. Besides, most computer files are either scanned or transcribed from paper files, and often edited down. This way I get the whole unabridged information. But I will do some research on the terminal."

Akira leaned on the box and looked over the mountain of files that dominated the desk. "Yes Mr…John. Does anybody ever call you Jack?"

"Not more than once," Morgan said, grimacing. "I tried it on for size when I was in college and decided it didn't fit. By and large I don't much care for nicknames." He rifled through the files in the box then asked, "Can you get me some information on the local government? Names, positions, backgrounds; that sort of thing."

"I'll check. Back when the Chartered Zarathustra Company owned the planet outright, people coming in had to get handprinted and supply background information. We should still have that, plus the news archives."

"That would be fine. I'm especially interested in anything we have on the Native Affairs Commissioner, the Colonial Chief Prosecutor and anybody who has ever been to Freya."

"Freya?" Akira thought it was an odd request but held her tongue. Maybe John was homesick. Akira stood close to Morgan then said, "I was thinking about going out for drinks after my shift. I was wondering if you would like to join me?"

Morgan smiled and replied, "Actually, I was thinking of asking you the same thing. Where did you have in mind?"

"The Bitter End. It's a lounge over in Junktown."

*   *   *   *   *   *   *   *   *

"Do you know what you are going to say, Darloss?"

"Relax, Dane…yes, I do. I've been rehearsing all morning." Professor Darloss, despite his affected calm, was very nervous. While he was an experienced lecturer from his time at Ares University, a small community college on Mars, he had never been on a broadcast show. Tonight he was going to be on CZCN, the major broadcast company on Zarathustra. The fact that the whole planet might see him did nothing to settle his nerves.

"Do you need a tranquilizer?" Dane reached into his pocket and produced a medicine bottle filled with pale blue pills. Darloss shook his head and Dane returned the bottle to his pocket. "Actually, it might help if you feel a bit shaky. We don't want you coming across as an experienced talking head. But you can't be too nervous. Just pretend you are teaching a class back on Mars."

"I was fired from Ares, if you recall," the professor snarled.

"For an impropriety with a student, wasn't it?" Dane suppressed a chuckle. "You should have waited for tenure before getting frisky with the co-eds. Be that as it may, your teaching and lecturing skills were never in question. This is well within your skill set."

Darloss fumed inwardly at being reminded of his indiscretion, but grudgingly admitted that Dane had a point. "Fine. I'll take one of those pills with me, just in case."

Dane smiled as he again produced the pill bottle.

* * * * * * * * *

Unlike what might be expected from a nightclub on the outskirts of Junktown, The Bitter End was not a dive. Originally intended to be a front for Raul Laporte's less-than-legal activities, it became popular with the young well-to-do. Laporte, knowing a good thing when he saw it, quickly expanded the lounge and improved the interior with an eye towards attracting even more such clientele.

As a front operation, Laporte was careful to keep all illegal activities out, even his own. Any connection made between himself and any crime on his property would get him quickly put under veridicator interrogation. While he couldn't be forced to answer any question, that failure to cooperate with the police would result in numerous search warrants and there was no telling what they might find. So, Laporte paid his bribes to the right people and normally kept the less savory elements out of his club.

"There's no way to get at him while he's in Medical House."

Anderson rolled his eyes in exasperation. "Ripper, when we get him, we will need him in reasonably good health. We can wait until he has recovered."

Raul Laporte, tired of sitting in his office with his off-world guests, suggested that the three of them continue their discussion in the lounge of The Bitter End. Like all of his enterprises, the lounge was equipped with anti-surveillance devices to keep anybody from listening in on what happened inside its walls. As the owner he had a private booth well away from the patronage so they could speak freely without being overheard and still keep an eye on things.

"Wouldn't he make a better bargaining chip if he was still sick?" Rippolone pulled a cigar out of his pocket and lit it. "Y'know, like if something went wrong and we needed an out?"

"Please explain to your associate the downsides of putting the bag on a sick man," Laporte said, as he rolled his eyes in exasperation.

"If he dies while we have him then we risk a bullet in the head for nothing." Anderson extracted a cigarette from a pack and lit it off Rippolone's cigar. "We need him healthy if we plan on taking him back to Terra for the pay-off."

"Yeah, I get that, but how long will it be before he gets better?" Rippolone retorted.

"We have two weeks until *The City of New Chicago* leaves for Terra," Anderson explained. "Waiting works to our advantage; it gives us time to plan."

Laporte took out his knife and inspected it. Since the two men from Terra arrived he had been working it quite a bit. By the time this whole thing was over he might have to replace it. A couple of patrons glanced his way and started whispering among themselves. Laporte quickly put the knife away. "Brannhard lives out in the country north of Mallorysport. He'll be easy to nab out there."

"After he gets out of the hospital, then." Anderson nodded. "We have time. Ripper and I have rooms in Mallorysport. You can reach us there if anything develops." He produced a business card from the Zoroaster Hotel. On the back, in handwriting, was a room number.

*   *   *   *   *   *   *   *

"I half-expected this place to be a dive," John Morgan admitted. He took in the atmosphere of the lounge as they looked for a vacant table.

"Why is that?" Akira asked.

"The neighborhood we came over on the way in."

"Oh! You mean Junktown. Yeah, it's pretty bad, but The Bitter End is the hottest place on Alpha continent. The owner is reputed to be some sort of mobster, so nobody messes with the customers or the parking lot. I wouldn't want to walk home through Junktown, though."

"I wouldn't think so." Morgan looked about and noticed that many of the patrons were armed. He had left his sidearm in his quarters while working and didn't bother to retrieve it before leaving with Akira. Now he wondered if that was a social *faux pas* for this world. "The owner doesn't have people check their guns at the door?"

Akira shrugged. "It's a colony world. People hand over their teeth quicker than their guns. But nobody would dare to start a fight inside The Bitter End." She jerked a thumb over her shoulder indicating two large men with noticeable bulges under their jackets. "Security."

She jerked her other thumb towards the back corner where an elevated table with three men were sitting. One of them was sharpening a knife. "The one with the bowie knife is the owner, Raul Laporte."

Almost on cue, the man with the knife glanced around the room and quickly put the blade away.

"There's an empty table over there," she said.

They selected a table near the dance floor. Akira grabbed a chair and plopped down before John could hold it out for her. The directional sonics that allowed the music to reach near ear-splitting levels for the dancers was barely a distraction off the dance floor, allowing John and Akira to converse without yelling.

"Do a lot of people come here after work?" Morgan asked.

Akira waved to somebody at the bar. "I come a couple of times a week. It helps me unwind."

A barmaid approached the table. "What are you drinking?"

"Do they serve Freyan ale here?" he asked. They did. "That will be good. You?"

"I'll have the same," Akira replied. "I've never tried ale before."

The drinks arrived and she tried an experimental sip. "It's like a strong dark beer but thicker."

"Best go easy on that until you get used to it," Morgan warned. "Back in college I used to win a lot of drinking contests with that ale."

"That's right; you mentioned you attended Mars Colony University. What was that like?"

He took a long drink then said, "A bit strange at first. The academics weren't so bad, but the free time took some getting used to."

"The free time?" Akira took another drink. She was already feeling the effects. "What was wrong with the free time?"

"They had some of the damnedest activities," he explained. "There was a huge fan-club, a term we never used on Freya, by the way, for post and pre-atomic fiction writers, especially the ones that wrote imaginative stories about Mars. They would hold big parties and dress up in these elaborate costumes based on characters from the books. The fraternities were even named after the writers. There was Epsilon Rho Burroughs and Rho Digamma Bradbury and Heta Beta Pi—"

"That sounds great!" Akira interrupted. "On Terra it was usually toga parties. Which frat were you in?"

"Epsilon Rho Burroughs. And we had our share of toga parties, too, though at least one person would dress up as Ares, god of war. But mostly we would stick to the Mars parties. My frat tended to do the Burroughs themes, mostly."

"That sounds like a lot of fun," Akira squealed. "I'll bet you would make a very dashing John Carter."

"Just between you and me, I did," Morgan admitted half-smiling. "My fraternity had a tradition of throwing what they called a 'Barsoom Bash' every semester and the part of John Carter went to the youngest freshman named 'John' or 'Carter'. May the Gods help the man with both names! He'd be stuck with the nickname "Warlord" his entire time at the university. Anyway, I had to spend the entire evening walking around half-naked with a rapier on my hip. Those ancient writers had odd ideas of what appropriate attire consisted of. I am surprised that you are familiar with the character, though. I had to look it up."

"I filled one of my electives with pre-atomic literature back in college. Oh! Tell me you have pictures of yourself in costume!"

"I do, though I've never shown them to anybody." John's face took on a reddish shade. "I also had to kiss all the sorority girls dressed up as Dejah Thoris." John shook his head. "Freyan society is a bit more reserved than what I was exposed to on Mars and it took a while to adjust."

"How did you pay your way through? I could only afford community college on Terra and I had to pay that off with the work-exchange program."

"Work-exchange?"

"Yeah. You sign on with an off-world company and they pay your tuition, then you have to work on a colony world for so many years. The Chartered Zzarathustra Company paid for my schooling, so I have to work here for seven years before I can go back to Terra." Akira took another drink then said, "Your parents must have been rich to send you to Mars from Freya."

The Freyan's face took on a serious mien. "Actually, I never knew my parents. I was raised by my mother's brother. He was fairly wealthy and saw to my education even though he didn't approve of my leaving Freya. I received a generous allowance while in college." John finished his drink and signaled for another before changing the topic of conversation. "When will you be going back to Terra?"

"Well, I have three years left on my contract, but I think I'll stay here. Zarathustra is my home now. All my friends are here and my parents are thinking of immigrating now that Zarathustra is a Class IV planet, subject to Federation law." Something caught Akira's eye and she waved. A woman at the bar waved back then started over to the table. "That's Betty Kanazawa from accounting."

Betty was a statuesque woman with glossy black hair, full lips, semi-Asiatic eyes and olive skin. When the light hit her navy blue blouse just right it became transparent. "Akira, who's the hunk?" Betty asked, as she took a seat. She turned to John. "You must be new here. I'm Betty."

"John." Morgan made a concerted effort to keep his gaze upon the woman's face. "I just arrived on Zarathustra."

Betty gave Morgan a visual once-over then said, "Welcome to Fuzzyworld, John."

Morgan looked at Akira with a raised eyebrow.

"That's what some people are calling Zarathustra. It's a slang-thing."

Morgan turned back to Betty. "Are you here with your date?" Betty nodded. "Why not have him join us?"

"We already have a table with some friends." Betty pointed to a table on the other side of the dance floor.

Morgan looked where Betty pointed. "Which one is yours?"

"The redhead, Frank Patel from administration."

"I thought you were still with Manuel." Akira glanced at the other table. "Although, Frank isn't bad looking. Snappy dresser, too."

"Manuel is back with his ex, again." Betty glanced at John. "Better be careful or I'll come after the stud, here. Nice to meet you, John."

John stood and bowed slightly before remembering that such niceties were rarely observed in Terran society…at least not in bars and lounges. "It has been a pleasure, Lady Kanazawa."

Betty smiled and bowed back before returning to her table. John took his seat and turned to Akira. "What is a 'stud' and a 'hunk'? I assume these to be slang-things, as well."

"Oh, right, Terrangelo is your second language, isn't it? You speak it so naturally I forgot. Well, those are archaic terms applied to particularly attractive men, usually."

John appeared slightly embarrassed and changed the subject. "I'll have to get a new primer on Terrangelo. I guess I am not as conversant as I had thought."

"Say, how many languages do you speak?" Akira asked. "I speak some Fuzzy and a little college Latin."

"Well, there is Terrangelo, Sosti, which is the Freyan language, ancient Martian, which was a requirement at Mars U, Khooghra, Barsoomian…"

"Barsoomian?"

John laughed. "Yes. It was an artificial language based on Burroughs' Mars stories created by my fraternity. Pledges were expected to learn it or they weren't accepted into the frat. Let's see, there is also Latin, Ullerian, Thoran and most recently some Fuzzy."

"Wow! You must have a real ear for linguistics."

"Well, if you speak the local tongue, you get more respect from the natives."

"I just remembered. Freyan women are supposed to be more beautiful than Terran women." Akira feigned a pout. "I must seem very plain to you."

John was taken by surprise at the sudden topic shift, but gamely rose to the challenge. "On the contrary, you would be considered attractive on any world," he said, smiling. "Would you be interested in teaching me some of the local dance steps?"

"How could I deny such a slick talking, not to mention fast thinking, man?"

VII

Miguel Courland ran a tight ship and everybody who worked for or above him knew it. Except for Bill Tuning. Tuning thought that on his show everything should be run his way. At most stations he would be right, but not on CZCN, a subsidiary of the Charterless Zarathustra Company. On CZCN, Courland was the final word on all telecasts answerable only to Victor Grego himself. So naturally when Tuning swapped the planned interview with a local celebrity for that of an unknown, at least locally, college professor at the last minute, Courland hit the roof.

"Miguel, the man has an interesting theory about the Fuzzies," Tuning argued. "Fuzzies are still a hot topic with the ratings. Would you rather we run another bit about a vapid actress trying to deny her latest cosmetic procedure, or an interview with a scientist with a new slant on the natives?"

Courland was no fool even though ratings were the Holy Grail of broadcast television. "What's this new slant, Bill?"

"He only says this will turn everything we think we know about Fuzzies on its ear," Tuning replied. "Look, even if he's a crackpot, Ghu knows we get plenty of those, he should be more interesting than that has-been Darla Cross. We can put her on tomorrow if you want to. She won't dare kick up a fuss."

"No, she needs all the exposure she can get," Courland agreed. "Rumor has it she's up for the part of Ruth Ortheris in that documentary, um, 'First Contact' or something like that." The station manager drew a deep breath and let it out slowly. "Fine, run the professor. I just wish these things weren't live."

"Relax, I can handle this guy," he said with a smile.

"You'd better. I'll go smooth things over with Ms. Cross." Courland glanced at his watch. "Two hours and twenty-five minutes. Go get ready."

*   *   *   *   *   *   *   *   *

Jan Christiaan Hoenveld was arguably the premier scientist on Zarathustra. His ego very nearly matched his scientific qualifications. As such, he was a difficult man to work for. Nobody worked *with* Dr. Hoenveld as he acknowledged no equals, at least on Zarathustra. As such, he was equally difficult to supervise. More than once Juan Jimenez found it necessary to remind the man exactly who worked for whom.

Jimenez mentally girded himself for battle as he entered Dr. Hoenveld's office. Not surprisingly the scientist was in his blindingly white lab coat. He believed the scientist bleached it twice a day to keep it that clean.

Juan Jimenez made his greeting and got right to the point. "Chris, I have a new project I would like you to work on."

Hoenveld looked up from whatever was on the computer screen with his normal expression, a look of annoyance. "And what would that be, Mr. Jimenez?"

Jimenez actually held a doctorate in his field but decided to forgo the correction. "We have a Fuzzy—"

"Almost everybody has a Fuzzy, these days," Hoenveld interrupted.

"Who chooses not to eat Extee-Three?" Jimenez finished as if nothing happened.

"I don't blame him," Hoenveld put in. "I tried the stuff once myself. Horrible thing to feed anyone."

"Chris, you do know that every Fuzzy to date has consumed as much Extee-Three as they could without exploding."

"A certain amount of deviation from the norm is to be expected in any species, Mr. Jimenez."

"He also passes on land-prawn," He added.

"Well, that's to be…" Hoenveld stopped in mid-sentence. "Land-prawn? Hmph…is he allergic, somehow?"

"Actually, we hadn't considered that possibility…"

"I'll need to run some tests, draw some blood, get stool samples… mmm…how soon can you get this Fuzzy here?"

He was almost stunned at Hoenveld's reaction, having expected a battle. "I'll call Mrs. Van Riebeek after lunch. If she can't bring Zorro in directly, I'll send an aircar for him."

"Yes, that will be fine," the scientist replied. "Zorro, eh? Well, I'll get everything ready by then."

"Don't hurt him, Chris."

"Mr. Jimenez, in addition to my various degrees, I possess an MD." Hoenveld actually looked indignant at the suggestion that he would injure a Fuzzy. "The first rule of medicine is 'do no harm.' I wouldn't even think of hurting another sapient being."

"My apologies, doctor. Zorro will be here as soon as possible."

*   *   *   *   *   *   *   *

The Fuzzies all gathered around as the large machine floating in the air scooped out large chunks of earth. They were careful not to get too close as they had been warned many times about the dangers of such things, but they were curious as to what it was doing. Little Fuzzy spotted Pappy Jack and ran over to him.

"Pappy Jack! Pappy Jack!" the Fuzzy yelled emphatically as he pointed at the earthmover. "What make do?"

Holloway patiently explained that the machine was digging a big hole. Little Fuzzy looked at his Pappy with an expression that said *I can see that.* "Why make big hole?"

Holloway puffed on his pipe for a moment as he considered his answer then said, "That is where we will put the new septic tank." As expected, Little Fuzzy inquired what a *sep-tik tank* was.

"You know what a commode is, right?"

Little Fuzzy explained that it was the made-thing that took Big Ones' bad smells away. To the Fuzzies it seemed both amazing and silly. It was a lot of trouble to go all the way to a special room to take care of one's business, but then there was no need to dig a new hole every time, either.

"Well, the bad smells don't just vanish, they are washed down into a big…um…box under the ground where they are broken down and returned to the ground."

Little Fuzzy looked dubious, at first. It seemed like a roundabout way to put something into the ground when Fuzzies did it in a more direct manner. Then Jack explained that the Fuzzies had used up most of the area burying their bad smells and had to walk further from the Reservation every day. With the new septic system and mini-toilets there would be no need for that. Little Fuzzy accepted this explanation and shared it with the other Fuzzies.

The Fuzzies were still debating the pros and cons when Holloway saw Gus Brannhard arrive. Gus set his aircar down well away from the Fuzzies and the digging. Holloway walked over to greet him.

"*Heyo,* Pappy Jack!" Allan and Natty yelled.

"Heyo, Allan, Natty. Should I be expecting a couple of hospital orderlies, too?" Jack called to Gus.

"Orderlies?" Gus lifted out Allan and Natty then turned to Jack.

"Yeah. You made a break for it, didn't you?"

Gus laughed then stopped himself and rubbed his torso over his surgical scar. "Nah, the sawbones cut me loose. He said something about my disturbing the other patients. I had to swear on my honor that I'd behave for the next few weeks, though." Gus glanced at the earthmover. "Putting in a swimming pool for the kids?"

Jack explained about the new waste disposal unit for the Fuzzies. "Why didn't you just requisition a matter converter for all that?"

"Because an M/E conversion unit costs about a hundred times as much," Jack explained. "Even my home still uses an atomic battery cartridge. Besides, we still don't know what a Fuzzy's tolerance for radioactivity is and even the most ecologically sound unit raises the background radiation a few milli-rads. This will work just as well, and the Fuzzies could learn how to make their own outhouses and whatnot for use in the villages."

"I think they're a long way from making a working septic system, but an outhouse wouldn't be out of the question, I guess."

Jack watched as Gus's Fuzzies scampered off to join the crowd. "Don't kid yourself. We have a few blacksmiths in the crowd and Henry Stenson's bunch can repair simple electronics."

"Humph." Gus looked back over at the crowd of Fuzzies and wondered how soon it might be before they started using everything Big Ones used. "Grego was right; no bet on what a Fuzzy couldn't do is safe."

Jack agreed, then asked, "So what brings you out here?"

"Oh, just figured Allan and Natty needed a little face time with their friends," said the big man with a dismissive wave. "They've been cooped up watching over me and I decided they needed a break. It's too soon for me to go hunting with them so I was hoping they could tag along with some of your crowd."

"Good idea," Jack said. "I'll fix up the spare room for you and the kids. Gerd, Ruth and Ben are coming out later tonight."

"Sounds like a party," Gus said. "Before they get here I want to talk with you about those provisions for the future you mentioned back at the hospital."

Jack was taken a bit by surprise. "Sure. Let's walk to my house and have some coffee while we talk."

The two men took seats at the kitchen table while they waited for the coffee to perk. Jack refused to use instant or microwave brands preferring it the old-fashioned way.

"Jack, after what happened with my liver I got to thinking how I won't be around forever," Gus started. "If something happens to me I need to be sure that Allan and Natty will be taken care of."

"Sound thinking," Jack agreed. "My bunch will be well provided for when I'm gone."

"But who's going to be the provider?"

"What? Oh. I guess I should appoint a guardian." Jack leaned back in his chair and reached for his pipe, only to remember Gus was still recovering.

The coffee pot buzzed and Jack poured two cups.

"My thoughts exactly," Gus said. He started to take the cup in front of him then remembered that caffeine was also *verboten* while he was on the mend. Damned doctors! "That's why I want to make you Allan and Natty's godfather."

"What? Gus, I've got, what, a good ten or twenty years on you? What makes you think I have even half a chance of outliving you?"

Gus shrugged. "If you don't, and I very much doubt that, then I'll appoint someone else. But, these days, your line of work is safer than mine."

"Ah, well, what the hell. Who's your second choice?"

"Ben, of course. He's younger than we are and I've seen how he treats Flora and Fauna." Gus threw a glance at the Fuzzies. "He'd be a good Pappy to them. What about you?"

"Me? Oh, I guess I would go with Gerd and Ruth." Jack checked his watch. "I'll drop that bomb on them later tonight when they come out for dinner."

*   *   *   *   *   *   *   *

"…So, professor, you are saying that the Fuzzies might actually be alien to this world," the interviewer asked.

"That is a very real possibility," the elder man replied. "The fact that *Fuzzy Sapiens Zarathustra* is the only known bipedal mammalian life form prior to our own incursion on Zarathustra makes them a zoological oddity. Take Terrans, for example; we come from a widely divergent family of primates."

The professor pontificated at length about how all life forms on any given planet tend to develop in accordance to their environment, splitting off into divergent species citing that wolves, dogs, coyotes, bears, foxes, etc, all shared a common ancestor. The Fuzzies were genetic orphans having no known kindred species…at least on Zarathustra.

"I think I've heard enough of this foolishness," Jack said, as he thumbed a button and shut off the vid. "Fuzzy astronauts for Ghu's sake." He leaned back and took a sip of water from his glass.

With him were Colonial Governor Ben Rainsford, Colonial Chief Prosecutor Gus Brannhard and the van Riebeeks. Out of respect for Gus, who was still recovering from his liver transplant, the gang was having soft drinks instead of their usual cocktails. Nobody wanted a run-in with Allan Quatermain and Natty Bumppo, especially after having heard of the hospital orderly that nearly became a patient.

The Fuzzies were all outside playing in the Reservation or hunting land-prawn so it was just Terran-type people for a change. Fuzzies were a lot of fun to have around but as any parent of active children knows; sometimes it is necessary to get away and enjoy the company of adults.

"Actually, that Professor Darloss brought up some interesting points," Ruth noted from the couch where she sat next to Gerd. "The Fuzzy's dependency on a substance that is not plentiful makes you wonder."

"Maybe they just used up all the titanium at some point," Gus suggested. He absently rubbed the right side of his abdomen, where the liver is located.

"Not possible, Gus," Ben said. "Titanium isn't altered in the body into something else the way organic compounds can be. It's an element and elements simply don't become something else. Well, granted, there are a few exceptions, like those produced in a cyclotron, but that's a whole other thing. It goes in as titanium and comes out as titanium. And even if it stayed in the body—which I very much doubt, it would turn toxic. When a Fuzzy dies, his body eventually breaks down and returns the titanium to the ground. It's an endless cycle."

"Well, maybe there was a plant or something that the Fuzzies would eat that provided something very similar to the long-chain titanium molecule but without the titanium," Gus argued. His litigious nature automatically spurred him on to win any argument.

"Now that is entirely possible. The environment might have had a dramatic alteration, causing this plant to die out," the Colonial Governor agreed. "However, it was far more likely that the NFMp countered some naturally occurring toxin in the environment. Whatever created the toxin might have died out leaving the NFMp nothing to counter, so it turned destructive."

"You said that titanium would turn toxic if it built-up in the body," Gus pointed out. "Maybe land-prawn and Extee-Three act like a poison that the NFMp counters."

"There's a thought," Gerd said. "But it doesn't explain everything."

"Did I mention that we found one Fuzzy that refuses to eat Extee-Three or land-prawn?" Ruth said. Everybody except Gerd expressed disbelief. A Fuzzy refusing Extee-Three was like the sun rising from the west. "It's true. Doctors Mallin and Hoenveld are checking him out. We don't know what to make of it yet."

"We're hoping it isn't a parasite or something catching," Gerd added. "We'll know more soon, I hope. We should pay more attention to what our own Fuzzies eat, especially the reservation crowd. No telling what they might have brought in from the wild."

"Good idea, Gerd. As soon as we know what to look for, we'll start looking for it. Back to this Darloss business, it seems to me that a simple DNA analysis would decide the matter pretty quick," Jack offered. He again fumbled for his pipe but left it in his pocket. It wasn't fair to smoke in front of Gus for the time being. "Compare the Fuzzies to almost anything else on the planet and the matter will be settled."

"Maybe not," Gerd put in. "If the Fuzzies did come from another planet then they must have been here for thousands, maybe even hundreds of thousands of years. After breathing the air, eating the local wildlife and just generally existing under the same sun as everything else on this planet their DNA may have drifted a bit to be closer to that of the indigenous life-forms. You are what you eat, so to speak."

"Is that even possible?" Jack asked.

"DNA does change over time," Ben said, "mostly through mutation. If it didn't we would all still be microscopic one-celled organisms. All living creatures adapt to their environment or die out. Fuzzies would have developed the same mutations as other Zarathustran wildlife, hence similar DNA strands. There is only about a two percent difference in DNA between a man and almost any other Terran mammal. About ninety-eight percent of your DNA is just to get you up and running as a viable life form. The last two percent or so determines what form that life will take."

"Is this theory or fact?" asked Jack.

"Well, mostly theory on the adaptive DNA," Gerd admitted. "We haven't been around and out in space long enough for a practical test. We would have to take a group of animals from one planet, drop them on another and track the changes, if any, over several millennia. The animals with the correct mutations would thrive while those that didn't would die out. The available DNA in the species would determine the survival rate and any mutations that enhanced their survivability would become the species norm. Since only the positive mutations would be adaptive to their environment it might mirror the DNA of the indigenous species."

"Like the Martians," Ruth added.

"What do you mean by that?" Gus asked.

Gerd looked to the ceiling and spread his arms in mock exasperation. "Here it comes."

"Here what comes?" Ben asked.

"You are about to learn our secret shame. My darling wife, Ruth, is a closet Martianist."

Ruth gave Gerd a little punch on his arm. "Actually, I just keep an open mind."

"Martianist?" Jack looked first to Gus, who shrugged and shook his head and then to Ben who put a 'don't ask me' look on his face.

"The Martianists were a small cult that started on Mars Colony," Gerd explained. "But they've been growing the last couple of decades. These crackpots compared Terran DNA to samples taken from those mummified Martians discovered back in, oh, late first century Atomic Era, I think."

"They found only about a point zero two percent deviation between Martian and Terran DNA," added Ruth.

"Is that a lot?" Jack asked.

"On the contrary," she said, "There is about a one percent deviation between humans and chimpanzees. Point zero two percent is barely a difference at all."

"So? We were similar," Gus stated. "We're pretty close to Freyans, too."

"Ah," Ruth said with a gleam in her eye. "There is only a point zero one five percent difference between Martians and Freyans. And about a point zero two five percent deviation between Terran and Freyan."

"Meaning that humans and Freyans could have interbred with Martians," Gerd added. "But wait; here comes the kicker."

Ruth shot a 'you're going to get it later' look at Gerd, then continued. "Well, the extremely close genetic structures between Freyans and Martians has given rise to speculation that the Freyans may actually *be* the Martians, but adapted to conditions on Freya."

"Oh, come on," Ben exclaimed.

"This conclusion assumes facts not in evidence," Gus said. "That is like saying all poodles are dogs so all dogs must be poodles."

"I read in a scientific journal that the Martians would have been dark skinned due to the intense radiation," Ben added. "Mars lost its planetary magnetic shield and much of its atmosphere long ago, so they lacked for protection against cosmic and ultra-violet radiation. But Freyans tend to be fair skinned and light haired."

"There's a helluva lot less UV getting through Freya's atmosphere, from what I remember," Jack told him. "If Martians did land there, I would imagine, they would have adapted."

"That's right, Jack. Just like the tribes that migrated from Africa to Northern Europe did. But, wait," Gerd said. "It gets better."

Ruth shot another look at Gerd then continued. "Well, from there the theory goes that since Freya is very similar to Terra and Terra was a lot closer, then Martians must have settled on Terra first by several thousand years. That would explain the greater Terran genetic deviation than the Freyan."

"If they did where are they now?" Gus asked.

"You're looking at them," Jack said. "Am I right, Ruth?"

"Bull's eye." Ruth nodded.

"Now wait a minute," Ben said. "We know Martians had atomic power but there is zero evidence that they ever developed a hyperdrive engine."

"How much evidence could there be after, what, fifty-thousand years?" Gus asked, switching over to play devil's advocate. "For all we know the thing might have gone straight from the drawing board to the workshop, or even been a government secret."

"Well, I've never been to Freya myself," Ben said, "but everybody who has, swears up and down that Freyan women are even more beautiful than Terran women are."

"I have been to Freya, and I would have to say that's pretty much the case," Jack said. "Present company excepted."

"Seconded," Gus added.

"Nice save," Ruth said with a smile.

Ben continued, "Well, if we are all one big happy Martian family shouldn't Terran woman be considered equally as beautiful to our eyes?"

"I choose to think they are," Gerd said, as he rubbed his arm and glanced at Ruth.

"Smart man," she offered, with a wink. "The Martianists believe that the Terran Colony might have mixed with the indigenous sapient race. The Neanderthals."

"This is the part that really makes my head hurt," Gerd groaned. "We are able to breed with Freyans because Terrans and Freyans all came from Mars but we look slightly different because we swapped a few genes with some primitive monkey-boys which should be impossible since they weren't Martians in the first place."

"Science does hold that some genetic exchanges between Cro-Magnon and Neanderthal man may have occurred," Ben offered, "but how would that be possible if Cro-Magnons came from Mars?"

"That takes us back to environmental adaptation," Ruth said. "If the Martians lived, say, ten or twenty thousand years on Terra adapting to the gravity, eating the local cuisine, breathing the air and toiling under the Terran sun they might have enjoyed, or suffered, depending on your point of view, a DNA shift that would make them compatible with the indigenous peoples…provided they were fairly close to begin with."

"Using that logic," Gus countered, "Terrans and Fuzzies could become compatible in about a hundred thousand years."

"Fuzzies are a bit further away from us, genetically speaking, than a Neanderthal might have been," she countered. "Unfortunately, science is still on the fence whether humans and Neanderthals ever mixed. The DNA debate has been going on since first century A.E."

"About a decade after the human genome was mapped some scientists managed to map the Neanderthal genome," Gerd pointed out. "They found possible evidence that humans and Neanderthals mingled and mated about 80,000 years ago."

"I think there is another issue we should consider," Ben Rainsford said. "If we find evidence that Fuzzies really did come from another planet, how would that affect the colonial government and the Charterless Zarathustra Company?"

"What do you mean?" asked Jack.

"He means that the Charatered Zarathustra Company lost their charter because this is now a Class IV inhabited planet," explained Gus, quick on the uptake. "If the Fuzzies turn out to be space immigrants the Charterless Zarathustra Company could argue that their charter was taken illegally since the Fuzzies never filed a claim of ownership to this world."

"That's ridiculous," Jack said. "They were here first; it's theirs, period."

"I wouldn't bet the farm that the courts would see it the same way," Gus replied.

"Victor Grego is a businessman," Jack pointed out. "When he was fighting to keep control of Zarathustra it was to defend his bottom line. Now, he has nothing to gain by rocking the boat. He's smart enough to know when to hold 'em, and when to fold 'em."

"I'll call Leslie Coombes and see what he thinks," Gus said. "He's way ahead of me when it comes to charter law. Just the same, I would feel a lot better if something like this had come out before and was dealt with. If something comes of this, it would be the first time I ever went to court without a lot of citable precedents."

"Hey, this is purely academic," Ben said. "Isn't it?"

"For now it is," Gus answered. "Let's hope it stays that way."

VIII

"Who authorized that interview on my station?" Victor Grego asked. He was entertaining Leslie Coombes, Ahmed and Sandra Khadra, Dr. Mallin, Juan Jimenez, the Company Police Fuzzies and Leslie Coombes' Fuzzies when Diamond scampered in saying that a Big One on the vid was making talk about Fuzzies. Grego said that was nice until Diamond asked what an astronaut was.

This piqued everyone's interest enough to stop socializing and join the Fuzzies in watching the program. The show was called "Tuning In with Tuning."

"Couldn't the other quasi-primates have died off as a matter of natural selection?' asked the interviewer, Bill Tuning. "On Terra the Neanderthals died out when Cro-Magnon came on the scene."

"Certainly," Professor Darloss countered, "yet countless varieties of apes and monkeys still exist in the wilds of Africa and South America. Where are the cousins of the Fuzzies, Mr. Tuning?"

"If they suffered from the same procreation problems caused by the NFMp hormone they might have died out fairly quickly," Tuning countered. "If not for the land-prawns Fuzzies would have become extinct as well. If they were ancient astronauts it would be a pretty extreme coincidence that the only means to their racial survival just happened to be on the same planet they landed on."

"That's enough of that rubbish," Grego said, switching the station to a western show. "Diamond, this is a better program. Much more fun."

"*Hokay*, Pappy Vic." Diamond started to explain to the other Fuzzies about the cowboys, Indians, bounty hunters and gunfighters in such programs, all of whom agreed that shooting the bad Big Ones was a good idea.

"Tomorrow I am going to have a talk with the station manager and ask him what that was all about," Grego fumed.

Sandra Khadra didn't understand what the problem was. "It was just another anthropologist with a crazy theory, wasn't it?"

"The problem," Juan Jimenez said, "is that some people will believe it, including stockholders. That could open up a very large can of worms."

"How so?" Ahmed asked.

"First, every scientist the Home Office could round up would descend on Zarathustra like a swarm of locusts all looking for proof that Fuzzies aren't native to this planet. The evidence, no matter how tenuous or circumstantial, would be turned over to the legal department. Next would come the years of court battles trying to prove that the CZC charter had been revoked illegally."

"Don't take this the wrong way, Victor, but don't you want to regain control of the planet?" Sandra asked.

"Two years ago, yes. Now, not so much," Grego replied. "Not with the lease that gave us back everything we had when we owned the planet outright, more or less. If Home Office decides to try to get the planet back by arguing that Fuzzies came from a different world, well, not only could we be tied up in court for several years but the current lease could be broken in the process."

"Meaning," Coombes interrupted, "that the Company will not be able to administer any of the holdings recovered in the lease until the court issues are settled and either the Company resumed control of the planet or a new lease agreement is signed."

"Well, in the long run wouldn't the company profit by getting back the planet?" Ahmed Khadra asked.

"Only if we outlast the current lease," Grego said. "We can't even be sure the Company would be around that long. Nifflheim, the Federation could collapse before then! As I see it, the only people who could benefit from rocking the boat are our competitors. Or stock speculators."

"Speculators?" Sandra and Ahmed said in unison.

"If stock drops while the Company's position is tenuous, speculators could buy up outstanding stock at low prices and then make a killing after the dust is settled and the stocks rebound," Coombes explained. "In fact, already existing stockholders would certainly take the opportunity to increase their holdings within the Company."

"Then it would turn into a power-play to gain control over the Company," Grego interjected. "I wouldn't be surprised if there weren't a few stockholders who would take a less Fuzzy-friendly approach to management, here."

"There is another aspect to the whole thing," Coombes said. "Let's say that it is proven in court that Fuzzies came from another planet. Fine. They still enjoy certain protections under Federation law. Any habitat that is provably theirs will still be nixed from external exploitation."

"I don't speak legalese, Leslie," Sandra put in. "What does that mean in laymen's terms?"

"It means that all lands that can be proven to be the Fuzzies' ancestral homes will be off-limits until a treaty can be worked out and signed by them," Ahmed supplied.

"No sunstone mining operation, no farming, no anything," Jimenez added.

"How would a Fuzzy prove he owned or used any land?" Sandra argued. "They don't have any kind of documentation. They couldn't even write until we taught them!"

"They would get the 'first come first served' treatment. Back on Terra

Pre-Atomic era gold miners would make a pile of stones or just drive a wooden stake into the ground to show their claim to an area. That is probably where the expression "stake a claim" comes from. Fuzzy funeral Cairns would carry the same weight in a court of law as almost anything else," Victor Grego explained. "Even if we got ownership of the planet back, most, if not all of Beta continent would become Fuzzy land. No sunstone mining, no nothing."

"There was a case like that on Magni. Two separate groups made planet-fall on opposite sides of the planet. Both groups mapped out a continent, planted a flag and then returned to Terra to file their claims; each completely ignorant of the other. The short story is that the group that made it back to Terra first got the planet after a long court battle and the second group got ownership of the second continent." Coombes took a drink then added, "Eventually the two groups came together to become the Chartered Magni Cooperative."

"So the Fuzzies would retain ownership of Beta continent?"

"Most likely, Sandra, the Fuzzies would get ownership of the planet and the CZC would only get Alpha. And anybody taking a Fuzzy off of Beta could be charged with kidnapping, enslavement and God only knows what," added Coombes. "I'll check with Gus Brannhard; the man has an encyclopedic knowledge of precedents in colonial law. There is a good chance that all adopted Fuzzies would have to be returned to Beta as well."

"What?" Sandra Khadra was horrified at the thought of Fuzzies being ripped away from their adoptive families and her face showed it. "Why?"

"Because a space faring race, even one that has been marooned on a planet and lost all their technology and history," Grego said, "couldn't possibly be considered incompetent aborigines, let alone minor children in the eyes of the law, at least not without a few decades of intensive scientific study and more court rulings."

"Is this really all possible?" Ahmed Khadra asked. "This was just an interview with one crackpot scientist who only has a hypothesis. How much trouble can he cause?"

"A hypothesis that sounds very convincing, Ahmed," Grego said. "It's just a matter of time before more so-called scientists jump on the bandwagon hoping to make a name for themselves."

*   *   *   *   *   *   *   *   *

Dr. Hoenveld rarely watched network television. He preferred the documentary, history and science channels. He was flipping between the History and Science channels when he noticed the interview with Professor Darloss. Out of curiosity he stopped and watched the interview. By the time the interview was over, Dr. Hoenveld was outraged. He decided to do something, but didn't know what. After some thought, he concluded that he would have to go to Juan Jimenez, his boss, the man promoted over him.

*   *   *   *   *   *   *   *   *

"Now that was an interesting piece of journalistic legerdemain."

With the canopy up and the robots doing most of the grunt work, the leader had called for a break. Past experience taught him that exhausted men were prone to error, something they couldn't afford on their current venture. As such, the men were gathered for a little vid time. Occasional entertainment also helped to keep them sharp.

"Space Fuzzies," Bronson said with a laugh. "Sure, they came from Nifflheim and adapted to conditions here."

"Naw, they came from Mars, like the Freyans," Henderson countered. "Just wait. Next it'll be Martianists claiming them as long lost brothers."

"Wait, I know," Nichols yelled, "they flew here on winged land-prawns from Uller."

"Okay, let's settle down," the leader ordered. "Too much noise might disturb the neighbors."

The crowd quickly quieted and discussed the show among themselves. Hendrix left the group and approached the leader. "Sir, do you think this will interfere with our operation, here?"

The leader turned to Hendrix and asked, "How?"

"Anthropologists, scientists, geologists, what-have-you could start combing Beta for proof right or left. That Darloss may have just sparked a match that will light a fire under every idiot amateur anthropologist and treasure hunter who saw that interview."

The leader considered Hendrix's words a moment before replying. "That could happen, but not before we are done here. Beta is mostly Fuzzy territory. You need all kinds of permits and government sanctions to come crawling around here. Governor Rainsford won't hand those out willy-nilly to just anybody. Plus, there will be counter arguments all over the vids. Most people won't get off the couch until they have more information. Anybody trying to sneak in will get nailed by the Native Affairs Police."

"And if somebody does come snooping around?" prompted Hendrix.

The leader stared levelly at Hendrix. "There's another use for the mass/energy converter."

IX

Victor Grego was tired and ready to call it a day at 1800 hours. He had called the head of the mass media division, Miguel Courland, on the carpet earlier. Courland's position was that he couldn't run an effective news organization if he had to get the okay from the boss on every story. While Grego was forced to agree in principle the fact remained that the Darloss interview was potentially damaging to the company. Courland couldn't see how a crackpot saying that Fuzzies came from outer space could be a threat and said so. Nothing short of finding a Fuzzy spaceship would be considered proof positive of the theory.

The meeting ended with the understanding that Darloss would not be given a second interview and any reputable scientist with an opposing view would be given equal airtime. Grego liked Courland and respected his ability to run his division effectively and even respected the man's ethics. He respected anybody who had a job to do and did it competently even if he was personally inconvenienced by it. Courland had been against the anti-Fuzzy slant of the news during the Holloway/Kellogg trial. The news was the news and should be free of all bias. Grego was inclined to agree but simply couldn't let his own media company do anything that might damage the CZC.

There was also the John Morgan business. The man was constantly digging through files, talking with the staff and just generally nosing around. That in itself was to be expected. However, Morgan was too polite and that worried Grego. Company hatchet men tended to be rude, arrogant types that had clear agendas. Akira's report said that Morgan was interested in market research, which was also to be expected, but more-so in anybody who had been to Freya. Records on Jack Holloway, Gus Brannhard and Chief Harry Steefer had been accessed from the main computer along with information about Epsilon Continent. Epsilon was about the size of Australia and used as a game preserve since the signing of the agreement with the government that leased the unseated lands back to the CZC. The company had never even seriously developed it.

John Morgan was up to something and he couldn't imagine what it could be. Akira also reported that Morgan was very interested in reports about radiation, particularly background radiation. In general, Zarathustra had the lowest background radiation level of any Terra-like planet. What was Morgan after?

Then, on a personal level, there was Diamond to worry about. While the bachelor life suited Grego, it was unfair to expect the same for the Fuzzy. Diamond should have a mate and Grego had no idea what was involved in a Fuzzy selecting a suitable partner. However, he did know— that at the very least—Diamond would need to get out of the penthouse and be placed in an environment where he could be exposed to unattached female Fuzzies.

I'll give Jack a call and see if he could let Diamond stay with him on Beta for a few weeks, Grego decided. A fine specimen of male Fuzzy-hood like Diamond should be able to attract a suitable female pretty quick there.

To wrap-up the evening there was the meeting with Akira O'Barre. She was less than enthusiastic about her side-job in intelligence.

"I think he suspects, Mr. Grego."

Victor Grego laid the report that Akira O'Barre handed him down on his desk and regarded the young woman. He knew when he assigned her to watch John Morgan that she wasn't espionage material, but she was intelligent and attractive and had an easy way with people that made them comfortable around her. She also had a bit of a reputation for jumping from man to man, though the term 'easy' had never been used to describe her.

"Of course he suspects, Akira," said Grego. "He seems like an intelligent man. In the business world he has to be suspicious of everybody. But suspicion does not constitute proof." Grego opened his cigarette case and offered one to the young woman. She declined and Grego lit one for himself. "John Morgan is a wealthy man. Wealthy men do not lend their trust easily. That is how they stay wealthy. Nonetheless, I understand you have been seeing him socially."

"We just had some drinks together. He's been a perfect gentleman."

Grego nodded. "Yes, Freyan men tend to be more…restrained…in their treatment of women, I understand. Dr. Mallin provided me with a cultural profile of Freyan society."

"Sir, I don't want to spy on him, anymore." Akira was on the edge of tears.

"Then don't."

"What?" This took the young woman by surprise. "I don't understand."

"Mr. Morgan is a stockholder, Akira. We don't spy on our own. However, as the CEO of this company, I need to know what files are accessed by whom and why. As an employee in Records Division, you need to keep track of that sort of thing. John Morgan should know that. If he doesn't, then he is a fool." Grego smiled. "That is all I require. That isn't spying. That's procedure. As for what you do on your off time, well, that is nobody's business but your own.

"However," he added, "if you find reason to believe he is up to something illegal or potentially damaging to the company, it is your responsibility to report it to me. Just like any other good employee. Is this understood?"

"Yes, Mr. Grego. Will there be anything else?"

"No, that will be all. Keep up the good work."

Akıra left in the private elevator leaving Grego alone with his thoughts. He looked over at his scale model of Zarathustra and realized it was late in the evening. He had guests coming and an interview to see on the vid.

*   *   *   *   *   *   *   *   *

"With us tonight is Dr. Jan Christiaan Hoenveld, the discoverer of Hoenveldzine." The speaker turned to the thin elderly man at his left. "Thank-you for being on our show, Dr. Hoenveld."

"Thank-you, Mr. Tuning."

"Please, call me Bill. Dr. Hoenveld, I understand that you are here to dispute the claims made by Professor Darloss last week."

"That is correct, Bill. Ah, call me Chris." Hoenveld cleared his throat and tried to sit up a little straighter. Anybody who knew the doctor would be able to see that he was distinctly uncomfortable in the gray suit he was wearing. No doubt he would have preferred his usual lab coat. "Well, to begin, Professor Darloss' hypothesis is based on the flimsiest of evidence. It takes years of research to properly catalogue scientific data, which he has failed to produce."

"Interesting," said Tuning, who in fact did not look particularly interested. "Are you saying that there are other bipedal mammals on Zarathustra?"

"No, nor am I saying that there aren't any, either. Nobody should say so one way or the other until every animal group on the planet has been properly identified and catalogued. The Terran gorilla was not catalogued until the first century Pre-Atomic. Terrans have been on Zarathustra for less than three decades. It takes time to get a complete zoological picture on any planet. In fact, we had colonized this world for twenty-five years before Jack Holloway discovered the Fuzzies. It might take another twenty-five before we discover another bipedal species."

"What about the Fuzzies' unique vocal and audio capabilities?" The interviewer's face broke out into a cat-who-got-the-canary grin. "No other mammal on Zarathustra can hear in the ultrasonic range."

Hoenveld, taken by surprise, nonetheless pulled out a ready answer. "On Terra the reverse is true. Numerous animals such as dogs can hear in the ultrasonic range while humans cannot. Does that mean humans came from a different planet?" Hoenveld put on a slightly superior grin. "Then there is the damnthing which is the only omnivorous carnivore ever discovered anywhere with hooves and horns. Mammalian carnivores and omnivores typically possess fang and claw while herbivores have hoof and horn."

The interviewer countered by asking, "What if no other bipeds are found on Zarathustra?"

"What about *pseudopterodactyl zarathustra,* or harpies as the layman might call them?" Hoenveld countered. "Across the entire planet there is only one species of harpy, and no other avian reptiles have yet been discovered. Should we assume that they, too, piled into a hyperdrive ship and got themselves stranded here? Pseudocrustaceans, or land-prawn as we call them, are also singular representatives of their species. Zarathustra's zoological makeup defies numerous conventions. A single bipedal species is barely a blip on the radar compared to the rest of the environmental picture."

"Professor Darloss conjectured that the land-prawn were brought to Zarathustra by the Fuzzies as a food animal," Tuning countered.

"Then at some point the land-prawns must have had wings that allowed them to cross the oceans," Hoenveld said with a laugh. The laugh sounded odd as if he had never done it before. "Pseudocrustaceans are distributed across every major land-mass on the planet while *Fuzzy sapiens zarathustra* are native only to Beta continent. If Fuzzies had brought them then they would only be endemic to Beta."

Hoenveld was getting the better of Tuning and Tuning knew it. While the interviewer had no personal interest one way or the other in the Fuzzy debate he had made his career by putting people off balance then tripping them up. It galled him that he didn't get the better of Darloss the week before and now he was being shown up by Hoenveld. It was time to play the hole card. "Then perhaps you can explain the NFMp hormone, Chris. Your own research shows that no other mammal on Zarathustra produces it."

"Well, the current wisdom is that it was designed to counter some toxin in the environment some hundred thousand years ago," the Doctor countered smoothly. "There was a great deal of volcanic activity at that time spewing noxious smoke. It is possible the NFMp countered the harmful effects. There may have been numerous species that produced the NFMp hormone at that time. They either developed a mutation that removed the NFMp, or died out. Fuzzies are the only known species that prey on the land-prawn, or *zuzora*, as they are called by the Fuzzies, which would explain their continued existence despite the hormone."

"Has any experimentation been done to test the toxic environment theory?"

"Certainly not!" Hoenveld actually looked scandalized at the suggestion. "That would entail subjecting a group of sapient beings to several toxic environments. Moral implications aside, a person could be legally shot for such a thing. However, the NFMp hormone might explain why the Fuzzies survived and all the other quasi-primates died off; the NFMp must have been a beneficial mutation that bred true only to turn destructive when the environment changed. I suspect that over time another mutation could occur in the Fuzzy genome that would remove or counter the genes that result in NFMp production.

"Hoenveldzine has a titanium base. Titanium was also found in the digestive tracts of the land-prawn. In humans titanium can become toxic requiring chelation treatment to remove it. In Fuzzies the NFMp hormone must perform the same function because all of my studies to date show that there is no titanium build-up in the Fuzzies bodies. Then there is the issue of fire, which is very significant…."

Hoenveld went on to explain the fact that Fuzzies never used fire until Terrans taught them as further proof that they were native to Zarathustra. Any race capable of space travel would be capable of producing fire. Since fire created warmth, cooked food and frightened off dangerous wildlife, any spaceship crash survivors would certainly hand down that piece of technology if they had ever possessed it.

"It defies the imagination that any race could regress to the point that they couldn't rub two sticks together."

*   *   *   *   *   *   *   *   *

"I never would have thought old Chris had it in him." Victor Grego was watching the viewscreen with Leslie Coombes, Ernst Mallin and Juan Jimenez in his penthouse.

"You never had to sit through one of his lectures on scientific method," Juan Jimenez said. "Once he gets going collapsium shielding won't stop him."

"I would love to get him on the couch for a couple hours," Ernst Mallin added. "I think he has some serious parental issues to work out."

"How did you talk him into doing the show?" Leslie Coombes asked.

"Actually, he came to me." Grego's eyebrows shot up and Jimenez explained. "He saw the interview last week and had kittens over it. If there is one thing Dr. Jan Christiaan Hoenveld, PhD MD MA, etc, cannot abide, it is sloppy scientific procedure. He even asked me politely…well, polite for him, if he could do the interview. I think his time with Zorro might be having a positive effect on his personality."

Dr. Mallin smiled and asked, "Did you prepare him for the interview at all? He was a lot smoother than I would have expected."

"Not at all. I just bought him that suit with my expense account. I didn't want him to look like he was coached but he needed to be, at the very least, well dressed."

Juan has come a long way since he took over Science Division, thought Grego. "Well, he did great. Three months from now give him a seven percent raise retroactive from this morning."

Jimenez didn't miss a beat. "Right. If we give him a raise now and it got out it would look bad. We wouldn't want anybody to think he was being paid-off to tout the company line. I'll let it be a surprise. I would like to give his expense account a bump, though. We might need him to publicly debate Darloss and he really needs to update his wardrobe. I swear he was born wearing that lab coat."

"Done," Grego agreed. "And get somebody to help him. I doubt if he knows an evening suit from a bush jacket. I hear that Frank Patel is a clotheshorse…."

The viewscreen interrupted Grego. Chief Steefer was staring out of it. Grego tapped the Receive button. "Yes, Chief?"

"Mr. Grego, I got those background checks you requested. Lansky is on his way up with them, now."

"Very good, Chief. Can you give me the highlights?"

"Yes, sir. Darloss was a professor at a small community college on Mars. There was some sort of scandal with a female student or two that resulted in his termination, there. Darloss has held a few teaching jobs and a lab position since. His last known position was in a lab on Loki. More than that will have to be sent for off-planet."

That meant a possible one year turn-around time. "Known associates?" he asked.

"Still looking into that," admitted the Chief with a grimace. "He's checked into the Alibi Inn. That's a 'No-Tell Motel' over in Junktown. I have Haynes there in mufti scoping it out."

"Haynes?" The name sounded familiar.

"Haynes was the guard who let Mr. Morgan in with that cannon on his hip…after taking his bullets."

That Haynes! Grego had to admit that Haynes had acted correctly. Powerful stockholders could destroy the careers of company people who annoyed them. Haynes had taken a very big chance just confiscating the ammunition from Morgan. "Good. What do we have on our Mr. Morgan?"

"Mr. Morgan is a Freyan native. His mother died in childbirth and there is no record of a father, though with his son being named 'John Morgan' I have to believe he was from Terra. His mother's brother raised him, a minor noble named Orphtheor Honirdite…I'm not too sure about that pronunciation. This uncle put him through school on Freya and Mars. When Honirdite passed on, Mr. Morgan inherited everything. He invested heavily in the Charterless Freya Company and later with the new Chartered Magni Cooperative and the CZC. Since graduating with a master's degree in business and a bachelor's degree in forensic science with a minor in criminology he's been all over the Federation. He touches down, invests in the local companies, learns the local language then moves on. His last stop was on Gimli."

"Either he's a Freyan Gypsy, or he's looking for something," Grego observed. "Any idea what?"

"I am afraid not, sir. I do have an idea that he invests in all of these companies in order to get access to their files."

Grego nodded at the screen. "That would fit. He invests enough to have some clout, gets into their files and looks for whatever it is he's looking for…I'm guessing he hasn't found it, yet, or he would stop looking…then moves on." Grego leaned back, then a thought hit him. "Where is he getting all that capital to invest?"

"His uncle was somewhat wealthy and already heavily invested in the

CFC. Mr. Morgan seems to have the Midas touch with his investments," replied the Chief. "Clearly he does his homework…I guess that master's degree in business isn't just for show." Steefer listed off John Morgan's known assets and investments. It was well into the billions of sols.

Grego whistled low. "If he rolled all that over into one lump and invested it with the Home Office, he'd own over half the company. Anything else?"

The Chief thought before answering. "Two things: I tried to get some info out of him on the way down to Science Division but he managed to turn it around and pump me for information. I hadn't even realized it until just now."

Grego was impressed. Chief Steefer was nobody's fool. "What kind of information?"

"Mostly lay of the land type stuff, and when I had been to Freya and if I knew anybody else who had been. He gave me the impression that he was a little homesick at the time, but now I'm not so sure."

Maybe Miss O'Barre would provide some illumination, thought Grego. "And the other thing?"

"He owns a private hyperspace yacht which is headed to Zarathustra as we speak."

Grego was impressed. "Now how did you find that out?"

"The ship is on his list of assets, and the Darius receiving station has it listed as incoming within the next month or two. As for why he took a commercial craft, or where the *Adonitia* is coming from, that I haven't found out as yet."

Grego began to wonder if Chief Steefer was being paid what he was really worth. "Thank-you, Chief. Please keep me posted."

The Chief vanished from the screen in a splash of color and Grego returned his attention to his guests. "This Darloss didn't just happen to land on Gimli and come up with that theory of his overnight. That interview was planned well in advance."

"You don't think John Morgan is mixed up with this guy, do you?" Jimenez asked. "According to the Chief, they came in on the same ship."

"I hadn't thought of that," admitted Grego, "but I won't rule it out."

*   *   *   *   *   *   *   *   *

"Nifflheim! That little Khooghra ripped me to shreds!" Darloss fumed after seeing the Hoenveld interview. Hoenveld, not even an anthropologist, had poked more holes in Darloss' theory than Freyan cheese. "He made me look like an idiot."

"Hardly," said Dane in an amused voice. "This plays right into our hands."

"How is that?" Dr. Rankin asked.

"I knew somebody would try to counter your claims, if only to get on the vid," said Dane. "But that was the CZC's lead scientist." He looked around at the blank faces. "Don't you all see? We'll smear him as spewing the company line! Everything he said will be put under a microscope by the general public and then dismissed as CZC whitewash."

"You want me to debate him?" Darloss jumped at the idea. "Maybe I can come up with something to refute his conclusions. That will take some research—"

"There's no need for a debate," Dane interrupted. "Public opinion will do the job for us. But track the web chatter and see if you can cull some useful theories while you do your own research."

Darloss' expression suggested he had little interest in the opinions of lay people. "Well, if you think it would yield useful results…"

"I doubt it, but it might give you some ideas of your own." Dane turned to the others. "Gentlemen, things are moving along perfectly."

X

Gus Brannhard was tired from the long flight back from Beta. He had planned on calling Leslie Coombes when he got in, but the three-hour trip left him too fatigued for a lengthy conversation, and two lawyers discussing law just didn't know how to have any other kind. Natty and Allan were already asleep so Gus had to carry them into the house. Fortunately they only weighed about twenty pounds each and did not cause him any undo strain.

Gus placed the two Fuzzies on the downsized bunk-beds that he had specially made just for them. Allan stirred but did not wake while Natty remained dead to the world. After the Fuzzies were tucked in for the night, Gus walked into his kitchen, reached into a high cupboard and extracted a bottle. He read the label and smiled: Old Atom-Bomb Bourbon. This stuff was hard to get anymore, he thought. The name was as appropriate as it was inane; one shot was enough to put most people out for the count.

Gus set the bottle on the table then sat down and stared at it. He didn't *need* a drink or even particularly *want* one; he was a heavy drinker because he chose to be, not out of any addiction. But being told he shouldn't drink made him want to take a few shots out of pure contrariness. As he sat looking at the bottle he could hear Allan and Natty breathing softly in their room. He idly wondered if any Fuzzies ever snored, then decided it was unlikely as it would attract predators.

Gus sighed then stood up and put the bottle back in the cupboard. Despite his protests he knew he couldn't afford to damage his new liver.

After all, he was a family man now. Gus had just decided to go to bed when he heard the dogs barking and howling. Normally they only did that if a contragravity vehicle flew by. The hypersonic whine of the engine hurt their ears. He turned in time to see two men holding sono-stunners take aim, then everything faded to black.

*   *   *   *   *   *   *   *   *

Natty Bumppo and Allan Quatermain found themselves jarred awake by a strange high-pitched noise and the barking of the dogs. Quietly, they slipped out of bed then collected their chopper-diggers and went to investigate. Peeking around the doorway of their room they could see two Big Ones carry Pappy Gus out the front door. Natty started to go after them but Allan stopped him.

"Big Ones strong," pointed out Allan lapsing into lingua Fuzzy. Rather than pitching his voice to the ultra-sonic that he knew Big Ones could hear some of if not understand, he whispered. "Fuzzy fight Big Ones, Fuzzy make dead. Follow, see what Big Ones do."

Natty was forced to agree and the Fuzzies followed the new Big Ones. Gus Brannhard and his family lived well outside of Mallorysport so there were no exterior light sources beyond his property, but Fuzzies adapted to living in the wilderness and were quite comfortable with the ambient light from Darius, Zarathustra's inner moon.

The two men shoved the still unconscious Gus into a contragravity vehicle, amid a great deal of grunting and swearing, and then secured his arms and legs with plastic ties. The taller of the two men looked about quickly then climbed into the craft followed by the shorter man. Not a single word passed between them as they closed the hatch and lifted off.

"Bad Big Ones take Pappy Gus," howled Natty. "Not follow cont'a-gav'ty vee'kle."

"Use *screeno*. Call Pappy Jack," said Allan. "Call Pappy Ben. Call Pappy Vic."

*   *   *   *   *   *   *   *

Jack Holloway learned to deal with a lot of unpleasantness in his seventy-six years of life: blistering heat, freezing cold, inimical wildlife and even more inimical low life. The one thing he never did learn to accept with grace was having his sleep prematurely interrupted. So when he was jarred out of a sound sleep by the viewscreen his first thoughts were: *somebody better be dead or dying.* Jack quickly pulled on a housecoat before activating the screen.

He bit off a sharp comment when he saw that it was two Fuzzies; Allan Quatermain and Natty Bumppo. It took a moment before the Fuzzies could settle down enough for Jack to understand what they were saying. They were so upset that they reverted to lingua Fuzzy though they remembered to keep their voices in the audible range. "Big Ones took Pappy Gus!" they finally cried in unison.

It took several minutes before Jack could settle the two Fuzzies down enough to get the whole story. Little Fuzzy, awakened by the noise, came to investigate. Jack brought Little Fuzzy up-to-date and asked him to talk to Natty and Allan and try to calm them down. While the Fuzzies spoke on the viewscreen Jack ran out to his contragravity vehicle and screened Ben Rainsford. Ben was just settling down for the night when he got the call.

"I'll issue a planet-wide alert," Ben said. "If we're lucky we can catch them in the air before they have a chance to hole-up. I'll call Victor Grego and let him know, too. He might be able to loan us some more men for the search. Are you coming over to Alpha?"

Jack considered for a moment. Ben would have oomphty dozen men scouring Alpha continent; one more wouldn't be much help, especially after the three-hour flight over. "I'll stay here and alert the Native Protection Force and the local cops in case our Gus-nappers try to hole-up on Beta."

"Good idea," Ben said. "If I bagged someone as high profile as the

Colonial Chief Prosecutor I would try to find someplace remote to hide. I'll have Natty and Allan picked-up and have them look through some mug-books. Maybe, we'll get lucky and know who we're dealing with."

Jack agreed and signed off then contacted Gerd van Riebeek. When he finished bringing everybody up to speed he went back into the house to get dressed.

Little Fuzzy stayed on the viewscreen until a team of men wearing the blue uniforms with shiny badges came and collected Natty and Allan. Jack arrived just in time to see Little Fuzzy turn off the screen. "Allan Quateh'main and Natty Bumppo went to Gov'men house-place, Pappy Jack."

"Good," Jack said, as he ruffled the fur on Little Fuzzy's head. He noticed the look of concern on Little Fuzzy's face and added, "Don't you worry. We'll find Pappy Gus and get him back." That seemed to satisfy the Fuzzy and he scampered off to spread the word.

*   *   *   *   *   *   *   *

Grego activated the screen to discover a distraught Ben Rainsford staring out of it.

"Victor, Gus has been abducted," the Governor said, without preamble or pleasantries.

"What? When?"

Rainsford filled in the Charterless Zarathustra Company CEO. "We're organizing search parties now. I contacted Lieutenant Commander Pancho Ybarra and he's sending down some troops to help the local police force go through Mallorysport. He'll also increase the satellite surveillance. I'm getting ready to head out and join the search myself."

"That would be a very bad idea, Ben." He said. Rainsford wanted to know why and Grego explained, "This might be a ploy to get you out where you are vulnerable. I don't want to worry you even more, but this could be an assassination plot."

"Assassination? Who'd want to kill me?" Rainsford never considered that he could be a target.

"The forty-nine percent that didn't vote for you would be a good place to start. I suggest you get a couple of men to stay with you and keep out of sight. I'll get Chief Steefer to take some men and join the search. Is there anything else I can do to help?"

"I'll let you know, Victor."

The two men discussed some details then screened-off. Grego immediately turned on the screen again, this time calling Chief Steefer's office. Instead of getting Chief Harry Steefer, Captain Morgan Lansky's face stared out of the viewscreen. Lansky usually worked the midnight to six shifts. He was an hour early.

"Mr. Grego," Lansky said, trying to keep the surprise out of his voice. The last time Grego caught him off-guard he made less than a stellar impression. This time, however, his uniform was picture perfect and his eyes wide and alert. "Is there something wrong, sir?"

"Where's Chief Steefer?"

"He's doing a surprise inspection of the night shift," the captain replied. "He asked me to come in and hold down his desk while he did so."

Chief Steefer was a retired Federation Army officer with an impressive record who tended to run the company police like a military organization. "Call him and ask him to contact me immediately." Captain Lansky gave Grego a 'yessir' and screened-off. Grego mentally counted to ten as he waited. He made it to six just as Chief Steefer screened in. He updated the Chief on Gus Brannhard's abduction and asked him to send as many men as he could spare to help out with the search. "I'll be down to join in as soon as I get a sitter for Diamond."

"With all due respect, sir," the Chief said, "I can't allow that."

What? "Excuse me, Chief, but I didn't quite get that."

"Sir, an important government official has been grabbed up," Chief Steefer explained. "This is a capital crime and will likely earn the grabbers a bullet in the head. That means they will not be playing nice. My first duty to the Charterless Zarathustra Company is to protect its interests. That means protecting you." Steefer jabbed an index finger at Grego through the screen for emphasis. "I will not have my boss getting shot at on my watch. You have your work and I have mine. This is mine."

He considered what Steefer said, then replied, "Chief, I would be very put out with you if I hadn't given essentially the same speech to the Governor a few minutes ago. Just out of curiosity, what would have happened if I fired you, put Lansky in charge, and then told him I was going out on the hunt?"

"Then Lansky and I would both be unemployed," the Chief answered. "Captain Lansky has his rough edges but I trained him well. Rule number one is to protect the primary at all costs, even if it means taking a bullet."

Grego didn't know that rule and realized he should have. "Okay, Chief, you win. Tell your men that there will be a hefty bonus for the team that finds Brannhard in one piece." He almost added that he wanted no heroics but realized that Chief Steefer didn't need to be told how to do his job.

*   *   *   *   *   *   *   *   *

Raul Laporte stared coolly at his visitors. Bad enough he had to deal with those mutts from Terra, now there were two men from Ghu-knows-where sitting across from him with an even more outrageous plan than his previous guests had ventured. He was tempted to just have them tossed into the M/E converter, but Laporte knew better than to kill somebody before he had all the facts.

"Gentlemen, I do not know where you got the idea that I could assist you on such a cape-, um, undertaking, but I assure you I have no interest in doing so," Laporte said in his most reasonable voice. "In fact, I should contact the authorities and have you both arrested for conspiracy."

The man on the left, Dane, laughed out-loud while his associate lost all color in his face. Dane was clearly a lawyer of some type. Likely a criminal defense attorney from the way he handled himself. The other man seemed like a tech-freak. He had soft hands and looked as though he hadn't been in direct sunlight in years.

"Mr. Laporte, We both know you have no intention of contacting anybody, let alone a law enforcement agency." Dane extracted an envelope from inside his jacket and handed it over to the gangster.

Laporte opened the envelope and extracted the papers inside. After a moment of perusing the pages he grew pale. "Where did you get this?"

"Suffice to say," Dane said, "we have a friend in common. Now, since neither of us wishes to have this particular information come to light, what do you say we put aside the posturing and talk business?"

Laporte nodded and took out his knife and whetstone.

"Good. Now, as we already explained, we intend to extract Leo Thaxter from prison…."

"Can't be done." Laporte worked the blade as his visitors stared silently at him.

Thaxter, his sister Rose, her husband Conrad Evins, the former chief gem buyer for the Chartered Zarathustra Company and Phil Novaes were serving ten to twenty for attempted grand theft of the CZC sunstones. When their sentences were up, they would be retried on the faginy charges, illegally capturing, enslaving, and forcing incompetent natives to commit a crime, and would likely be shot in the head for it, except for Novaes, who died in prison. Moses Herckerd, the fifth member of the gang, got himself conveniently dead in a shoot out with the company police.

Hugo Ingermann, the penultimate shyster on Zarathustra, had promised to get them off on the faginy charge, then skipped planet with 250,000 sols worth of stolen sunstones. When the four conspirators arrived in court, their defense counsel was aboard the Terra-Baldur-Marduk liner *The City of Konkrook* in hyperspace headed to Terra, leaving the four defendants nowhere in terms of legal council; so much for crooked lawyers and their promises.

"Oh, come on," the younger man argued, possibly to break the silence, "Nothing is impossible with sufficient study and planning."

Laporte stabbed his knife into the top of his desk for emphasis. "Fine, say you bust Leo out of the pokey. How do you plan to get him off Zarathustra? Leo has a very memorable face."

"Plastic surgery—"

Laporte interrupted. "Once Thaxter was processed into the prison system they took his DNA, did a retina scan, mapped every scar and blemish, X-rayed his teeth and skeletal structure, then, just for laughs, implanted a microchip in his brain that allows him to be tracked anywhere on the planet. Fingerprints can be altered, retinas can be covered with implants, scars can be removed, teeth and bones can be worked on and, as I recently learned, DNA can be masked under the correct circumstances, but that microchip comes with a lifetime guarantee."

"Microchips can be disabled," the younger man volunteered.

"Maybe back in the old days when they were vulnerable to an electro-magnetic pulse, but these days you need the exact code and frequency combination…"

"I can hack it," the younger man said with a smug expression.

"Hack?"

"My associate likes to use archaic terminology," Dane explained. "He means that he can override the security protocols on the microchip and disable it."

"Really," Laporte said slowly. *Now that's a useful talent*, thought the gangster. "I see. Now all we have to do is get Thaxter out of prison, fit him with contacts, do a series of surgeries and arrange for a new identity. Sure, nothing to it."

"Really, Mr. Laporte, there is no point in—"

"The point is that we have no way of breaking into or out of the prison. The perimeter walls are all lined with collapsium, as are the cells. The perimeter guards are all armed with 10 mm auto-fire Martian Express machine guns."

"We could gas them and grab Thaxter while they're all asleep," the younger man suggested.

"The guards all have oxy-masks with them. Anybody passes out; they all mask-up and put the place on lockdown. The warden used to run a prison on Uller. He was there during an attempted jailbreak fifteen years back," Laporte explained. "The cons had outside help that lobbed anesthezine gas bombs over the walls. Unfortunately, they failed to account for the wind and the gas was dispersed before it took effect. Afterwards, the warden made it a policy for all of his guards to carry protective gear at all times."

"Do they have any kind of prisoner employment program?" Dane asked.

"They didn't used to but after the attempted land-grabs and veldbeest rustling they had to pull a lot of workers off the farms and shift them to security," Laporte said. "Rainsford signed off on the prisoner work detail plan and the CZC put a lot of the able-bodied prisoners to work."

"What kind of security do they have on the farms?" the younger man asked.

"Collar and pole," Laporte said. When he saw the blank expression on the two men's faces he elaborated. Prisoners were each fitted with a thin metal collar that could only be removed with a special magnetic key. Any prisoner wearing such a device had to remain within a perimeter of electronic poles. Anybody wearing such a collar that escaped the confines of the perimeter would find himself suddenly and violently bereft of his head when the electronic signal from the poles was interrupted. Without the steady signal emitted from the poles, a preprogrammed command within the collar would ignite a fifty-milligram capsule of cataclysmite. "The last time somebody tried to make a break for it, the body kept going for six steps after the head ceased to exist. That was one Phil Novaes."

Dane's associate let out a low whistle.

"Hmm. Then we will simply have to arrange for Mr. Thaxter to be taken out of the prison for us," said Dane.

Laporte pulled his knife out of the desktop and set it aside. "And how do you expect to manage that?"

Dane smiled. "I have a few ideas…"

XI

Hoenveld was happy. It was a rare state for the elderly scientist. With him were Dr. Ernst Mallin and the Fuzzy named Zorro. Hoenveld extracted a hypodermic needle from the Fuzzy's arm and said, "There now. That wasn't so bad, was it?" The Fuzzy disagreed, rubbing his arm. "Tell you what, how would you like something nice to eat? We have land-prawn, goofer, pool-ball fruit…Ernst, what is the Fuzzy name for that?"

Dr. Mallin had to admit that he didn't know.

"Well, pick anything on this table you would like and you may have it, Mr. Zorro."

Zorro looked over the offered fare and selected some taffy from Odin. Mallin scribbled something on his pad and resumed his observations.

"I would have expected him to go for the goofer," said Hoenveld. "We know he disdains land-prawn and Extee-Three, but he is still a carnivorous omnivore."

"Actually, he had some veldbeest for lunch, so he was more interested in dessert," explained Mallin. "Although most human children at twelve years of age would automatically go for the candy first."

"I should be kept abreast of his dietary habits, at the very least, Ernst," Hoenveld said tartly. He picked up a compu-pad and tapped in some notes.

"I agree," nodded Mallin, "that is why I have this list of everything Zorro has eaten in the last three days." The psychologist handed Hoenveld the paper with a small grin.

"And of course you had to wait until I complained about it to give it to me," Hoenveld observed. "Always with the brain games."

"My stock and trade. I must say that you are being far more solicitous of Zorro's care than I would have expected."

Before Hoenveld could respond, Juan Jimenez entered the lab. "How is our favorite patient, today," he asked, as he ruffled Zorro's head.

"Unka Chris give taff-ee," the Fuzzy exclaimed.

Jimenez and Mallin both stared at Hoenveld.

"Unka Chris?" Jimenez asked.

"Everybody is either unka, pappy, mummy or auntie to the Fuzzies," the scientist replied. "I saw no reason to argue the point with him."

"No. Of course not," Jimenez agreed, "Unka Chris."

Juan and Mallin chuckled and even Hoenveld smiled a little.

"Have you found anything significant in our little friend's bloodwork?" he asked.

"Actually, yes. So far, I have ruled out pathogens, allergies, parasites and physical trauma. Mr. Zorro, here, is as healthy a Fuzzy as I have ever seen."

Mallin added, "And there is nothing to suggest that he has suffered any kind of psychological trauma that would explain his aversion to Extee-Three and land-prawn."

"I do have one more avenue of research I would like to follow, but would rather not say anything about it until I have determined whether or not it will lead anywhere," Hoenveld said. "I just took some more blood for analysis and will need a day or two with this young person to follow-up on it."

"I'll talk to Ruth and see if she can get the Garzas to agree," Jimenez said. "Where will you keep him? Not in the lab, I hope."

"Certainly not," Hoenveld exclaimed. "I would never lock a sapient being up like an animal…unlike some people I could mention."

Jimenez visibly winced at the comment. Of everybody in the room, only Hoenveld had nothing to do with putting Fuzzies into cages for tests back before their sapience was established. And neither did Zorro, of course.

"He can stay with me," Hoenveld explained. "It…will give me a chance to observe him under non-clinical conditions. I have familiarized myself with the care and feeding of Fuzzies and promise not to let him come to harm."

Jimenez stared for a moment, then said, "Welcome to the Friends of Little Fuzzy, Chris."

Hoenveld simply 'harrumphed' and made a display of going to work on the blood sample.

*   *   *   *   *   *   *   *

"…A 25,000 sol reward for information leading to the safe recovery of Mr. Brannhard. To repeat; the search for Colonial Chief Prosecutor Brannhard who had been reportedly kidnapped by persons unknown at this time…"

"Oh, this is just too perfect," Dane said as he shut off the radio. "This is an opportunity we can't miss. Everybody will be focused on getting that drunken caveman Brannhard back. They're probably pulling men away from the prison force right now. Is Mr. Clancy ready to do his part?"

"Yeah. How'd you find this guy so fast?" Murdock inquired. "He's almost a dead ringer for Thaxter."

"Not almost. Now he's an exact match," Dr. Rankin added. "Just a little minor plastic surgery on his ears."

"I've been to Zarathustra before," Dane cut in. "I know my way around and who to contact. Clancy arrived on-planet after I left, but my contacts found him for me when I asked for them to provide me with a double for Thaxter." Dane turned to Lundgren. "Where are we on disabling the collar?"

Lundgren held up a card attached to a miniature computer by a long, thin cord. "Without an actual collar to test it on I can't guarantee that this will work, but it's the same principle as any other security lock that uses an encoded card—"

"You want to be very sure about this," Dane interrupted. "If you're wrong the plan blows-up…along with Thaxter."

* * * * * * * *

"…Colonial Chief Prosecutor Brannhard was abducted from his home. According to eyewitnesses, two men broke into his home, used a sono-stunner and took him in an aircar at around 2400 hours Alpha time. There is reason to believe that Brannhard is still alive and a major manhunt is underway. Victor Grego, CEO of the Charterless Zarathustra Company, has volunteered the assistance of the company police force in the search for the Colonial Chief Prosecutor. To repeat; the search for Colonial Chief Prosecutor Brannhard, who had been reportedly kidnapped by persons unknown at this time…."

The leader signaled for the radio to be turned off then called some men over to him. "You all heard the radio?" They had. "This is bad, no getting around that. They'll tear apart Alpha Continent atom by atom if they have to, then they'll turn to the rest of the planet. Satellite surveillance will be stepped up and we have no way of getting the sweep schedule, now."

One man spoke up, "Do we abort?" It was the same man who wanted to pack up earlier when the Fuzzies were spotted. Some people didn't have the stomach for extra-legal activities.

The leader shook his head. "We can't. Not with the increased satellite activity. The only thing keeping us from being spotted now is the canopy. No way will we be able to pack up and light out without being spotted until Brannhard has been found, alive or dead, and the satellite schedule returns to the normal routine. Any suspicious activity will bring the wrath of Ghu down upon us. They'll think we're connected to the disappearance of this Brannhard. Even if we're cleared of that they'll still nail us for trespassing and illegal mining. We'll have to stay under the canopy and work as best we can on the dig."

"The canopy won't block a ground search," a dark haired man said. "Since we are here illegally no excuse will satisfy anyone who stumbles upon us. We'll likely be arrested under suspicion of complicity in this Brannhard's kidnapping. Then we'll each be put in the polyencephalographic veridicator and questioned. Then we have a choice; don't speak and be assumed to be part of the kidnapping, or talk and give up our operation and everybody involved."

Then their whole mission would be revealed. "Is there any way we can camouflage our position well enough to withstand scrutiny from the ground?" he asked. Not against anybody with significant wilderness experience was the answer. Especially not against Fuzzies whom all possess superior hearing, vision and maybe even sense of smell. "I need options, people."

A tall blond man spoke up. "Let's do the best we can with the camouflage then send some men out to join the ground search if they start one. If we get lucky they'll be able to get assigned to this area and will lead any others safely around us."

"How do you propose to get anybody out of here and back to Alpha without being spotted? We're on the far edge of the Fuzzy Reservation. Anything larger than a Fuzzy will set off the infra-red alarms."

"Wait a second," Hendrix said. "This is Fuzzy land so the police have to be real careful not to disturb the Fuzzies, right? Well, let's just encourage that group over the hill to stick around."

"How would that benefit us?" the leader asked.

"I read that Holloway wants the wild Fuzzies out here to be left alone, let them develop and evolve without interference from Terrans," Hendrix explained. "That means the cops won't be allowed to get too close if there are Fuzzies in the area. Chances are they'll just do an infra-red and sonic sweep, spot the Fuzzies, and move on."

The leader quickly grasped the implication. "The fibroid weave deflects infra-red and muffles most sound. We just shutdown the equipment and stay quiet if they move the search into this area."

"How do we encourage the Fuzzies to stick around?" Stewart inquired. "I heard they lead a nomadic lifestyle."

"That's because they are always searching for food," Hendrix said. "So, we give them some Terran Federation Armed Forces Emergency Ration, Extraterrestrial, Type Three."

"Excellent idea, but we'll remove the tins," the leader said. "We don't need that kind of evidence lying around. Meanwhile, we'll have to speed-up our time table. Beta is a big continent; we might be able to finish here before somebody stumbles over us."

"Sir, there are about a dozen Fuzzies out there," Jagger, the sound tech, reported. "At one tin per Fuzzy per day, they'll go through our entire supply of XT3 in about two weeks."

"Good point," the leader agreed. "We'll leave three tins worth a day and add some local game to the buffet. I'll need two volunteers to suit up in camou-suits with sonic rifles. Not very sporty, I'll admit, but we don't want any shell-casings left behind…"

* * * * * * * *

It was morning and everybody was hungry and tired. No one had slept well the night before. Strange noises from the direction of the Big Ones' camp frightened the young Fuzzys, forcing the adults to comfort them. Climber wanted to go out and see what was making all the noise but Red Fur stopped him. Some of the noises were just like the ones they heard when the *shimo-kato* made dead, the same noise that hurt Makes-

Things ears.

Red Fur was gathering the tribe together to go hunting when Little One came running with something strange in his hands. Everybody looked at the strange thing Little One carried. It was a never seen before thing. Red Fur sniffed it and wrinkled his nose. He had never smelled anything like it. Runs Fast took a piece of the strange thing and tasted it then put the whole thing in his mouth and grabbed for more.

"*Kii-mossii!*" Runs Fast cried out, after he swallowed. "This is wonderful food!"

Red Fur tried a piece and spit it out, as did Little One, Tells-things, Stonebreaker and Healer. The rest attacked the golden stuff and devoured it as fast as they could.

"Where you find?" Red Fur asked. Little One took Red Fur to the hill by the Big Ones' hidden camp. There were two more golden cakes placed on some leaves. "The Big Ones left this."

"Big Ones?" Little One asked. "Why?"

"Not know," the Fuzzy leader admitted. "Maybe want to make friends. Or maybe try to trick us, like *shimo-kato*."

"*Shimo-kato* trick?"

Little One hadn't learned how a *shimo-kato* would fool its prey by leaving the area and circling around to attack its victim from behind. Red Fur was afraid the Big Ones might trick the *Jin-f'ke* into thinking they were friends, then making them all dead. If the Big Ones wanted to be friends why didn't they simply come out and meet the tribe? Why hide in their burrow? The Big Ones behaved very strangely, thought Red Fur.

* * * * * * * * *

It was good to get out in the field for a change. Normally, Chief Harry—never Harold—Steefer spent most of his on-duty time at Company House supervising the men and double-checking the security tech. And as always, there was paperwork, lots and lots of paperwork. Occasionally he would get out to the farms and ranches for inspection, and a once a month trip to Yellowsand to make sure the sunstone mining operation was secure. On average that got him out of Company House about four days a month.

Steefer was used to action. During his time in the Federation Army he had seen his fair share of combat, mostly against rebellious aliens who didn't appreciate what the Federation had to offer. There was the separatist group on Uller who favored the hit-and-run tactics of first century A.E. terrorists, and the mess on Freya when a small principality declared its independence from the kingdom of Taalstahk and took several Terrans hostage. But the one that ended Major Steefer's career was the uprising on Yggdrasil when three tribes of Khooghras banded together and attacked the Chartered Yggdrasil Company. The attack was so sudden and so well executed nobody could believe the Khooghras had planned it.

The native sapient population of Yggdrasil sported the lowest intelligence of any known sapient species. Harry Steefer distinguished himself by rallying his men into an effective counter-force that wiped out the lion's share of the attackers. Unfortunately, he sustained severe injuries that resulted in the loss of one kidney, the spleen and two feet of intestine. While the Army readily paid for the organ replacement surgery, his military career was over. Officers were held to high standards of physical fitness and any officer who had had major surgery of any kind fell below those standards. Forced retirement with disability compensation was his only option.

With his military career over Harry Steefer decided to put his criminology degree to good use and tried to join the police force in his home town on Terra only to find that his age worked against him. He had missed the cut-off by two years. While he could live well enough on his military pension, Steefer wasn't ready to retire. He kept an eye out for employment opportunities and jumped at the chance to go into off-world security.

When the word went out that Zarathustra was looking for men, he got on the next ship and never looked back. When he arrived on Zarathustra he was assigned a position as captain of security. There he caught the eye of one Victor Grego, who knew a good man when he saw one. When Chief Tanaka put in for retirement, Steefer was promoted on the spot.

Now, eight years later, Chief Steefer was feeling the walls close-in. He missed the action and change of scenery that was a part of military life. When Victor Grego asked him to join the Colonial Police in search of Gus Brannhard it was like an answer to a prayer. He put Lansky in charge of Company House security and left him a skeleton crew to supervise. The rest went with him to join the police effort.

At first Chief Steefer enjoyed the change of pace. He and his men joined the police in serving warrants and searching suspect homes and businesses. While police regulations required civilian deputies to carry non-lethal weapons, the cops didn't make a peep about the CZC security force packing firearms. Steefer appreciated this breech of protocol and said so.

"No problem, Mr.- uh, Chief Steefer," Officer Chang said. "We appreciate the extra manpower and Colonial Marshal Max Fane signed off on it. If any shooting starts up, I like having lots of guns on my side."

Steefer, Chang and a mixed squad of Colonial and Company police along with a squad of Terran Federation Marines, on loan from Lieutenant Commander Ybarra, were taking squad cars to an abandoned warehouse in the area formerly titled to Hugo Ingermann.

"I like your thinking, son," the Chief said with a wolfish smile. "Say, weren't you one of the cops with Marshal Fane when he stormed through Company House looking for Jack Holloway's Fuzzies?"

"Yeah, me Piet and Miguel," Chang replied. "I don't recall seeing you there, though."

"I wasn't. It was my night off, but I reviewed the security tapes after debriefing my men." Steefer grimaced. "Just my luck to miss all the fun."

"I hope there's no hard feelings."

"Not to worry. I understand following orders and doing the job you are supposed to do. I doubt Mr. Grego holds a grudge, either. He even tried to re-hire Ruth van Riebeek, and she'd been spying on the company. Now if you want me to be mad about something, do a half-assed job while I'm around to see it."

"I'll pass," Chang said, laughing. "Marshal Fane takes the same dim view of sloppy police work."

The aircars settled to the ground a short distance from the warehouse. Chief Steefer stepped out and organized the men. By unspoken agreement, Chang deferred to the chief's greater experience.

"Okay, since this is CZC property, now, we won't need a warrant," Steefer said. "What say we split off the men with one of yours, one of mine and a marine or two per group?"

Chang thought about it and agreed. Two aircars with four men each covered the sky while the ground contingent surrounded the building. When Chang gave the signal, they all kicked in a door, tossed in an anesthezine gas bomb and then entered the building with gas masks on and guns at the ready. They found half a dozen men slumped over a card table. The men had been in the middle of a poker game when the gas overcame them. One man had a Royal Flush.

"Too bad we didn't wait another minute," Chang said, after glancing at the cards. "It looks like this one was ready to clean-out his buddies."

"Guess his luck isn't all it could be," agreed Steefer. "See what happens when you don't post a look-out?" he said to the unconscious man. He then said into his radio, "all teams report."

"Team Alpha, all clear."

"Beta Team, nothing to report."

"Gamma Team. Chief, you might want to see this."

"Brannhard?" Chang asked. Chief Steefer relayed the question.

"Negative, sir. Something else."

The Marines clearly preferred to answer to Chief Steefer rather than the resident police. This was due partly to Steefer's military background, but mostly because of the Space Federation Medal of Honor he proudly wore on his uniform along with the rest of his numerous military awards and citations. When the three teams had first met up, the Gunnery Sergeant called his men to attention and saluted the chief. Though no longer required to return the salute, Steefer did so out of habit.

Steefer and Chang walked over to Gamma Team's position while receiving the rest of the reports. No Gus Brannhard. What they found instead was a treasure trove of vid-screens, Extee-Three, computers and other merchandise. Most of it was still in the original packaging with the CZC logo on it.

"Well, it's not Brannhard, but we've been looking for these guys, anyway," the Chief sighed. "A couple of our warehouses were coming up short on inventory. It looks like we just found it."

"Did you recognize any of those mugs back there?" Chang asked.

"No, but they might be newly hired. The CZC has had a high turnover rate in personnel the last couple of years." The Chief looked over the assorted loot. "You and your men can have credit for this bust. I figure you would have found all this with or without us." Something occurred to the Chief. "That's an awful lot of Extee-Three. We should do another sweep for any signs of Fuzzies being held, here. I don't think any of these clowns were eating the Extee-Three for dessert."

Officer Chang issued the orders and the men started a second more thorough sweep of the building. After a moment Beta Squad found a hidden trap-door. One man pulled the door open while a second covered it with his machine gun. When nothing happened, Chang took the lead down the stairs followed by Chief Steefer and two Marines.

The room was completely devoid of light. Chang and Steefer turned on the wrist lights that were standard issue for company and colonial police and scanned the area.

"Great Ghu! Chief, do you see this?"

"I wish I didn't. Let me get this light switch." Steefer flicked a switch and the room was illuminated from several sources. Revealed in the full light were four dozen cages, each occupied by one or two Fuzzies. Steefer turned to the Marine closest to him and told him not to let anybody else down until the prisoners were safely locked up. "We don't want this to turn into a bloodbath."

Chang called for reinforcements and ordered that the prisoners be immediately taken to the police station. "And don't let anybody down here except medical personnel."

Chang swore in old Terran Chinese as he walked over and started opening cages. The Fuzzies were afraid to come out at first. Steefer noticed dark marks on their fur that resembled the electrical burn marks from high-powered cattle prods like the ones used on veldbeests.

Steefer put a hand on Chang's shoulder. "We better wait for Fuzzy Protective Services personnel to get here. These Fuzzies are going to have a hard time trusting anybody for a while."

Reluctantly, Chang pulled back from the cages. "You think they're pets or slaves?"

"Either one will get those idiots a bullet in the head. You can't make a pet out of a sapient being, so it would come under kidnapping or enslavement. The Governor takes a very stern and final approach with guys like this."

Chang nodded in agreement. "He isn't the only one. I have a pair of

Fuzzies at home. Fred Astaire and Ginger Rogers. I see this…" Chang took a deep breath and switched topic. "You figure Brannhard might be in one of these other abandoned buildings?"

"No. We've been sweeping this and the surrounding areas with infrared and sonic detectors with no results until we found this bunch." Steefer sighed again. "If the door-to-door doesn't yield any results it may be time to move the search out of Mallorysport and Junktown."

XII

When John Morgan awoke he was momentarily startled to find that he wasn't in his suite at Company House. The room was much smaller and decorated with relics he didn't recognize. After some thought he realized that the smaller items that looked like tiny weapons made of wood and bone had to be Fuzzy crafts. As his brain got up to speed he also realized that one of them was a chopper-digger made of wood. Morgan had seen Diamond carry a similar one made of metal.

On another wall was a sword similar to those used on Freya but of a design he was unfamiliar with. Next to it was a cloth garment like a plaid skirt, but also of unfamiliar design. A third wall had a sword that Morgan recognized from his college days. It was a Katana. Morgans's roommate at the Epsilon Rho Burroughs fraternity had a collection of ancient Japanese weapons. There were also a number of throwing stars, a Kama, a Tanto, a Bo staff, Nunchaku and a matching set of Tonfa.

That's right, Morgan thought, *I had drinks with Akira last night and accompanied her to her home. This must be her bedroom.*

The door opened and Akira walked in bearing a tray. "Good morning, sleepy-head. I have some breakfast for you."

Morgan got up and started getting dressed. "…uh…I don't want to sound like a…jerk…but did we do something I should remember last night?"

Akira laughed and set the tray on the nightstand. "Yeah, but not what you're thinking. I slept on the couch. How much do you remember?"

"Well, we were having drinks at The Bitter End when we bumped in to some people who had been to Freya. We all got to talking, but then it gets a bit fuzzy."

"Well, this is the right planet to get fuzzy on."

Morgan looked blankly at Akira.

"Sorry. Bad joke. You and Mark Szymanski got into a drinking contest. Mark said he could keep up with any Freyan…"

"Mark?"

"Big guy with dark hair," explained Akira. "He had worked construction for the Charterless Freya Company before coming to Zarathustra. Anyway, you and Mark started throwing down Freyan ale like it was soda pop."

"That explains the hydrogen fission process taking place in my head." Morgan grabbed the coffee and took a drink. He didn't like it but the warmth and caffeine helped his headache. "Did I at least win?"

"Oh, yes. Mark passed out around the twelfth round. You both had quite a following and the betting got pretty heated."

"Betting?"

"Don't you remember? You had me bet one hundred sols that you could put Mark under the table." Akira took some bills out of her purse. "Here are your winnings."

"Gods above and below, I haven't done anything like that since college." Morgan looked at the money with distaste. "Keep it. You earned it."

"What?" Akira took a step back "What do you think I am?" She was afraid that Morgan knew about her keeping tabs on his actions at the CZC.

Morgan's head renewed its earlier pounding. "Gaaah! Please, stop yelling. I mean that you got me out of that lounge in one piece when I was in no condition to defend myself. That couldn't have been easy with that crowd. And as I recall, you loaned me the money to bet since I never carry much cash. Your risk, so your reward."

Akira fought to keep the relief she felt off her face. "Oh…I thought it was…something else."

"You mean watching me for Victor Grego?"

Akira fell back into a chair. "How did you find out?"

Morgan grinned then winced as his head pounded even more. "You just told me. Frankly, I was prepared to suspect any assistant Mr. Grego sent to help me. A major stockholder comes out of nowhere and wants to dig through his files…how could he not have me watched? I would be very disappointed if he didn't."

Akira slumped further into the chair. "So, what happens now?"

"Nothing." Morgan drank more of the coffee and grimaced. "I don't suppose you have any tea? Maybe some Earl Grey Green?" She didn't. "You should just keep doing what Mr. Grego tells you to do and I'll keep going on about my business."

"What…what is your business, here? You don't really seem all that interested in the company." Akira leaned forward. "Oh, sure, you've looked through the financials, mostly for my benefit, I think, but you seem far more interested in Epsilon Continent and certain Terrans that had been to Freya than anything connected to the Company."

"Hmm. You are very observant. I thought I had managed to hide that. Ah, do you have any headache pills?" Akira pulled a packet out of the nightstand and handed them to Morgan. After washing two capsules down with the coffee he continued, "No, I don't have any real interest in the Company. Mr. Grego has been working miracles considering what he has had to deal with since the Fuzzies were discovered. There is a Terran expression that has caught on with Freyans: If it ain't broke, don't fix it. My interest in Epsilon Continent will remain my secret for now. As for the Terrans that have been to Freya, well, that is personal." John took in a breath then let it out slowly. "I'm looking for my father."

"Your father? But you're Freyan…."

"My father is Terran."

Akira absorbed that revelation then asked, "Have you found him, yet?"

John picked at the breakfast on the tray that Akira brought in. He recognized the Terran chicken eggs and home fries—presumably made from introduced Terran potatoes—but the sausage was a mystery. Likely something local with 'zara' in its name, like zarapig or something. "I don't know. I've been hopping from planet-to-planet for fifteen years since I finished college. The man I am looking for is between fifty-five and eighty Terran years of age, by now. If he is on Zarathustra, I've narrowed my search down to five people."

Akira was interested and her face showed it. "Anybody I know?"

"Maybe. Right now Gustavus Brannhard is my chief suspect."

Akira again leaned forward. "Gus? I met him once in a bar. Now, there's a man you wouldn't want to engage in a drinking contest!"

"Right this second I couldn't out-drink a Fuzzy," said Morgan as he downed a second pill pack. "I plan on making an appointment to see him later today…."

"Haven't you heard? Gus has been kidnapped. It's been all over the news."

Morgan stopped eating and stared at Akira. "Have there been any… what's the word?"

"Leads? No. Only that it was two men with a sono-stunner. Gus's Fuzzies saw the abduction, and they are working on a better description, but they didn't get a good look at the men's faces."

"Damn!" Morgan jumped up and grabbed his jacket and started to race out, but stopped himself before he reached the door. He turned to face Akira. "I have to go. Maybe I can join one of the search parties…they are using search parties, aren't they?"

"Yes, they are," she said.

"Then I'm going to join one of them. I have to find him, Akira."

"You said you weren't sure if he was your father or not…."

"True. He may not be. But I can't take the chance."

Before Akira could say anything further, Morgan was though the door and out of the apartment.

*   *   *   *   *   *   *   *   *

"Sir, Zarathustra is a big planet," said Colonial Marshal Max Fane. "Larger than Terra, in fact, with more temperate land masses. A ground search is simply impossible."

"How can we make it possible?" Colonial Governor Bennett Rainsford asked.

"How? Borrow about ten million men from other planets. I would even settle for a massive force of Yggdrasil Khooghras. They're all dumb as stumps, but at least they know how to track." Marshal Fane realized he was raising his voice at the Governor and stopped himself before he did or said something he would regret.

"Max, I think you have something, there." Ben turned away from the confused Colonial Marshal and punched in a code on his communications screen.

"Governor, I was kidding about the Khoo…"

Ben signaled for quiet as the connection was made. "Jack, the search of the city hasn't turned up anything."

"What can I do to help?" replied Jack from the screen.

"How is the dog rider program coming along?"

Eighteen months earlier Sandra Khadra noticed two Fuzzies riding on the back of a large mixed breed dog and mentioned it to Victor Grego, Jack Holloway and Ben Rainsford at a dinner party. That started a discussion about the merits of Fuzzy mounted dogs since Zarathustra lacked for any animal that could do the job of a horse, especially for the diminutive natives. Eventually, it was decided to bring in a number of breeding pairs of sturdy dogs and train them as 'horses' for Fuzzies.

This opened another debate about what breed of dog would be best suited to the task. One of Gus's friends, Larry Wolvin, a handyman and mechanic who also bred dogs, suggested the Curtys, a relatively new breed dating back to second century A.E. The Curtys were smart, strong, quick and good trackers. Larry later demonstrated the Curtys' potential and Victor Grego arranged for two hundred breading pairs to be brought in from near-by planets, along with five hundred Curtys' embryos to be grown in artificial wombs.

"We have over one hundred trained dogs here on Beta," Jack reported. "They're grown enough to carry a Fuzzy and some supplies. I'll check with Larry Wolvin and see what he's got—"

"I'll do that, Jack," he said. "Do you think it would be possible to start a ground search in suspect areas using Fuzzy cavalry?"

"That's a cracker-jack idea, Ben," Jack agreed. "Can you send over some of Gus's dirty laundry? The dogs might be able to sniff him out."

"Good thinking. I'll send that along with Natty and Allan. They need some happy time on the Rez. Maybe letting them join the search will help perk them up."

"I'll be sure to keep them too busy to worry about their old Pappy Gus," Jack said. "Why don't you send Flora and Fauna along, too? They might enjoy seeing my little mob here."

"That's a good idea, Jack. I hate to admit it, but since Gus went missing I haven't spent as much time with them as I should." The two men said their good-byes then Ben cut the connection and pulled up the code for Mr. Wolvin.

Larry Wolvin had the kind of face normally associated with Pre-Atomic era prospectors. Thin to the point of being gaunt, balding, bushy mustache, chin covered in stubble and widely gapped teeth. In a galaxy where cosmetic surgery and hair replacement was widely and inexpensively available he chose to be as nature had made him. He even wore prosthetic vision enhancers rather than get corrective surgery on his eyes.

"Governor! This is a surprise," Larry said from the screen. "What can I do you for?"

"Mr. Wolvin, I need to know how many trained dogs you have available right now?" Ben asked, without preamble or pleasantry. The Colonial Governor quickly explained his plan. Larry explained that he had one hundred and eighty dogs ready to go if there were Fuzzies with the training to ride them.

"Nifflheim! How long does it take to train a Fuzzy to ride?"

"Two days for the basics and a week to get fancy. Fuzzies are fast learners and take to dogs like ducks to water."

"All right, we'll get as many Fuzzies into training as we can. Mr. Wolvin…"

"Call me Larry, Governor."

"…Okay, Larry, but you have to call me Ben…see if you can borrow some dogs from your private sales to boost the numbers. We need every dog we can get."

Larry assured Ben he would pull out all the stops then screened-off.

"Fuzzies on dogs will cover a lot of territory, but they'll need back-up," Marshal Fane pointed out. "I'll organize the force to ride herd on the Fuzzy search parties. Hmm…you didn't check with the Fuzzies to see if they would volunteer."

"I very much doubt that will be a problem, Marshal."

*   *   *   *   *   *   *   *   *

"…Fuzzies on dogs are expected to join the search on Alpha and Beta Continents. Colonial Native Affairs Commissioner Jack Holloway had this to say: "Eighteen months ago we started training some dogs to accept a specialized saddle. The average Curtys can hold two Fuzzies plus saddlebags without strain and they can run rings around a damnthing. While they don't have any bloodhound in them, they are still superior trackers and hunters. If Gus is out there, we'll find him."

"In other news actress Darla Cross has been dropped for the part of—"

Anthony Nicholovich Anderson turned off the radio and let out a long breath. He was bracing himself for what he knew must surely follow.

"Nobody said anything about dogs!"

And there it was. "Ripper, calm down before you wake our guest."

Rippolone started pacing back and forth yelling. "Tony, you know how I feel about dogs…"

Yes, Tony knew how Duncan felt about dogs, especially large breeds, ever since that time on Baldur. "Relax, Duncan. These dogs do not have our scent and they couldn't track an aircar even if they did."

"You can bet they'll get Brannhard's scent, somehow," Rippolone snarled. "They'll get something out of his house and stick it under those damn dogs' noses—"

"And still not find us," Anderson interrupted. "I never heard of a dog that could track a contra-gravity vehicle through the air. Plus, this hideout Laporte provided for us is shielded seven ways from Sunday and in a place nobody could ever find. The cops have been past here a dozen times already and never suspected a thing. Now sit down and let me think in peace."

"Why don't we just stuff Brannhard in a mass/energy converter? We can record it and take it back for proof to collect the bounty."

"The contract says he has to be delivered alive and in one piece. Besides, he's our insurance policy," Anderson explained. "If things go south, we have a bargaining chip. Until we can be sure we're in the clear we need him alive."

"Fine, it's your show. There just better not be any damn dogs comin' around here," muttered Rippolone.

* * * * * * * * *

"How much do you think is in there?"

The leader shrugged. "By volume I would say around 25,000,000 sols, give or take a mil. Of course, I'm no expert and none of these were professionally appraised, but I think that's a safe estimate."

There were excited mutterings and somebody let out a low whistle.

"Don't spend your bonuses yet. There's a lot more stones to dig up, and we have to ship these out without getting caught."

The room fell silent. The leader turned to Hendrix. "What's the word?"

Hendrix stood up and walked over to a hover-board resting on the floor in the back of the room. It was a special model designed for unmanned transport over long distances. "Gizmo here is all set to go. Charged up, fully cloaked, hypersonic sound baffles on-line, set for low-level flight, submersible, and programmed to avoid everything until it reaches its destination."

The leader nodded. "How long will that take?"

"Barring unforeseen complications, 30 to 40 T-hours."

"All right, let's get it done and get back to work. Hendrix, send the signal to the Alpha Party. Use encryption three on a burst transmission."

It was always a burst transmission but Hendrix simply nodded. For his cut of the thirty percent bonus he could stand a little redundancy.

* * * * * * * * *

Red Fur watched in amazement as a hole opened in the Big One's burrow and a strange looking made-thing slowly moved out. It floated at about waist level, for a *Jin-f'ke*, and moved out at increasing speed. It was silent and its colors rippled, matching that of the terrain. It was long and shaped like the melon-seed flying things, but with a large lump on its back. In a hand of heartbeats, the strange made-thing accelerated out of sight.

XIII

John Morgan was, to all appearances, sitting comfortably with his hot green tea from a bucket-sized mug, but inside he was an emotional tempest. Victor Grego had invited him, along with Dr. Mallin, Leslie Coombes and Juan Jimenez, to his penthouse for drinks. Morgan didn't want to insult his host by refusing to attend and realized the best way to join the search for Gus Brannhard was with Grego's help. Still, after the previous night's debauchery he refused to drink any alcoholic beverages.

Instead, he brought along a supply of Earl Grey Green tea that he had picked up on his last trip to Terra. As it turned out, Grego had an impressive supply of tea varieties including the Earl Grey. When Grego asked if Morgan would like a small or large cup, Morgan quipped, "A bucket would be perfect."

Grego again surprised Morgan by producing a two-liter novelty mug with a logo on the side that said "Fuzzy Con One."

"Fuzzy Con?"

Grego laughed. "I'm sure you've seen conventions on Mars…"

"Oh, Nifflheim, yes! Burroughs Con, Wells Con, Bradbury Con…" John explained that Mars colonists were completely obsessed with early science fiction writers, especially those that wrote fanciful stories about Mars.

"Well, Gus Brannhard made an offhand remark that we should host a Fuzzy Convention. I'm sure he meant it as a joke, but I ran with it. I invited non-company vendors and used an empty warehouse to throw it in. I'll have to show you some footage of that. Most people were dressed up like giant Fuzzies with homemade chopper-diggers to scale. One enterprising young man made a contra-gravity surfboard into a giant mechanical land-prawn and stuffed it with various cooked meats. He made quite a show of killing and eating it. The real Fuzzies were very excited about the whole thing and only a little disappointed to learn that under all the fur was just another normal Big One. I use the word 'normal' a bit loosely, of course."

"And you made a killing on these mugs, I'll bet." Morgan hefted the mug he was holding and concluded it was made of super-insolating plastic. The tea would stay hot for quite a while in there.

"Not just the mugs. Where do you think the vendors bought most of their supplies?"

Morgan began to wonder if there wasn't anything that Grego couldn't make profitable. He was about to say so when the communication screen beeped. Grego excused himself.

"Gus had quite a time at the convention," Ernst Mallin said. "He came in wearing bush gear that showed off his incredibly hairy legs and arms."

Morgan was surprised. Dr. Mallin didn't seem like a conventioneer. "You attended the con?"

"Surprised?" Mallin smiled. "It was a joy to observe people in that situation. You can learn a lot about people when they let their hair down… in a manner of speaking."

Grego returned looking grim. "That was Chief Steefer. They are moving the search out of the city. They've already sent men to Beta and Gamma continents."

"Maybe you should rethink allowing us to join in on the search," Jimenez suggested. "I know the terrain on Beta better than just about anybody short of Gerd or Jack."

"I wouldn't mind joining in," Morgan added. He couldn't believe his luck. It took an effort not to look too enthusiastic. "I was a fair tracker back on Freya. I got in some hunting on other planets, too."

"I'd like to get out there myself, but Chief Steefer won't allow it," Grego said, "and I have to back him up on this. Anybody high in the company as well as the Colonial Government could be another target. And Zarathustra is a lot more hazardous than Freya when you get out into the wilderness, John. You're still too green to be running around in the wild. Damnthings aren't the only dangerous fauna out there."

"He's right about that," Jimenez agreed. "I've been out there enough to know. You don't want to run afoul of a nest of tunnel-worms, believe me! Are your vaccinations up-to-date?"

"I can take care of that, today." Morgan made a mental note to look up tunnel-worms before heading out to Beta.

"Well, I am a little embarrassed to admit that I am not at all anxious to go wandering about in the bush on a manhunt," Dr. Mallin said. "I possess neither the training nor the physique for such an endeavor. I know my limitations."

"I'm afraid that applies to me as well," Leslie Coombes added. "But I will cheerfully step into the role of prosecutor when we find the miscreants. With yours and the Governor's permission, of course."

"You have mine," Grego said. "I just hope it won't be a murder trial."

"I just realized something," Jimenez said. "Jack Holloway would also qualify as a high government official as the Native Affairs Commissioner. Maybe he shouldn't be out on the hunt, either."

"A good point, but a moot one," Grego said. "Nobody but nobody would get anywhere telling Jack to stay home. Besides, if he finds the kidnappers first, they'll be the ones needing protection."

"Perhaps I could go to Beta and join Jack's team," Morgan suggested. "I'm a fair hand with a gun and Jack could keep me out of trouble."

And technically, John Morgan doesn't work for the Company; he is a part owner, Grego mused, *making him immune to orders.* "If Jack is fine with it, and Chief Steefer doesn't hear about it, I guess that would be okay."

* * * * * * * * *

"The ground search hasn't yielded any results, yet," George Lunt explained. "We still have a lot of area to cover, but I think the wilderness areas are a dead-end."

Jack Holloway leaned closer to the viewscreen. "Why is that?"

"If I was going to grab somebody up, I'd hide them in the city where satellite surveillance had no chance of spotting me." He went on further to explain the advantages of being in a crowded city where confederates could give the abductors support that would be unworkable in an isolated area. "We have come across some illegal sunstone miners and a few poachers on the reservation, though, so it hasn't been a total waste of time."

"Well, we'll keep sweeping the area anyway," Jack said. "It can't hurt and you never know what anybody crazy enough to grab up the Chief Prosecutor might be thinking. They could hole up in the wilderness thinking that the police will concentrate on the city for the reasons you mentioned. Besides, we might catch some more illegal miners and poachers if nothing else."

"What do you want me to do with the confiscated sunstones?"

"Tag them as evidence for now and turn them over to the prosecutor's office." There will be a lot of debate what to do with the stones later. Technically, only the CZC was authorized to dig up sunstones on the Reservation, and Fuzzies, of course, if they ever bothered. The question would be; who gets the stones, the Fuzzies or the CZC? Jack was surprised the issue never came up before. Chalk that up to George Lunt's efficiency; he tended to catch the illegal prospectors before they broke ground. Searching for Gus Brannhard has stretched his manpower to the breaking point allowing trespassers to get in. He would have to discuss the sunstone and manpower issue with Ben and Victor. "We'll talk some more tomorrow, George."

George Lunt said his "good night" and screened-off. It had been a long week of flying around, coordinating part of the search and sleeping in the aircar. But Jack was the Native Affairs Commissioner and had work to do so he came back to do it before returning to the search. He glanced at the clock and saw that it was just after midnight. He'd missed cocktail time and dinner.

He was still debating on having a sandwich before turning in when the screen beeped. Late for a call, he thought. He turned on the screen and found Victor Grego staring out at him. "Jack! I thought you would still be out on the search. I was going to leave you a message."

"I just got in to catch-up on paperwork."

"I know how that is. I was wondering if you would mind my sending John Morgan over to join you?" Victor asked without preamble. "He says that he's a fair tracker and good with a sidearm."

And a tenderfoot as far as Zarathustra was concerned. Well, so was I once, Jack thought. "Sure, why not? We'll be in the air more than on the ground and I'll keep him out of trouble when we land. As long as he doesn't take a 'how bad can it be if a Fuzzy can survive out there' attitude."

"I don't think that will be a problem." Grego turned from the screen and spoke to somebody out of range then turned back. "He promises to be on his best behavior and do as he's told."

"I'll settle for his not shooting himself in the foot," Jack said with a smile. "When will he be out?"

"Is 0800 Beta time good?"

"He would have to get up mighty early in the morning over there. Make it noon so I can get some work done before heading out," he suggested. "No point in his sitting around waiting for me to finish shuffling papers."

The two men exchanged a few pleasantries then screened-off. Jack got up and walked into the bedroom. Just before sleep took him he remembered that he'd never had that sandwich.

XIV

Juan Jimenez sat in his office trying to concentrate on work, but was unable to do so. As a general naturalist he was accustomed to spending most of his time outside in the open air. In the last two years since his promotion he spent most of his work time behind a desk. He had seriously wanted to go on the search for Gus Brannhard on Beta. He understood Chief Steefer's position, and by extension Victor Grego's, in not allowing him to go, but the idea of staying behind while a stockholder went made him restless.

He had just finished signing the reports from the day before when Dr. Hoenveld walked in with Zorro on his shoulder. On his heels came Dr. Mallin. Neither of them thought to knock before entering.

"Gentlemen, is there something I can do for you?" he added a touch of irony to his voice, but neither man seemed to pick up on it. "Heyo, Zorro."

"Heyo, unka Juan," the Fuzzy replied.

"Dr. Jimenez," Hoenveld stated, remembering the proper honorific for a change, "I have discovered the reason our little friend here dislikes Extee-Three."

"Late onset sanity?" Jimenez quipped. Dr. Mallin chuckled but Hoenveld failed to get the joke. "What is it, Chris?"

"Zorro, here, does not produce the NFMp hormone." Hoenveld set the Fuzzy down on Juan's desk. "I ran every non-invasive test I could think of and couldn't find a trace of the NFMp."

Juan stood up and came around the desk. "That's amazing, Chris! Wait, previous tests showed that disabling the glands that produced the hormone led to sterility. Is that the case, here?"

"Not at all." Hoenveld actually smiled. "I expect this fellow to father many strong children." He turned to Zorro. "Do you have a gir…ah, mate?"

The Fuzzy looked confused.

"Not yet. Well, a fine figure of Fuzziness like yourself should find a mate in no time."

Zorro didn't appear to understand what Dr. Hoenveld meant, but nodded anyway.

"But what caused this?" Jimenez pressed. "Environment, steady infusion of hokfusine, mutation—"

"There's no evidence of any chemicals in his body that don't belong there," Hoenveld interrupted. "Of course, many things are flushed through the body that leave no trace after a couple of days, so we cannot be sure that isn't the cause. We also can't rule out radiation exposure or beneficial mutation."

He thought for a moment before asking, "Is there a chance that this is permanent, maybe even hereditary?"

Hoenveld's smile faded. "We won't know any time soon, I'm afraid. First, Zorro here will have to produce progeny, then we'll have to wait for them to get through puberty which is generally when their bodies begin to produce the hormone…"

"Wait, they don't start producing the hormone until puberty? When did we learn this?"

Hoenveld shifted into lecture mode. "Oh, a few months ago. I was measuring the NFMp levels of various Fuzzies hoping to find a better solution to the problem than hokfusine. I found that while the levels matched the mothers in newborns, which was very low, of course, or the fetus would not have developed normally, it dropped off sharply in the next few weeks down to zero, then began to buildup again with the onset of puberty. I documented and filed the report on my findings."

And I missed the report because it was buried under a hundred others, he thought. "In the future, please deliver any reports connected to the Fuzzies directly to me, Chris. Good job with Zorro, by the way."

He addressed the Fuzzy, "Are you ready to go back home to your Pappy and Mummy?"

"Yes, *unka* Juan. Can Zorro come back an' visit *unka* Chris?"

Jimenez suppressed a laugh and looked at Hoenveld, who told Zorro that he could visit as often as he liked. He had a mental image of Hoenveld becoming Pappy Chris. It wasn't as bizarre as he thought it would be.

*   *   *   *   *   *   *   *

Jack Holloway signed the last paper then dropped it into the out box. He looked up at the wall clock and saw it was 11:30. *No time for anything fancy for lunch*, Jack thought, *before John Morgan gets in*. He got up to make something to eat when he heard the sound of an aircar coming in.

Outside a Native Protection Force vehicle was coming to rest next to Jack's personal aircar. George Lunt and a dark-haired man in his mid-twenties to early thirties stepped out of the vehicle.

Lunt waved. "Hi, Jack, I brought in your visitor."

"Mr. Holloway," the dark-haired man said, as he extended a hand. "I am John Morgan. It is a pleasure to meet you."

He took the hand and shook it firmly. He noticed that Morgan had a good firm grip, the type of grip a man who is accustomed to working with his hands develops. "Pleased to meet you, too, Mr. Morgan."

"John will do," insisted the younger man. He stared intently at Jack's face for a moment.

"Then call me Jack. I understand you fancy yourself a fair tracker.

What planet?" *Now what is he staring at? Do I have something in my teeth?*

"Freya and Terra, mostly, though I've done some tracking and hunting on several other worlds. I've tracked wild oukry and kholph on Freya."

"Now what would anybody track a kholph for," Lunt asked. "Not to eat, I hope."

"Lab animals, intelligence tests, exotic pets," Morgan explained. "That sort of thing."

"You must be pretty good to get a kolph," Lunt said. "I hear that they're smarter than Terran chimps."

"For my money kholphs are smarter than Khooghras," Jack added with a smile. "I used to have one for a pet. What did you track on Terra?"

"A jaguar, once. It was a rogue so the usual protections didn't apply. Some antelope, rabbit, whatever wasn't on the endangered species list."

"Maybe we can bag some zarabuck after Gus is back," Jack suggested. "Hope the trip over wasn't too rough."

"I came in with some Junktown volunteers last night and slept on the ride over."

"You were able to sleep surrounded by that crowd?" Jack shook his head. "I hope you kept one hand on your wallet and the other on your gun."

"It wasn't as bad as all that. We were accompanied by NPF rangers after all."

John Morgan is either very confident of his abilities, or not as bright as he looks, Jack thought, *guess I'll find out which.* "I was just getting ready to make lunch. Fancy some zarabuck, John?"

"I'm game. I try to sample all the local cuisine on every planet I visit, provided it has been declared safe for consumption. Back on Alpha I've tried veldbeest and some sort of pig-like animal somebody gave me with my breakfast."

"Domesticated river pig, probably," Jack said. "Leaner than the Terran variety."

"Careful," Lunt warned, "the Fuzzies will have you eating raw goofer and land-prawn."

"I might be open to goofer, properly cooked, but I think I'll pass on the land-prawn," Morgan said with a smile. "I tried grasshopper and chocolate covered ants on Terra. That was quite enough bug food for me."

"There is a restaurant owner over on Alpha who claims he tried a land-prawn dish looking for a new item for the menu," Lunt added. "He said it tastes a bit like haggis."

"Haggis?" Morgan asked. "What is that?"

"A traditional dish served by Scots on old Terra," Jack supplied, as he extracted cold sliced zarabuck from the refrigerator. "You would have to visit Australia to get it made right, these days. Kind of like *guarmor* on Freya."

Morgan cocked an eyebrow at Jack. "You've tried *guarmor*? Most Terrans wouldn't touch it."

"A…woman of my acquaintance…served it to me a few times." Jack paused a moment before laying out the rest of the food. "I won't say that I particularly liked it, but I would eat it whenever she prepared it."

"Is that a Freyan dish?" George Lunt asked.

"Yes. The intestines and various organs of the oukry are shredded and broiled in the skin of the beast," Morgan supplied. "Some Freyans have taken to adding Terran cheddar cheese and hot sauces, but I prefer it made the traditional way."

Lunt looked a little green but recovered in time to accept a hot sandwich from Jack. Without any cheese. After the quick lunch George returned to his duties.

No sooner had Major Lunt left, than an airbarge arrived and settled in the open field away from the Fuzzy training grounds. Jack hustled over to meet the tall, thin balding man and four Fuzzies who stepped out of the forward cabin.

"Pappy Jack, Pappy Jack!" It was Flora, Fauna, Allan Quatermain and Natty Bumppo. They surrounded Jack and his guest. After much ruffling of heads Jack pointed to Little Fuzzy and the foursome ran over to make talk with him.

"Mr. Holloway? Governor Rainsford asked me to escort these dogs out for the search."

"Nifflheim! I had forgotten all about it," Jack admitted. "Good thing you got here when you did or I would have been out in the field. I'll call Gerd and Ruth and see if they can help get things arranged around here."

"Actually, Mr. Grego leased us some robots to setup an electric corral and some prefab shelters for them. Just show me where they go and I'll get them started."

"How friendly are they?" Morgan asked.

"Oh, friendly enough if you are a human or Fuzzy," Larry Wolvin replied. "When they were pups they spent a lot of time with Fuzzies and human children. The overly aggressive ones are separated out and used in security work. All of these were trained to obey human and hypersonic Fuzzy voices. These dogs are all unattached so whichever Fuzzies work with them will be able to keep them. I have some other dogs coming in a few days from my private sales, so they'll have to go back after we find Mr. Brannhard."

Jack noted that Larry didn't say "if." He liked that.

"I'll have some more dogs in a week or so after they come out of heat, Mr. Holloway. It's too risky to have them out here with all these studs around. I only do selective breeding to get the best mix in the next generation."

"Well, I sure appreciate your coming out here, Larry," Jack said. "Don't forget to put in a voucher for your time and trouble."

"Nope. Gus is a friend of mine. I want him found, too." Larry smiled. "Besides, it's his turn to buy the next round."

Jack turned to Morgan. "John, I'll have to stick around until Gerd or Ruth gets here. Why don't you take a look around while I deal with this?"

"Sounds good. Do I need an escort to keep me out of trouble?"

Jack looked around and noticed Mart Burgess lugging a crate on his shoulder. "Hey, Mart, can you spare about thirty minutes to play tour guide?"

Morgan went with Mart Burgess over to observe a mob of Fuzzies at the firing range. The Fuzzies were using down-sized 8.5 mm and .22 rifles. Their aim was impressive. One Fuzzy was zeroing his weapon and put three rounds into the paper Canadian Bull. The Fuzzy hit the target low and to the right of the bull, but the bullets made a single hole smaller than a ten centisol coin. Morgan was impressed and said so.

"I'll have to adjust the sights on that rifle down and to the left." He shook his head. "I knew a guy back in the army who could shoot like that."

Morgan inspected the guns that Burgess had just carried in. "Aside from being smaller, these rifles look very different from anything I ever saw before. What model are these?"

"Oh, I based these on the first century A.E. M16A1. I left out the fully automatic setting until I'm certain the Fuzzies won't abuse it. These rifles are good for them because they are easy to load and recoilless, and not as loud as normal hunting rifles."

"They're a lot quieter than my Baldertec 10.3," Morgan said. "I noticed the Fuzzies are still wearing the ear protection."

"Well, overuse of any pistol or rifle can damage your hearing, and Fuzzies are particularly sensitive to loud noises." He passed out the new rifles and took Morgan to the next range. "Here we are trying the Fuzzies out on crossbows."

Morgan watched intently as a Fuzzy set the nose of his crossbow down against a rock, cocked the string back with a lever, locked it in place and loaded a bolt. He then raised, aimed and fired in a single fluid motion. The bolt missed dead-center of the bull's-eye by half a centimeter.

"Great Galdor, that was a beautiful shot," Morgan exclaimed. "But why train the Fuzzies with a crossbow when you make guns for them?"

"Not all Fuzzies like the rifles," Burgess explained. "They don't like the loud bang so close to their ears. So, Mr. Holloway has crossbows and standard archery equipment made-up for them. All Fuzzies learn archery, then the ones that are interested can learn to use the rifle and crossbow."

"Are they taught to make bows and arrows?"

"You betcha. Follow me."

He showed Morgan several other classes: how to make voice like Big Ones, learn Terran language, fletching, weaving, clay pottery, and smithing.

"A Fuzzy blacksmith?"

"Oh, we have lots of those, now," he laughed. "This little fellow here makes the arrowheads for the fletchers. Gerd dubbed him Vulcan."

The Fuzzy blacksmith wore a leather apron to protect his fur from being singed as he hammered out a red-hot arrowhead. When he finished shaping the metal, he cooled it in a bucket of oil and handed it over to another Fuzzy who sharpened the edges on a peddle-powered grindstone.

"I think I understand," Morgan said. "You are teaching them mostly things they can do without the aid of Terran technology."

"Right. Jack has been adamant that we not let the Fuzzies become a lot of welfare bums. Many of the Fuzzy villages we set up have become almost completely self-supporting."

"Farming? Ranching?"

Mart nodded. "Farming, yes. Ranching is stalled until we can find a food animal small enough for the Fuzzies to handle."

"Goofers?"

"No, they tried that, but the goofers are able to climb over, and burrow under, corral fences. About a year ago an island was surveyed off the coast of Gamma continent. The fauna on that island had adapted to the limited living space by becoming pygmies. Veldbeests, damnthings, zarabucks and even harpies were all about a third the size of their Beta continent counterparts."

"Ah, I learned in college that there were similar cases with dinosaurs sixty-odd million years ago on Terra."

"Oh, right, the Bristol Dinosaurs. There were also the Malta elephants and, um, the *Homo floresiensis* of…Flores, I think. I heard Gerd say that the Gamma islanders were one of the more extreme cases he had ever come across. The size reduction is almost perfectly uniform among the various species. Anyway, Jack had a couple dozen veldbeests and zarabuck brought out and distributed among the Fuzzy villages hoping to get their numbers up enough to work as a food source for them. Not that they are starving, now. Come check this out."

He led Morgan to a prefabricated building with second door sized for Fuzzies. They walked through the front door to find several heavy-duty refrigeration units. Burgess opened one to reveal shelves filled with plastic wrapped meat.

"What animals were these?"

"Goofer and zarabunny. These are the kills made by the Fuzzies while they were clearing out the farmlands and transplanting trees for the Company."

"Why bother keeping all this meat? Don't the Fuzzies prefer Extee-Three?"

"Fuzzies do not live by Extee-Three alone," he said. "Fuzzies are carnivorous omnivores. They eat pretty much anything, but prefer meat. No point in wasting all this, anyway. I heard Victor Grego is thinking of canning goofer so that Fuzzies adopted by city folk can still get some.

Victor Grego seriously never misses a trick. Morgan was about to ask another question when a Fuzzy ran in yelling his name.

"John Mo'gan! John Mo'gan! Pappy Jack ready to go."

"That means go with him," Burgess supplied. "I have to get back to my workshop, anyway."

"Thank-you for the tour, Mart."

Morgan followed the Fuzzy out and started running. He hadn't thought a Fuzzy could move so fast on such short legs. The Fuzzy noticed Morgan was lagging behind and slowed his pace.

Jack had waited until Gerd and Ruth came in to supervise the setup, said his farewells to Larry Wolvin, then Jack and Morgan loaded up the aircar to rejoin the hunt for Gus.

During several hours of flight time Jack pointed out various landmarks and wildlife and gave a crash course on Zarathustra. John took careful note of everything the elder man said. It was getting late and the two men started scouting for a campsite.

"How long were you on Freya," Morgan asked after a while.

"A few years," Jack said tersely.

Morgan pressed, "Why did you leave? Most Terrans I have spoken with who had been there claim they wished they never left."

"You can add me to that list," Jack admitted. "Why did you leave, John?"

"Well, when you are raised there it doesn't seem all that special, I guess. I wanted to see other planets, get an education, that sort of thing."

Jack nodded. "That was why I left Terra. Only I wanted more than the education I received in school. It's a big galaxy out there, and we've barely scratched the surface of it."

"So you left Freya to see more of the galaxy?"

Jack considered for a moment before answering. John Morgan was awfully curious for somebody he'd just met. Still, there was no harm in answering the question. "No, I was prepared to settle down and stay put by that time. I met a pretty little thing that was willing to put up with me. She was something special."

Jack stopped talking and Morgan was about to press for more when he spotted a large beast charging across the veldt. It was a monstrous thing with a long straight horn protruding from its brow like some demonic unicorn, and two tusk-like horns jutting from the sides of its lower jaw. It had to weigh 3000 pounds if it weighed an ounce.

"What the hell is that thing?"

"*Shimo-kato*," Jack replied. "What us Big Ones call a damnthing."

"The book description doesn't do it justice. They still range this close to your place?"

"We're a fair pace from there, by now, but no, not usually. We cleaned them out pretty good. This is the first one I've seen around this area in over a year." Jack pulled out a set of old style binoculars. "Hey! There's a family of Fuzzies out there."

Before Jack could turn around Morgan grabbed the 12.7 Express and took a bead on the charging damnthing through an open portal. The first shot caught the beast in the right shoulder but failed to halt it charge. The second shot caught its center of mass causing the damnthing to stumble and fall. Jack circled around for a better view. The beast was trying to get back up.

"What does it take to stop that thing?" Morgan asked, as he lined up a third shot.

"Try for the head," Jack advised. "Body shots just make him mad."

"He doesn't look very cheerful as it is." John did as Jack suggested and fired. The slug caught the damnthing just above the eye and took off a sizable portion of its skull. "That should do it."

"We'll land and make sure. Anytime you think a damnthing is dead you want to shoot it again. You check on that and I'll check with the Fuzzies to be certain they're all right."

Jack brought down the aircar and the two men left the vehicle. John carefully approached the damnthing making sure to keep the rifle at the ready. He was almost convinced it was dead when he noticed a small cloud of dust arise from in front of its muzzle. Without hesitation Morgan put another round in its head.

Jack and the Fuzzies came at a dead run until they noticed Morgan working on the damnthing with a Freyan dagger. "Taking a trophy?"

"Good idea. That center horn will make a good walking stick, but first I'm skinning, gutting and stripping it of meat."

"You're planning on eating that?" Jack was surprised. Typically, he would just haul the carcass out into the wilderness and dump it for the scavengers.

"Is it poisonous?"

Jack said he didn't think so.

"On Freya we generally eat what we kill." Morgan nodded towards the Fuzzies. "Are they okay?"

"Yeah. They're some of my gang from the Rez out on the search."

"Maybe they would like some of this meat?" Morgan nodded towards the rifle. "By the way, my apologies for using your rifle. I didn't think my .457 would do the job."

Jack inspected his rifle, then the dead damnthing. "Clean it and we'll call it even. That was some real nice shooting."

"Your rifle really pounded the hell out of my shoulder." Morgan said.

"Yeah, it takes some getting used to. You'll be sore for a few days. Remind me to give you some ointment for that when we get back." Jack pulled out his own knife and joined in skinning the damnthing. He knew enough about Freyan tradition not to offend his guest.

"We may as well make camp here." The Fuzzies joined in the skinning effort. It was a rare opportunity for a Fuzzy to skin a damnthing.

"This should make a nice wall decoration," Jack observed. "Are you planning on eating the heart?"

Morgan smiled and gestured at the Fuzzies who were nibbling on loose pieces of meat as they worked. "Only if we cook it first. Wait, why aren't these Fuzzies on dogs?"

"There weren't enough dogs to go around until Larry Wolvin brought out that barge-load, today," Jack answered. "This group was dropped by aircar and supplied with a set of radios a few days ago. If I had known this big fella" –Jack stabbed the damnthing with his bowie knife– "was out here, I would have killed it first."

"Well, I don't think any harm was really done," Morgan observed. "These Fuzzies don't seem worse for wear, and they are getting a rare treat of…*shimo-kato*?"

"Yeah, generally speaking a live Fuzzy is a happy Fuzzy. Well, I'll set up camp while you carve out dinner."

"Good idea," Morgan said, "but leave the tent to me. I have a special self-erecting model."

XV

"Do you think there is anything to it?" Governor Riansford asked.

Colonial Marshal Max Fane took a deep breath and let it out slowly. "I can't be sure of anything at this point, Governor. It's just a couple of rumors we picked up while doing the door to door."

Ben Rainsford swore under his breath. "This is the sort of thing I would normally talk over with Gus. He understands all this cops and robbers stuff way better than I do. Actually, he would be talking with you, if . . ."

"I understand, sir."

"Marshal, would you do me a favor?"

"Governor?"

"Take off that gun belt and join me on the terrace." Before the Marshal could react, Rainsford got up and walked out to the terrace where he took a seat. Max Fane hung up his belt and joined him. He indicated a seat and Fane sat down. "Now we can talk like normal people, Max. I want your sincere opinion."

Marshal Fane thought for a moment before speaking. "Well, as a cop I chased down a lot of leads based on rumor. Here we have it that Leo Thaxter knows something about Gus being grabbed up and that he is the target of a prison hit because of it. Before he was arrested and convicted nobody would have dared breathe a word about him or his activities. Now people feel safer to talk about him. That doesn't prove anything."

"What do you suggest, Max?"

The Colonial Marshal shrugged. "Normally, we would interrogate

Thaxter in protective custody, under veridication, of course. If he knows something, we make a deal. Maybe add a few years to his sentence," he chuckled. Any other convict would want less time on his sentence. More criminals should have a death sentence waiting for them at the end of their term of incarceration. "If it's a wild goose chase, we dump him back at Prison House and move on to the next lead. Frankly, the leads have been few and far between. I'm ready to grab at some straws."

"Why not question him at the prison?"

The Marshal let out a long breath. He had to remind himself that this was all new to the Governor. "If there is a hit out on him, it would be a guard or fellow inmate who would carry it out. For that matter the warden himself could be in on it." Fane anticipated Ben's next question. "We can't question the warden under veridication without either just cause or his cooperation. If he refuses, that doesn't even prove he's up to something since most people would do the same. But if he is crooked and we ask him oh-so-politely to please sit down in the hot seat with the glowing globe on top and he refuses, we not only fail to prove anything, but we have now warned him that we think he may be dirty.

"In that case, Thaxter's life expectancy could go way down. It's just too big a risk. No, sir…we have to bring old Leo in and question him ourselves. Then, while Thaxter is safe with us, we can have somebody have a chat with Warden Redford and see which way he leans."

Rainsford sat quietly as he considered Marshal Fane's words. After a minute he turned to the top cop. "Max, as of this moment you are off the leash. Frankly, I really had no business butting in on your investigation, anyway. You do what you have to and let me worry about the fall-out. Try not to trample too many civil liberties in the process, but find Gus. If you need something, just ask. After you pick Thaxter up, I'll call the warden and ask him to come in for a quiet chat."

"Thank you, Governor. For what it's worth, you've been more of a help than a hindrance." He stood up. "I'm going back to work, now. I'll have Thaxter brought in for questioning immediately."

"One more thing," Rainsford said, "I'll arrange for a military transport. I suspect you'll have less trouble that way."

The Colonial Marshal rushed off leaving Ben Rainsford to his thoughts.

*   *   *   *   *   *   *   *   *

Leo Thaxter, regardless of his current circumstances, was a man to be reckoned with. Even in Prison House he was respected and, more importantly, feared. Other prisoners gave him a wide birth when he walked by. His prior position as a mob boss rendered him immune to many of the tribulations of prison life. Nobody attempted to take 'liberties' with him in the shower room, for example.

Even without his reputation and standing in the criminal community, Leo Thaxter would make a poor target for his fellow convicts. Thaxter stood a solid six foot two inches and tipped the scales at 230 pounds, all muscle, which he maintained in the prison weight room. In the two years since being sentenced, only one person had ever started a fight with him. It was an off-worlder from Baldur who was busted on a larceny charge by the name of Ricardo Profit. Profit saw how everybody deferred to Thaxter and decided to make a name for himself by taking down the top dog. This resulted in the off-worlder being treated in the Prison House hospital for numerous broken and fractured bones. Thaxter didn't have a mark on him.

He feared only one thing; the end of his sentence. The mobster didn't like prison, but it beat the alternative. He considered trying to find ways to get his sentence extended but the only way he could pull that off would be to turn stool-pigeon. That was the one line he would not cross. The Warden knew this but kept trying to flip him anyway.

"Leo, Warden wants to see you."

Thaxter turned to see Guard Williams standing over him. The Warden always seemed to call for him when he was eating, probably on purpose since that was the time most of the cons were gathered together and would see it. Thaxter wolfed down the remainder of his meal before following the guard out.

"What's he want, now?"

"He doesn't discuss these things with me," Williams replied. "He tells me to get somebody, I get him. Period. Guard at the gate!"

Bixby, the gate guard at checkpoint alpha looked the two men over. "Where you goin'?"

"Warden's office."

"Why isn't this convict in cuffs?"

"Whoops! Sorry, Leo, gotta do this." Williams quickly placed the restraints on Thaxter. It was prison policy, but everybody knew that Thaxter was a model prisoner. Unlike other convicts, he had no hopes of getting out for good behavior. What could happen was that every infraction might result in time off for bad behavior. Every day subtracted from his sentence was a day closer to a bullet in the head, and everybody knew it.

"All right, you can pass." Bixby placed Thaxter's left hand on a scanner plate that registered his prints, pulse and body temperature. After a light flashed green he pressed the button that shut down the electric current and opened the gate. The two men passed through and the gate automatically closed. A faint hum indicated that the electrical current was reactivated.

Three more checkpoints and a collapsium-laminated door later, Leo Thaxter was face-to-face with Warden Paul Redford. Redford was a slim, medium height man with thinning gray hair. He gestured to Williams and the guard removed Thaxter's restraints. Thaxter rubbed his wrists as he took the indicated chair.

"Mr. Thaxter, do you know why I've called you to my office?"

"Same-old same-old. I'm still not a rat." Thaxter took in the office. It was always different to some degree every time he was brought in to see Warden Redford. This time there was a display case with a collection of Fuzzy artifacts secured to the wall next to the bookcase. Last time there was a display of Thoran weapons. The glass was likely bulletproof. The Warden was extremely security conscious and left nothing to chance. "We've been doing this dance for the last two years. I don't know why you think I'd ever turn stoolie."

Redford smiled and said in a soft casual voice. "That isn't what this is about, Mr. Thaxter."

"No?" Thaxter was surprised but didn't show it. He was used to hiding his feelings.

"No." Redford dismissed the guard then returned his attention to the prisoner. "It has come to my attention that somebody has taken a contract out on you."

"On me?" Thaxter considered all the people who might want him dead. The list was an extensive one, but nobody would bother to pay out the kind of money it would take to swing a hit in prison. Especially on a man who would never leave there alive. Raul Laporte would no doubt be happy to see him dead since that would pave the way for him to take over the business concerns Thaxter once ran. But Laporte was too cagey to let word of a hit get out. In his organization loose lips ended up being converted to Em-See-Square.

"I gather from your expression that you have no idea who would want you out of the way." Redford leaned back. "Well, we'll get to the bottom of this, one way or another. For now you are going to be transferred to the Mallorysport holding center for questioning."

"What? Why? I don't know nuthin' about this." Transfers were always a pain; being shackled the entire time, put in a cage smaller than his cell, surrounded by prisoners who might not know who he was and the potential for a fight. Then there was the questioning under veridication.

"There is also a rumor that you have some knowledge in the matter of the Brannhard abduction." Redford watched Thaxter's face for any indication that he knew something. Instead, the mobster's face grew puzzled despite his usual control.

"Warden, I've been in stir for the last two years, remember? You've got this place wired like an electric light strip-joint. Nothing comes in or gets out that you don't know about. How the Great Gehenna would I know anything about Brannhard without you knowing it first?"

Redford leaned back in his chair with a wolfish grin on his face. "I think we both know better than that. But you'll have your chance to state your case under veridication."

I knew it, thought Thaxter. "Fine. As long as we don't talk about what goes on here or about any of my prior, um, activities, I'll tell you anything you want to kno—hey! You mean in Mallorysport?" Thaxter rolled his eyes. "You dumb screw! That's how they'll try to get at me."

"We considered that," the Warden said, ignoring the disrespectful tone. "You'll be transported in a collapsium shielded military transport borrowed from the TFN. If anybody tries to get at you they'll just waste a lot of ammunition and reveal themselves."

"And of course if they do get me you'll be all broke up about it," the mobster sneered.

"Yes, I will," Warden Redford countered. "I haven't lost a single prisoner through escape or assassination since I took over this facility. I would very much hate to see my record blemished by the likes of you."

Thaxter scowled at the Warden. "Under the circumstances, that makes two of us."

XVI

Red Fur was worried about the tribe. There were always things to worry about; bad hunting, *shimo-kato*, too much rain, injury, sickness and just plain making-dead. But this was a new worry, something that had never happened before. It all began when the Big One started leaving food on the hill. *Hat-zu'ka*, *shikku*, *zuzoru* and the strange food that some of the tribe couldn't get enough of. So much food that nobody needed to hunt. Everybody was happy to sit around the camp or play.

Red Fur sat down on a log and shook his head. *What would happen if the Big Ones went away? Would everybody be too fat and lazy to hunt for themselves? Something would have to be done.* Red Fur thought for a while. The problem was the Big Ones. If they wanted to be friends, why didn't they come out of their burrow and meet the tribe? Why just leave food for the people to find?

Maybe the Big Ones wanted the People to be lazy and fat? The Big Ones were people. People didn't hunt the way animals did. *Shimo-kato* killed everything it could catch, big or small, when it was hungry…and it was almost always hungry. People hunted for animals big enough to feed the tribe. Slow animals, like the *hat-zu'ka*, were easier to catch than a *shikku*.

Slow animals.

Fear stabbed deep into Red Fur's chest. *What if the* Big Ones *thought the* people *were animals? Maybe they wanted the people to be fat and slow so they could hunt and eat us! The people did not eat their own kind…but the* Big

Ones *are not the same as us....*

Red Fur thought hard on what to do, and finally came to a decision.

*   *   *   *   *   *   *   *   *

The Armored Personnel Carrier settled down outside the gates of Prison House where Colonial Marshal Max Fane was waiting. The APC settled to the ground though the contra-gravity engines continued to hum. Flying the APC directly behind the prison walls was completely out of the question. In a world where everybody had access to contra-gravity special precautions had to be taken. The entire facility, especially the exercise yard, was situated below a canopy of crossed bars made of collapsium. The bars were too close together to allow anything larger than a small child through them. Between the bars was a monofilament mesh, also made of collapsium, which would slice through anything that fell through it into neat ten centimeter meter pieces.

The side hatch opened and two men in military camouflage stepped out. The Marshal noticed that the CGUs, or Computer Graphic Uniforms, changed in appearance to reflect what was behind the wearers. It was the most effective all-terrain cloaking attire ever developed and more than a little expensive. The common foot soldier could never afford such gear, so it was issued to them upon completion of basic and advanced training. When the soldier or marine de-mobbed, the uniforms were returned to the quartermaster. The fabric was impregnated with thousands of monofilament cameras that collected data from every direction and relayed it to the opposite side of the wearer where microscopic LEDs changed color to simulate the terrain. Such uniforms, Max Fane knew, were typically only used in combat and demilitarized zones.

One of the men approached the Marshal and saluted. "Gunnery Sergeant Stryker reporting for prisoner transfer detail, sir!"

"At ease, Sergeant. You boys look ready for serious trouble." He pointed at the helmets, ballistic goggles and lower face-shields plus the heavy rifles. "You expecting any?"

"Always, sir," the Gunny replied. "So is the Governor or he wouldn't have requested our assistance."

Good point. "All right, let's get this show on the road." he pulled a radio from his belt, stepped away from the Marines and covered the mouthpiece then whispered, "We're ready, Warden Redford. Code alpha-six-niner-gamma-one-one-epsilon."

The Warden's voice replied from the radio, "Code confirmed. We're sending him out, now."

He could hear a gate open then close, then a second one. As Colonial Marshal, one of his duties was to inspect the Prison House security, even though it was a privatized institution run by the Charterless Zarathustra Company. As such Max knew that all three gates were laminated with collapsium. The triple redundancy was to keep anybody from getting in if one of the gates were open. The security design was such that only one gate would open at any one time. Finally the outer gate opened and Leo Thaxter was escorted out.

As per protocol, Thaxter's hands and feet were fettered with magnetic shackles. For security, Thaxter was also wearing a protective helmet and bulletproof vest in case the rumored threat against his life was genuine. There were four guards, two on each side. The forward guards were armed with truncheons while the rear guards had sono-stunners. This was in case the prisoner attempted to seize a weapon and fight his way free. It was unlikely he would be able to grab a truncheon without being stunned, and almost impossible to twist around and get a sono-stunner. The guard towers were more than adequately equipped to deal with any hostile third parties that might attempt to free or kill the prisoner.

The procession halted before the APC and the left forward guard produced a magnetic key card that was quickly snatched up by the Gunny.

Wolfgang Diehr

Max let it slide. It didn't matter who held the card and the Gunny's ass was in a sling if anything went wrong. There was no way out of the shackles without that card and the Gunny was hardly likely to surrender it.

"Marshal Fane, do you accept custody and responsibility for this prisoner?" inquired the right front guard.

"Yes, I do."

The guard produced an electronic pad and indicated the place where he would press his thumb. The print was verified and he produced the paperwork, which the guard accepted. "Okay, we're good."

The Gunny gestured and two men took Thaxter by the arms and hustled him into the APC. There, he was placed in a cell a little larger than a closet. The Gunnery Sergeant caught the Marshal's expression and explained, "We use those cells to transport prisoners of war, sir. Would you care to ride up front with the pilot, sir?"

"Thank-you, Sergeant." *Why not*, thought Marshal Fane, *Thaxter isn't going anywhere.*

Before the Colonial Marshal entered the Armored Personnel Carrier, he saw a CZC company car settle down outside the gates. The Gunny and one of the Marines quickly drew their weapons and trained them on the newcomers. He watched intently as Chief Harry Steefer and a uniformed policeman stepped out of the vehicle. Max Fane and Chief Steefer often inspected the Prison House facility together as it was a Charterless Zarathustra Company concern.

"At ease, men," he said. "They're on our side." Marshal Fane waved, then stepped into the APC. He decided to give Steefer a call later when he wasn't busy.

*　*　*　*　*　*　*　*　*

Gus Brannhard was feeling restless, nauseous, frustrated, hungry and angry. There were no windows in his room, so he had no way of knowing where he was being kept. In fact, up until today he had been kept in a drugged stupor. He didn't even know how long he had been kept in the room. His clothes were gone, along with several pounds of his own substantial *corpus delecti*. His mind was a bit fuzzy which annoyed him to no end. Gus Brannhard had a huge reputation as a man who could drink without visible effect, but even his worst binges failed to appreciably dull his remarkable mind.

He examined his surroundings with an eye toward escape. The room was easily sixteen feet by twenty feet. The ceiling had to be at least eight feet high. He had a light fixture just out of reach overhead that stayed on constantly. In one corner was a pile of trash; rags, empty boxes and cans, candy wrappers and even some small bones that must have belonged to some form of large rodent; a goofer, maybe. The boxes and wrappers all had the CZC logo on them, but then, so did almost everything else on the planet.

He listened carefully as he knocked on the dingy gray walls. The dull thud and pain in his hairy knuckles suggested heavy reinforcement… collapsium, most likely. The door also appeared to be reinforced. It was an old style door, with a doorknob and hinges, instead of retracting into the wall, for the use of engineering personnel in the event of a power-outage. Gus examined the hinges, but they were recessed into the door-jam. No way to pry out the pins without a special tool, and the door would have to be open in order to do that.

"At least they put a sanitary closet in here with me," the Colonial Chief Prosecutor in absentia grumbled. Gus inspected the waste disposal unit hoping to find something he could use for a tool or weapon. It was a micro M/E converter in a collapsium casing. *Somebody is willing to spend a lot of sols to keep me here*, thought Gus. M/E converters were expensive at best. Micro units were obscenely pricey and were considered an impractical luxury. A unit like this would typically be found on a private yacht…or in an office where extremely sensitive material could not be trusted for normal disposal. Like most M/E units, there was a heavy cable connecting the sanitary closet to a wall to draw off surplus energy. Where the energy went, he had no clue.

He re-inspected himself. His extremely hairy body was relatively clean and unscarred; or rather there were no new scars. He hadn't been forced to lay in his own filth or been tortured. There were reddish bands around his wrists and ankles suggesting he had been restrained. He re-opened the closet and saw hooks where he could have been shackled and left on the commode.

Stacked next to his cot were several cases of Terran Federation Armed Forces Emergency Ration, Extraterrestrial, Type Three, bath tissue and at least a hundred liters of bottled water. Gus grimaced at the offered fare. Water was bad enough, but it was possible that the Extee-Three was intended as a torture device since nobody except Fuzzies could stand the stuff, though just as likely it was simply the easiest to get and didn't require cooking. It would be safe enough to eat, of course. Jack Holloway had told him that he lived on the stuff for a solid month, once. Granted, Jack showed no physical signs of harm from the Extee-Three as it was designed to be healthful if not delectable, but Gus couldn't help but think that it contributed to the Native Affairs Commissioner's notoriously short temper.

Okay, they want me alive and reasonably healthy, if not happy about it. They may also want me to lose weight. Why? Unless it's because they want to make me harder to recognize. Twenty-odd pounds or so with a good shave and haircut would do the job pretty well. They might even force me to have cosmetic surgery. Now the question is, just whom have I annoyed lately?

Gus couldn't think of anybody on-planet who would go to this kind of trouble. Sure there was Ivan Bowlby, Spike Heenan and, worst of all, Raul Laporte, but Bowlby lacked the spine for wet-work, Spike wouldn't act on his own and Laporte wouldn't bother keeping him alive. On Zarathustra anybody wanting revenge would just kill him and dump him in the wilderness for the scavengers to work on. Or, if they had the means, dump the body in an M/E converter.

He glanced at the sanitary closet. Whoever these people were, they had money, or access to people with money. The kind of money Victor Grego had, but Grego didn't make the list of his personal enemies. And even if he did, Grego would never have risked keeping him alive, he was much too smart for that; he would have just sent Gus to Em-See-Square and be done with it. Laporte certainly had the kind of money to swing abductions like this, not to mention the stones and probably the hidey-hole, but he wouldn't bother to keep Gus alive, either.

So, it had to be somebody from off-world that wanted him alive and functional, more or less. That only left Terra. While the hirsute attorney had visited several planets since leaving Terra, he hadn't made any enemies of note on any of them, at least as far as he knew. He had spent most of his time bouncing planet-to-planet defending petty thieves and doing the odd divorce case before being appointed Colonial Chief Prosecutor of Zarathustra. Granted, he had passed on defending several high-end mobsters, but they just went and found themselves another shyster.

Terra was a different story. It had been well over thirty years since he left the world of his birth. He had been a young lawyer working as an assistant district attorney. Not the youngest in the office, but close to it. Prosecuting attorneys collect enemies on a near daily basis. So, the question was which one wanted him alive and healthy?

Actually, he had no doubt as to whom and why. At the top of his suspect list was the Hoshi Campanili Family, the premier criminal organization of Australia. Gus had run afoul of the capo and his crew back when he was a young ADA.

He had been only twenty-three, fresh out of law school with a wife and two year old daughter when Gus had caught the attention of the chief prosecuting attorney of Sydney. After passing the bar he was offered a position with the DA's office. He accepted and worked zealously, often at the expense of his home life. His wife, Yennisa, understood and supported him. In his second year as an ADA, an informant brought him evidence of several different crimes committed by the Campanili Family, and by Hoshi Campanili personally.

Gus had worked day and night building his air-tight case. By the time Campanili was brought to trial, even the capo's lawyers knew he wasn't getting off. He had called for the jury to be sequestered to avoid bribery or intimidation, rooted out another Assistant District Attorney on the take and even managed to get a judge who could not be bought. At trial's end, Hoshi Campanili received twenty years in maximum security.

Two months later his wife and child were killed in a freak aircar collision. The other driver had fled the scene. That was when Gus started drinking in earnest. Word came down from Investigations that an open contract had been taken out on Gustov Banner. After a great deal of discussion, Gus was talked into going into the witness protection program. He was given a new identity, money, and an open ticket to any planet he wanted to go to. Marlon Gustov Banner became Gustavus Adolphus Brannhard. He had started growing a beard and shipped out to Mars, where he remained for a couple of months before moving off-world again, though not before exacting a little additional revenge of his own.

For the next twenty years Gus went from planet-to-planet, drinking and defending petty criminals, never staying on any world longer than two years, and never defending any client involved in organized crime. Shortly after making planet-fall on Zarathustra, Gus learned that Hoshi Campanili died a month after his release. Brannhard finally felt he could stop running and settled down. After a near legendary celebration at the Damnthing Bar and Grill, where he met Jack Holloway, Gus hung up his shingle where it remained until his appointment as Colonial Chief Prosecutor.

But it was possible that the contract was still in effect. Hoshi had sons who might want to make good on the father's wishes, and when the news of Zarathustra's shiny new status as a Class IV Inhabited planet hit Terra, news pictures of the new Colonial Governor and his appointees put Gus back in the crosshairs, beard or no beard.

So why take me alive? It was possible the Campanili heirs wanted to administer their retribution personally. Of course, there was also that little thing Gus did before leaving Terra. That meant either taking him back to Terra, or bringing the Campanilis to Zarathustra; assuming they were not already here. *No, if they were here I would already be dead,* thought Gus; *I have to get out of here, but how?* He looked about at the trash, Extee-Three and the sanitary closet. A desperate plan began to form.

XVII

"Name."

"Thaxter, Leonello S."

Blue light.

"What does the 'S' stand for?"

"Sylvester."

Blue light.

"Good, now answer 'yes' to the next question. Are you a member of the species *Fuzzy sapiens zarathustra*?"

"Yes."

Red light.

Dr. Mallin turned away from the veridicator controls to address the man on his left. "Okay, we have our baseline. You can ask your questions, Mr. Coombes."

Leslie Coombes, the Colonial Chief Prosecuting Attorney *pro tem* stepped forward. "Thank you, Dr. Mallin." While Leslie Coombes covered for Gus, he wanted somebody familiar with the psycho-sciences and veridicator operation he could trust. Dr. Ernst Mallin qualified on all three counts.

"Mr. Thaxter, it has come to our attention that you may possess some knowledge regarding the whereabouts of the missing Gustavus Adolphus Brannhard. Do you know where he is?"

"No. How would I? I've been in the pokey for the last two years," Thaxter snarled. The steady blue light of the polyencephalographic veridicator indicated he was telling the truth.

"Do you have any idea who might possess this kind of information" Coombes asked.

Thaxter considered his response while the light fluttered between blue, red and shades in between. Finally, the light settled on blue and Thaxter asked, "What's in it for me? I ain't no rat, y'know."

Coombes expected something like this and had discussed it with Governor Rainsford in advance. "For your cooperation, provided the information proves useful, we can make certain concessions regarding your sentence."

"I'm not lookin' for time off," the mobster barked. With a possible death sentence hanging over his head at the end of his current sentence time off was the last thing he wanted.

"Of course not, Mr. Thaxter," Coombes said. "But we could add to your time. A year or two, maybe more if your information is good enough."

"Thanks, but that ain't what I'm after." Thaxter looked around at everybody in the room. There was the Colonial Marshal, a few uniformed policemen, Dr. Mallin and Leslie Coombes. "I want Rose safe from retrial at the end of her stretch. When her twenty is up, she goes free. That's the only cheese I'll bite."

Coombes was taken aback. He had expected Thaxter to look out for himself, not his sister. "I'll have to speak with the Governor before I can make a deal like that. But even if he goes for it you will have to give us something that will lead to our recovering Gus Brannhard. Alive. No guesswork or theories."

"Why do I gotta keep remindin' you mooks that I've been locked up for the last two years? Mallin here helped put me there! Even with the prison grapevine guesswork and theories are all I've got."

Coombes knew Thaxter was telling the truth even without the steady blue of the veridicator globe. Still, nobody knew the ins and outs of the local underworld better than the former crime boss.

"We'll come back to that. Do you know anything about the rumored threat to your life?"

Thaxter laughed. "Aside from the legal one in eighteen years? Nah. Nobody would dare. Even in jail I have some juice. Enough of my former associates are in there with me that I am well protected."

Coombes was curious. "Wouldn't one of them want to take over your operations when they get out?"

"Assuming they ever get out, you mean. Look, when one of my boys gets nabbed, they clam up and leave my name out of it. The veridicator can't catch a lie if they don't talk. As a reward, they get their full pay to take care of their families while they sit in stir. Anything happens to me, the money goes away. Even while I am in prison." Thaxter could see Coombes' next question in his eyes. "Call it a trust fund. All set-up by my brokerage business and all very legal. But if I die, the money goes into probate and the payments stop. All those cons still drawing pay won't stand for me getting killed and everybody who matters knows it."

"According to Warden Redford, somebody already tried to kill you in the pen," Marshal Max Fane pointed out.

Thaxter chuckled. "You mean Ricardo Profit, that son of a Khooghra? A small-time off-world punk who didn't know who he was messin' with. The only reason he's still breathin' is because I put out the word not to change that. He makes a real nice example of what could happen to the next brain donor who wants to try and take me on."

Coombes had wondered how Thaxter avoided jail as long as he had, not to mention survived after his conviction. Now he knew. "All the same, can you think of who might want you out of the way?"

"You mean aside from Victor Grego, Jack Holloway and all those Fuzzy lovers?" Thaxter considered. In fact he had a very good idea who would want him dead, but doubted he would act on it. Still, the threat was out there, and as his brother-in-law Conrad Evins liked to say, nothing exists in a vacuum. "The only guy I can think of in a position to profit from my death is Raul Laporte. I don't see him trying for it, though. Too much risk for too little gain."

"Wouldn't he be in a position to take over all of your former… businesses?"

"Too many people would be after his ass if they found out he was the one who ordered the hit," Thaxter explained. "People still loyal to me. Even more so since I never ratted any of them out in the plea bargain that bought me twenty more years of breathin'."

Coombes started to realize that Leo Thaxter was far smarter than he had given him credit for. "Very well, Mr. Thaxter. The Governor is expecting my call. I'll return in a moment with his decision."

Coombes stepped out and quiet conversation went back and forth in the room. Dr. Mallin took the opportunity to ask Thaxter what triggered his antisocial tendencies. Thaxter was in the middle of explaining what a drunken bastard his father was when Coombes returned.

"Mr. Thaxter, I have the Governor's approval. If your information leads to the recovery of Gus, alive, the death penalty is off the table for Rose Evins."

"Okay, good, the only mugs I can think of who might be willin' to try to put Brannhard in a box are Ivan Bowlby, Spike Heenan and Raul Laporte. Bowlby doesn't have the stones for it by himself, but I wouldn't put it past him and Spike to cook somethin' up together. But they don't have the leg-breakers to do the job. For that they would have to go to Laporte."

"What about Laporte?" Coombes prodded. "Would he be up for it?"

"Maybe, but Laporte is the smartest and slickest of the bunch, and he doesn't take unnecessary chances. Even I don't know for sure if he ever killed anybody. He doesn't like kidnappin' on general principles. If he grabbed up Brannhard personally, then Brannhard is dead and gone. You'll never find a body. The only other way he would get involved would be as a facilitator, or middleman."

Coombes leaned forward. "Middleman?"

"Yeah. Say somebody came forward and said, 'Hey, we need to grab this guy, can you help us?' Well, Laporte would provide transportation and a hidey-hole, for an unreasonable fee, of course, but he wouldn't get within a country mile of the actual crime. And anybody ready to implicate him would come up missin' fast."

"Yet you don't know if he ever killed anybody?" Dr. Mallin asked. He found the criminal mind fascinating.

"I never seen it, and he never told me if he did," Thaxter said.

The veridicator globe remained a steady blue.

"Bowlby or Spike would brag on it to me if they ever whacked somebody, but Laporte keeps his mouth shut."

"I'm guessing you didn't get the word," the Marshal said. "Ivan Bowlby was found dead in his studio three days ago. Overdose. We kept it out of the news until today."

Thaxter shrugged. "Hmph. Sounds like the way he'd go. That son of a Khooghra didn't have the sense to leave his own product alone."

"Do you have any idea where this 'hidey-hole' of Laporte's might be," Coombes asked.

"No." The globe stayed blue. "Only that he once said it was one-hundred percent secure and impossible to find. That was all he would ever say about it. Like I said before, Laporte keeps his mouth shut when it comes to business."

"Okay, anybody else?"

Thaxter thought for a moment then shook his head. "Was there a ransom demand?"

"None."

The mobster shook his head. "Then, no. Gus Brannhard's dead and I doubt you'll ever find his body. Somebody as big as Brannhard is good for only two things; gettin' out of the way or holding for a payday. No ransom demand, then no more Brannhard."

Coombes was afraid that Thaxter might be correct. "Are you absolutely certain nobody would have another motive that would require Brannhard being kept alive?"

"Not on this planet." Thaxter considered other possibilities. "Back on Terra or Baldur or Thor a prosecutor might get grabbed for questionin', say, for information about an upcoming case, or to shake up the prosecution. Occasionally there might be a bounty, in which case the target would be kept alive…until the bounty was paid, of course. Nobody on Zarathustra would try nuthin' like that. Especially Spike or Laporte. The only other guy I can think of who would be crazy enough to try somethin' this big is Hugo Ingermann."

"Ingermann skipped planet," Max Fane said.

"You think I don't know that?" Thaxter yelled. "He was my damn lawyer when he took off. But maybe he came back."

"Ingermann would be pretty easy to spot," Fane pointed out. "Between defending your little crew and making off with the CZC sunstones, he's the most hated man on Zarathustra. That 50,000 sol bounty Grego put on his head would keep him as far away from this planet as he can get."

"Ha! No wonder you cops never seem to catch anybody." Thaxter laughed.

"We got you," said Max with a smile.

Thaxter looked around the room. "Yeah, after how many years? Look, ain't any of you ever heard of cosmetic surgery? Ol' Hugo could walk through this room right now and you wouldn't know him from Adam."

"Do you know he did this for a fact," Coombes asked.

"Nah. If I had anything on that rat-bastard I'd give it to you for two centisols and a tin of Extee-Three. But if I was him, I'd do everythin' I could to be unrecognizable, and 250,000 sols can buy a lot of high-end work." Thaxter smiled wryly. It didn't look pleasant. "I thought about gettin' some work done myself someday. Figured it would make my retirement safer."

* * * * * * * * *

Out in the Armored Personnel carrier a different conversation was taking place.

"Remember the deal, Clancy," the Gunnery Sergeant warned. "You sit pat for one month and you cash in big. Open your mouth before then and you'll never see your daughter again."

"Yeah, I got it," Clancy said. He was a large brutish man with an unpleasant face that bore a striking resemblance to one Leo S. Thaxter. Clancy Slade had made planet-fall nine months earlier from Gimli in the hopes of cashing in on the open lands only to find that out they had already been leased back to the Charterless Zarathustra Company for the next thousand or so years. Having no place else to go and a family to support, Clancy took any job that came his way; ranch hand, farm hand, stock man and security guard. It was that last job that brought him to Raul Laporte's attention.

At first Clancy's resemblance to Leo Thaxter went unnoticed due to the thick beard that framed his face. Then, two weeks earlier, Clancy shaved off the beard hoping to get a better job at the Charterless Zarathustra Company. After his interview he went to his job as a security guard at The Zoroaster, a mid-level hotel in Mallorysport.

Raul Laporte was exiting the hotel after *interviewing* a new secretary and almost slammed into the glass door when he saw Clancy walking up the stairs. Laporte quickly had the security guard checked out and learned he had a wife and daughter and was in need of cash.

Initially, Laporte had played with the idea of using Clancy to trick Leo Thaxter's old crew into thinking he had broken out of prison and was picking up where he left off. Unfortunately, Clancy was insufferably honest and wanted nothing to do with Laporte. Then Laporte met Ivan Dane and his associates. Dane wanted Thaxter out of Prison House and needed a double to pull off his caper. Since Clancy was of no use to him personally, Laporte accepted the finder's fee and turned Clancy over.

Clancy, finding himself in a room faced with six men, all wearing masks, knew he was in over his head and refused to cooperate. That's when his daughter was kidnapped. Now he was waiting to change places with a convicted felon.

"Annabelle will be returned once I'm in the pen, right?"

"Yes, Mr. Slade," the Gunny answered. "We have no interest in harming your little girl. But if you get cute before the month is up, we can still get at her and your wife."

"Yeah, I got it. I'll play along."

"Okay, everybody," the Gunny barked, "get back into character. They're on their way out."

XVIII

On the return trip to the prison, one of the Marines shed his uniform and headgear to reveal a face only a mother could love; Leo Thaxter's mother. He was a dead ringer for the mobster. The Gunnery Sergeant produced the magnetic key card that deactivated Thaxter's shackles and quickly removed them. The mobster and the look-alike swiftly swapped their clothes and then the shackles were placed on the double.

"What about the microchip in my head?" Thaxter asked.

"It is only active while outside of the prison," the Gunny explained. "It will be turned off as soon as 'you'," the Gunny nodded at Thaxter while pointing at Clancy, "re-enter the main gate. The frequency can't penetrate collapsium shielding, and this APC is lousy with it. We stand outside until Clancy here clears the first gate, then you hustle back into the APC. Once we are airborne again we'll try to disable the chip."

"Try?" Thaxter became livid. "*Try* could get me a bullet in the head! Look, I just made a deal for my sister. I don't want to screw that up. I didn't ask for this and I'm not sure I want it."

"Please, be calm, Mr. Thaxter. My associates are very competent. You will stay in this APC where the signal is blocked until the chip has been deactivated. Nobody will even know that you are missing with Clancy here keeping your cell warm."

"Yeah, he looks like me, but what does he sound like?"

"They adjusted my vocal cords when they did the fine touches on my ears," Clancy replied. "When I get to the prison I will request segregation."

"Why would they give you that?" Thaxter looked back at the Gunny.

"Because there is a rumor that somebody took out a contract on you," the Gunny said with a smile. "Remember?"

The Gunny further explained that the original plan was to abduct the mobster from a farming detail, but the disappearance of Brannhard allowed for a smoother and safer Plan B. With no exploding collar to deactivate there was far less risk of immediate detection or messy demise.

Thaxter had to grudgingly admit that these men, whoever they were, were slicker than snot on a doorknob. Then something occurred to him. "Hey, are you the guys that grabbed up Brannhard?"

The Gunny shook his head. "We have no interest in him. We simply took advantage of his abduction. Now, why don't you give Clancy a quick run-down about prison life? He needs names and descriptions of friends and enemies, daily routine, cell number and location. Oh, and let him know where you fit in the prison hierarchy and how you talk to people. So far he's only been coached off of the trial vids. If he's gonna pull this off, he needs to be updated about your life in prison."

*　*　*　*　*　*　*　*　*

Two hours later, in a new set of clothing, dark glasses, false beard and a deactivated homing device, Thaxter was hustled into the hotel room in Junktown with the six strange men.

"Welcome, Mr. Thaxter."

Thaxter looked around at the six men and shabby hotel room he now found himself in and then returned his gaze to the obvious leader. "I'll give you credit for having collapsium plated big ones, pal."

The leader nodded.

"Fine," Thaxter said. "Now that you got me, what are you going to do with me?"

The leader, Dane, stepped forward and answered. "We are going to help you get off-planet, Mr. Thaxter. You will be given extensive cosmetic surgery; smooth out that face, add a couple of inches to your height, maybe add a few pounds to that waistline. Then we will give you enough money to support yourself on some out-of-the-way planet. Loki is nice this time of year, though I imagine Freya would be more to your liking...."

"Yeah, I get it, you're a freakin' criminal genius," Thaxter said, as his voice rose. "How did you pull this off, anyway?"

"I intercepted the call," the dark-haired one with the pasty complexion said. He was the other 'marine' on the APC. "When Rainsford put in a call for the TFN base on Xerxes, I rerouted the call here."

"How'd you know he would call?"

The leader smiled as he poured himself a drink, then a second one which he offered to Thaxter. "We spread the rumor about the hit on you. Rainsford is a big fan of over-kill, so I knew he would want military support to transport you to Mallorysport."

"What if he didn't buy the rumor, or just had a couple of cops question me at Prison House?"

"Then we would have tried something else." Dane said. "We had several contingency plans ready to go, but this was our best bet."

"I'll admit it worked, but where did you get all that military stuff?" Thaxter took a drink. It was a twelve-year-old double malt scotch, neat, the way he always drank it.

"That was the easy part. Back when this planet first became classified as a Class IV inhabited world, a couple Terran Federation Naval Marines stole an Armored Personnel Carrier with a plan towards striking out for Delta continent and staking a claim. They never made it off Alpha. Instead, they were caught while stocking up on supplies and arrested for unauthorized absence. I...knew the man who defended them. He couldn't beat the UA charge, but the TFN failed to make the connection between the two Marines and the missing APC."

"Don't military hardware have a tracking device like civilian vehicles?"

"Ha!" Brandon Murdock, who had played the Gunnery Sergeant, cut in. "Military vehicles don't use theft protection devices like that. If the TFN can track an APC, so can the enemy whoever that might be. Besides, military vehicles tend to stand out in traffic."

Thaxter could see the logic, up to a point. "Then why did those two Marines steal it in the first place?"

Dane chuckled. "Because they were certified brain donors. The only reason they got away with stealing the Amored Personnel Carrier is because they never had the chance to use it. The uniforms and most of the gear came with it as a sort of package deal. The weaponry was acquired from the local black market. And, their attorney arranged for some long-term storage for the APC in Junktown where nobody would ever find it."

"Except you."

"Like I said, I knew their attorney," Dane stated.

"What do you need me for, anyway?" the mobster demanded. "I'm done on this world no matter how you slice it. My old crew wouldn't touch me with a ten light-year pole. A few might even try to turn me in for a reward and a chance to go straight."

"We want you to sign over your loan brokerage and private financier operation. We also want your…ah…client list to go with it. It will go nicely with Ivan Bowlby's entertainment enterprises. Oh, and anything you can tell us about Spike Heenan's operation would be very helpful."

"So that's it! You want to take over the local underworld." Another thought struck the mobster. "Somehow, I don't think Bowlby's overdose was an accident. How do I know I won't end up the same way?"

Dane sat down and lit a cigarette. After a couple of puffs, he spoke. "Mr. Bowlby proved reluctant to cooperate with us. You do not have that luxury, Mr. Thaxter. Besides, our aims are set much higher than simply running this planet's illicit enterprises."

"Higher? What? You tryin' to take over the whole freakin' planet?"

Thaxter's only answer was the sudden silence in the room.

*   *   *   *   *   *   *   *   *

"Anything?"

"Afraid not."

Jack Holloway and John Morgan had spent the greater part of the day crossing back and forth over Beta continent looking out for anything out of place. Jack couldn't remember the last time he put so many hours of air-time at a stretch. While he manned the controls, John Morgan split his attention between the scanner that would register any unusual energy output and the viewscreen that captured and recorded several hectares of land.

Jack glanced at the power gauge and swore blasphemously in Freyan. Morgan looked over and asked what was wrong. Jack pointed at the gauge.

"We're going to have to land and recharge for a while," Jack explained that the nuclear battery was near the end of its warrentied lifespan and getting replaced soon and that the solar collector, though an antique, would keep them from getting standed."

"I could use a little solid ground time, myself," Morgan said. "I didn't want to say anything, but I was starting to get a little airsick…whoa! I just got something on the scanner."

"Let me set down then I'll take a look." Jack expertly brought the contra-gravity vehicle to ground then joined Morgan at the scanner. "Hmm…that's a lot of power for an illegal prospector. Maybe we just found something big."

Though Jack didn't say it, Morgan knew 'big' might mean Gus Brannhard. "The power signature is about one point three seven kilometers northwest of our current position." Morgan switched to the viewscreen and adjusted the image then pointed at the upper left section. "Just over this hill."

"If we're lucky they didn't hear us coming." Jack drew and inspected his sidearm. Satisfied it was loaded and the safety was off, he reached for his big 12.7 double express and repeated the process. He noticed Morgan was following his example with the .457. "John, I can't ask you to get involved in this…"

"I came to help with the search," Morgan countered. "Mr. Brannhard might be over that hill, so I'm already involved."

Jack had to admit that the kid had stones. No telling what could be hiding behind the hill. "It might just be some trespassers doing a little digging…"

"Then you'll need a little back-up in case you're outnumbered."

Jack shrugged in defeat. "Fine. Take the rifle and be ready to play sniper. Just follow my lead. Oh, and one more thing…"

"Yes?"

"Yes." Jack smiled. "Let an old man finish a sentence once in a while. All right. Let's do this."

Before the two men started walking toward the suspect location, Jack set up the solar recharger. If things got too hot, he wanted a ready avenue of escape. John Morgan suggested calling for the police, but Jack said no. Whoever was on the other side of the hill might have police band scanners. No point in giving them a heads-up. Jack made a mental note to requisition an aircar with sound baffles and a secure radio for situations like this in the future.

Over the hill was an encampment of small equipment, two aircars, and a tattered fibroid weave canopy, numerous metal boxes with holes on the top and three men doing something around a portable electric grill. Jack grimaced. The trespassers used the grill rather than an open fire so as not to give away their position, but the damaged canopy failed to block the energy signature from up close. Jack quickly outlined his plan to Morgan, rechecked his sidearm, holstered it and then started down the hill several meters away from where he left Morgan. No point giving away his back-up's position.

It wasn't until Jack got within ten meters of the three men that they noticed that they had company, and then the dirty one with the scraggly beard spotted him and told the other two. Their hands crept close to their guns, but didn't pull them out right away.

"Where'd you come from?" the short man with red hair demanded.

"Just passing through and noticed your campsite." Jack did a quick glance then returned his focus to the three men. No mining equipment was in evidence. That left out illegal prospectors. The shabby condition of the canopy and general appearance of the trio made Jack doubt the men had anything to do with Gus's abduction, either. So what were they doing?

"You do realize that you are on the Fuzzy Reservation, right?" Jack asked.

"Who are you?" the large man with the shaved head asked. "The Native Affairs Commissioner?"

"Yes."

If Jack had grown a second head the three men couldn't have been more startled. What happened next surprised Jack. The three men all put their hands on their heads.

"Don't worry yourself none, Mr. Holloway," the redhead said. "We ain't about to give you no kind of trouble."

These men knew Jack's reputation, apparently, and had no interest in testing it. That suited him just fine. He could tell that two of the men were right-handed and the third was a southpaw by how they wore their guns. "You two reach down with your left hand and unbuckle those gun belts, and you do it with your right hand, Lefty."

After the belts hit the ground Jack pulled some plastic tie-wraps from a pocket and tossed it to the ground in front of the short man. "Slip those on your buddies'…."

The native Affairs Commissioner was interrupted by a loud noise and the sound of something striking the ground behind him. He successfully fought off the urge to spin around choosing to keep his attention on the men in front of him. The trio were disconcerted by Jack's calm bearing.

Jack continued. "As I was saying, slip those on your buddies' wrists then come over here and turn around." The man obeyed and Jack slipped a tie-wrap around his wrists. By the time he finished John Morgan had joined the party rubbing his shoulder. "What did I tell you about interrupting me?"

"Didn't think you would mind, this time," Morgan said with a smile. On the ground behind Jack was a fourth man with a machete and a whole lot of air where a head used to be. "You never even glanced back after I made the shot. How did you know it was me doing the shooting?"

"Easy…I'm still breathing," Jack replied. "And I know the sound of my own rifle. I couldn't take my eyes off of these idiots, anyway. If I had, they might have gotten brave and gone for their guns."

"You put a lot of trust in my aim," Morgan pointed out. "I might have missed. Damned thing kicks like an oukry during mating season. I think I'm getting a bruise."

"After that demonstration with the damnthing from a moving aircar, the last thing I was worried about was your aim." Jack heard a muffled sound from one of the metal boxes. "Besides, if you hit me we wouldn't be having this conversation. Mind taking a look at what's in the boxes while I watch these boys?"

Morgan hustled off and inspected the boxes then hustled back. Jack was about to ask what he found when he felt a tug at his belt.

Jack turned and snarled, "What the hell?"

"I'm sorry, Jack, but I know a bit about your reputation, too. Go look in those boxes and you'll see what I mean." Jack hurried off and Morgan repositioned himself closer to the prisoners. "If you three have any hopes of seeing tomorrow morning, I strongly advise you all to keep your mouths shut."

When Jack returned it was easy to see he was ready to kill somebody, three men in particular. Morgan interposed himself between Jack and the prisoners. "I read up on Zarathustran law on the way in, Jack. These men are dead, already."

It took several minutes for Jack to reassert control of himself. When he did he went back and opened the metal cages and spoke soothingly to the Fuzzies as they climbed out. Morgan and Jack had stumbled into the other half of the Fuzzy slavery ring that Chief Steefer and the police found a few days earlier. Jack told the Fuzzies that they were safe now and could leave if they wanted to, or they could come with him to a wonderful place where Fuzzies were safe and happy.

The Fuzzies were unsure if they could trust the new Big Ones until all of the cages were opened and a couple from Hoksu-Mitto bounded up screaming, "Pappy Jack! Pappy Jack!"

The slavers had caught some Fuzzies out on the Gus hunt. While the Hoksu-Mitto Fuzzies told the rest about all the wonderful things the good Big Ones did for them, Jack returned to Morgan and the prisoners.

"Okay, I've calmed down. I'll take my gun back if you don't mind."

Morgan returned the weapon and Jack inspected it. Still loaded. "I'm not saying you were wrong, but you took a mighty big chance, there."

"Victor Grego warned me how you feel about Fuzzies," Morgan explained. "And that you have a bit of a temper."

"He's not wrong on either count, but I've never killed an unarmed man." Jack glanced at the prisoners. "Though, I'll confess to being real tempted, this time." He took in a long breath and let it out slowly. "Let's turn these Khooghras over to George Lunt and arrange a ride for the Fuzzies. I'm afraid we'll have to cut short the search for Gus for today. These kids will need to be checked-out by the docs, processed in and reassured that we won't eat them."

Morgan gazed out over the open plain. "Do you think there are any more slavers out here?"

Jacks face grew dark. "If there are and I catch them, I hope they make a fight of it."

XIX

Everybody was arguing. Red Fur wanted the tribe to stop taking the food the Big Ones were leaving for them and the tribe could not understand why. Red Fur told them about his fears that the Big Ones were fattening the *Jin-f'ke* up for slaughter but the Fuzzies could not grasp the concept. People did not eat people, and the Big Ones were just big people. Red Fur argued that it was possible the Big Ones did not know that the *Jin-f'ke* were people like them, only smaller and less wise. Or maybe they were like the *gouru* that ate their own dead.

"These Big Ones do not behave like any people we have ever known," Red Fur said. "The people do not hide in burrows or fly in the sky in made-things. People do not leave food out for other people while hiding from them. People make friends!

"These Big Ones know we are here, but do not come out to make friends. They leave food for us, but do not meet us in person. Why do they hide from us? Are they afraid? How could they be afraid of us when they are so big? They even made a *shimo-kato* make dead!

"If they are not afraid and do not want to make friends, why do they leave us food?" Red Fur asked. He looked about at the tribe. "When is the last time any of you hunted? Climber has become…"—Red Fur thought hard for a word—"big around his middle. We are all becoming slow and big around the middle. What would we do if a *shimo-kato* came here? We not run fast. *Shimo-kato* come, we all make dead!"

The tribe muttered among themselves. Red Fur was right about how slow they were becoming. "What we do?" asked Makes-Things, who was still in the splints.

"We stop taking the Big One's food," Red Fur replied. "We hunt, we find food for ourselves. No more Big One's food."

Some of the Fuzzies yelled that they wanted the Wonderful Food. The tribe argued back and forth until Red Fur called for quiet. He wanted the people to hunt for their own food, but only the Big Ones had the Wonderful Food. After many heartbeats he made a decision. "We take the Wonderful Food, but hunt for *hat-zu'ka* and *zuzoru.*"

The tribe discussed it for a while and then finally agreed. They would accept the Wonderful Food, but not the Big One's meat offerings. Red Fur breathed a sigh of relief. All was well…for now.

*   *   *   *   *   *   *   *

"…Yeah, old peace loving Jack."

"How many did he kill before you got there?" Colonial Marshal Max Fane's voice came out of the viewscreen in Major George Lunt's office. Lunt could see on the Marshal's face that he was more worried about the resultant paperwork than any number of dead Fuzzy slavers.

"Actually, there was only one fatality," Lunt replied, as he fought to keep a smile off his face. "And it wasn't Jack that caused it. It was some off-worlder by the name of John Morgan. Ahmed Kadra took the statement. He told me he went through the details with Jack Holloway and John Morgan three times to make sure he had it straight. One of the slavers tried sneaking up on Jack from behind and this Morgan sniped his head clean off with Jack's 12.7 double express from over one hundred meters."

Max Fane let out a long low whistle.

A 12.7 wasn't designed for sniper work. In fact, it kicked like a re-branded veldbeest. Lunt wondered if even Jack Holloway could have managed that shot. Probably.

The Marshal gave Lunt a quick rundown on everything he knew about John Morgan, which wasn't much. "I'm going to have a talk with Harry Steefer and see if he did a background check on the off-worlder." The Marshal looked up from the note he was writing. "Wait a second, this story isn't adding up. Jack found a Fuzzy slavery cell practically in his own backyard and didn't express his annoyance with a few well placed rounds?"

"He said that Morgan talked him out of doing anything rash," George Lunt explained. "But I've known Jack as long as anybody on Beta and I can tell you he doesn't kill people just to make a point…or even for revenge."

"Still, that must have been some talk! Ah, well, these slavers will likely get the death penalty, anyway. No point in Jack doing all the work," Marshal Fane chuckled. "And I didn't mean to suggest Mr. Holloway kills people for fun, George, though in this case I can't think of anybody who would blame him if he did."

Lunt agreed then shifted the topic of conversation. "Any word on Mr. Brannhard, yet?"

The Marshal filled Lunt in on the details of Leo Thaxter's interrogation. "I'm afraid Thaxter may be right; Gus Brannhard was disposed of right after being grabbed up. But we won't stop looking until we either have a body, live or dead, or the people that grabbed him."

"Glad to hear it. I've met Gus a few times when he came over to go hunting. Eats what he kills, doesn't hunt from an aircar and obeys the rules. A true sportsman."

"No slouch in the courtroom, either." The Marshal started to say some more then realized that they were talking about Brannhard as if he were dead. That was no way to conduct a missing person's case. "We're going to find him. Alive, damn-it. I'll talk to you later, George. Time to go back to work."

"Sure thing, Marshal. I'll transfer the prisoners, body and depositions to you first thing tomorrow. Oh! What should we do with the slavers aircars and equipment?"

"They were seized as assets in the commission and/or furtherance of a crime, right? Well, as I see it, they're now the property of the Native Protection Force. Or will be after the trial. Hold it all as evidence, have forensics go over it, then put it in secure storage until sentence is carried out. Make sure the aircars have clear titles then ask Jack what he wants to do with it all after the slavers are executed."

"Will do, Marshal."

George Lunt screened-off and Marshal Fane punched in the code for Chief Harry Steefer at the CZC. A youngish man with captain's bars on his uniform appeared instead.

"This is Captain Lansky, how may I help...oh, Marshal Fane. Chief Steefer is out right now."

Damn, I should have expected that, he thought. "Any idea when he'll be back?"

"Actually, he should be at police headquarters, right now," Lansky explained. "He and Piet and some company security men are reviewing new search strategies to find Mr. Brannhard."

"Oh, well, I'll just stroll on down and say hi in person, then. Thanks." he screened-off. *No point trying to get any information from one of Harry's men*, he thought, *they'll just clam up. Better to go to the source.*

*   *   *   *   *   *   *   *   *

Raul Laporte organized the receipts into neat little piles then poured himself a drink. In truth his accounting skills were somewhat lacking, he had a man for that, but he liked to look them over all the same. It kept the people working for him honest, in a manner of speaking. Nobody wanted to risk the boss catching them skimming the take. Besides, whether he understood it all or not, the desk computer collated the data and gave a nice, concise readout of the end product. What the computer couldn't do was play with the numbers. This was a talent only human type calculators could do, hence the need for the accountant. Laporte's quasi-legal activities generated significant revenue, and that revenue had to be accounted for if he were ever busted for something he couldn't bribe his way out of.

Laporte had just placed a fresh cigarette into a holder and lit it when there was a knock at the door. He grimaced in annoyance; his people knew he was never to be interrupted when going over the receipts, which meant it had to be something important for them to dare disturb him. He pressed a button on his desk and the door retracted sideways into the wall. From the outside it took Laporte's own handprint to open the door. Eric Mugami entered with a distressed look on his face.

"What is it, Eric?"

"Boss, there's a man outside who says he has to see you and that it is very important. We would have sent him away, but he said he knows about your involvement in that Thaxter business."

"Really? What Thaxter business is he referring to?"

"He said you wouldn't want him to say anything to anybody but you. You want I should give him the bum's rush?"

Laporte considered doing just that, then decided it was better not to take chances. No telling what this individual might know, and how it would affect him, personally. "Send him in, but check him over real good. He might be a cop fishing for something. Can't take any chances that he might be carrying something nasty." Laporte's office was shielded against external surveillance but a portable recording device carried in by a guest was a different matter.

Mugami nodded and left, then returned with a large man with a beard wearing a bush hat and dark glasses. Laporte gave the man a quick visual once-over then asked him what his business was.

"I think we should speak privately, Raul."

Laporte nearly dropped his cigarette holder when he heard the voice. "Eric, wait outside and make sure we aren't disturbed." Mugami left and Laporte sealed the door after him. "I'll be damned, they pulled it off!"

Leo Thaxter removed the hat, shades and phony beard. "Hiya, Raul, I got a business proposition for you."

*　*　*　*　*　*　*　*　*

Akira O'Barre was bored and lonely. She didn't feel like going out even though she had some time off while John Morgan was off in Beta continent. To keep herself busy, she decided to do a little research on Freya, Morgan's home planet.

As a Charterless Zarathustra Company employee, Akira had limited access to the Company library through her home computer station. Victor Grego encouraged his employees to read and do private research; something or other about well-informed workers being more productive. Akira scrolled down through the information on her screen.

Roger Baron and company first discovered Freya in 223 A.E. They immediately established relations with one of the princedoms and started trade with Yggdrasil; gunpowder for foodstuffs. Some of the details were sketchy. There was some interaction in the local politics resulting in a friendly government signing a treaty with the Charterless Freya Company. No doubt the Yggdrasil gunpowder played a part in that. The claim was filed on Yggdrasil for the entire planetary system. Unlike most planets with indigenous sapient life forms, Freya had a fairly sophisticated if mostly pre-industrial society. Some of the natives grasped the advantages of investing in the Charterless Freya Company. Of course the only ones who could were successful merchants and the land holding noble class.

John Morgan mentioned that he was the nephew of a minor noble with substantial holdings in the CFC. How minor the noble and how substantial the holdings?

After an hour she located a list of Charterless Freyal Company stockholders in the CZC data files. As it turned out, a lot of the same investors with the CZC were also invested with the CFC. Companies often bought stock in each other. Sometimes it was just to diversify, other times it was a takeover bid. Either way, the CZC had a lot of background information on CFC stockholders as well as the company itself.

Xeterus Honirdite invested with the Chartered Freya Company in 227 A.E. Each generation increased their holdings in the company and none took out more than half the dividends, choosing instead to roll most of the profits back into the company. Unfortunately, while the Honirdite line enjoyed considerable financial gains, the family suffered greatly from illness, war, and intrigue. By the time of Orththeor the Greater, the family consisted of only himself and his sister.

John had mentioned he had no cousins or siblings. His entire family was reduced to just him and his uncle.

Akira shifted the focus of her research from historical to cultural. Freya, when first discovered, was a feudal society. While they had progressed considerably technologically and socially under the aegis of the Federation, at heart they still retained a feudal core.

Akira perused the various facets of Freyan life until one section in particular caught her eye. She re-read the page from the beginning. As Akira read more, she began to become uncomfortable with the subject matter and how it might relate to what she knew of John Morgan.

According to the research, dueling was a common manner of dealing with a perceived insult in Freyan society. Such insults could include cheating at some sport or game of chance, allowing cattle to graze in a neighbor's pasture without permission, failing to meet family obligations, engaging in conversation with another man's wife or sister in a private setting…the list went on, as did the appropriate responses. For minor offences, a sound thrashing was acceptable. A duel to the death was deemed necessary for more serious offences.

Akira went further down the list until she came to one passage in particular that caught her eye. The eldest son could challenge a man who abandoned his family when he came of age. In such cases a duel to the death was considered to be appropriate, and even necessary.

John is going to kill Gus Brannhard…or whomever his father may be!

Akira shut down the computer then poured herself a glass of wine with unsteady hands. As a resident of a colony world the idea of a duel was far from shocking. Dueling licenses were issued on an almost daily basis on Alpha continent alone. But the idea of a fight to the death with your own father was a difficult concept for her to grasp. Even though she didn't know Gus Brannhard personally, he didn't seem like the kind of man who would willfully abandon his family.

Akira sat for a while drinking her wine. Around the halfway point of her second glass she had an idea. She threw back her drink and headed for the door. John Morgan was good, but Records Division was her job. She would dig through the files and see if she couldn't find proof one way or the other who John's father really was. If he was on Zarathustra she would talk to him herself, maybe even warn him. She would at least learn why he abandoned his unborn son.

Akira had one other thought as she hailed a taxi: what if John's father was the kind of man who needed killing?

*   *   *   *   *   *   *   *   *

"They took the Extee-Three but not the meat?"

"Yes, sir." Hendrix held up the goofer carcasses before throwing them into the M/E converter.

The leader considered the new development. "Any chance the meat wasn't fresh enough? Or maybe diseased?"

"It was no different from the previous offerings, sir."

Hendrix activated a viewscreen and called up a surveillance file. The image of several Fuzzies out hunting filled the screen. Hendrix fast-forwarded the footage to show the Fuzzies returning to their encampment with two goofers and three land-prawns. The two men watched the screen as the Fuzzies skinned, gutted and shared the meat. One thing struck the leader as odd; some of the Fuzzies ignored the land-prawns.

"I thought land-prawn consumption was a species wide trait. The Fuzzies need something in the land-prawn digestive tracts in order to successfully reproduce," the leader observed.

"That is the common belief," Hendrix confirmed. "Wait a sec…the ones not eating the land-prawns are the same ones passing on the Extee-Three. The titanium stuff in Extee-Three is supposed to be more effective than what is found in the digestive tract of land-prawns."

The leader reviewed the footage. "Check the archives and see if there is any other footage of this nature. This could be significant."

Hendrix leaned forward. "Maybe, but significant of what?"

"Damned if I know, but transmit the image files with the next report. Maybe upstairs can do something with it."

Granger entered the cabin in time to catch the end of the conversation. "You'll want to send this, too."

The leader inspected the photo images Granger handed him. They were of some sort of quasi-primate skeletons. According to the legend at the bottom, the bones would have made up a being roughly four feet in height when standing fully erect. "Are these what I think they are?"

"Beats me," Granger admitted. "Best to check them with Anthropology. It just looks like leftovers from a barbeque to me. There are at least three different skeletons, judging by the skulls."

"This keeps getting better and better," Hendrix said.

*   *   *   *   *   *   *   *   *

"How in Nifflheim did somebody beat us to it?"

"As soon as the news broadcast hit the airwaves the stock in all of his legitimate enterprises dropped like a rock," Jacque DeCarr from Acquisitions Division reported. "It dropped even further when Bowlby's illegal enterprises came to light. Every single stockholder dumped his shares on the market hoping to avoid any suspicion of being connected to either his death or his illicit activities. Well, some as-yet unknown person snapped up all of that stock for about two centisols on the sol. It was all gone before my people had a chance to move."

Victor Grego wanted to yell at somebody, but CEOs don't yell. It makes them look like they have lost control. "Jacque, Ivan Bowlby's death was broadcast on CZCN, meaning we were the first people with any foreknowledge that the stock might drop. Why did you wait for the actual broadcast?"

Jacque let out a sigh. "To avoid the appearance of impropriety, Victor. We had to wait for the broadcast to air or risk being accused of unfair trading practices. The Company has become very popular with the general public since Science Division discovered Hoenveldzine, but any perception that we were manipulating the stock market and PR Division starts having nightmares at noon."

"Damn straight we do," Edgar Burlisson from Public Relations division agreed.

Jacque was right, which made it all the worse. Grego personally accepted responsibility for the bad PR during the Colony of Zarathustra versus Kellogg and Holloway trial. The fact that his actions afterward resurrected the Company's image didn't mitigate the potential for more damage.

"How soon after the broadcast did you try to acquire the B.E. stock?"

"Thirty minutes. I thought that gave us plenty of time to beat any possible competitors and still look like we weren't using foreknowledge of the event." Jacque slumped a bit in his seat. "I truly didn't expect anybody else to be interested in it."

Grego leaned forward. "How fast did the other group get there?"

"They were in and gone before I even arrived," Jacque said. "I tried to find out who bought the shares up, but as you know stock transactions are not public knowledge."

Victor Grego considered the implications of that. The only people on the planet that knew Ivan Bowlby was dead were the police, the secretary that discovered his body and the Company when the information was released to the news services. And, of course, the other broadcast companies. Yet some mysterious group of investors appeared out of thin air to snatch up Bowlby Entertainment the second the news was aired.

"Jacque, you're off the hot seat," Grego declared. "You acted correctly. Had you been there any sooner it would have looked bad. Gentlemen, if you don't mind, I would like to adjourn the meeting early, today." Nobody objected. "Thank-you, gentlemen. If there are any issues to be dealt with before next week's meeting, we can do a special session later this week. Meeting adjourned."

As the men filed out of the conference room, Grego signaled Miguel Courland to stay behind. "Miguel, we both know those stock transactions aren't as confidential as they're supposed to be. More often than not either a reporter or some paid-off stockbroker gets the low-down on all those transactions. I've seen enough of them end up on the news."

"True," Courland agreed. "I'll have to call my reporters in for a meeting, listen to everybody deny that they have anything, then wait for one of them to come see me privately."

Grego raised an eyebrow. "Really?"

"Good Ghu, yes!" Courland threw his arms up in exasperation. "Reporters are all like selfish little children trying to out-scoop each other on every story and they don't want to share resources. Not a chance in Nifflheim that any of them will admit anything in front of his colleagues."

Grego developed new respect, as well as sympathy, for the work Courland did in his division. "All right, do what you have to but get me those names. Put whatever carrot on the stick you think will work."

"You got it, Victor. I'm sure I'll have something by tomorrow at the latest."

After Miguel Courland left Victor Grego moved quickly out of the conference hall to his office. It wasn't until he was past Myra and through the door to his office that he realized that Juan Jimenez had followed him from the hallway. "Oh, Juan, was there something you needed?"

"Actually, I thought you might need something."

"Me? What would that be?"

Juan smiled broadly. "A sounding board. You almost never close a meeting early, at least not in the two years since you made me a division head, and Jacque DeCarr's report lit a fire under you."

Grego nodded, "It did. Whoever bought out B.E. knew the stock was going to drop and was there to snap it up. That makes me think the late Mr. Bowlby's overdose may not have been accidental. Somebody wants control of one or all of Bowlby's businesses."

"I agree, but which one? Ivan Bowlby was into everything from television to prostitution and drugs."

"I'm putting Chief Steefer on it. It wouldn't hurt if he tickled Marshal Fane's ear, too."

"The only business concern that B.E. had that could have any impact on the Company was his television interests," Juan observed. "Specifically, the news and talk show programs."

"Exactly." Grego punched in the code for Chief Steefer but waited to press the SEND button. "Remember the Darloss interview?"

Juan admitted it was still fresh in his mind.

"Imagine a network company owned by someone with an axe to grind against the Company. First thing they'll do is stick another crackpot like Darloss on, maybe even Darloss himself, looking for ways to punch holes in our government contract. We might be seeing the opening gambit of a land-grab scheme. Land we hold the lease on for the next ten centuries."

Juan took in the possibilities and then added another one. "Interesting how all this is happening at the same time."

"What do you mean?" Grego's finger still hovered over the SEND button.

"First John Morgan hits town to dig through our files, then the Darloss interview. Next Mr. Brannhard is abducted, then Bowlby is found dead and his stocks are instantly grabbed up the second they hit the market."

Grego didn't like where Juan's train of thought was going. "You think this is all tied together?"

Juan shrugged. "Don't you?"

Grego hit the SEND button.

XX

Akira was up to her backside in work. While off the clock, she was still hard at it, digging through the computer files and news archives. She tracked the men on John Morgan's potential father list from when they first left Terra to the present. Morgan had only tracked the men from their time on Freya to the present, but a lot could be found out about a man by going into his background.

She set up multiple screens and tracked the histories of the five men on each one of them. John Morgan had told her only that his chief suspect was Gus Brannhard, but by tracking the research the Freyan had already done she quickly put together the other candidates for paternity. Using a password she got from a friend in Security Division, a young man she used to date, she pulled up the personal information on Chief Harry Steefer, Jack Holloway, Markus Rikitake, Gus Brannhard and Morgan Richards. She put the files with photo I.D.s up and looked them over. Gus Brannhard, Harry Steefer and Markus Rikitake looked nothing like John Morgan, but that didn't prove anything as he might take after his mother's side.

Akira was about to get busy when she noticed that each of the men's blood types were listed on the I.D.s. Gus Brannhard was O positive, Jack Holloway AB positive, Chief Steefer B negative, Markus Rikitaki O negative and Morgan Richards A negative. Next she called up John Morgan's I.D. file. AB positive. She tried to find out what Morgan's mother's blood type was, but the file was not in the computer.

Of course not, though the young woman, only people that were processed through Zarathustran customs would be on file. She saved the information on a microdisc and shut down the computer screens. Somebody had dropped the ball in John Morgan's education. Basic medical knowledge was taught in high school on most worlds. But perhaps this was not the case on Freya. Of course blood typing was nowhere near as accurate as comparing DNA, but it would eliminate a lot of people from consideration.

Then another thought struck her; Morgan might already know the name of his father and set a false trail for her benefit. He admitted that he always suspected that she was watching him for Mr. Grego. Jack Holloway was on the short list and John Morgan was currently on Beta with him. Was he really over there looking for Gus Brannhard, or had he already found what he was looking for?

*   *   *   *   *   *   *   *   *

"Just hang your hat next to mine, John."

The two men had just returned from the police station where Jack collected one of the aircars seized from the Fuzzy slavers. John Morgan went along to fly the second vehicle back. Morgan placed his hat on the indicated peg and accidently knocked Jack's hat to the floor.

"*F'troogt*! Sorry about your hat, Jack," Morgan quickly scooped it up and brushed it off with his bare hand before replacing it on the peg.

"No worries. That hat has been through a lot worse. It looks like we'll have to pick up the search tomorrow, though." Jack grimaced. "Damned paperwork is going to kill my evening. I'll set you up in the guest room."

"Actually, I was planning on pitching a tent for the night, if that's not inconvenient." Jack asked why and Morgan explained that he liked to camp out at least a few nights under the stars of every planet he visited. "Except on Nifflheim, of course. We didn't get the chance to really camp out last night since we were stuck at the police station filling out depositions and introducing the new Fuzzies to the Rez."

He was still aching from the catnap he took on Major George Lunt's office couch. Some days he felt his age more than others. John Morgan didn't even get the chance to take a nap since he had twice as many papers to fill out and a veridicated statement to make. Anyone killing somebody in the commission of a crime was immune to prosecution, but it needed to be verified. Especially in the case of a little known off-worlder.

"It looks like a nice night for it, but the local wildlife might make getting any sleep a challenge," Jack cautioned.

"Oh? Should I worry about another damnthing?"

"Nope." Jack smiled. "Fuzzies. Somebody new is going to get them curious. Don't be surprised if you wake up with a dozen Fuzzies sawing logs next to you."

Morgan laughed. "Sounds like a good way to stay warm!"

"I'll mix-up some dinner before you start roughing it." Jack went into the kitchen. Before he could open the refrigerator Morgan declined saying he was too tired to eat. He bid Jack a good night and went out to set up his tent.

Jack considered offering to help put up the tent, then remembered from the first night out that Morgan had one of those fancy self-erecting fibroid weave jobs that cost almost as much as an aircar. This particular model could become almost invisible, much like TFN CGU uniforms. He could even set the opacity of the top so as to appear open to the sky, which he did. Jack shrugged. *To each his own.*

* * * * * * * *

In his tent with the walls opaque and the ceiling transparent, Morgan quickly stripped off his clothing and sat down on his sleeping bag. He extracted a small device from his field pack and opened it. Inside were five clear glass tubes, the first three with hair strands in it. Each had a name label on it except for the last two. Morgan extracted the fourth tube and dropped in a few white hairs, then replaced the tube in the device and wrote a name on it. He then extracted the fifth tube. After plucking a few hairs from his own head he placed them in the tube and returned it to its position in the device and filled out the label.

Morgan stared at the device for several heartbeats before he let out a long sigh and pressed a button. Several minutes later it pinged and displayed two green lights and three red ones. He stared at the lights for an hour before exhaustion overtook him.

*   *   *   *   *   *   *   *

Victor Grego finished his breakfast and ruffled Diamond's fur affectionately. With everything that had been going on he had neglected to spend real quality time with the Fuzzy. He resolved to do something about that as soon as he reasonably could. Maybe Diamond would like to spend a few days out at the Rez. Grego made a mental note to speak with Jack about that later in the day.

Diamond no longer needed a sitter to keep him out of trouble. Fuzzies learn fast what they should and shouldn't do in a Big One's home or business. But Fuzzies were also gregarious and needed a great deal of social interaction. For that reason, Grego arranged for Diamond to be taken on play-dates with Fuzzies who were adopted by CZC employees in a specially equipped room on 12th level.

After dropping off Diamond, Grego went up to his office and checked his messages. Nothing from Harry Steefer or Miguel Courland, yet, but there was a new text message from Akira O'Barre. Grego hit the intercom button on his desk.

"Myra, would you please call Miss O'Barre up from Records Division? Have her take my private lift up."

"Yes, Mr. Grego."

Grego was a quarter-way through his cigarette when Akira entered his office. He indicated a chair and she took a seat. Grego remembered that Akira didn't like cigarette smoke and stubbed it out. *It seemed more people were refraining from tobacco, these days*, reflected the CEO, *well, these things run in cycles.*

"Miss O'Barre, I received your message that you needed to see me," Grego said conversationally. "Dare I assume this is connected to our Mr. Morgan?"

"I think he's going to kill somebody, maybe Jack Holloway," Akira blurted. "I can't be one hundred percent certain, but I think that's what he intends to do. Either Mr. Holloway or Mr. Brannhard…I mean if we find Mr. Brannhard alive…."

The young woman was extremely upset but she wasn't breaking out in tears, Grego noted. "Why do you think he wants to kill Jack or Gus?"

Akira related what Morgan had told her about searching for his father and then what she discovered in her research on Freyan society. Next, she admitted to accessing confidential files with an illegal password, leaving out where the password came from, and what she suspected based on the blood-types of the men on Morgan's list.

Grego stabbed a button with his finger. "Myra, call Dr. Mallin, Chief Steefer, Juan Jimenez and Leslie Coombes to my office right away!"

"Yes, Mr. Grego." Myra noted that her boss failed to use his normal manners and summoned the men quickly. *Something big must be up.*

Five minutes later everyone but Leslie Coombes entered the office. Coombes was in court dealing with a larceny case in his capacity as Colonial Prosecutor *pro tem*. Akira was asked to repeat her suspicions, which she did in more concise terms.

Grego turned to the chief Fuzzyologist. "Ernst, what do you think?"

Juan Jimenez interrupted, "Wait, if Gus or Jack is Morgan's father, why isn't his last name Brannhard or Holloway?"

Dr. Mallin screwed up his face as he considered the ramifications of Akira's research. "He may not know it, Juan. Or the father might have changed his name. I think Miss O'Barre is on the right track, though. My own cursory examination of Freyan culture tells me that things like family honor are paramount, much like Pre-Atomic feudal Japan. Without a father in evidence, John Morgan has no real name. Were he not raised by his uncle he would have been a virtual pariah. To claim the family name he has to take it from the father who abandoned him. That usually means a duel to the death."

"Usually?" Grego prompted.

"A severe wound can also satisfy the requirement," he said, "provided it either prevents the party from continuing the fight, or the challenged party accepts defeat and admits his fault in the matter. At the minimum, blood will be spilled."

"Do you think either Jack or Gus could have abandoned their families like that?" Jimenez asked.

"From what I currently know of them now, no," Dr. Mallin said. "But a lot can change in thirty-five years. Look at us; we've all changed significantly in the last two years alone. It could even be argued that both men were ready to accept the responsibility of adopting their Fuzzies as a way of making up for abandoning their own natural offspring."

Chief Steefer shook his head. "I don't buy it. I don't know Jack as well as any of you, but Gus is a drinking buddy and in my opinion the man would sooner abandon his own gonads than his family."

"Gus Brannhard is a remarkably heavy drinker," Dr. Mallin countered. "That is often an indication that he is trying to drown a traumatic memory. Abandoning one's wife and child easily qualifies as such a reason. The fact that he significantly reduced his intake after adopting Allan and Natty suggests that he has found a surrogate family to replace the one he lost."

Grego considered Mallin's words carefully. Nobody was more qualified in the psycho-sciences on Zarathustra. But he knew both Jack Holloway and Gus Brannhard and could not bring himself to believe either of them was capable of leaving their families. Jack was a wreck when his Fuzzies came up missing before the famous Fuzzy Trial, mostly due to Grego's interference, and again when Little Fuzzy went missing while visiting Diamond at Yellowsand. Still, as Dr. Mallin had pointed out, a lot can change in thirty-five years.

"We won't get anywhere trying to psychoanalyze two men in absentia," Grego said, "and what they may or may not have done three and a half decades ago is not the issue. John Morgan is. Ernst, how do you think John Morgan will handle his little affair of honor?"

"Handle?" Dr. Mallin mulled it over. "He'll do everything in as legal a way as possible, I would have to guess. He is currently operating within the strictures of his culture, a fairly law abiding people. If he plans on challenging anybody, he'll most likely purchase a dueling license, hire a second to go through, set a time and place—"

"…all the niceties according to Colonial Law," Harry Steefer interrupted.

"If he is following the law, then can't Jack or Gus legally refuse to accept the challenge?"

"Yes, Juan," Chief Steefer replied, "But there is a social stigma attached. Refusing a challenge will get a man branded a coward. Then there is the hit to Jack's reputation as a man not to cross. Besides, I never heard of Jack or Gus backing down from a fight."

"Less importantly, perhaps, is that the challenged party would be barred from ever returning to Freya," Mallin added. "While I doubt that either man ever plans on leaving Zarathustra, just knowing he was forbidden to return there would, ah, 'stick in his craw'."

Grego had to agree. Jack Holloway was a man who didn't like restrictions being placed on him. Gus would likely handle it better, but it would still rub him the wrong way. But could either of them kill their own son?

"Mr. Grego, I need to use your screen." Without waiting for permission the Chief quickly moved to the communications screen and punched out a code. In a Technicolor splash Colonial Marshal Max Fane appeared. "Max, I need something quick, fast and yesterday."

"Sounds big," Fane said. The fact that Steefer ignored normal view-screen protocol was significant. "What do you need?"

"Has John Morgan purchased a dueling license since arriving on Zarathustra?"

The Marshal's eyebrows shot up at the question, and then he turned to the computer terminal on his desk and banged some keys. "He purchased an open dueling license the day after he hit dirtside."

Grego, Mallin and Juan said in unison, "Open dueling license?"

"That means the name of the opposing dueler can be added later," the Chief explained.

Fane added from the viewscreen, "To be legal it has to be signed by the other party and witnessed by at least two people, usually the seconds. Does somebody want to bring me up to speed, here?"

Chief Steefer gave a concise account of the situation as he understood it.

"Great Ghu on Nifflheim! Well, Morgan gets points for style; I'll have to give him that. He even saved Jack's life so he could kill him himself, if that's what it comes to."

"And why he was so determined to join the search for Gus," Juan added.

"What can we do about it?" Dr. Mallin asked.

"Nothing," the Marshal replied. "Morgan has yet to break any laws, and seems determined to do everything all nice and legal."

"I saw Jack kill Kurt Borch," Juan interrupted. "One second he was beating Leonard Kellogg to a pulp, the next he pumped three rounds into

Borch's chest. I've never seen anybody move so fast. If Jack is the father, maybe it's Morgan who'll be in trouble."

"Don't count on it," Akira said. "Freyans are trained from a very young age to handle firearms. John took me to the company firing range and we did some target practice and fast drawing. One time I blinked and completely missed seeing the gun go from holster to hand."

"Mr. Morgan is very motivated, as well," Dr. Mallin added. "If he is Jack's son he may have inherited his father's reflexes. And, I hate to add, Jack is well into his seventies. He's no spring chicken."

Grego started to swear, then remembered that a lady was present and swallowed his words. "Wait a second…Jack is the Native Affairs Commissioner. Isn't there a regulation to keep him from dueling?"

"That only applies to high officials, judges and prosecuting attorneys," Max Fane said. "That helps Gus if he chooses not to waive it. But, Mr. Holloway refused to let it be applied to him. He said if somebody had a problem with how he managed his office, they were welcome to discuss it with him through seconds and with witnesses."

Yeah, that was Jack, all right, Grego thought.

"Too bad Jack isn't a stockholder," Jimenez said. "Company policy forbids top staff and stockholders from dueling. At least with each other."

"I'm afraid that only protects his Fuzzies," Grego pointed out. Everybody stared and he explained. Shortly after the murder of Goldilocks, Leslie Coombes and Victor Grego arranged for Jack Holloway's Fuzzies to be brought to Mallorysport under the guise of being held as evidence in the upcoming trial. While the Fuzzies had escaped and been secretly taken to Xerxes, Zarathustra's outer moon, by a TFN agent, Gus Brannhard filed a lawsuit naming the CZC responsible for the illegal seizure and imprisonment of Little Fuzzy, Mama Fuzzy, Ko-Ko, Mike, Mitzi and Cinderella for seven million sols. After the Fuzzy Trial, Gus was appointed Colonial Chief Prosecutor and wanted to clear his old caseload, so he settled out of court for 140,000 sols and 60,000 shares of common stock. Jack paid Gus his fee and banked the rest in the Fuzzies' names, then a few months ago he issued each of them debit cards with the plan of teaching them financial responsibility. "So the Fuzzies are stockholders and Jack isn't. Gus also soaked me for Jack's legal fees in the process, though I drew the line at his hotel bill."

Chief Steefer couldn't suppress a grin. "You have to give Jack credit for style, too, and forward thinking on that one." Then the grin ran away as he added, "It must run in the family."

"Government officials can't own stock in a local company, anyway," Fane added. "Conflict of interest. We nailed former Colonial Governor Nick Emmert on that charge. When Gerd van Riebeek was sworn in as Deputy Commissioner of Native Affairs, he had to divest himself of his Company holdings. Say, if stockholders aren't allowed to duel, won't that be the way to stop John Morgan?"

"Not allowed to duel with other stockholders," Jimenez explained. "They sign agreements to that effect. The idea is to keep anybody from applying pressure on other stockholders."

Marshal Fane grumbled how he knew it was too easy and then asked, "What did Jack say when you told him about John Morgan being his possible son?"

"We haven't, yet," admitted Grego. "This all came out just now."

"Good God, man!" the Marshal roared. "Call him, already." The screen went dark.

Grego punched in the code for Jack, but only got a message stating he was out. "Chief, grab the yacht and get over there. Take anybody along that you think you might need, but get over there and warn Jack. Stop the duel if you can."

"There's a storm out over the ocean, right now," Juan Jimenez said. "It won't clear for several hours. The yacht won't be able to navigate it safely."

Grego swore under his breath. "And it will take just as long or longer to go around the storm or the other way around the planet. Damn! Chief, get as far as you safely can, then wait it out. No heroics! I don't want to lose you or the crew."

Without a word Chief Steefer hotfooted out of the office, Akira O'Barre close on his heels. Grego almost called her back then refrained. She might be able to talk Morgan out of it, he thought.

XXI

"Look, he's served his purpose. Now he's a liability. We need to get rid of him."

"I already bought a ticket to Gimli and enough cash for him to start over or stay hiddin'."

Brandon Murdock sneered at the idea of wasting the money on Leo Thaxter. "It's quicker, cheaper and safer just to kill him."

Dane shook his head as if frustrated with a small child. "It is also more permanent. Thaxter is useful as long as he is alive. Dead he ceases to be a source of useful intelligence. Never underestimate the value of information. And here at the B.E. studio we have plenty of room to hide him."

"Alive he is a dangerous liability," Murdock countered. "Say he gets pinched on Yggdrasil or whatever rock he settles on? First thing he does is rat us out for a deal. And the former owner of these buildings was a known felon. It's just a matter of time before that Coombes guy finagles a warrant to go through these places."

"Bowlby is dead, hence his crimes died with him," Dane replied. "The only way they get a warrant on this place is if we give them an excuse, which we won't."

The two men went back and forth until finally Dane agreed that Thaxter should be eliminated. Eventually. What the two men did not know was that the subject of their discussion was listening in through a secret video feed in Bowlby's old office. Thaxter had come there many times before he was imprisoned and knew most, if not all of Ivan Bowlby's little secrets.

He wasn't surprised that his liberators would also plan to become his executioners; he had been waiting for that shoe to drop since they busted him out of Prison House. For this reason he had taken some precautions of his own. He had contacted Raul Laporte earlier and arranged for some different accommodations. Laporte knew about the caper, of course; nothing happens in Mallorysport without the owner of The Bitter End hearing about it first.

Laporte was only too happy to give Thaxter anything he needed; with the understanding he turned all of his less than legitimate enterprises over to the lounge owner. Thaxter neglected to mention the details of his interview with the police. He didn't completely trust his old colleague, of course, and planned on getting the Nifflheim off of Zarathustra before Laporte came to the same conclusion as Dane and Murdock.

Thaxter didn't need the money that Dane and his goons were dangling in front of him though he wouldn't have minded taking it. He had several hundred thousand sols stashed away before his arrest, plus the substantial amount of money he had just received from Raul Laporte. There was always the chance that he would have to skip planet and he had planned accordingly. Thaxter had also stopped shaving. A good beard and dark glasses went a long way towards a disguise. It helped that nobody was looking for him, either. Yet.

When he had taken the chance of going out to see Laporte, a man on the street waved and called him 'Clancy' and even said growing the beard back was a good idea as 'it made him look less like 'that Fuzzy Fagan Thaxter.' Thaxter had actually laughed out loud and shook the man's hand. It also gave him the idea to get a forged identity card in Clancy's name.

Thaxter packed up his few belongings, mostly clothing given to him by Dane's crew and the money he had stashed, then headed out to the hidey-hole Laporte provided for him. He made one stop along the way to the Mallorysport spaceport where he rented a storage locker under his alias of Clancy Slade to store a duffle bag full of most of his money. He took one other thing with him that he had also hidden away; his old .45.

*   *   *   *   *   *   *   *

"What the hell is that?" Bronson exclaimed.

Hendrix came over to look at the tachyon scanner readout. According to the image, something roughly one hundred meters long and forty meters wide was twenty meters down from the lowest excavation point. It was some sort of metal alloy, at least partly iron.

"It looks like a missile," Bronson said. "I never saw one that big, though, short of a planet buster."

"Take a radiation reading," Hendrix ordered. Granger flipped a few switches then manipulated a joystick. Radiation was nominally higher than normal background levels for Zarathustra. Well within safe levels, at least for Terro-humans. Hendrix exhaled slowly. He hadn't realized he was holding his breath. "Okay, let's get an interior read and see if we can find out about this missile."

"Already done," Bronson said. "It's mostly hollow. There is some machinery, or something, but except for dirt and rock it's mostly empty. I'm afraid that's all we can determine without digging down to it."

"Granger, can you construct a basic blueprint from the scans?"

Granger typed on the keyboard with rapid steady strokes for several minutes. "That should do it."

"Crosscheck it with the database," Hendrix said, "see if there are any matches."

Granger again attacked the keyboard. "No exact matches. Closest we can get is early interplanetary spacecrafts. Hey, Bronson, it looks like we got an old-fashioned rocket down there."

"I saw one in a museum on Terra once," Bronson said. "I wasn't impressed."

"What era would that depth indicate?" Hendrix asked. "How long has that ship been there?"

Bronson checked the geological data. "Assuming it didn't bury itself on impact, it would be about…ah…that can't be right…according to the chart that thing has been buried for about 50,000 to 80,000 years."

Nobody spoke for several minutes. Finally Bronson spoke up. "You think maybe Fuzzies came to Zarathustra in that rocket? You know, like that Darlock said in the interview?"

"Darloss," Hendrix corrected. "Maybe. Or maybe some other species we know nothing about."

"Wait!" Granger became excited. "Those skeletons might be the original crew of that ship."

"Great Satan!" Hendrix reached for the short range radio. "Let's get the boss in here and let him decide what to do next."

* * * * * * * * *

Allan Quatermain and Natty Bumppo were having fun. Though they missed their Pappy terribly, riding about Beta continent on their big dogs looking for Gus was keeping their spirits high. With them were Little Fuzzy and some as-yet unnamed Rez Fuzzies.

Contrary to popular belief not all Fuzzies wanted to be adopted by Big Ones. The ones waiting to be adopted only accepted names from their new *pappies* or *mummies*. The ones that remained at the Rez or went into one of the Fuzzy villages took new names from the Big Ones that taught them so many new things. And, while rare, there were Fuzzies that came to learn new things that eventually left and returned to the wild, though they would visit to trade furs for Extee-Three and metal tools. Some groups of nomadic Fuzzies even traded only with other Fuzzies at the villages spread throughout Beta continent.

Unlike most Fuzzies, Allan and Natty were armed with miniature 8.5

mm rifles. Gus Brannhard had them specially made by Mart Burgess, the preeminent gunsmith on Zarathustra, after he adopted the two of them. Burgess was to gunsmithing what Stradivarius was to violin making. The 8.5 mm would stop anything up to and including a zarabuck, but would be almost useless against anything as big as a veldbeest or, far more dangerous, a damnthing. Still, these were sapient beings that had survived uncountable centuries without the benefits of Terran technology. They knew what to watch for and what to avoid.

On foot a Fuzzy being chased by a damnthing had little chance of escaping, but on the back of the Curtys, the powerful dogs used as mounts, escape was all but guaranteed. The average damnthing, a creature of significant bulk comparable to a Terran Bison, though several hundred pounds larger, had been clocked moving as fast as thirty miles per hour, somewhat slower than its Terran counterpart. The Curtys, unencumbered, could do thirty-eight. With Fuzzy and gear, the Curtys still managed better than thirty-four miles per hour over short distances and thirty at a steady trot. In addition to the speed advantage, the dogs enjoyed greater endurance and maneuverability than the 3,000-pound damnthing.

Even if the giant beast caught up to the mounted Fuzzies, the dogs would run circles around it. While the 8.5 mms had little chance of doing serious damage, enough stings from them could possibly drive the damnthing away in search of easier prey. Short of flying over Beta in an aircar, the Fuzzies were as safe as they reasonably could be.

A few days earlier, a large shipment of dogs was brought over from Alpha continent, including Allan and Natty's personal mounts, Hottentot and Chingachgook. The Fuzzies with their dogs were dropped at various grid points, according to the probability that somebody could hide there from satellite surveillance, and equipped with a radio and GPS to track their movements. Each group consisted of six Fuzzies with dog mounts, or eight Fuzzies on foot, depending on terrain and dog availability. Since

Allan and Natty were already trained with their own dogs, they were placed in charge of a group exploring high up on the Fuzzy Reservation.

Along the way the search party met other Fuzzies. Unlike most other Fuzzies, these had never heard of the Big Ones and the wonderful things they gave to the people. These new Fuzzies were also different in other ways; they were taller and their fur was different colors instead of the uniform golden typical of the species. One had fur that was the color of the setting sun. Another was as dark as night. One was even the hue of the clouds. And their language had many words new to the Rez Fuzzies. Not like Big One words, but different from words known to them. Even more surprising was that some of them did not like the *esteefee*, the Wonderful Food.

At first the wild Fuzzies were afraid of the dogs, and surprised to see the strange new things that Allan and Natty carried, like the shoulder bags and metal weapons. Little Fuzzy passed out some Extee-Three, which was accepted first with suspicion, then with delight by some of them. According to the new Fuzzies, there were strange noises coming from the land behind the tall hills where the sun rises. A few nights earlier a strange not-live thing that flew went toward the direction where the sun goes to sleep.

Little Fuzzy, Natty Bumppo and Allan Quatermain discussed it and decided to see the place with the strange sounds. After they told the wild Fuzzies about the Rez and how to find it, they pointed their dogs towards the tall hills and raced off.

* * * * * * * *

Everybody was busy when the leader walked into the operations room. Hendrix was scanning the buried rocket, a few men were cleaning and polishing sunstones and another was separating glowing rocks from what appeared to be ordinary gravel.

"We have new instructions." Everybody stopped what they were doing and turned to look at the leader. "It's time to close shop. We are not to replace the dirt and debris back into the dig. Throw it all into the M/E converter after we get off the reservation."

"Why after?" Bronson asked.

Hendrix spoke up. "That much mass conversion will light us up like a supernova on the satellite scanners. Off the Rez it won't matter, but we don't want to give away our position while we're still here." Hendrix turned to the leader. "I am curious why we went to so much trouble to hide our activities only to fly away with a big hole that screams 'illegal miners were here'."

"Upstairs wants the artifact, missile, rocket or whatever, to get noticed by the legal authorities. And no, I don't know why." The leader walked over to the sorting station and picked up a small stone. "They also want us to send back these duds." That created a stir among the men. "Again, I don't know why, they just want them. Load 'em up with the sunstones and send them out, now. We break camp immediately afterwards. The last thing we want is to get caught with these sunstones in our possession.

"Oh, one last thing; we need to get some samples from those Fuzzies that don't like the Extee-Three. Hair, blood, anything we can get from them. Nichols. That will be your job while we get packed up here. Use stun-bombs or sono-stunners. I know I've said this before, but it merits repeating: trespassing gets us a fine, illegal mining gets us a few years jail time, but a dead Fuzzy buys us all a bullet in the head. Clear? Good. Let's do this fast and get the Nifflheim out of Dodge."

*   *   *   *   *   *   *   *   *

Sun Fur was out hunting for *hat-zu'ka* on her own. She saw a land-prawn off to her left and ignored it. Like Red Fur she would only eat land-prawn if she was very hungry and nothing else was available. *Hat-zu'ka, shikku* or even wild berries or nuts were more to her taste. *Shikku* was much too dangerous for a single hunter, and all the wild berries and nuts had been eaten by the tribe since the Big Ones came and frightened away most of the game. But *hat-zu'ka* could still be found if one was careful and smart.

Sun Fur knew that Red Fur would be angry that she went hunting alone, but since he had convinced everybody not to eat the meat that the Big Ones left for them, there was less food for everybody. Some of the people wanted to move away in search of a new place where there were always good-to-eat things, but the others did not want to leave the Wonderful Food that the Big Ones left with the meat. That had caused much fighting and some almost left the tribe, but Red Fur managed to keep them together for a few more days.

Off to her left Sun Fur heard a sound, like a large animal. It wasn't a *shimo-kato*; they made more noise, and *shikku* tended to be much quieter when moving through the tall grass. Sun Fur hunched down behind a boulder and waited for whatever-it-was to pass by. The sound stopped for many heartbeats. After a while Sun Fur could not resist peeking around the boulder to see what was happening.

It was a Big One. None of the tribe had ever seen a Big One so close before. This one had dark skin like the night, and fur on its face that was even darker. There was a strange made-thing on the Big One's head that shaded its eyes. Maybe Big Ones didn't like the sun, like the screamers that only came out at night, she thought. She didn't know if the Big One was male or female as the strange outer coverings it wore disguised its gender, but she suspected that it was male…if the Big Ones had such distinctions.

The Big One also carried two made-things in its hands. It looked at one while keeping the other pointed in front of its body. The made-thing emitted strange noises, like the chirping of birds. The noise got faster and louder as the Big One turned in Sun Fur's direction. Sun Fur suddenly became very afraid; what if the made-thing was looking for her?

She turned to run when a high pitched sound, like many-many people all screaming at once, hurt her ears. It was the worst pain she had ever felt. In a few heartbeats darkness overtook her.

XXII

Nichols returned to the camp and headed straight for the operations cabin. Bronson and Granger noticed the worried look in his eyes and Granger asked what was wrong.

"I don't know. I followed orders and used the sono-stunner on the Fuzzy, but look at her!"

Nichols laid the limp body down on a counter. Everybody immediately saw the trickle of blood coming from her ears. The leader swore luridly in Sheshan, but not at Nichols.

"I should have realized this could happen," the leader said. "Fuzzies speak and hear mostly in the hyper-sonic range. That sono-stunner must have been like sitting in a sound chamber set for a thousand decibels. Is she still alive?"

"She's breathing," Granger said, "but I don't know what a Fuzzy's respiration rate is. This could be good or bad."

The leader swore some more. "Get Henderson in here. He was a medic during his stint as TFN corpsman. Bronson, get the med-kit and have it ready for Henderson."

Bronson rushed to the back of the cabin while Nichols spoke quietly to the leader. "I had the stunner on its lowest setting. What do we do if she doesn't make it?"

"I'm thinking. Normally I would just dump her in the converter and get the hell out of here, but there are the other Fuzzies out there. They can testify under veridication that we were here when this female disappeared.

Even an idiot like Marshal Fane can add two and two."

"You mean we wipe out those other Fuzzies, too?"

"Nifflheim, no!" The leader looked down at the Fuzzy. A few days earlier he was prepared to kill some Terrans if they were discovered, but Fuzzies were a much smaller threat. They were like small children, in fact. "I'm not about to pile one mistake on top of another. I didn't sign on to do murder. We'll do what we can for her then return her to the tribe. We'll make an offering of the rest of the Extee-Three by way of apology and hope they accept it. Besides, this is why we kept our distance from them and used aliases, even with each other. Fuzzies can't finger us if they can't give a clear description or name."

Henderson hustled into the cabin and made straight for the Fuzzy on the counter. "What happened?"

"Sono-stunner."

Henderson swore in archaic Terranglo. "Short of shooting her with a rifle, this is probably the worst thing you could do to a Fuzzy."

The leader shook his head. "I should have consulted with you before sending Nichols out. Can you do anything for her?"

Henderson looked the Fuzzy over with a portable medi-scanner. "She has ruptured eardrums, no surprise there, and possible brain-damage. I can pack her ears with med-gel that will protect her from more loud noises as well as provide general antibiotics. The ears have a good chance of recovering. That's not what I'm worried about."

"Can we do anything for the brain?"

"Not a damn thing." Henderson shook his head. "Even if I had the equipment I don't have the medical training to do anything. I can give her some anti-inflammatories to reduce the chance of brain swelling or stroke, but that's the limit. The only chance this Fuzzy has is to get her to a hospital."

"Damn. The nearest town is Red Hill, right?" Granger asked.

"That's the nearest one with a hospital, anyway," Hendrix added.

The leader started to say, "All right, I'll take her down and tell them I found her like this…"

"No need," Henderson interrupted, "she's gone."

The room fell silent. After a few minutes Nichols asked what they should do with the body.

"We could make it look like she was killed by a bush goblin," Granger suggested.

"Who does the mutilation," Hendrix asked. "Any volunteers?"

There were no takers. Finally, the leader spoke up. "We're going to give her back to her family. I saw a documentary on Fuzzy funeral rites. We'll wrap her in grass and set her on the ridge where we've been leaving food for them. Make sure you leave her weapon with the body. Put the rest of the Extee-Three next to her. Hopefully, they'll understand that it was an accident." He turned to Henderson. "Get all the samples you can, but try not to damage the body any more than you have to. We'll send them off with the final shipment."

The leader moved to the communications consul and composed a report to be sent in. His fingers moved very slowly across the keyboard.

* * * * * * * * *

Jack Holloway had just completed filing his paperwork when John Morgan walked in. Jack closed the cabinet where he kept the hard-copies and turned to say hello when he noticed the somber look on Morgan's face.

"Is something wrong?"

Morgan hesitated, as if searching for the proper words, then just laid a document on Jack's desk. Jack picked it up and read it. It was a dueling license, all filled out with only the seconds and challenged party information left blank.

"In accordance with Freyan tradition and the laws of the Federation, I hereby challenge you, Jack Holloway, to a duel of honor. As the challenged party it is your right to choose the weapon, time and place, provided the weapons are available on this planet and lethal in design and the duel takes place no more than two weeks from this notification. You have the right to name your second as I will name mine. If you choose a second that is dead or off-planet, you forfeit the right to choose the weapon and time in accordance with Freyan tradition and the Federation/Freyan treaty of 302 AE.

"Will you sign the dueling permit or must we forego the legal niceties?"

Jack was stunned. He had been challenged to duels before, though not in the last two decades, and those were for reasons he understood. "I don't understand? What have I done?"

Morgan was silent for a moment, as if considering his answer. "You abandoned my mother and me before I was born. As such, I have no name and no honor until I have faced you in honorable combat. I ask again that you sign and name your second."

"John, I think you have me confused with another man…"

"I compared our DNA last night. You are my biological father. I have been searching for you for over fifteen years." Tears began to form in Morgan's eyes.

Jack stared for a moment before speaking. "What was your mother's name, boy?"

"Adonitia Honirdite, daughter of Orphtheor the Greater."

Adonitia! Jack felt the air go out of his lungs. "But…she died while I was working on Nifflheim…I…" Jack picked up a pen and signed his name, then took out an inkpad, pressed his thumb on it, then on the document.

"And your second?" Morgan prompted.

Jack named Gustavus Adolphus Brannhard.

"I see. Clever. We do not know if he is dead or off-planet, so technically he is acceptable. Unless he fails to appear in two weeks, then you will be required to choose a new second. I will not contest this, as it is honorable for you to continue the search for your friend. I will now return to Mallorysport to secure the signature of my second. I will refrain from filing for two weeks unless Mr. Brannhard is located and is able to fulfill the role of your second, or he is determined to be dead or off-planet. I wish you good hunting. Until we meet again."

Morgan turned and walked out. Jack wanted to pepper him with questions but he couldn't make his voice work. He plopped down into a chair and became lost in his thoughts. When Chief Steefer and a young woman showed up he was only vaguely aware of them. On some level he noticed that they collected John Morgan and left, but for the most part he was lost in his thoughts and memories. Memories of a beautiful young woman he had met and married and then lost forever.

*　*　*　*　*　*　*　*　*

Unlike many companies, the Charterless Zarathustra Company encouraged initiative. Other companies claimed that they did the same, but failed to follow through. Not Victor Grego. Grego was always willing to lose a few sols if the justification was there. Shortly after he arrived on Zarathustra, the expense account of one of the gem buyers caught his eye. There was a payment of several thousand sols to one Benjamin F. Sunn for some glowing pebbles. Grego became curious and called for the gem buyer to explain the purchase. The gem buyer nervously laid out several dull stones of various colors. Grego was unimpressed until he picked one up and the heat from his hand caused it to glow brightly. The gem buyer was given a promotion and a raise and the glowing pebbles were named after their discoverer: sunstones.

Word quickly traveled through the company grapevine that the new CEO was a man who rewarded initiative. There were times when the initiative of some well-meaning employee ended up costing the company, as was the case when a couple of cops receiving under-the-table money from the Company arranged to frame some Fuzzies for assault before the Great Fuzzy Trial in an attempt to get the Fuzzies branded as hostile, but more often than not it worked to the benefit of the CZC.

Peter Davis considered himself to be a person who took initiative. Unfortunately, there was little opportunity to use that initiative in his position as a power control specialist. His day-to-day job required that he watch for anomalies in power generation, distribution and utilization. In a building as overbuilt as Company House, that meant he mostly watched for gauges that malfunctioned. Davis suspected that were it not for the Federation regulations requiring such a position, he wouldn't even have the job.

Davis only had one complaint: no real opportunity for advancement. He worked alone and, he had to be honest with himself, nobody expected much from him. The entire building was virtually self-sustaining. In his ten years working for the company only one gauge was ever found faulty. Davis simply called maintenance and a new gauge was installed in ten minutes. Nothing exciting ever happened, until Davis spotted a gauge reading higher than it should.

"Now what's going on with you?" Davis tapped on the gauge then called up the specs on his electronic reference guide. "Within safe parameters, but where is that extra power coming from?" A second check of his ERG showed that this particular gauge registered a minor power loss over the last few days. Davis pulled out his comlink and punched in the code for the Power Division. When they picked up he asked if anything unusual was going on. There wasn't. "I need a trace on…" he read the plate under the gauge, "…line 77398210."

"Are you for real?" the voice from the comlink asked. "That line is well-within safe levels."

"I'm not down here for my health, damn-it." Davis took a moment to get control of his temper. He went through the same scenario every time he asked for a line trace. Not everybody was as dedicated to his job as he was. Usually, like this time, it was something minor, but protocol was protocol. "I'm seeing several terawatts of energy coming in from that line. According to the manual, that is not a power generation station. So where's all that juice coming from?"

That got through loud and clear. Unexplained energy sources could be a leak in the M/E converter, and that could lead to the entire building being blown straight to Nifflheim. After a couple of tense minutes the voice from the comlink gave Davis a probable energy source.

"We'll send a couple men down to check it out."

"Don't bother. That's just two sub levels below me. I'll check it out myself and call back if I find anything." Davis was almost excited. Nothing interesting ever happened in the sub levels of Company House. Davis checked his sono-stunner and Baldertec 9mm. Sometimes there were unpleasant vermin in the sub levels; land-prawns, pygmy bush goblins, quarter-meter long zaraspiders and other things still lacking classification. Nobody knew how they got into the building let alone how they thrived, but Davis preferred to be ready for anything. One never knew what they would find down in the sub-levels. Still, it would be nice to look at something other than a bunch of digital readouts and gauges for a while.

* * * * * * * * *

Rippolone checked his face in the mirror and nodded in satisfaction. His beard had grown in and his hair had been dyed a dark brown. His normally deep tan had faded considerably during his time in hiding. Contact lenses changed his pale blue eyes to dark brown. As a final flourish,

Ripper placed a gold cap on a tooth.

"Perfect. My own mother wouldn't know me."

"She doesn't want to know you, Ripper," said Anderson. "Last time you saw her she kicked you out and said don't come back."

Ripper shrugged. "Ehn. She didn't approve of my career choice. That never stopped her from cashing the checks I sent."

Anderson rolled his eyes. "What exactly are you doing?"

"I'm going out on the town. We've been cooped up in here since we bagged the shyster and I'm going stir-crazy."

"Rip, we ship out in two days…."

"And spend the next three weeks locked up in a cabin takin' care of our 'sick friend' in there." Rippolone jerked a thumb towards the door behind him. "Besides, Laporte forgot the depilatory cream for the sasquatch. I ain't about to try and shave him with an electric razor."

Anderson had to agree with the sentiment. "Still, even in disguise it's risky."

"Get real, Tony. This planet is lousy with new immigrants. We're unknowns around here. The only…uh, hell, call them *people*…that saw us were those two Fuzzies. What's the odds I'll run into them?"

"That's what you said on Baldur…"

"Stop harpin' on Baldur!" Rippolone roared.

"Keep your voice down…"

"I don't have to! This whole damn room is lined with collapsium. I could explode grenades and Brannhard would never hear a thing. Or anybody else!" Rippolone grabbed his hat and stormed out of the room.

* * * * * * * * *

Davis turned the corner just as a door was opening ahead of him. Out of reflex he ducked back around the corner out of sight. He drew his sono-stunner and set it on high. After a few seconds he heard the footsteps moving away. Davis risked a glance around the corner in time to see a strange man disappear into a wall. He carefully stepped over to the door and tried to listen, but the collapsium lamination prevented him from hearing anything. Davis considered his options and decided to play it smart. He punched the Security button on the comlink.

"Security, Captain Lansky, speaking."

"This is Peter Davis on sub-level three, floor four, section nine, corridor thirty-two. I need a security detail to get down here fast."

Davis could hear some muffled voices then Lansky's voice, again. "State the nature of the emergency, Mr. Davis."

"I saw an unauthorized person come out of a room and leave by way of a…well, a secret panel, really." *Damn, that's going to sound like something out of a spy novel.* "The man was wearing civilian attire, not work clothes. I'll stay here and keep an eye on the door until your people get down here."

Up on the ground floor of level one Captain Lansky quickly assembled five men to accompany him down to sub-level four. "Glazier and Hoffa, you use sono-stunners, Smith, Schröter and Matedne, grab automatics, but keep the safeties engaged until there's reason not to. Clear? Okay, let's go."

XXIII

Red Fur was worried. Nobody had seen Sun Fur since sun highest time. He organized the people and sent them out to search for her. Makes-Things stayed back with the young as he was unable to walk yet. Red Fur selected the ridge near the Big Ones for himself. He suspected Sun Fur went to the place where the Big Ones were leaving food, even though she was told not to. That was the way of the young when they were close to being adults; they pushed their limits and defied those who were wiser. Eventually, she would learn and behave responsibly.

Red Fur climbed the ridge to the place where they first saw the Big Ones. There was a pile of the strange food that some of the tribe liked to eat. Next to it was something wrapped in grass. Red Fur approached to investigate and recognized the wrapping that the people used when one of the tribe made dead. Though fear gripped his chest, he opened the wrapping to look upon the face. It was Sun Fur.

Red Fur examined the body and discovered the tell-tale blood coming from the ears. Sun Fur was killed by the noisy made-things the Big Ones used on the *shimo-kato*! He collected the body and raced back to the camp screaming at the top of his hypersonic voice for everybody to gather together. When the tribe was assembled they all wailed at the sight of Sun Fur's body. Red Fur explained to them how he found the body and what he believed caused her death. Everybody talked at once about what to do.

"Big Ones made Sun Fur dead?"

"We make Big Ones dead!"

"How? Big Ones big-big! Big Ones very wise!"

"We leave this place. Get away from the bad Big Ones!"

Red Fur called for quiet. "Big Ones made a *Jin-f'ke* dead. We must make Big Ones dead."

Everybody wanted to know how when the Big Ones were so powerful. Red Fur admitted he didn't know how. He asked Makes-Things if he had any ideas. Makes-Things had had a lot of time to think while he was healing and had an idea for a new weapon for hunting shikku. He told Red Fur about it and then the entire tribe began to make plans on how to make the Big Ones dead.

"First we bury Sun Fur," Red Fur said. "Then we make the Big Ones dead."

* * * * * * * *

"The camp is broken down and the shipment sent off," the leader said into the viewscreen. "The skeletons have been reburied near the artifact. We'll dump the debris into the M/E converter after we are safely off the Reservation—"

"No," said the voice from the viewscreen. "Convert it now. We want to draw attention to the dig. By the time anybody gets there to investigate, you'll be long gone."

"That's a little risky with the search for Brannhard going on, don't you think?"

The man in the screen laughed. "Great risks can bring great rewards. Once off the Reservation, just have everybody scatter and use their cover stories if caught. In fact, dump the robots and mining gear into the converter as well. That will remove any evidence of what you were up to."

The leader considered the orders. M/E converters could only contain so much power without numerous secondary systems. He said so.

"Use the surplus energy to power all the vehicles back up to full.

The rest can be expelled as heat into the atmosphere. That, too, will draw attention to the artifact. This will be our last communication…until you return to Mallorysport."

The screen exploded in a kaleidoscope of colors then went dark. The leader didn't like the orders. Not one little bit. Still, he knew there were big plans in action he wasn't privy to, yet. He left the cabin and relayed the orders to the men.

"I'm going to walk the perimeter, collect the cameras and make sure we didn't miss anything that could lead back to us." The leader armed himself with a rifle, pistol and sono-stunner, and as an afterthought, a hypersonic hearing aid, then walked out of the camp and started a slow circle around it.

Back in Mallorysport a decision was made and ten minutes later a well-manicured finger depressed a very special button.

*　*　*　*　*　*　*　*　*

The Fuzzies were gathered near the ridge when they spotted one of the Big Ones. Climber wanted to use her new long-arm thrower, but Red Fur said no. "Wait for Big Ones to come close."

The new 'long-arm throwers' were branches cut and carved so that a Fuzzy could place the base of a pointed throwing stick on it and get a longer arc when launching the missile. It was arm's length with a hook-shape at the end where the pointed throwing stick would be seated. The throwing stick had to be shorter, but could be delivered with more force.

The plan was to try and catch the Big Ones off-guard. Stonebreaker and Climber would use stone axes to chop at the Big Ones' lower legs while the rest of the tribe used the pointed throwing sticks. Once down, a few chops to the head would, hopefully, make the Big One dead.

The Big One, perhaps hearing the hypersonic yeeking of the Fuzzies, turned toward the ridge and approached the waiting tribe. Red Fur was prepared to attack when he noticed the Big One had moved his arms out and was holding his hands up, away from the noisy made-things at his sides.

The Big One had just come around a large tree when something no *Jin-f'ke* had ever seen before happened: the big melon-seed flying thing exploded with a flash of light like the sun and big noise like thunder. The Big One was knocked off his feet and the tree behind him broke apart leaving only the thick trunk the height of three *Jin-f'ke* behind.

The Fuzzies were knocked back from the ridge and showered with dirt and shiny hard things. Red Fur gathered his people together and took refuge under a tree that blocked most of the falling debris. It was many-many heartbeats before things stopped falling, though the air was thick with dust. There was also a strange sound in everybody's ears, like many-many feekee birds singing at once.

Red Fur checked his people. There were some minor cuts and bruises, and people had a hard time hearing each other, but nobody was seriously injured or made dead. The Fuzzies picked themselves up and cautiously ascended the ridge.

All of the made-things and Big Ones were gone. There was just a big hole in the ground. There were also patches of fire on the ground. This made everybody afraid. Fire was a bad thing for the *Jin-f'ke*.

"Big Ones gone! Made-things gone," Climber observed. "What made do?"

"Not know," Red Fur said. He looked over the area and saw the Big One who had walked toward them before the thunder noise. Stonebreaker also saw the Big One and wanted to make sure he made dead.

Red Fur stopped him. "No. Take his made-things. See if he alive."

The tribe argued. Hadn't they come to make the Big One dead for what they did to Sun Fur?

"Big One not dangerous, now," Red Fur insisted. "Wait for him wake up. Then we make talk. May be other Big Ones who come. Want to know more about them before come."

*   *   *   *   *   *   *   *   *

Little Fuzzy, Natty Bumppo, Allan Quatermain and the other Fuzzies were nearly knocked off their mounts by the explosion. Little Fuzzy dropped his radio and it struck a rock. After that, it didn't work.

"What that?" Allan asked. "Sound like Pappy Gus gun, but big-big."

"Ex-plo-shun," Little Fuzzy said. "Big Ones make ex-plo-shun to find things in ground, like sunstones. Pappy Vic make many-many big ex-plo-shun at Yellowsand."

"We go look at big ex-plo-shun," Allan said. "See what make-do."

Little Fuzzy thought for a moment then decided against it. "Dangerous. No radio. We go back and tell Pappy Jack."

Reluctantly, the Fuzzies turned their dogs around and started back toward home.

*   *   *   *   *   *   *   *   *

Captain Lansky took the lead as he approached Peter Davis's position. Davis held his sono-stunner in both hands aimed at the ceiling. When he heard Lansky's security detail behind him, he swung around, aimed his weapon at the six men, recognized the CZC security uniforms, then quickly returned the stunner to the neutral position.

Good, thought Lansky, *this Davis has had proper weapons instruction.* Lansky introduced himself and requested an update. No change since last communication.

"Do we know if anybody is still in that room?"

Davis explained the impossibility of hearing anything through collapsium.

"Hmm. That means no secret knock or special signal, too. Can you show Matedne and Schröter and Hoffa where that secret panel is? Good. Smith, Glazier, you're with me. Let's get us some squatters."

Matedne, Schröter and Hoffa went with Davis to the hidden panel. Careful examination revealed the outline of the door, but not how to open it. It was decided that they would simply wait for the squatter to return. The plan was for Hoffa to open fire with the sono-stunner the second the door was fully opened. Davis agreed to act as back-up with his stunner if things got hairy.

Captain Lansky led the rest over to the service door. Back when he was in the security academy he was taught how to kick in a door to take a suspect by surprise. Kicking a collapsium laminated door was a sure-fire ticket for a broken bone or two. Looking over the door he noticed that there was no locking mechanism. That made sense; this deep into the CZC sub-levels there was nothing worth stealing, and no way to get it out of the building if there were. Or, so it was believed before Peter Davis spotted the secret passage being used.

Chief Steefer nearly went nuclear when he learned people had been sneaking into the upper levels and setting up tea pads and supernovas over the attempted sunstone robbery. Security had been tightened up significantly since then. Steefer had even talked Grego into putting a rush on sealing up the open levels.

"All right, on three we go in," Lansky ordered. "Glazier, stun the whole room whether you see anything or not as soon as the door opens. I'm not taking any chances, here."

"What if there's a Fuzzy in there?" Glazier asked. "They have hypersonic hearing. Won't the sono-stunner hurt them in an enclosed area like that?"

Lansky considered that. He had never heard of Fuzzies being stunned, at least not with a sono-stunner. But bullets were a lot more lethal all around and he wanted whomever was in that room taken alive. "We'll have to risk it. Let's just hope there aren't any Fuzzies in there and do our damn jobs. On three. One…two…THREE!"

Smith shoved the door open and jumped back as Glazier sprayed the room with sonic waves. A man inside the room had jumped up and was immediately dropped by the stunner. Lansky and Smith rushed into the room in search of others. To the left was another door, but this one had an iron bar across it. The door was designed to swing into the adjoining room, so the squatters used super-epoxy to attach hooks to the collapsium lamination on the door, and placed the iron bar across it.

"Looks like they want to keep something from getting out," Lansky said. "Could be anything in there, but I doubt it'll be armed. Smith, get the bar. Glazier, stand ready but don't shoot unless you have to."

Smith pulled the bar and Lansky pushed open the door then jumped back.

"Great Ghu's gonads!" yelled Glazier. "It's a giant Fuzzy."

The Fuzzy stepped into the room where everybody could see him better. Lansky looked closer at the face and his eyes widened in amazement. "That's not just any giant Fuzzy, that's Brannhard!"

"It's about time you lot got down here," rumbled Gus. "Uh, I need a drink, some pants and to call my family. In reverse order."

*   *   *   *   *   *   *   *

The Fuzzies carefully approached the still form lying by the shattered tree. The Big One was cut in several places and had a large gash on its forehead but was still breathing. Red Fur noticed the noisy made-thing lying next to the Big One and picked it up. He handed it to Tells-things and told her to throw it into the river. The other made-things were unknown to Red Fur but he took them as well.

Stonebreaker, Climber and Silver Fur wanted to kill the Big One, but Red Fur would not allow it. He explained that the Big Ones could no longer hurt them. The other Big Ones must have made dead when the big thunder noise thing happened.

"Help Big One," Red Fur declared. "Healer fix. Take back with us."

That opened up another argument but Red Fur was firm. People did not kill helpless people. "This Big One sick. Hurt. We help. Learn about Big Ones. Try to hurt us, then make dead."

*   *   *   *   *   *   *   *   *

Ripper entered the Last Chance Bar with his bag of supplies and waved to the man mixing drinks. The man nodded and Ripper walked past him to the restroom. In the last stall he pressed three bricks on the wall in the sequence Laporte had shown him and a section of floor opened to reveal a narrow staircase.

Fifteen years earlier when the CZC Company House foundations were being laid, one of the senior architects, Hikaru Schwartzen, arranged for a special modification to the plans. This modification created a hidden passage to what was then a prefabricated cabin. The plan had been to have a secret entryway into Company House allowing him to help himself to whatever was stored in the lower levels.

Unfortunately, a few years later as Mallorysport grew and certain undesirables immigrated to Zarathustra, Schwartzen ran up significant gambling debts to one Spike Heenan. To get the money to payoff Spike he borrowed from Leo Thaxter, at a rate of six-for-five. When he ran behind on his payments Raul Laporte sent his men to collect. Having nothing else to pay with, Schwartzen told Laporte about the secret passage into Company House. Laporte immediately saw the advantages and paid-off Schwartzen's tab, then set up a bar where Schwartzen's cabin had been.

Schwartzen had since met an untimely end in a freak construction accident, as did his confederates who helped him construct the secret corridor. Only a very few select people knew about it and they all stayed healthy by keeping their mouths shut.

Ripper descended the long staircase wishing Laporte could have arranged for some kind of elevator or escalator. It was a long way down to sub-level three, floor four, and a two mile walk to the hide-out. *Maybe Laporte will upgrade with his cut of the bounty on Brannhard*, he thought with a chuckle.

Ripper pushed open the hidden door into the corridor and carefully looked both ways and listened for any voices. Nothing. The first time he came through he almost soiled himself when he saw a giant twelve-legged spider skitter past his legs. He drew his gun but held his fire, remembering Laporte's warning that the noise would travel a long way through the corridors. Collapsium was good for soundproofing out noises on the opposite side, but it also allowed for a lot of sound wave rebound and echoing. The mobster didn't understand the physics, but readily grasped the need for silence.

Satisfied that the corridor was empty, he stepped out and sealed the panel behind him. He then walked directly to the storage room where he and Anderson were hiding out. Ripper opened the door to find a strange man pointing a sono-stunner at him. The last thing he knew was that the man said "nighty-night" and everything went dark.

"Nighty-night?" Lansky asked with a wry expression.

Davis shrugged. "Thanks for letting me do that. This has been the most excitement I've had since I took this job."

"Well, don't let anyone know about it," Lansky warned. "The Chief would skin me and use me for a welcome mat if he found out I let a civilian take a risk like that."

"Oh, relax," Gus grumbled. "If Steefer makes a fuss, tell him it was my idea. Now let's get the Nifflheim out of here."

After finding Brannhard, Lansky's first inclination was to hustle Gus upstairs and call the colonial police, but he realized there was a second man still on the loose. There was also the possibility that the kidnappers had confederates in the CZC since they were hiding out in the bowels of Company House. Lansky decided that it was best to wait for the other man and take him when he returned. To this end he sent two men around the corner of the corridor, two more down the opposite end around the next corner, and kept Gus, Davis and Schröter with him. Gus Brannhard was asked to wait in the adjoining room where he would be safe from possible gunfire.

"The only way you'll get me back in that damned room is on a gurney," Gus replied. "Maybe not even then."

Lansky relented provided that the Chief Prosecutor would wait in a corner behind the entry door and added, "Take my back-up pistol, just in case."

It was over an hour before the door opened again. Peter Davis, who had been pacing back and forth, was standing in front of the door when it opened. Without thinking he raised his sono-stunner.

"Well, now we can get these mutts out of here," said Lansky. "Smith, go get some proper clothes for Mr. Brannhard—"

"'Mr. Brannhard', hell," Gus interrupted. "You boys can call me 'Gus'. In fact you can call me a hairy sonuvabitch and I'll still buy the first round after this."

"Yes, sir…uh…Gus," Lansky turned to Davis. "How would you like to let Mr. Grego know we just found the missing Colonial Chief Prosecutor?"

XXIV

"I would have put him in the best suit we had but he wanted to avoid the appearance of impropriety." Victor Grego spoke into the four-way split screen to Jack Holloway, Ben Rainsford, Max Fane and Leslie Coombes. "He's getting into a pair of workman's overalls, right now. That and getting some veldbeest steak into him. Those sons of Khooghras kept him out for days then left him nothing but Extee-Three and water to survive on."

There was a babble of voices as everybody spoke at once, then Jack Holloway took the lead. "How did they get into the Company Building in the first place? Where did that secret entrance come from?"

"Chief Steefer is looking into that, but it had to have been made when the building was in the construction stage. We won't be able to ask the prisoners for several hours, I'm afraid."

"By that time they'll be in one of my cells," Marshal Fane cut in. "But let's keep a lid on this until then. We don't want some ambulance chaser looking to make a name for himself by getting underfoot."

"You be sure to send that Peter Davis over here first thing tomorrow morning for his 25,000 sol reward," Ben Rainsford said. "I'll want to congratulate him in person."

"He's also getting a bonus, raise and promotion here at the company," Grego added. "I can't believe he was left working in the same position for ten years. He's overdue in any case. Lansky and crew all get the bonuses I promised, too. I'll talk to Harry and see if we should promote Lansky to major. He really handled himself like a pro on this one."

"Where is Lansky?" Jack asked. "I want to thank him personally."

"He took a team into the secret passage to the Last Chance Bar in Mallorysport and secured it until the Colonial police showed up," said Grego. "The owner was Ivan Bowlby, according to the property title, and all the employees knew nothing about the passage."

"We'll see if they remember anything under veridication," Fane said. "I have a BOLO out on the manager."

"BOLO?" Ben wasn't up on cop acronyms.

"Be On the Look-Out," Coombes explained.

"Oh. Personally, what I would like to know is who sent the kidnappers?" Rainsford asked. "From the pictures you sent they seem too young to have known Gus on Terra before he left."

"They were sent from Terra, all right," Gus Brannhard interrupted, as he walked in wearing ill fitting coveralls. "By the Hoshi Campanili Family would be my guess. I helped to send Hoshi up for twenty years when I worked for the DA's office back there. Hoshi died a month after he was released from prison, the same year I arrived on Zarathustra, but I would guess his sons wanted revenge for that and…another little thing I did before leaving Terra."

"What did you do?" Rainsford asked without thinking.

"As an attorney I would advise against answering that question if you did anything actionable," Coombes interjected.

"The statute of limitations expired over twenty years ago," Gus said, "and these aren't the kind of people who swear out complaints." Gus took a seat, glanced at the bar, and shook his head slightly, and then related the events leading up to his departure from Terra. "Before I left Terra I used much of the information we had gathered while putting the case together. There were several account numbers from various banks that we were unable to seize as they were outside of our jurisdiction. Well, I just accessed all those accounts and re-routed the funds to a local bank."

"What did you do with all that money?" Marshal Max Fane asked.

"Well, I donated most of it to several charities—anonymously," Gus said with an evil grin. "The rest I stuffed into a duffle bag and took with me. That's how I supported myself while planet-hopping for twenty years."

Victor Grego let out a low whistle, then scribbled a note to have all the Company account numbers changed and to increase the security on them. As an afterthought, he added to have the account activity checked for the time around the Fuzzy Trial.

"How much did you get away with?"

"Around three hundred and fifty million sols, Jack." Gus turned to Grego and asked if he had a cigar. He only had cigarettes in the office and he declined. "Let me think…I left planet with only ten million. It was all I could carry in the duffle. That was one of the reasons I gave most of it away. The other was that if they ever caught up with me, they wouldn't get much of a refund." Gus chuckled. "I emptied every account I could. They had maybe five million left in liquid assets by the time I was done. The idea was to cripple them as long as possible. Well, that and some revenge for my family."

Everybody was quiet for a moment before Jack spoke up. "Ben, is this going to cause any trouble as far as Gus's position as Colonial Prosecutor?"

"I don't see why it should. Mr. Coombes?"

"Well, legally Gus has never been charged or convicted with a crime. Moreover, nobody even swore out a complaint against him, as far as we know. As I recall, there is no law on this planet stating that a criminal suspect cannot hold office."

"Only convicted felons are barred from public service," Gus added. "However, if this gets out, I'll resign my position and leave Zarathustra to save the Colonial Government any embarrassment." Gus focused on the screen. "Leslie, would you mind prosecuting my abductors? Obviously, as the victim of the crime, I can't be directly involved in the legal proceedings."

"With your permission," Leslie Coombes replied.

"You have it, Leslie," Grego said. "Ben?"

"Works for me. Leslie, you've been doing a fine job in Gus's absence. No point in rocking the boat." Ben had a thought. "Hey, is that where the shrapnel in your liver came from?"

"That? Naw, I was in a courtroom on Odin when somebody set off a bomb. We never learned who or why, but the suspicion was that somebody was out to get the judge. They pulled so much metal out of me the doc called it iron mining. No wonder he missed such a small piece. I was off-planet a month later or he might have found it on a follow-up visit."

The six men spoke for a while bringing Gus up-to-date on what he had missed, then Jack asked to speak with him privately. Grego graciously vacated his office while Coombes, Rainsford and Fane screened-off.

"Gus, I've been challenged to a duel," Jack said without preamble. Gus smiled and asked who the future corpse was. "My son."

"What?"

Jack explained about John Morgan challenging him and why.

"Mugawd, Jack! I didn't even know you had any children. Why did you sign the permit?"

"Freyan tradition," Jack explained. "Frankly, I didn't know I was a father, but I have to face him or he'll never have any standing in Freyan society. Besides, I have it coming. I should have gone back to Freya and seen for myself whether he was alive or dead."

"Freyan standing, hell! One of you won't be standing at all after the duel. "Who's your second?"

"You."

"Ahh. With me missing you bought some time. Sorry I got found so fast...."

"Don't talk like a fool, Gus! You were my only choice, regardless. Ben can't be involved in something like this as Colonial Governor. I doubt that Harry Steefer would allow Victor to get involved, even if it wasn't a conflict of interest. Gerd has to watch things back on the Rez while I'm gone and none of my friends in law enforcement can be involved. And besides, I've known you the longest of anybody on this planet."

"Fair enough." Gus nodded thoughtfully. "Are you going to kill him?"

"I don't know if that will even be possible. I saw how he handled my 12.7. I hear the kid is good with a pistol, too. I guess we'll find out tomorrow after I bring your kids and dogs back over. But before then there's a few things we need to do."

*   *   *   *   *   *   *   *

Like most services on Zarathustra, satellite control was run mostly by the Charterless Zarathustra Company, save for the military satellites operated by the Terran Federation Naval base on Xerxes. Communications, broadcast entertainment, non-military police surveillance and planetary security all filtered through the command center in Science Division.

Several hours earlier, Jason Cosby had noticed a sizable release of energy in the far northeast of Beta Continent. Lacking in imagination, Cosby simply noted the event and wrote a report, which eventually found its way to Sub-Division Chief M'Bato san Giacomo. Giacomo saw the report and immediately contacted Xerxes Base.

"No, Mr. Giacomo, we haven't had any mishaps with explosive ordnance," Yeoman Perry replied. "We would have contacted the colonial government if we had. Could you give me the coordinates, please?"

Giacomo did so.

"That's at the far northeast edge of the Fuzzy Reservation." The Yeoman spoke to somebody off-screen then returned. "We have a satellite scanning the area. It looks like a baby-nuke or an M/E converter exploded. I suggest you speak with your superiors at Science Division while we contact the colonial governor. Could be something serious. Thanks for the heads-up."

The screen went dark. Giacomo put in a call to Juan Jimenez. He had a feeling there was going to be hell to pay for somebody.

*   *   *   *   *   *   *   *   *

"As the Native Affairs Commissioner, this falls into your court, Jack."

Jack Holloway swore up a blue streak at the viewscreen. "That's what Little Fuzzy, Allan and Natty were trying to tell me about. This damn fool dueling business is distracting me from my job. I'll have to send Gerd out, Ben. I'm already on my way over to Alpha with Allan and Natty. George Lunt and his gang should be able to handle everything, anyway. That's what a native protection force is for."

"I would have thought you'd be more concerned, Jack."

"I am, but I have to let my people do their jobs. I suspect it was illegal prospectors or more Fuzzy slavers. If I had paid better attention to Little Fuzzy, I would have already been out there. Either way the explosion likely killed whomever was fooling around up there. I'll just have to hope no Fuzzies were hurt in the process. When I came across those slavers the other day I was ready to kill the lot of them. I might have if John Morgan hadn't taken my gun when I wasn't looking. That's no way for me to do my job. So, I'll let other people do theirs and try to keep my perspective. I do have a few other things on my mind, just now."

The duel, Rainsford thought. "You're going through with it?"

"I have to. And I don't want you interfering, either. As Morgan sees it, he has good cause to want me dead."

"As he sees it," Rainsford repeated. "Does he, in fact?"

Jack grew silent and broke the connection.

* * * * * * * *

"Why can't you just talk to him?" Akira pleaded. "Maybe it's not what you think."

Morgan said nothing. All the way from Beta he had been silent while she tried to convince him not to go through with the duel. When Chief Steefer announced that Gus Brannhard had been found, alive and well, Morgan had just nodded. After docking at Company House, Morgan went to his quarters, barely aware that Akira followed him. Without a word he stepped into the bathroom.

Akira could hear the shower running as she sat in an overstuffed chair. She looked around the tastefully decorated room until her eyes settled on a file folder sitting on a desk. She went over to the desk and quickly flipped through the folder. There were numerous hand-written notes in a language she didn't recognize. She decided it had to be Sosti, the Freyan language. There were also typed pages and photos of some aliens she wasn't familiar with. One of the pages was a document relating the effects of radiation on Ullerians and possible treatments to restore fertility. The document went into detail about treatments, fertility drugs and even attempts at cloning. All with little or no success.

There were more reports on Terran animals suffering from similar reproductive failings. The conclusions were much the same; exposure to excessive background radiation damaged the DNA.

Akira heard the shower cut off. She quickly restored the papers to the folder and returned to the over-stuffed chair. John Morgan stepped out wearing a towel around his waist and using another to dry his hair. It would seem that Freyans had yet to embrace the hot-air drying system popular with Terrans. She noticed a large bruise on his chest near his right arm.

"John, please talk to me."

"I can't, Akira. Not about the duel."

"Do you have to kill him? Isn't there another way?"

Morgan looked down and into her eyes. After a few moments he explained that once the challenge is given, it must be followed through. By facing his father he would gain proper recognition in Freyan society, but to make the challenge and flee would leave him forever a pariah, or even worse, a coward.

"But do you have to kill him?" Akira repeated. "Many duels are settled by 'first blood.' You could just wound Jack…"

"Damnation, woman! Were you a Freyan we wouldn't even be having this conversation. Fine! Yes, it is true, that first blood would satisfy Freyan honor, but it could also get me killed. I know all about Jack Holloway and his reputation on this planet. From the moment I suspected him, I dug into every piece of information I could find. Victor was only too ready to tell me about how Holloway beat Leonard Kellogg half-to-death, then spun and shot Kurt Borch *all the way dead*. I can't hold back in the hopes that he won't kill me. If by some miracle we both survive, then I'll be happy to discuss things with him in a more civil matter. But the duel must come first. It is the Freyan way."

"You already knew he was your father before you went out to Beta, didn't you?"

"I suspected."

"Why?"

Morgan sighed. "I have been looking for him for fifteen years. All I could really go by, to be sure I had the right man, was his DNA. Names and faces can be changed easily, though he did still look a lot like his photograph. But his name caught my attention the second I saw his birth certificate on the company computer. It was too much of a coincidence not to be him."

"What? Why his name? Jack is a pretty common name…."

"It is also a nickname, I think that's the term, for 'John,' Akira. On his birth certificate he is named John Morgan Holloway. I was named for my father, though my uncle hid that from me. Morgan is actually my middle name. I have no last name until I face my father and claim his."

Akira didn't know what to say. She knew Jack Holloway only by reputation. But from everything she ever heard about him he seemed like a decent man. Even Victor Grego liked him and Holloway had played a big part in the Chartered Zarathustra Company losing its charter. She didn't want to see him killed. Moreover, she had strong feelings for John Morgan and didn't want to see him killed, either.

The viewscreen beeping interrupted her thoughts. It was a CZC operator. "Mr. Morgan? There is a call from a Mr. Holloway. Shall I patch him through?"

"Yes, please." The screen exploded in Technicolor fragments and reformed to show Jack Holloway's grim visage. "Mr. Holloway. How may I be of service?"

"Mr. Morgan, as per our agreement, my second is now available and I am prepared to settle our business. Will tomorrow at noon be satisfactory?"

He nodded.

"Then tomorrow it is. I choose the place to be the Goldilocks Memorial Park. The weapon of my choice is the Baldurtec 8mm revolver."

"I would have expected you to choose something heavier, Mr. Holloway."

"The Baldurs are lethal enough to satisfy the Freyan rules, and won't make as much of a mess to clean-up afterwards. Besides, either one of us is good enough that it won't matter."

"Very true, Mr. Holloway. Tomorrow at noon, then." Morgan cut the connection.

"You may die, tomorrow," Akira said in a soft whisper.

"Or I may finally live."

Akira thought for a moment about how she felt towards John Morgan. She knew she loved him, and that he might die facing Jack Holloway. There was something she wanted to do and this might be her last opportunity.

"I did a little research on Freya. One of your traditions is to, um, spend time with a woman the night before a duel or marching off to war. Well, John Morgan, tonight you are going to really live," Akira said, as her skirt and blouse fell to the floor.

XXV

Colonial Marshal Max Fane was not happy. This had been his normal state since the disappearance of Gus Brannhard, and the chief Prosecutor's return only slightly elevated his mood. While he was glad Brannhard was found alive and well, it was CZC security that did it. That, in and of itself, was a minor annoyance. The way he was found pretty much guaranteed only a CZC employee could find him.

Brannhard had somehow figured out he was inside of the CZC building, so, he dumped everything he could into the sanitary closet. The M/E converter performed its function transforming matter into energy. Energy that had to be diverted back to the company power plant where Peter Davis noticed the reversed power flow.

Damned clever of Brannhard. And it was a good catch by Davis, too.

What stuck in his craw was his inability to extract any information whatsoever from Brannhard's abductors. They both refused to so much as give their names. Not that it mattered. Fane had a doctor extract blood from each man and ran the DNA. The men were Anthony Nicholovich Anderson and Duncan Rippolone aka Ripper. They were suspected hit men from Terra, but with no convictions. Both were known to have worked for various crime families, but kidnapping was a bit out of their usual routine.

"Let me spell this out for you, Ripper," Fane said in his most reasonable voice. "We have eye witnesses to the abduction. You were captured with

Brannhard in your company. You can stay mute all you want. You both still get a bullet in the head after you are convicted. And believe me, the twelve lowest IQs on the planet can't help but convict you. Your only chance to stay alive is to cooperate. Tell me who sent you, and who set you up in that hideout. Then I'll be able to help you. Life in prison is a long time, but you'll be dead a whole lot longer."

Ripper stayed as silent as the grave. A cop walked in, handed Fane a piece of paper and walked out.

"Well, it looks like your friend is a bit more cooperative. He says that the Campanili crime family on Terra hired you both. Oh, look, it says here that Raul Laporte set you up with the hideout. Loyalty is a wonderful thing, don't you think?"

Rippolone stayed silent.

"That's right. You just sit still and stay quiet. We don't need your help anymore." Fane left the interrogation room and walked into the adjoining one. There, he met up with Leslie Coombes. Coombes had watched the questioning from behind a hidden window.

"Do you think he bought it?" Coombes inquired.

"Nah," Fane grunted. "He never even twitched. The globe didn't so much as flicker on the veridicator. This guy's a pro. He knows that Mr. Brannhard told us who he thinks set-up the grab. And on a world with so small a population, the list of suspects capable of acting as middleman for a job this big is damned short. That phony note didn't fool him for a second."

"Too bad. Getting Laporte would have been a nice bonus. I'm more worried about the Campanilis sending another team that won't bother grabbing Gus. They'll just shoot him and catch the next ship off-world."

"Well, that's at least a year away. We might be able to shake these mutts up before then." Fane watched Rippolone through the glass. "It's easy to act tough when somebody is only shooting questions at you. It's a different story when there is an actual gun pointed at your head."

Coombes nodded. "Keep them separated. If their lawyer wants to talk to them, he can talk to them one at a time. I don't want any collusion between them."

"You got it, Mr. Coombes."

*　*　*　*　*　*　*　*　*

Deputy Commissioner of Native Affairs Gerd van Riebeek, Major George Lunt and a squad of police waited patiently while the science team scanned the area for radiation. After several tense minutes Juan Jimenez, wearing a white radiation suit with a CZC logo on the chest and back, approached and removed his protective headgear.

"All clear, Gerd," Juan Jimenez said. "Looks like an M/E converter ruptured. If I were to hazard a guess, I would say they overloaded it… whoever they were."

"No baby nuke, then," Gerd said. "That's a relief, but what were these vaporized idiots doing out here in the first place?"

"Mining would be my guess," George Lunt observed. "That hole doesn't look like any blast crater I ever saw."

"Good guess, George." Juan pointed at one of his crewmen. "Francoise West over there figures the blast went straight up. There was a relatively minor shockwave at ground level, but the bulk of the force went up like a Roman Candle."

"Minor?" George pointed at a tree near the ridge. "That tree is a pile of toothpicks."

"From about six feet on up," agreed Juan, "but a man crouching behind it would have had a good chance of surviving."

"Did you see any evidence of Fuzzies being killed?" Gerd said.

"I'm not sure that's even possible, this close to the blast. But there are no signs of metal cages." Jimenez, like most people who watched the news, had heard about the Fuzzy slavers.

"Those idiots that Jack and that Morgan fella caught claimed they were the only team live-trapping Fuzzies on the Rez," George said. "The veridicator backed them up."

"Okay. Illegal sunstone or gold or whatever miners, then." Gerd looked at the hole and the metal scrap. "This had to be a pretty big operation. How did they stay hidden?"

"Military grade fibroid weave would be my guess," George Lunt said. "We use it on stake-outs in the bush when we suspect poachers or prospectors are trespassing on the reservation. It blocks almost everything except loud noises up close. Plus, this is a pretty isolated area. Very little chance of somebody tripping over them out here."

Jimenez's radio beeped. "Yes?"

"Mr. Jimenez, you need to see this," said the voice from the radio. "I think you'd better bring your friends, too."

Juan, Gerd, George and the rest all hustled over to the dig site. There, a man in a radiation suit, though bare-headed, pointed down into the hole with a high-powered flashlight. Something metallic glinted in the light.

"I'm running a tachyon scanner to get an idea of what that is," the man said. "Whatever it is, it's big and artificial."

"How can you tell, Rolf?"

"Raw ore doesn't shine like that, Mr. Jimenez. Or have a smooth shape like that. That is some sort of refined metal, probably an alloy. And before you ask, no, these dead miners didn't bury it. I think they exposed it. The dig pattern and surrounding terrain are undisturbed…well, except for the shockwave damage from the explosion, but everything below ground level was protected from the blast. There is also a lack of dirt and debris that had to have been removed from the hole. I think all that must have gone into the M/E converter and caused the overload."

"Whatever it is, we'll have to dig it up," Jimenez said. "I'll authorize a company excavation team from Science Division to do the heavy lifting on this one."

"Are you sure Mr. Grego will go for that?" Gerd asked.

"Well, I'm responsible for Science Division expenditures, so I don't need Victor's approval, but this might be a major scientific discovery. I'm sure he'll agree that it's better we find it than somebody else, especially after last time."

"Last time?" Rolf asked.

"The Fuzzies," Gerd explained.

Rolf laughed. "Yeah, Mr. Grego would definitely rather be in front of a new discovery than learn about it after the fact."

* * * * * * * * *

In accordance with Colonial and Federation regulations, the park was cordoned off and only the seconds and witnesses and those directly involved in the duel were allowed in. Gus Brannhard and Mark Szymanski signed the dueling papers as the seconds, followed by Larry Wolvin and Peter Davis as witnesses. A professional referee was retained to oversee the duel. Among the other witnesses were Chief Harry Steefer, Pancho Ybarra, Colonial Marshal Max Fane and Akira O'Barre. Peter Davis was asked to attend by Gus Brannhard as he knew neither of the dueling parties personally and could be completely impartial. There was also an ambulance in attendance as required by colonial law. The Fuzzies were told to stand behind the police tape, but they had to be watched carefully. They knew that Pappy Jack was in some sort of trouble and wanted to help.

With the papers signed by the seconds and attending witnesses, Frank Marshal, the referee, met with the duelists and seconds to discuss the rules. "Gentlemen, as I understand it, this duel is a matter of Freyan honor and tradition. Is this correct?"

Everybody nodded in the affirmative.

"As such, are we to go by Freyan rules of conduct?"

Gus discussed the matter with Jack, then both men agreed. Morgan and Szymanski simply nodded.

"Very well. In accordance with Freyan tradition, the duelists will face each other at a distance of twenty meters. The guns will remain holstered until I fire my starter gun. At that time both men are to draw and shoot a single round. In the event that neither party sustains injury, you will both be asked if you wish to continue. Freyan tradition allows that honor is settled if both men have fired once and agree not to continue. If you choose to continue, then guns will again be holstered until I fire the starter gun a second time. We will repeat this procedure until either one of you chooses to withdraw, or one of you is no longer able to continue.

"In the event one or both of you are injured, will you both agree that honor is satisfied and withdraw from the field?"

Both parties discussed this and finally agreed. First blood would be acceptable.

"Very good, sirs. Now, understand that anybody firing a second shot during any round will be disqualified and removed from the field. As it violates Terran Federation law and Freyan rules of conduct the transgressor can be charged with a felony. I could prevent this by removing all but one bullet from each of your guns and piecing them out one at a time per round. I will not do so as I have it on good authority that you are both men of honor and good character. Additionally, any man firing before I discharge my starter gun can be charged with homicide, or attempted homicide, depending on the accuracy of the shot. In this event the opposing second is within the law to fire upon the transgressor. Is this understood?"

Both parties nodded in the affirmative.

"Very well." Frank Marshal produced and opened a black box containing two pistols. "The challenged party will choose his weapon first, then the challenger will take the remaining pistol."

Jack selected the pistol closest to him. Morgan took the second weapon without comment.

"The seconds will now inspect the weapons and, if they so choose, fire a test round into the ground."

Gus and Mark accepted the pistols, fired a round into the ground, reloaded the weapons and returned them to their primaries who then holstered them.

"The seconds will now escort the primaries to their positions."

Gus walked with Jack to the white box chalked onto the grass. "Jack, I know this is supposed to be your son, but you can't hold back. It's either him or you. Don't let it be you."

Jack took a deep breath and let it out slowly. "I know, Gus. Don't worry. I plan on being around for a while longer. I have a family to take care of, you know." Jack nodded to the mob of Fuzzies behind the police tape.

"Damn straight," the Colonial Prosecutor agreed. "Why did you choose the Baldurs? You normally use a much heavier sidearm."

"Yeah, but I'm experienced with lighter pistols, too. You ever see that cannon John Morgan lugs around?"

"Heard about it. 0.457, right?"

Jack nodded. "I figured the lighter gun might throw his aim off a bit. Besides, I imagine either one of us can take an 8mm round and survive, provided the other guy doesn't get lucky."

"You're planning on winging him." It was a statement, not a question. "That's real risky. Hell, why not just fire a round into the air?"

Jack chuckled. "Facing him at all is risky. Firing into the air is against Freyan rules. The thinking is that if you didn't want to shoot the guy, you shouldn't be in a duel in the first place. Winging is the best I can hope for. He's my son, Gus."

"Let's hope he feels the same way."

Jack pulled two envelopes out of his shirt. The referee saw this and started to protest until he saw what it was and stayed silent. Duelists often gave important documents to their seconds; like a last will and testament. "Give this letter to John after…well, just after. The other letter is for you; my power of attorney and living trust with instructions of what to do in the event I can't speak for myself. I tried to cover every eventuality."

Gus accepted the letters and stuffed them in a pocket. "You get yourself killed out here and I'll kick your cold dead ass myself, damn-it."

"Duly noted. I'll try to save you the trouble."

At the opposite position Mark was giving Morgan a pep talk. Morgan had selected Mark to be his second because of his background of working on Freya and his understanding of the culture. "I've heard how good you are from Akira. Don't let it make you cocky. Holloway has killed more men than cancer from what I've heard."

"Didn't Terra cure cancer?"

"Yeah, about three hundred years ago. It still killed a helluva lot of people before then. Don't let his age fool you, either. He spent a lot of time in hyperspace jumping from planet-to-planet. He might actually be ten years younger than his birth certificate suggests. And Terrans don't age the way Freyans do. Medical science keeps us healthy long after our natural expiration date."

"Freyans enjoy those same benefits since we joined the Federation, you know."

"Are we going to talk about the man who could kill you or history? Now, remember that the last man he killed, a Kurt Borch, I think, had a gun pointed at the broad of his back and Holloway still put three in his chest before Borch fired a single shot. Do not underestimate him. It could be very hazardous to your health."

"Don't worry, Mark. I plan on making it at least to his age."

"You sure picked a strange way to go about it, John. May the gods be with you."

The seconds withdrew and the duelists faced each other. Behind each man was erected a temporary wall designed to catch and hold any bullet that failed to hit its target. This was for the protection of the general public. It also removed any distractions that might enter into the background during the fight.

Frank Marshal called for silence then addressed the duelists. "In accordance with Federation Law and Freyan tradition I ask one last time if both parties wish to continue or withdraw in favor of an alternate solution to your disagreement."

Both parties agreed to continue.

"Very well. When I have fired my pistol, both parties may draw and fire. I wish you both luck."

Unlike the dueling weapons, Frank Marshal's starter pistol was loaded with blank rounds. This was for two reasons: so that he could not aid one of the duelists with an 'accidental' discharge, and to allow him to fire into the air without fear of hitting a bystander with a falling round. Marshal raised his pistol into the air, mentally counted to three, then fired.

When asked about the duel later, the witnesses would swear that the guns almost magically appeared in Holloway and Morgan's hands. They would also swear that the two men fired simultaneously.

The only thing they would be unable to agree on was who fell first.

XXVI

"Yeah, I'm waiting for word on how it turned out, Gerd. As Colonial Governor I'm not allowed to be around duels or shooting in general, according to Max."

"My money is on Jack, Ben," Gerd said from the viewscreen. "Back to this suspicious dig, I was wondering if you could ask the TFN if they would like to poke around and maybe provide some extra security. We haven't rounded-up all the search volunteers and the police are still spread pretty thin."

"Sure thing. I'll call Pancho Ybarra and see what he can do. I'll have to wait until he gets back from the duel, though. Hopefully, he'll bring good news."

*   *   *   *   *   *   *   *   *

John Morgan awoke in the hospital amid the smells of disinfectant and the soft beeping of the medical monitor above his head and a sharp pain in his shoulder. The last thing he remembered was being hit by Jack's bullet. He had gone down bleeding heavily. Morgan assumed that he had passed out either from blood loss or shock.

Morgan was also more than a little surprised that he was still alive. Jack Holloway didn't usually leave his targets breathing from what he had heard. He thought harder and vaguely remembered that Jack also fell to the ground.

Did I kill him, or is he in another room here at the hospital? Federation medicine could repair almost anything short of a direct hit to the heart or brain.

A nurse walked in and saw he was awake. "How are we feeling, Mr. Morgan?"

Morgan grimaced at the plurality of the question. A Freyan would have simply asked how *he* was. "I can't speak for you, but my shoulder feels like somebody shot me."

The nurse laughed. "Indeed, and with impressive accuracy. The bullet hit you right in the middle of a rather large bruise. It looked like you were hit with a hammer, then shot. The doctor was amazed you could even raise that arm with all of the swelling you had, there."

"Yes, well, a 12.7 Martian Express hammer, in fact," Morgan replied. "It wasn't quite that bad, but I do think it may have slowed my draw or messed up my aim a bit."

"You'll have to leave that kind of thing alone for a while, Mr. Morgan. The surgical team repaired the damage, but you'll need time to heal before you go around shooting anything, especially something as heavy as a twelve-seven." She checked the readout over Morgan's bed and nodded in satisfaction. "Are you feeling up to some visitors?"

"I guess so." Morgan shrugged and instantly regretted it as pain shot down his arm and side. The nurse walked out and Akira O'Barre practically flew in, almost falling onto the bed with him. Morgan reflexively caught her with his good arm, though his hand landed on a surprising location on the young woman's chest.

"Hey!" Akira recovered her balance and Morgan's hand fell away. "None of that until you recover. Maybe not even then. I should slap you for taking a chance like that."

"I...didn't mean...it just...you fell, and I..."

"Not that, you Freyan idiot," Akira said. John Morgan was a very intelligent and capable man, but in some ways he was so much like a little boy. "Dueling with Jack Holloway. I'll bet you're the only person he ever shot that's still breathing. Don't you dare take another chance like that."

"Yes, Akira." Morgan nodded, then winced as more pain shot through his shoulder. "I don't have any other affairs of honor to settle, so I think I'll be able to avoid dueling for a while. Provided nobody insults my lady, of course."

Tears welled up in Akira's eyes. "I can take care of myself, John. Terran women aren't all helpless little flowers like the women on Freya…"

Morgan laughed, then grunted in pain. "I can see you never met a Freyan woman. How long have I been here?"

"Just since yesterday." Akira explained about the surgery and sedation afterwards. In all, Morgan was unconscious for about sixteen hours.

The nurse returned. "Miss O'Barre, I am afraid you will have to go, now. Mr. Morgan's readings suggest that you are over-exciting him."

"You bet she does," Morgan said with a wink. "We'll talk later, Akira."

"You better believe it, Bubba!" Akira gave him a soft kiss then walked out of the room. Morgan noticed that she gave an extra wiggle as she left.

"I know a taxi driver that calls people 'Bubba'," mused the nurse. She again checked the readings over the bed. "If you can behave yourself, I'll let another visitor in. Normally I wouldn't do this, but he claims that it is extremely urgent."

Morgan nodded then winced as he received a shock of pain. I have *got* to stop doing that, he thought. He received another shock, of a different kind, when his next visitor was shown in. It was the recently recovered Gus Brannhard.

"Thank-you, nurse," Gus said. "Say, was that Darla Cross in the room across the hall? Is she getting more face work done, or something sucked out?"

"I can't comment on other patients, Mr. Brannhard," the nurse said, as she rushed out of the room. Gus noticed she went straight to Ms. Cross' room.

Gus turned his attention to John Morgan. "I think she'll be gone for a while, so we can talk privately. I have a letter for you from Jack. He told me to deliver it after the duel if he was indisposed."

Morgan thought a moment then said, "Is he dead?" There was a surprising amount of emotion in his voice. He had grown to like the old man.

Gus picked up a chair and set it down by the bed and took a seat. "No. Not yet, anyway. Your bullet ricocheted off a rib and nicked his heart and collapsed one of his lungs. It barely missed hitting a vertebra as it exited. He lost a great deal of blood on the way to the ambulance, and they had a lot of trouble stabilizing him. Fortunately, they had plenty of synth-plasma and a blood oxygenator on board. They patched the lung and re-inflated it, and the heart is repaired enough that it will last until it can be replaced. Right now he's in a coma. There's talk of growing him a new heart and lung versus a mechanical replacement, or just doing a more permanent repair on the existing organs when he's stronger."

"Growing the heart and lung…That can take about three months, I believe."

"That is what I thought, too," Gus said. "My new liver took that long. But a heart is simply a muscle and easier to grow, or so the doctors tell me, and can be replaced in about a week. The lung is a little more complicated and will take six to eight weeks. Fortunately, Jack can get by with just one in the meanwhile if the patch job doesn't hold. Assuming he makes it."

"Assuming? Federation medicine can work miracles…."

"Jack isn't a young man, anymore, and this isn't the first time he's taken a bullet. Not by a long shot. At one time or another he's been shot, stabbed, beaten, poisoned, starved and, one time, nearly drowned in freezing water. There's a lot of scar tissue he never had removed or repaired all over his body. Half of his teeth had to be regrown after six men ambushed him on Freya. That's right, Freya!

"And that stupid Freyan rule of not giving a duelist medical aid until he is removed from the dueling field cost him a lot more blood than he could afford to lose. That means possible brain damage, and there's damned little Federation medicine can do about that. We can't grow and replace his mind, damn-it!"

Gus took a moment to regain his composure. "I have instructions to terminate medical treatment if his brain is irreparably damaged. Jack has no desire to spend his last days with the mental capacity of an Yggdrasil Khooghra. Or worse." Gus extracted the letter from his shirt. He started to hand it over then remembered that Morgan's right arm was immobilized. "I'll open it for you. I haven't read it and I'll leave if you want privacy."

"No. As his second you act in his place while he is incapacitated. Please, stay while I read this."

Gus agreed and extracted several papers; an old parchment, three documents, several papers and a microdisc from the envelope.

The first document was a Freyan birth certificate for Donareus Honirdite. Gus could see the confusion on Morgan's face as he reviewed the certificate. The second and third documents were death certificates for Donareus and Adonitia Honirdite. Morgan's confusion quickly turned to anger. He snatched up the parchment, quickly read it and swore blasphemously in Freyan and Sheshan.

"It was all a lie, damn-it!" Morgan fought to keep the tears from his eyes. "I shot my father for nothing. Nothing! All because of my uncle."

Gus was surprised at the outburst and unsure what to say. "What do you mean?"

Morgan held up the certificates. "This birth certificate isn't mine. It's my cousin's. He was born a week after I was. Stillborn. He would have been my uncle's only progeny had he lived, his only heir. These death certificates are my cousin's and my mother's. This letter," Morgan held up the parchment, "is from my uncle explaining how both my mother and I died in childbirth. Jack didn't abandon us, he was told we were dead!"

Gus digested that, then asked, "Wait, why do you have Jack's name? Wouldn't your uncle have changed that?"

"He couldn't. My mother named me before she died. Before I was born, really. This was recorded by the midwives and physician. To change my name he would have had to face my father and either get him to sign away his rights or beat him in a duel. Orphtheor was no duelist. Instead, he raised me to believe Jack had abandoned my mother and me."

"I don't want to stir the pot, but how do you know that letter is legitimate?"

"This is my uncle's stationary. The writing is in Sosti, the Freyan language, and I can recognize Orphtheor's handwriting. I won't say I couldn't be fooled by a clever forgery, but there would be no point in it after the duel. Honor is satisfied, I don't have to challenge him again."

Gus nodded. It all made sense. "Had you seen all this before the duel, would you have gone through with it?"

Morgan took a deep breath and let it out slowly. "Had I seen all this before the duel, I would have thought them fakes. Besides, the challenge, once given, cannot be revoked. Freyan tradition, again."

"If you don't mind my saying so, you Freyans seem a little trigger happy."

"This from a representative of a race that turned half their planet into a radioactive wasteland," Morgan said with a smile. Gus laughed and agreed that Morgan had him on that one.

"Are you going to read Jack's letter?"

Morgan nodded and started reading. It was written in passable Sosti. Some of the tenses were off, and Jack confused a few of the nominatives, but the meaning was clear:

John Morgan,

I, John Morgan Holloway the Greater, also known as Jack Holloway, hereby recognize the son of Adonitia Honirdite, known as John Morgan, as my legitimate son and heir, with the right to bear the family name of Holloway, work the family lands, defend the family honor, and make war on those allied against the family.

John Morgan will be known as John Morgan Holloway the Lesser until such time as John Morgan Holloway the Greater is unable to fill his role as patriarch, at which time the Lesser will assume those responsibilities as the new Greater Holloway.

John, by now you have read the documents and the letter from Orphtheor Honirdite and know that I did not knowingly abandon you. Still, I find myself filled with shame that I did not return to Freya to see for myself what had become of you. For that I blame myself and no other. I knew that Orphtheor never approved of me. He had even black-balled me from getting a decent job while on Freya. You wouldn't believe how many oukrey stalls I mucked out to put food on the table. Your mother was pregnant, I knew that, but I was offered a job on Fenris working for the Hunter's Co-operative. The money was good and we would have been set for the next five-years when I got back.

I wanted to take her along, but she would have been alone on a strange planet while I was out on the seas. Have you ever been to Fenris? Damned nasty place for a Freyan woman used to the open air. We agreed she would be better off with her family while I was gone. I knew I could count on Orphtheor to take care of her, and bad talk me, while I was gone.

I had completed my one year commitment and was preparing to return to Freya when I received the letter from Orphtheor. In the letter he claimed that you and your mother died in childbirth and provided the certificates to prove it. I should have realized your mother would have named you after me, not some relic from the family tree. I should have gone back to Freya and seen for myself. Instead I bounced around Baldur, Loki and Fenris for the next five years. I met Pancho Ybarra, an ensign then, during one of my visits to Fenris. If you have any questions, he may be able to help.

Assuming I am not dead, I intend to pay a visit to Orphtheor on Freya *the first chance I get. I owe him a severe beating at the bare minimum.*

If you succeeded in killing me, do not mourn. I lived a longer and happier life than I expected to.

On the microdisc is a video recording of me in a veridicator verifying my story in this letter. I don't want there to be any question in your mind about what is true. If you have to be mad at me, be mad for the right reasons.

Your father,

Jack Holloway

P.S. I hope my Sosti wasn't too bad.

Morgan set the letter down. "I have to admit that I didn't want to believe he would abandon me or my mother," Morgan said. "But I was raised on Uncle Orphtheor's stories about him." He examined the microdisc then stuffed it back into the envelope in disgust. Jack Holloway had faced him with honor. On Freya, the word of such a man was beyond reproach. No fancy Terran machine was needed to support his word.

"I think Jack will want a word or six with your uncle when he recovers," Gus mused.

"No need. He left this plane of existence thirteen years ago. Freyan years, that is. He left everything to me as he had no heirs of his own."

Gus grunted then shook his head. "Title and everything? And he put you through school, I imagine. Well, the lies aside, I think he did a fair job of raising you."

"Were he still alive I would shoot him myself," Morgan snarled. Gus couldn't help but notice how much he looked like Jack at that moment. "Gus, would you do me a favor? Call Jack's doctor in here. I'm going to make it very clear how badly I want my father to pull through. And since you currently have his power of attorney, we're going to fix those other little things he'd been neglecting, too. As soon as he is strong enough, of course."

"Jack's coverage is good, but I don't think all of his pre-existing—"

"I have it covered," said Morgan. "After we speak with the doctors, I want to go see him."

XXVII

The leader awoke to the sound of birds warbling in the trees. He tried to open his eyes but couldn't; they were swollen shut. He tried to move but found he was bound from head to toe.

Where the hell am I? I was outside the camp, saw some Fuzzies, then boom! The Fuzzies! They must have found me and tied me up. They blame me for the one that got killed. Well, why shouldn't they? It is my fault. So why am I still alive?

He struggled a bit and some of the bindings fell away. It was only grass, not ropes or vines as he thought at first. Didn't the Fuzzies wrap their dead in grass then bury them under stone Cairns? Maybe the Fuzzies thought he was dead and rated a funeral. But then, where were the stones for his funeral Cairn?

"Yeek!"

The leader could not understand the yeeking he heard, but suspected a Fuzzy just announced that he was awake. He could hear the sound of several Fuzzies scampering over to investigate over the ringing in his ears. He freed an arm and searched his pocket. The hypersonic hearing aid was still there. The leader fumbled it into his ear amid more excited yeeking.

"*Bal-f'ke! Kannii! Ashkii-Koo-wen dohla!*"

Now he could hear what the Fuzzies were saying, if not actually understand them. He tried to concentrate and remember what little he knew of the Fuzzy language. "Me…Joe Quigley," he croaked out. *How long was I unconscious?* "Me…ola." *Ola is friend, right? Ghu, I hope I didn't just tell them I'm a harpy or something.*

* * * * * * * * *

"There are new *Koo-wen* at the thunder noise place," Climber said. "Give this *Koo-wen* to them."

"Big Ones made Sun Fur dead," Tells-things argued. "Maybe make us dead."

"Kill the bad Big One," Stonebreaker yelled.

"No!" Red Fur glared at the tribe. "People do not kill people without cause. People make friends. We sometimes fight, but we always try to make friends. Not know if this *Koo-wen* killed Sun Fur."

"You say we make Big Ones dead, now you say we not make *Koo-wen* dead," Silver Fur said.

"Many *Koo-wen* made dead when the thunder noise thing happened," Red Fur countered. "Only one not dead. We help him…"

"Him?" Makes-things asked. The strange not-fur covering of the *Koo-wen* made it difficult to identify their gender.

"Him," Healer said.

"What do we feed this Big One?"

"The strange food they left with Sun Fur's body." Some of the *Jin-f'ke* grumbled about that. "We help him and learn from him," Red Fur continued. "*Koo-wen* are a new thing. We must know if they are bad for us or good for us."

"Bad," Stonebreaker said.

"Then we must learn how bad," Red Fur said. "We watch the hurt one. We watch the others at the big thunder noise place. See what they do."

"And if they make bad things for *Jin-f'ke*?"

"Then we find more people," declared Red Fur. "We gather together and become ready to make the bad Big Ones dead."

* * * * * * * * *

"Mr. Morgan, this is extremely irregular," Doctor Drogan argued. "Mr. Holloway is in a deep coma. You can't go barging into his room."

From his contragravity chair, Morgan glared up at the doctor. "Jack Holloway is my father. I will not be barred from seeing him, especially if this could be the last time I see him alive. If I have to, I'll buy this damn hospital, fire you, then see him anyway."

Gus whispered something in Morgan's ear. "Really?"

Gus nodded. "As it turns out, this hospital is owned and run by the Charterless Zarathustra Company, of which I am a major stockholder. That means I already own this hospital, more or less. Now step aside."

Flustered, Dr. Drogan stepped out of the doorway and allowed Morgan and Gus to pass, then followed them in. It was a small private room crowded to overflowing with Fuzzies. Jack's entire family was there; Little Fuzzy, Mama Fuzzy, Baby Fuzzy, Mike, Mitzi, Koko and Cinderella. Gus's Fuzzies, Allan Quatermain and Natty Bumppo and Victor Grego's Fuzzy Diamond accompanied them.

Morgan turned to Dr. Drogan and demanded why the Fuzzies were allowed in when he was denied access.

"Mr. Grego insisted. However, I made sure each and every one of these Fuzzies were bathed and checked for parasites and pathogens before I allowed them in. I even had their chopper-diggers disinfected."

Morgan glanced at Gus who nodded.

"Very good, doctor." Morgan steered his chair to the left of the bed where he wouldn't accidently run afoul of any medical equipment.

The Fuzzies, who had seemed oblivious to everything but Jack, became aware of the newcomers. After a moment, Little Fuzzy screamed something in his hypersonic voice, jumped up and leaped over the bed, chopper-digger swinging wildly. It was a jump any human athlete would have applauded.

Morgan tried to catch the Fuzzy with both hands forgetting that the right was immobilized. Despite the pain the act caused him, he still managed to catch his attacker's weapon before it connected with his throat.

By this time the rest of the Fuzzies realized that Morgan was the man who had hurt Pappy Jack and scrambled to collect their weapons.

Dr. Drogan slapped the security button then joined Gus in trying to corral the furious Fuzzies.

Morgan's good arm was occupied with Little Fuzzy while he fought to use the right hand to adjust the elevation of his chair. The restraints on the arm made it difficult to move his fingers, but he managed to work the contra-gravity controls and raise himself to the ceiling, bumping his head in the process. The sudden jarring caused another surge of agony through the shoulder and down the arm.

With one arm and his weapon held by Morgan, Little Fuzzy punched and kicked any target he could reach. He launched a particularly vicious kick into Morgan's injured shoulder. Morgan screamed in pain and dropped Little Fuzzy. Gus barely managed to catch him before he fell onto the unconscious Jack.

"That is enough!" Dr. Drogan roared. The Fuzzies and humans alike froze in place. "This is a hospital room, not a war zone. Fuzzies there," Drogan pointed to one side of the room, then pointed to the other, "and humans there. Move it!"

The Fuzzies filed over to the far side of the room and glared at Morgan. Morgan floated near the ceiling unconscious. The pain from Little Fuzzy's kick to his shoulder had caused him to pass out. Gus, being the tallest, had to reach up and fumble with the chair controls until it lowered back to floor level. Dr. Drogan examined Morgan's head for signs of a concussion, then tapped a few buttons on the back of the chair to revive him.

"You hurt Pappy Jack!" Little Fuzzy cried. "Go 'way!"

Through the haze of pain, painkillers and stimulants Morgan fought to remember what he'd learned of the Fuzzy language and explained himself as best he could.

Dr. Drogan, unable to follow what Morgan was saying, asked Gus to translate. "Morgan is saying that he is not here to kill Pappy Jack. He wants to talk and make friends."

Gus turned to the Fuzzies who were still yelling and yeeking at John Morgan. "People, be quiet! Let John Morgan make friends."

Slowly, the Fuzzies quieted down, though they kept their chopper-diggers at the ready. Jack's family took up protective positions around his bed while Natty and Allan stayed near Pappy Gus. Diamond, who had met John Morgan at Company House, was uncertain what to do. He had liked the new *Koo-wen*, but he liked Pappy Jack, too.

"I'm afraid Mr. Morgan will have to wait to make friends with, um, Pappy Jack," Dr. Drogan said. "Pappy Jack is in a coma. A deep sleep. Mr. Morgan can make friends when Mr. Holloway wakes up."

Drogan tactfully omitted the possibility that Jack might never regain consciousness.

"*Mo'gan* go 'way," Little Fuzzy repeated. "Big One not like *Fuzzies*. Big Ones say not-so things. I not trust *Mo'gan*."

Little Fuzzy had a point; Big Ones lie to each other all the time. Morgan slumped in his chair and started to leave, then had an inspiration.

"Gus, are you familiar with the Freyan Blood Oath? You were on Freya for a while. Surely you picked up some of the culture."

Gus stroked his beard for a moment. "Yes. Yes, I am. That's the one where two parties swear an oath, usually to defend something or enter into a binding contract. As I recall, to break such an oath means exile or death on Freya."

"Death. Exile is no longer considered sufficient punishment with a whole galaxy of planets to run to." Morgan turned to Dr. Drogan. "Doctor, is there anything in my system that would be harmful to a Fuzzy?"

"What? Well, no. The drugs I just pumped into you leave the

bloodstream and enter the soft tissues almost instantly. But why would… wait. Blood Oath? Are you going to…?"

"Yes. Gus, would you explain to Little Fuzzy what the Blood Oath is and what it entails? I suspect he won't take my word for it."

Gus nodded explained about the Oath and what they would have to do to make it binding. Little Fuzzy was a bit shocked. "Why you make oat'?"

"I will pledge my protection to Pappy Jack," Morgan explained. "That means I will not hurt Pappy Jack. If I do, then I make dead. Gus, as the witness, it falls to you to carry out my execution if I renege."

"Like I said before; you Freyans are way too trigger happy," Gus grunted. "Oh, Nifflheim, if it will keep the peace, I'm in."

"Doctor, we need a cup."

"Now see here, I will not just stand here and let you—"

"Doctor, you get to fix it when we are done. Would you rather we did this outside away from your ready care?"

Drogan grumbled and grabbed a coffee cup from the nurse's lounge, washed it, doused it with alcohol, washed it again and returned with it.

"Thank-you, doctor," Morgan said. "Little Fuzzy, as the *kin'sha* of your family, will you take the oath with me?"

Little Fuzzy didn't hesitate. "Hokay."

"May I use your chopper-digger, please?"

Little Fuzzy handed Morgan the weapon and watched with fascination as the Freyan carefully held the blade with his immobilized right hand and sliced open the palm of his left by dragging the hand over the blade. He then held the open wound over the cup let the blood flow into the receptical. After an ounce or two he pressed a cloth to the wound, which Dr. Drogan quickly wrapped, and held the weapon out for the Fuzzy to take. Drogan seized the chopper-digger before Little Fuzzy could take it.

"I can't stop this barbaric ritual, but I won't risk this Fuzzy getting an infection." Drogan quickly used an alcohol wipe on the blade then turned it over to Little Fuzzy.

Little Fuzzy duplicated Morgan's palm cut and held his own hand over the cup. After several drops joined with the Freyan's blood, Drogan quickly wrapped the wound.

Morgan held the cup between himself and Little Fuzzy and said, "I, John Morgan Holloway the Lesser, swear in the name of Min'tro, god of Truth, to act in defense of John Morgan Holloway the Greater, also known as Pappy Jack, that I will not do him further harm, and that I will make friends with him when he awakens."

Gus translated the oath into Fuzzy for clarification. He omitted the part about Min'tro as Fuzzies had no concept of gods or religion.

"What I do?" Little Fuzzy asked. Morgan explained in the simplest terms he could. "I, Li'l Fuzzy, accep' the vow of John Mo'gan Hollow-way the Less'r. Hokay?"

"Okay. Now we drink." Morgan drained half the contents of the cup, then turned it over to Little Fuzzy who drank the remainder. Dr. Drogan looked a little sick at the act, though Little Fuzzy had no problem with the ritual. It had only been two years since he had learned to cook his food, after all.

"Is that all? Good. Now let's disinfect and stitch up those cuts…" The swarm of security men that barged into the room interrupted Drogan. "*Now* you show up?"

XXVIII

Colonial Marshal Max Fane entered the Colonial Governor's office, saw he was speaking with somebody on the viewscreen, and waited quietly near the desk.

"…Yeah, Gerd thinks the military might want to be involved in whatever is buried out there," Ben Rainsford finished.

"I appreciate your bringing us in on this, Governor," Lieutenant Commander Ybarra's voice replied from the screen. "Any update on how Jack is doing?"

"Oh, hell, Pancho, call me Ben. Still in a coma, Pancho, but the docs are doing everything humanly possible. Oh, and I want to thank-you all again for sending that APC to transport Thaxter to and from Prison House…"

"Wait. What?" Ybarra spoke to somebody off-screen. "Ben, when was this?" Rainsford told him. "Sir, we had a communications snafu that day. No APC or personnel were dispatched to Prison House. Who did you speak to?"

"A Captain Bjork," Rainsford replied. "What seems to be…."

Pancho spoke with somebody out of camera shot of the vid, then said, "Ben, we don't have a Bjork on Zarathustra or Xerxes base, captain or otherwise." Ybarra barked a series of orders at somebody off-screen. "Ben, we've been hacked. I suggest you get your people to work on it there and we'll check our end. I'll be in touch as soon as I have something. Ybarra out." The screen went dark.

Rainsford turned and noticed Max Fane. "Max, you heard all that? What the Nifflheim is going on?"

"I have to admit it makes no sense to me," Fane said. "If somebody went to all the trouble of passing themselves off as military personnel, which is a hanging offence, by the way, why pick up Thaxter, let us question him, then take him back to prison?"

"Maybe we should ask him," Rainsford said, as he tapped in a combination for the viewscreen.

"Ask who? Thaxter?" Marshal Fane thought it over. *It makes sense to talk to the prisoner who had been schlepped back and forth by the imposters. Whoever it was, they didn't want him dead. Or did they? Who knows what had gone on in the back of the APC while he rode in front?* Fane realized he should have stayed with the prisoner. There would be hell to pay for that lapse, he knew.

"Warden Redford," the Governor said, as he clasped and shook his own hands by way of greeting.

"Governor. To what do I owe the pleasure?"

"I need you to do something for me…."

*   *   *   *   *   *   *   *   *

Leo Thaxter was ready to skip planet. He had his beard, dark glasses, off-world ticket, money and forged papers. All he needed was to get on the next shuttle and he was free. It was unfortunate that the ship out was headed to Gimli, but he could sit around in the spaceport there until the next ship came in. The only thing that bothered him was that he had to leave Rose behind. At least he managed to arrange to have her death sentence rescinded. She does her twenty and gets out without worrying about being tried on the faginy charge. Her husband, Conrad Evins, was on his own, of course. Well, Rose would understand.

Thaxter walked to the street corner and pressed the button for a taxi. The days of hailing a cab by whistling and waving were long past on any world where aircars were the norm, which was the vast majority of Federation planets. A cab came down and the door retracted into the frame. Thaxter tossed his two bags in then took a seat.

"Where to, Bubba?"

"Spaceport," Thaxter said tersely.

"Getting out of Dodge, eh?" The cab rose up into the air and spun in place a full 180 degrees before moving off. "Headed out for business or pleasure?"

"A little of both, I guess." *Why were taxi pilots always so chatty?*

"Good for you." The cabbie glanced into the mirror situated for looking at passengers, partly for sociability and partly to watch for trouble. "Say, haven't I seen you before? Let me think a sec…."

The mobster broke out in a cold sweat. If the cabbie recognized him, there was nothing Thaxter could do to stop him from just flying over to the police station. Taxis had been equipped with bulletproof partitions for centuries.

"Now I remember! I picked you up from the spaceport, what, nine months ago? Clancy, right? I remembered because you looked a lot like that Leo Thaxter guy that was all over the news a couple of years ago. Yeah, you had that pretty little wife and cute little girl with you. How are they doing?"

"Uh…fine." Thaxter breathed a mental sigh of relief. "Real good. The wife has a job working for the…CZC. I'm just going off-world to settle some business back on, uh…Gimli. No use dragging the girl out of school, y'know."

"Yeah. Kids don't take to hyperspace travel all that well," the cabbie said. "I remember when I first came over from Loki with my family. The kids were bored stupid…."

The cabbie regaled Thaxter with the story of his life on Zarathustra until they arrived at the spaceport. Thaxter was happy to let him ramble—it saved him from trying to make up any more stories about Clancy's family. At the spaceport Thaxter tipped the cabbie fifty sols. He wanted to make sure the pilot remembered 'the guy who looked like that Thaxter guy' and who left the planet.

Once inside, Thaxter quickly went to his rented locker, pressed his thumb to the pad next to the locking mechanism, and extracted the duffle with his money. He had over one million sols in cash plus a fistful of sunstones from Laporte plus the money from his stash. Laporte had been generous with the buyout of Thaxter's underground enterprises. It was worth it, though. Laporte was now positioned to take control of the entire Zarathustran underworld.

The loudspeakers announced that the shuttle for *The City of Port Sandor* was now boarding. Thaxter filed out with the other passengers. The steward accepted his ticket without comment and Thaxter went directly to his seat. Gimli was a two month space normal flight. Less than a week in hyperspace relative time. Just a few days then he would be safe. He considered staying to help Rose, but he didn't have the resources. Plus he would be in constant danger of being captured. He kept telling himself that his sister would be fine, that he had no choice. He had given up telling himself that an hour later when the ship entered hyperspace.

*   *   *   *   *   *   *   *   *

Colonial Governor Bennett Rainsford stared at his viewscreen with a mounting sense of dread. In calling the warden of Prison House his worse fears were realized.

"Clancy Slade? This was verified by the veridicator?"

"Yes, Governor," Warden Redford said on the viewscreen. "A group of men threatened his family if he didn't cooperate. They even forced him to have cosmetic surgery."

Ben Rainsford leaned back in his chair. "Great Ghu on a goat. The worst felon on the planet just escaped on my watch. Warden, we need to keep this quiet. Make sure your men keep this quiet, too. We have a better chance of catching Thaxter if he thinks we don't know he's on the loose."

"Will do, Governor. I should report this to Mr. Grego. Prison House is a CZC property—"

"I'll take care of that, Warden."

Redford nodded. "What do we do with Mr. Slade? Technically, he shouldn't be here."

Rainsford turned and looked at Max Fane, then back to the screen. "I'll send the Colonial Marshal over to collect him. Make it look like another prisoner transfer." Redford agreed with him and screened-off.

"Governor, that prisoner transfer was my responsibility. My letter of resignation will—"

"Will be refused, Max." Rainsford stood up and came around the desk. "I set up the transfer. That makes me as culpable as anyone. No. I plan on laying the blame squarely where it belongs; on the bastards that pulled the wool over our eyes. I want their asses nailed to that wall." Rainsford pointed at the west wall for dramatic effect. "Go collect this Clancy Slade and bring him right back here. First get your people looking for Thaxter… quietly. I…we don't need this getting into the newscasts. Once we have him, we can look for those Khooghras that got him out."

Fane scooted out as fast as his considerable bulk would allow him. Rainsford returned to his desk and punched out the combination for Grego's office. Victor Grego appeared on the screen with his toothy grin.

"Ben! Have you heard about the—"

Rainsford cut Grego off. "Victor, I have some bad news…"

* * * * * * * *

Raul Laporte was worried. It was a feeling he didn't like, to be sure, but it came with his career choice. One of his hidden cameras at the Last Chance Bar transmitted the image of CZC security and regular cops tearing the place apart. That meant either they were looking for the secret passage into Company House, or they already found it and were looking for other passages or evidence in general. Either way, the Last Chance Bar was blown as a front.

Laporte opened a panel in the wall behind him and pressed several buttons. *That will take care of the cameras.* The manager of the bar had no idea who he was working for and the title of the establishment was filed under the name of a former associate, now deceased. When the cops investigated they would find that the bar was registered in Ivan Bowlby's name, though the late entertainment mogul never knew it. A trick like that wouldn't have worked on most other planets, but the CZC deal with the colonial government meant no taxation, hence Bowlby never had to explain the property he never filed for.

Laporte hated losing his secret entrance into the CZC and the hideout it provided, but that was secondary to the fact that it also meant Anderson and Rippolone had to have been caught and arrested. No official announcement had been made to that effect, but there were rumors that someone who looked like Brannhard, though somewhat thinner, had acted as a second in the duel between Holloway and some rich off-worlder.

Brannhard didn't concern him, though the mobster wouldn't have minded had he stayed missing. The problem was Tony and Ripper. Could they be trusted to keep their mouths shut with a gun to their heads? So far, they had to either be dead, unconscious, keeping mum or the cops would already be swarming all over the place. Kidnapping in general was a capitol crime. Grabbing up a government official was a guaranteed bullet in the head, no discretion of the court about it. Their only out was a plea deal that served up somebody higher in the food chain, like Raul Laporte. As a facilitator to the abduction, he would be just as dead as the kidnappers.

Laporte considered his options. He had been handsomely paid by Dane for his help in getting Thaxter out of prison, in sunstones, no less, and Thaxter signed over all of his extra-legal concerns to Laporte in exchange for some money, papers and a safe hideout. Fortunately, he used a different safe house than the one Brannhard was being held in. Laporte finally had it all; Thaxter's business, minus the front operation that went to Dane, his own lucrative businesses, legal and not, plus he moved in on Bowlby's gambling, drugs and prostitution. He would have gone for Bowlby's studios and television business, but somebody beat him to the stock exchange. Only Spike Heenan was left and Laporte would quickly bring ol' Spike to heel and run the entire Zarathustran underworld.

Provided Tony and Ripper kept their mouths shut.

It was coming together. It was also one thread away from coming apart at the seams. One good tug by the prosecution and it all comes unraveled. Unless the thread was cut by the right tailor. Laporte smiled for a moment as he considered the metaphor. The problem in this case was finding the right set of scissors to do the job…if it wasn't already too late.

Or, he could sign everything over to Richard LaRue and quietly disappear. Laporte had always planned for that eventuality from the day he boarded the ship for Zarathustra. Laporte turned and regarded himself in the mirror. He couldn't help thinking that the years had been kinder to him than he deserved. Still, maybe it was time for Richard to take over.

XXIX

The heavy-duty contra-gravity lifters slowly rose up into the air gently pulling the load out of the earth. As soon as the load cleared the surface, the operator smoothly shifted location and lowered it onto the barge. Several men swarmed over it and secured the load with nylon straps.

"Damned if it doesn't look like an old style rocket ship," George Lunt observed. "Like the ones used to get to the moon back in the early days of interplanetary exploration."

"More like the ones initially used on the early Mars missions," Gerd said. "This one is a single unit, not multi-stage like the early Apollo crafts."

"Sure it isn't an unexploded missile?" Jimenez asked. "Like the planetbuster models used on rogue asteroids."

"I've sent Ahmed Khadra a photo image and he's running a comparison against all known spacecraft and ordnance back at the station," Lunt said. "So far there's no match."

"I sent the depth analysis back to Science Division. According to geology it was buried for somewhere between 50,000 and 85,000 years, give or take a millennia. Of course that assumes it didn't dig down on impact," Jimenez said.

"You don't sound like you buy the impact theory."

"Easy to see how you became a cop, Major." Jimenez extracted a metal shard from a box at his feet. "This is an alloy, to be sure, but not a very strong one, at least compared to poly-steel or collapsium. Any impact forceful enough to bury this…missile, for lack of a better word…would have destroyed it and spread it all over the countryside. I'll run some analysis when I get it back to Science Division, but for now I'll stake my reputation that this artifact is at least 50,000 years or more old." His radio beeped and he walked a few feet away to talk.

George whistled. "That would mean somebody was tooling around the galaxy when we were still pounding on each other with wooden clubs and stone axes."

"This is huge," Gerd said. "Too bad we don't have the pilots."

"Ah…actually, we might," Jimenez said. "Come this way."

Juan escorted the two men to the barge where three men in CZC fatigues were arranging some bones. The skulls looked more than a little familiar.

"Good God!" Gerd exclaimed. "Those are Fuzzy skulls."

George Lunt looked and rubbed his jaw absently. "Well, is that really strange? Fuzzies have been stomping around this area for oomphty-thousand years. What's so special about these?"

"Look how big they are," Gerd said. "Here, let me help with those bones…"

The men looked at Jimenez, who nodded slightly, and made room for the xenonaturalist. Gerd quickly and carefully separated the skeletons and arranged them on the tarp.

"There's a lot of pieces missing, and some of these bones appear to be from different skeletons. Notice the length of the femur, here, and the tibia and fibula below it. This femur is too long. No animal on any planet I have ever studied has a leg design like that. It would make them a very slow runner. From the teeth in the skull we can tell that this was an omnivore. The eye sockets are set forward and close enough together to create stereoscopic vision…useful for gauging the distance between itself and its prey. Hunting omnivores tend to be good runners or they starve."

Jimenez looked at the bones and nodded. "Yeah, the lower leg must have come from a smaller body…possibly a female. Look at the skulls. I'm not as up on Fuzzy physiology as you, Gerd, but these both look like males. Note the thicker brow ridge."

"Right. Fuzzies are a lot like Terrans in that respect."

George Lunt looked at the bones and mentally measured them. "No way are these Fuzzies. These bones belonged to something at least four feet tall. That's twice the size of any Fuzzy I ever saw, and in my job, brother, I see a lot of Fuzzies."

"Major Lunt makes a good point, Gerd." Jimenez looked closer at the skull. "I'll have to admit that it looks like a Fuzzy skull, though. Does the brain pan seem a little smaller, in proportion, compared to current Fuzzy physiology?"

"Yes, it does. Good eye, Juan. It could be another species of Fuzzy… call it Fuzzy Gigantus or something like that…on Terra there was a super-ape, for lack of a better term, that stood around ten to twelve feet tall, depending on the specie."

"Right, the *gigantopithecus*," Jimenez said.

George Lunt looked blankly at him.

"It existed from about 300,000 to 1,000,000 years ago in lower Asia. We still don't know all that much about it beyond the fact that it existed and was big. These bones might be from the Zarathustran equivalent to the *gigantopithecus*."

"You mean like Bigfoot?"

"The Sasquatch was never scientifically proven to actually exist, George," Gerd said. "Though a lot of crackpots back in the first century A.E. held up the *Gigantopithecus* as proof it was possible. Don't even get me started on the Yeti."

"Or these bones could have belonged to the pilots of that rocket," one of the men suggested with a short laugh. "This here is Captain Fuzzy,

Lieutenant Hairy and Yeoman Furry."

Gerd and Jimenez both swore, then Jimenez said, "Do not repeat that joke to anybody, Kendle. That's how rumors get started. Next thing you know, that Professor Darloss is back on the news yelling, 'see, I told you!' Bag up the bones for transport to Science Division. We'll see what Dr. Hoenveld makes of them. With your permission, Gerd." Gerd nodded and Juan glanced at his watch. "Excuse me, gentlemen, while I make a call."

"I'd better call Jack, too. Oh, damn…I hope he's out of the hospital. He might still be in a coma, for that matter," Gerd started for his aircar and added, "I'm also calling in more cops. Maybe ask for some more Marines. I have a feeling things are going to get very complicated real soon."

* * * * * * * * *

Ivan Dane was having a good day. Leo Thaxter was out of his hair without having to go through the messy business of killing him. Murdock had tracked Thaxter to the spaceport and watched him board the shuttle. It took a little time, but Dane soothed Murdock's fears that Thaxter might get caught and spill what he knew.

"Don't let his looks fool you," Dane added. "Leo is a lot smarter than he looks and likely had an escape plan of his own in place long before he was busted and sent to Prison House. I wouldn't be at all surprised if he had a stash of money hidden away for just this sort of thing. We've seen the last of him."

"What about Clancy Slade? We leave him in the pokey or what?"

"Hmm. He can't identify us, so he isn't a threat." Dane shrugged. "Send his wife the money we told him he'd get if he stayed quiet. He's done his part; we have Thaxter's brokerage company and Clancy no longer needs to sit where he is. Still, there is no point in risking exposure by trying to communicate with him. Let him earn the money we promised him. He can sit tight until either the warden finds out on his own that he's a fake or

Clancy screams his head off at the end of the month. I never counted on his long-term cooperation, anyway."

"We're still gonna pay him?"

"We said we would, didn't we? The money was the carrot, his daughter the stick." Dane saw the disgust on Murdock's face and elaborated. "Brandon, if we want to get anywhere on this planet, we need to build our reputation. If word gets out that we don't keep our word, nobody will be willing to work with us, no matter which side of the law they operate on. In fact, breaking a promise can get you challenged to a duel.

"While nothing can force you to accept the challenge, the additional damage to your reputation pretty much guarantees that you are through on this world. So, yes, we pay off Clancy, we don't kill people unnecessarily, and we don't give people any reasons to want to shoot us. At least until we have them under our thumb. Understand?"

A bald ebony-skinned man entered what used to be Ivan Bowlby's office. He spoke breathlessly through a big smile. "Dane, the last shipment just came in. I would estimate we have fifty million sols worth of sunstones, total. The advance crew did well. They've more than earned that thirty percent bonus."

"Excellent. Did they send the extra items we requested?"

"Indeed. One complete skeleton—more or less—about one hundred kilos of non-fluorescent stones, blood and tissue samples from a Fuzzy, and full scan data on the buried artifact. Joe did a top-notch job. I can't wait to tell him when he returns."

"What? Quigley, haven't you seen the news?" The geologist shook his head. Murdock turned on one of the screens above Dane's desk and surfed through the channels until he hit a news show.

"—ent the police and scientists on the scene have yet to give a comment on what may have caused the explosion at the far northeast of the Fuzzy Reservation, saying only that the situation is under control and under investigation. It has been speculated that another Fuzzy Slaver cell or illegal prospectors were trespassing on the Rez using high explosives. At this time it is believed that there are no survivors. Governor Rainsford has been si—"

Murdock flipped off the viewscreen. "That's been running almost non-stop on the news channels. The boys out there weren't using explosives, high or any other kind, since they where trying to avoid detection. The only thing that could have happened was a core-breach of the M/E converter."

"No! No…" Quigley, shaken, plodded out of the office and down the hall.

"Very nice, Murdock," Dane said in a condescending tone. "Would you like some kittens to strangle for dessert? You do recall that his son was supervising that job, right?"

"Oh, hell. I did forget. I never even met the kid." Murdock turned to go. "I'll go talk with him. Apologize…."

"No. Better to let him work through his feelings," Dane cautioned. "You'll just make things worse if you bother him now. We need him too much to antagonize him."

Murdock actually managed to look sorry for Quigley. "Yeah. Okay. Hey, he said you wanted those sunstone duds. What are those for?"

Dane smiled slightly. "Dr. Quigley will explain when he's feeling better. I think it is almost time to start our own broadcast. Is everything ready?"

"Yeah. I expected the news staff to give us more guff, but they accepted the script without comment."

"You can thank their former employer for that. Mr. Bowlby tended to play fast and loose with the facts…and his personnel."

Murdock was about to say more when Lundgren entered whistling. He was holding a notepad, which he held up high for all to see. "You'll never guess what I have here."

Murdock wasn't in the mood for guessing games and said so. "Who put a tunnel worm in your bed? Anyway, one of the surveillance cameras survived the explosion."

Murdock grunted dismissively while Dane sat up and leaned forward. "Anything interesting?"

"You betcha."

Lundgren held out the notepad and Dane took it. After a few seconds of scrolling through the images, he looked up with an amused look. "Can you disable the camera remotely?"

"Sure. I can send a command to overload the power cell and it will just overheat and melt into a plastic blob."

"Do it. But first get as many images as you can before Beta sundown," Dane ordered. "If it looks like somebody is walking toward it, don't hesitate. Destroy it immediately. As for these images, get them to the news crew. They can use the pictures for the backdrop of the lead story."

Murdock took the notepad and scrolled through the images. "What's the big deal? They dug up an old missile."

Dane shook his head. "Brandon, you need to get a new imagination installed. The dirt they just dug off of that missile will bury the Colonial Government and the CZC."

*   *   *   *   *   *   *   *   *

"It's definitely a cockpit, Dr. Jimenez. Over here is the helm...or rather what's left of it." Jim Stabenow from Science Division took Juan, Gerd and George through the artifact sections that had been cleaned out and made accessible. "This is where the pilot, or pilots, would have sat."

"There's no seats, here," George remarked. "What did they sit on? Did they even sit?"

"Oh, there must have been some kind of seating here. Look at the floor," Stabenow kneeled down and pointed at the crusted indentations in the metal deck plating. "They're corroded, and the seats rotted or rusted away, but these have to be where the support brackets would have been. It's not much different from what we use in aircars."

Gerd looked at the instrument panel, which was canted like a draftsman table instead of flat like Terran designed hyperships. It was covered in rust and corrosion. "What did they use for a power source?"

"No way to tell, yet. We haven't cleaned out the back sections, yet. Plus, if any hatches, doors or whatever were sealed at the time of the crash, they'll likely have to be cut open with laser torches." Stabenow waved a sweeping hand at his surroundings. "If this, oh, hell, call it a rocket, used anything like atomic power there's a good chance the radioactive elements would have completely decayed by now. This rocket has been here for a very long time, after all."

Juan Jimenez asked the question that was on everybody's mind. "Any idea who, or what, the pilots really were?"

"You mean: 'Did Fuzzies fly this thing here?' I don't know. There are no bodies inside any of the sections we've accessed. Everything organic has long since rotted and turned to dust. Paper, cloth, even plastics, if they had them, are all long gone. I would hazard to say this section was exposed to the open air for centuries before it was buried by time. That's plenty of opportunity for the local wildlife and bacteria to destroy anything organic inside."

Jimenez pointed at a corroded metal plate on a wall.

"My guess," Stabenow said, "is that this is some sort of sign or placard, possibly even the ship's registry, like what we put up on hyperships. It'll take a lot of careful cleaning before we can tell what it says, assuming it's even in a language we can decipher. I haven't seen any Rosetta Stones lying around."

"Do *you* think it was flown by giant Fuzzies?" asked George Lunt, half joking.

Jim Stabenow started to laugh, then stopped and gave it some hard thought. "Major, I have no way of even making an educated guess on that. Fuzzies, Thorans, Martians or even super-Khooghra could have flown it for all I can tell at this stage. Whatever they made the seats out of are long gone. Without the seats we can't get a clear idea of how they sat."

Gerd looked over at the instrument panel. "What about the height of the control panel?"

"That panel could be used by anything over three and a half feet, I would guess, but without the seats we can't get a clear idea of the leg length. Every sapient species we've ever come across designs his furniture so that his feet are close to the floor when sitting…well, those species that are developed enough to make furniture, anyway."

"With the exception of the Ullerians, sapient races tend to be built along humanoid design, more or less," Jimenez said. "It would be a safe starting point to assume the same for who, or what, crashed this thing. Keep me up on any developments, Jim."

"Yes, sir."

Juan, Gerd and George walked out through the hull rupture and wandered down to the end of the craft. Gerd observed that the exhaust system was clearly designed for solid fuel thrust technology, making any form of hyperdrive unlikely. George looked closer at the hull and noticed a series of fine lines in the metal. He pointed it out to Jimenez.

"This is way outside of my field, but I would guess that those are stress fractures, Major." Jimenez started to say more when his radio beeped. "Yes? Good. I'll be right down. Good news. The Marines are here."

*　*　*　*　*　*　*　*　*

A quarter mile away from the excavation site, a camera disguised as a rock took in and transmitted images of the artifact and the men working around it. The images were immediately transmitted to Mallorysport.

XXX

The yacht hovered at two meters above the thick grass well away from the excavation crew. Victor Grego, Leslie Coombes, Max Fane, Harry Steefer, Ernst Mallin and numerous Fuzzies; Diamond, and Leslie Coombes' Fuzzies, Lane Fleming, Gladys Fleming, Jeff Rand, David Rand, Kathie O'Grady, Carter Tipton, Humphrey Goode, Nelda Fleming, and Philip Cabot, all named for characters from a first century Pre-Atomic mystery novel.

The hatch opened from the side and a contragravity platform floated out holding most of the passengers, Big Ones and Fuzzies.

Not far from Victor Grego's yacht hovered a military transport carrying Commodore Alex Napier, fresh off the ship from Uller, Lieutenant Commander Pancho Ybarra and Captain Conrad Greibenfeld. In military fashion, the officers exited the transport on an extended ramp, the accepted wisdom being that contragravity platforms were theoretically vulnerable to extreme electro-magnetic disruption. The fact the transports themselves used contragravity technology was pointedly ignored.

The two parties gathered around the rocket ship where Gerd and Juan Jimenez met them.

"Word came down from Metallurgy; this thing is seventy-five thousand T-years old if it's a minute." Jimenez led the party into the craft through the hull rupture. "The alloy is unlike anything ever used on Terra. Lots of titanium and iron in it, though, so we know it isn't of local manufacture." There were a few polite chuckles from the crowd. "The stress fracture pattern throughout the hull is very unusual. Rigby over in Astrophysics thinks it may be from entering and/or leaving hyperspace without adequate protection. He said there are records of early hyperspace probes with the same damage. That was before collapsium was widely available."

"Wormhole, maybe?" Commodore Napier suggested. "I've heard stories about ships disappearing in space without any evidence of wreckage…"

"Wormhole?" Victor Grego asked.

"A theoretical shortcut through space, Victor," Jimenez explained. "A breach in space that opens into hyperspace and connects to another point in space. It's not my field so I don't know if it has ever been proven."

"We might be looking at the proof," Gerd put in. "I don't know any more about hyperspace ships than Juan, here, but I'll swear that this rocket used solid fuel propulsion technology. The exhaust ports on the back-end of this thing are very similar to what we used back during the exploration of Mars."

"So an accidental shortcut through hyperspace is how this craft got here?" Grego asked. He looked around the cabin and tried to imagine making such a trip without a hyperdrive engine and lots of collapsium for protection.

"It's too early to say, Victor," Juan replied.

"What about those skeletons? I saw the pictures."

"What about them, Pancho?" Gerd escorted the mob back out of the ship to three coffin-like containers and opened the first one. "This is the most complete of the three we found so far. He stands four feet high, or would if he were still alive…."

"How do you know it's a 'he'?" Grego asked.

"We can't be completely certain, of course," Juan Jimenez said, "But the thick brow ridge and relatively narrow pelvis are typical of male bipedal mammals. These fossils are very similar to that of the typical Fuzzy skeletal structure, with a few deviations normally associated with greater size; thicker femur in proportion to the body, more pronounced ribcage to allow for greater lung capacity and to support more muscle mass. I could go on, but I think you get the idea."

Captain Greibenfeld looked over the bones, then said, "Could these be the pilots?"

And there it was: the question everybody dreaded.

"The brain case seems a bit small for anything with higher cognitive abilities," Pancho Ybarra offered.

"Don't be too sure, Pancho," Gerd said, "Neanderthal man had a larger brain case than Cro-Magnon man, and we know who the winner was, there. Fuzzies have a smaller brain than the Yggdrasil Khooghra, and we all know which one is smarter."

"Albert Einstein, one of the most brilliant men of the 20th Century, that's Pre- and Post-Atomic era, had a smaller than average brain," Jimenez added. "How the brain is arranged is more telling than the size of the organ."

"So these *could* be the pilots?" Commodore Napier went a little pale.

"It's much too early to say, Commodore," Gerd said. "We'll be burning a lot of midnight oil on this one."

"For my money, I think these are simply a form of giant Fuzzy, not space travelers," Jimenez said. "The carbon-dating hasn't even come back on these, yet, so it's possible these bones pre-date the rocket."

"I hope they do. Mr. Van Riebeek, Mr. Grego, I need to speak with you privately for a moment. Lt. Commander Ybarra, please join us."

"Yes, sir."

The four men moved out of earshot, then Napier laid it out plain. "We need to keep a lid on this until we know what we've got. Mr. Grego, can I count on your discretion?"

"Absolutely, Commodore," Grego nodded. "Word of something like this gets out and there's no telling what could happen. Gerd, what about you?"

"I'm in as long as Jack doesn't countermand me," Gerd agreed. "Provided I still have access to the dig, artifact and fossils. I also have an investigation to run on the cause of the explosion and who was involved."

"You do and I'll send all the help I can. So do you, Mr. Grego. Just both of you keep your people quiet, if you can."

"My people are all professionals, Commodore." Grego smiled and added, "Besides, no scientist worth his microscope wants to release his findings until he can nail down his share of the credit."

"And the NPF know's how to keep a secret," Gerd added.

"Excellent. I'll call the governor and bring him aboard with this."

XXXI

The *Jin-f'ke* were coming together. The word was out that strange, almost hairless giants had killed a *Jin-f'ke* female. While most of the Big Ones who did the killing had made dead, new Big Ones had come and were doing incomprehensible things at the place of the old Big Ones. Many, many tribes had already arrived and more were coming.

Red Fur stood on top of a log and called for everybody's attention. It took several heartbeats before the Fuzzies were able to focus on Red Fur; there had never been so many *Jin-f'ke* in one place before.

"*Jin-f'ke!* The *Koo-wen* over the hill are dangerous. They use noisy made-things that made dead a *shimo-kato* and hurt our ears. They made dead Sun Fur. Big Ones worse than *gouru*, worse even than *shimo-kato*. Must drive away!"

"What Big Ones look like?" shouted a voice from the crowd. "Is people like us?"

"Not people like us!" Red Fur yelled back. "Here a Big One." The Fuzzy pointed to the side where Climber and Stonebreaker were removing leafy branches and brush to reveal the *Koo-wen*, Joe Quigley. Vines bound Quigley though otherwise he was unhurt. "See? Not people like us. Big big! Very strong! Very wise! Very dangerous!"

There was a stir among the gathered Fuzzies. They stared at the strange *Koo-wen* much like an exhibit in a zoo. They were all frightened and fascinated at the same time. Much like the object of their attention.

Joe Quigley could only catch a few words with his hypersonic hearing aid. The aid worked fine, but his knowledge of the language was limited. For as far as he could see, there was nothing but Fuzzies. Joe remembered a documentary on Thoran culture. There was one segment where the Thorans of one tribe gathered together to prepare for war on another tribe. It looked a lot like what he was seeing now, only there were a helluva lot more Fuzzies.

Before coming to Zarathustra, Joe had read up on Fuzzies. They were typically gregarious, friendly, and curious. Fuzzies were nomadic and tended to travel in groups of four to eight. Physically, pound for pound, a Fuzzy was three times as strong as a human, able to carry twice their weight when needed. On average a Fuzzy was two feet tall and weighed between fifteen and twenty pounds. They operated at a low Paleolithic level in the wild.

In short, nothing like what he was seeing before him. These Fuzzies were taller, heavier, and angrier than any Fuzzy he had ever read about. Some carried atlatl for throwing short spears farther. There were the chopper-diggers as well as stone axes, stone knives and, in one case, a particularly robust Fuzzy that Joe privately named 'Thor' wielded a heavy stone hammer.

Granted, against a single human with a machine gun the Fuzzies would be massacred, but in a sneak attack they could do a lot of damage. Thor could kill a man with that hammer of his, Joe thought. But no species was a match for Terran technology. Pistols, rifles, cannons, bombs…weapons of stone and wood were useless against them.

These Fuzzies are planning on making war against the humans. They're as good as dead already. And it's all my fault.

* * * * * * * * *

Little Fuzzy was trying to understand how Pappy Jack could eat while he was asleep. Even more confusing was that he was being fed through a tube in his arm.

"The food is made very small and put in…water that is run through this tube that goes into Pappy Jack's arm and into his blood," John Morgan explained.

"How make food small?" Little Fuzzy demanded.

Now, how does one explain about hyper alimentation, vitamin supplements, saline solution and glucose to a Fuzzy? "To be honest, Little Fuzzy, I really don't know. Four hundred and fifty years ago it would have seemed like black magic on my world." That started Little Fuzzy on what black magic was. Morgan was in the process of trying to explain it when he was interrupted.

"Who do I have to shoot to get some quiet, around here? Can't an old man sleep in piece?"

"Pappy Jack! Pappy Jack!" The Fuzzies swarmed around Jack's bed, all trying to get his attention at the same time. Little Fuzzy yelled something hypersonic and they settled down.

"How do you feel, fa…Jack?"

"Like somebody shot me," Jack grumbled. "Oh, wait, that was you. I'm surprised Little Fuzzy hasn't killed you, yet."

Morgan laughed. "Not for lack of trying. We've managed to come to an understanding."

"What did you do? Take a Blood Oath?" Jack looked down at his chest and saw the bandages, then looked at Morgan's shoulder. "Looks like we got each other pretty good. How long have I been out?"

"A week." Morgan explained about the damage to Jack's heart and lung. "Victor says you'll have a replacement for the heart in a few days. The lung will take another month or so."

Jack grimaced. "I had hoped to die with all my original equipment.

Ah, well, I guess I can pickle the leftovers in jars and have them cremated with me."

"That's very Freyan of you, John Morgan Holloway the Greater."

"Gus came through, I see. Little Fuzzy, could you take the family out while John and I talk?"

"Hokay," said the Fuzzy. He then called everybody's name and told them, "Leh's go." The Fuzzies filed out and closed the door behind them.

"The letter explained everything, father," said Morgan. "The fault was Orphtheor's, not yours."

"Oh, not that. I'm glad you read the letter, though. And the mircodisc?"

"No need. The word of a man of honor is beyond reproach. So, what do you wish to talk about?"

"I've missed out on your entire life, John…."

"Morgan. I'll use my middle name…now that it is my middle name."

"Morgan, then. Are you planning to stay on Zarathustra for a while? I've missed a whole lot of your life and would like the chance to get to know you better."

Morgan smiled. "Well, I was planning on visiting the outer colonies. You see, I was looking for my deadbeat dad. But, as things turned out, my schedule is suddenly free for a while."

"Great! Maybe after I'm patched up we could visit Freya. I have a few things to settle, there."

"Not anymore." Morgan explained about Orphtheor's death.

"Hmph. Just like him to cheat me out of the pleasure of sending him to Lo'thur's seventh circle, personally."

The two men spoke for a while, catching Jack up on the events of the past week and of Morgan's life in general. Morgan was just getting all the latest in on the rocket discovered in northeast Beta when the door slid open.

"Gus, welcome to the party."

"Jack, good to see you awake. You haven't seen the newscast on B.I.N., have you?"

"No, just woke up about an hour ago. What's up?"

Gus said something under his breath and flipped on the viewer suspended in the corner of the room. "Hell's come to breakfast, Jack."

On the screen was a vapid redhead talking about Darla Cross and her latest nose-job. Jack was about to inquire what Gus was all worried about when he caught the text-line at the bottom of the screen.

…FUZZY ROCKETSHIP FOUND ON BETA. MILITARY AND NPF INVOLVED IN COVER-UP. NATIVE AFFAIRS COMMISSIONER UNAVAILABLE FOR COMMENT…

Jack swore in Sheshan, and then said, "Morgan, I'm starting to wish your aim had been a bit better."

THE END

CPSIA information can be obtained at www.ICGtesting.com
Printed in the USA
BVOW070209151211

277753BV00003B/2/P

Lily and the Ghost of Tillie Brown is a work of fiction.

Edited by: RW Vincent

ISBN: 151738446X
ISBN 13: 9781517384463